THE GODWIT

JAMES McNEISH was born in 1931. He attended Auckland Grammar School and Auckland University College, and after writing for the New Zealand Herald, sailed for Europe in 1957. He published his first book, *Tavern in the Town*, in that year and achieved an international reputation with the success of his second, *Fire Under the Ashes* (1964), about the anti-Mafia reformer in Sicily, Danilo Dolci. He taught in London and travelled extensively for the BBC. In 1970 his prize-winning novel *Mackenzie* was published, a landmark in New Zealand fiction and the first of McNeish's seven novels.

James McNeish returned to New Zealand in 1967 to inhabit a sandspit in the Tasman Sea, recalled in *As for the Godwits* (1977) and *The Man from Nowhere & Other Prose* (1991). His work has been translated into several languages. He has called himself 'just a storyteller', but critics point to the originality in his writing and a gift for defining the universal in New Zealand themes. Professor Lawrence Jones writes in the 1994 *Journal of New Zealand Literature*: 'What unifies his novels (and his non-fiction), despite the diversity of subject and mode, is (that) they all focus on the place where politics and personal morality meet, whether it is with Danilo Dolci in Sicily, with Mackenzie and Amos Polson in nineteenth-century Canterbury. . . Jack Lovelock in Berlin. . .'

James McNeish's works include *The Mackenzie Affair* (1972), *Larks in a Paradise* (1974), *The Glass Zoo* (1976), *Belonging* (1980), *Joy* (1982), *Walking on My Feet* (1983) and *Penelope's Island* (1990). He has been a visiting writer under the Berlin Artists-in-Residence programme and was the 1973 Mansfield Fellow in Menton, France; he has twice been awarded the New Zealand Scholarship in Letters. He is married and lives near Wellington.

MACKENZIE

James McNeish

THE GODWIT COLLECTION

First published 1970

This edition published 1995 by
Godwit Publishing Limited
P. O. Box 4325, Auckland 1
New Zealand

© James McNeish 1970, 1995
© This edition Godwit Publishing Limited 1995

ISBN 0 908877 58 7

Cover illustration: 'Mackenzie and the Judge'
(detail) by Trevor Moffitt
Cover Design: Christine Hansen
Back cover photograph: Helen McNeish

for
HELEN

Women and land are the reasons why men die
—native proverb

The story has its origin in James Mackenzie, an illiterate drover whose illegal exploits led in 1855 to the discovery of the Mackenzie, some two million acres of grazing country hidden between the foothills and the southern alps. In 1856 the first settlers arrived, naming the land for him. But by then Mackenzie had vanished, together with his dog. Of the legend, as it has grown today, I have kept only the name. The other people in the story are fictitious.

J. McN.

Contents

Book One
THE STATION 9

Book Two
THE JOURNEY 261

BOOK ONE
THE STATION

HE had been walking for five days and now he heard the noise of the sea. He stopped at the edge of a clearing leaning against a tree, and listened. The bole of the tree went up straight, like a mast, then changed its mind and spread an olive-grey shade. He noticed the underleaf was turning ashen with the first cool of evening. A bird with blue plumage screeched in the branches. He let down his bundle and swung his arms free, making his fingers click. The clicking was answered by a spurt of leaf-mould ahead of him. The black dog that was his companion swung on her haunches half-immersed in bracken scree, and regarded him. Then she yawned, the blaze on her chest suddenly revealed. Together they listened. The bush was sodden. The thunder of the sea was muffled, far off.

He imagined kelp slapping and the tang of cuttle fish came to his nostrils. Then two keas started up, swallowing the thunder with demon laughter. A rail sounded to his left. 'Swamp country,' he muttered. Perhaps it was not the sea, only another creek. A man lived by crossing creeks. In this land the creeks ran like jugular veins from the rain forests of the interior to the sea. 'Creeks an creeks,' he said, and kicked off his boots which were full of water. He was a tall gangly man with a streaming beard which showed yellow against the black tree. He sat down with his back to the trunk and his toes twitching. Eventually he spread a patched coat across his legs. His feet stuck out into the clearing and he fell asleep with his mouth open, like a peasant.

He dreamed he was in a pit, falling. He drifted through clouds, falling through watery sunlight and bands of heather. Below on a moor he saw people running. Behind them came waves of white animals. The animals poured over the black ground. They had clean silky faces and they herded the people to the edge of a cliff. As the people fell from the cliff into the sea the waves opened and swallowed them as if they were stones. The children made no splash at all. Finally only the sea remained. The cuttle fish came out and danced on the sea and the animals receded, spreading sheets of whiteness over the land. Then a piper sat up, he climbed on the roof tree of a charred cottage and sat up there, blowing a lament.

The black dog crossed the clearing and crouched down with her jowl between the man's feet. The smell was unpleasant, so the dog receded a foot or two and regarded the toes of the man's feet, which were still twitching, from there.

The man stirred, fingering a keepsake at his neck. He went on dreaming about his childhood.

The native Wiremu walked onto the clearing carrying a kit and a stick, to the end of which was attached a dead robin on a string. Wiremu was followed by a scarred lurcher, the sort of dog that natives use for pig hunting. He noted the sleeping figure and kicked the lurcher so that it shouldn't bark. The animal sidled away and sat on a log. Presently it began to gnaw on the bark, making a grating sound. The black dog turned her head then and fixed the lurcher with glowing eyes. The grating stopped. Wiremu dropped his load and squatted. He considered whether he should wake the man. Wiremu wore a grass skirt over his trousers and a broken panama hat in the style of the Anglo-Maoris of the time; but his hair, which was long and straight, hid no cross at the neck to signify that he was a baptised Christian. His face was an inked bowl, inked in ugliness; had he been a pug or a pekinese he would have looked the same — but it was age, not deformity. Wiremu was of that age when nothing any longer can clarify the mind, not even a Baptist missionary. And 'Why is it,' he wondered, 'that white men sleep like that with their toes, their senses, their sex, all the living parts pointed at Rangi, the sky father?' He supposed it was to do with their religion. Wiremu kept to his own gods. He supposed nothing was the same, not even in sleeping. This man carried the Book. Yet he knew the sayings without the Book. Then why did he need the Book? Wiremu picked up the stick and made the dead bird dance before the dog. The black dog yawned at him.

He did not disturb the sleeper. He lit a fire and spread the contents of the kit. There were two wingless birds he had snared with the robin. He split the birds down the back, removing the bones, and when the fire had embered let them baste in their own juices. Then he gathered fern root and began to pound it, and the man woke.

Later they shared a pannikin of tea and conversed in Maori. The man had an accent, a boyish lilt which liquefied even further the already soft, Italianate sounds he had learned from Wiremu's people. The broken tributaries of his speech made the old Maori laugh.

The man had been sick. His grey eyes had the glaze of fever. But the pockmarks on his neck were signs of an earlier illness in his Gaelic childhood. He had forgotten the Gaelic. Yet he still said the psalms in that language, despite himself he still thought in it. It conditioned his actions. Like Shem, he carried his soul with him.

Apart from the smallpox on his neck, he carried scars, small depressions on his wrists from a time in Australia. But deeper than these was scored the mark of nomadism upon him. His patchwork coat which he wore as a plaid and his beard, a billowing haggardness, suggested the desert, as it suggested his calling. By calling he was a shepherd, he lived apart. To such men the luxuries and comforts of the world are a burden. He did not covet, since he had never known. He had missed the counsel of elders, the ceilidh, the fair-ground, the waulking frolics and the rich oratory of the hearth, the folk tales and the love songs. These had been denied him. All but the half-crazed blearing of the pipes and the milking croon of his sister, Mary, had been denied him. Had it not been for crossing the world, for small acts of kindness shown him in Australia and now here, among Wiremu's people, he might have grown up barren as the desert stones of his youth, quite natural and barely sane. But now he had learned something about men, about their longing.

The longing of Wiremu's people was for land. The cry of the dispossessed—and he could understand that. Yet he was ignorant. He did not understand the call that led him on. Therefore it is pointless (since he was ignorant) to concern ourselves with the man's purpose. And in any case it is only God who comprehends the soul of our calling.

They sat on. Before them stretched the beeches of the rain forest. Beyond they heard the noise of the sea, since Wiremu had proclaimed the sea, stuttering above the windrush of the branches. The smoke rose in spirals, carrying with it the aspic odours of their supper and the odours of the bush, leaf-mould, sap and pollen, mikimiki and liverwort and the woody fragrance of manuka. It was as if the forest were divesting itself of pain, that it might be worthy to be clothed in the new day. When they stood up the bearded man dwarfed the other. They cast about for a sleeping place, pausing in their separate ways to read the night, the bubble of stars, the mesh of noises seeping into the clearing. Behaving suddenly with abandon: throwing themselves on the mossy floor and throwing up bird cries, a wild ululation, *hup, hup, hup,* which released a bedlam of tree voices. Then lying back cheeping like mice with their hands cupped, not to let the voices die unhindered. And finally rolling over on the warm earth and sleeping as they lay. There was this bond between them, the bond of children who are preternaturally of the land.

They slept like mice in the warm antipodean night.

In the morning, long before the sun had warmed the hollows where they had lain, they moved on. The native, easy and fluent, slipping quietly through the hardfern and lawyer vines that wired the tunnels of the beach. The younger man was noisier. There was this difference now: the native moved with a quiet complacency whereas the other man, the bearded one, retained an urgency in his limbs.

About noon, emerging on a hillside of rotted timber, they saw the sea. It lay beyond the inevitable range of scrub, stretching to the north in a long blue pencil. From the base of the hill a river drove a grey arc towards the coast. It passed through a devastated landscape: hillsides fired by surveyors striking inland, thickets of scorched flax and the stunted char of dipping lowland plain. Here and there in a clearing a plough showed new furrow and wisps of smoke broke hazily from some settler's camp or riverman's hut.

The man made a face. 'Mangy country,' he thought. His eye, over-reaching the river, followed a long spur parallel to the coast. But the clouds were low in the north and the spur's end was thwarted by the torpid light.

Wiremu was drawing on the clay ground with his stick. He marked the coastal features and put crosses where the rivers ran to the sea from the gorges they had left behind. He explained that the crosses showed native settlements or trading posts; and that if the man found a banner and flew it, the Queen's ferry would pole him across for a charge of 1s 6d; but if he was fly, the natives would raft him across on dried flag for nothing. He marked a village a yard up the coast and, beside it, a reach of shingle where the dog might lap up whitebait. There Wiremu's knowledge ended. 'Where is Christchurch?' the man said. Wiremu put a forefinger to his nose, which covered half his face, and pressed the nose even flatter. He measured the coastline with his eye, pondered, and stepped forward. Then he planted the stick. Between the village and the stick was a space of fifteen yards. 'Kreiss-town,' Wiremu said, and placed his panama hat upon the stick, in sign of grace, since the bishop lived there.

The man was satisfied. Clearly the spur was his way. Beyond Christchurch he would find the open places that he sought. He needed to go to Christchurch, anyway, he needed new boots. But size eleven or ten, he could not remember.

Wiremu gave him a greenstone pendant he was wearing and made the man bend down to touch noses. Wiremu hung the pendant at his neck.

Soon they parted.

The man descended the hillside, glad to be free of the incubus of bush and walk once more on the crust of the land. He moved cleanly, head down, neck clinking, for Wiremu's pendant jostled the other thing he wore. The dog too moved freely, sliding amble-footed down the incline. She carried the brush of her tail gaily.

IN Christchurch they were building a civilisation. Polson had tried to explain it to Droo. But he couldn't explain it. Amos Polson was anxious.

'Are we late, Droo?'

'Late, thir. Past ten.'

'Damn,' Polson said, glancing over his shoulder. 'Then get on, get on.' Droo had stopped to water the horses. The dogcart rattled on.

'Tragic, Droo,' Polson muttered, 'if he beats us.' But it wasn't tragedy, he reminded himself. It was only a race with a missionary to reach the Land Office. Tragedy never happened to him. 'Tragedy?' his father had said once. 'The only sort of tragedy that will happen to you, Amos, is that you will hit a fly and hurt yourself—you're soft.' Soft was right. And on the day Polson had left Norfolk for New Zealand three years ago he had done just that. He had swatted a fly and sprained his finger. No. Tragedy never happened to him, only misfortune.

Containing his impatience, Polson fell to thinking again about what Droo had just said. But how, he thought, as the pilgrim town loomed on the edges of the plain, do I explain it to a bullock driver?

'Wot's a Pilgrim, thir?' Droo had just said.

'They're building a civilisation, Droo. A pilgrim, Droo —' Polson stood up in the dogcart and gazed on the plain at the approaches to Christchurch. Beneath the plain lay the omnipresent pebbles of ages, glinting wherever the tussocks were bare. 'All the world,' the plains seemed to say, 'is built on sand. But we are strong; we are upright. Only we, the plains of Canterbury, do not crumble. Only we are built on Anglican pebbles of the past.' Polson smarted and sat down again, for the dust was in his face and this last bit of plain was the worst.

'Get on, Droo, get on. We're nearly there.'

Droo's rheumy eyes were stuck together. 'Very effiekayshus that wheel, thir,' he said, and screamed at the horses. 'Skinflint!' Droo screamed. He drove the cart as if it were Nero's chariot, hurtling into a river. He crossed the fifth river of the morning in spate without bothering to find the ford and Polson clung on grimly, hoping that the wheel would hold: it had broken the previous day and Droo had held it up with wire. Polson's right eyebrow twitched as it always did when he was anxious. The smoke from Droo's pipe blew in his face, making him cough, and he smiled as the bullocky screamed again, firing the whip with one horny hand while the other attacked a boil on his neck with a pruning knife.

'If you don't know a Pilgrim, thir,' Droo said, 'then wot's a Infidel?'

Polson did not reply. As they crossed Ely Bridge and went down Cromwell Street towards Halifax he was smarting again — there it was in blue and white, 'Little Britain of the South'. It was only a sign recommending a teashop, but it made him snort. And a little further on, the town motto, waving from the Ladies' Glee Club. '*Ourselves Alone*', waved the banner. As they passed the signs neat and tuppy and crossed the square crisscrossed streets, square as a draughts board, the whole surfeit of nostalgic pride on which the town was built struck Polson with force — and he thought, looking on the new cottagey churches, 'Yes, they've converted even the pebbles.'

'Even the pebbles,' he said aloud; and was amazed at the industry of the pilgrims. He wondered why they had built here and not there, nine miles away, on the steep and iron coast of the Pacific. But no. They had landed from the Pacific, following the axis that Dana signified as that ocean's greatest depression, and they had come here onto the flat plain. The thought depressed him, it always happened. He came down to Christchurch and he was depressed. Polson lived in the mountains, he and a few score others who had climbed up and squatted. Polson was the rawest of squatters. As for the pilgrims—they had sailed from England to the Hollandic flatness of Christchurch, were moving from an Anglican past to an Anglican future without pain; they looked neither to the sea nor to the mountains; their adventure was over; they were enclosed. 'And I can't tell them what they've lost, Droo,' he said, speaking his thoughts aloud.

'Not that I've gained,' he thought, buttoning his top waistcoat as they entered a dingy street leading to the Land Office, 'by escaping into the mountains.' Yet he had, he knew very well; if only for the feeling he experienced each morning as he stumbled onto his verandah and blinked at the snow caps, like a half-witted Gurkha shepherd: a feeling of distinct spiritual superiority. Whenever Polson came down to Christchurch he was conscious of making a moral as well as a physical descent.

He continued talking up to the door of the Land Office. 'Droo, I can't tell you about the pilgrims without being rude. And anyway I'm as prejudiced as they are—' Certainly he was as English as they, as fastidious in starching his collars as they were in laying out their streets and plots of indian corn. Though he professed austerity, he was himself far from Spartan. He saw this. It was Polson's tragedy not that he saw too clearly, but that he allowed it to disturb his peace of mind.

'Skinflint!' Droo's inexplicable cry, which meant all things to all animals, seemed to sting the horses and they stopped. The bullocky got down, screwed his neck this way and that and banged with his mallet fist on the door of the office. Normally he wore a tall bumble-shaped hat like an oast-house—but now he was swathed in a hood, with slits for the eyes and nose, to protect his face from the dirt. He might have been a bear pawing up a tree.

'Clothed, thir.'

'Closed?'

Droo wiped his hood down and sucked his bottom lip. It was twisted by a scar running to the chin which made him lisp and sound even more lugubrious than he was. 'Clothed,' he repeated.

'But where is everybody?' Polson stared about him. 'Try the

newspaper office,' he said. But that too was deserted. So was Boppard's tavern and the Mechanics' Institute. They drove east towards the sea, traversing the square and the shuttered shops until vistas of hedgerows and farming strips appeared on the outskirts, rolling to a dull lake. 'Skinflint!' Droo whooped, and made at a cabbage tree. Looking up, Polson saw an object couched in the top-most branches.

'Halloa,' it cried, without getting down. The owner of the voice, a farmer called Trotman, continued to scan the bushes skirting the lake through a telescope.

'Seen Mabel?' he called. A hearty little man with pink whiskers.

'No,' Polson rejoined.

'Black bogger?' Droo stood up. 'Some black boggers over there.'

'No, no man. Them's ballocks. Mabel—it's Mabel I want. I ave to milk er.'

'Trotman, get down.'

'Please,' Polson added when he didn't move. 'I want to know why everything's shut.'

'Ey-hh?' Trotman made a noise like a wool bale coming unstitched. Then he folded the telescope and got down. 'Festivvitieweek Mister Polson—Festivvitieweek. You means you aven't a noshun?' Polson shook his head. 'Lorblessmasole,' Trotman began to titter. 'Lorblessmasole Mister Polson—it's Zbastiepole, Zbastiepole, Lorblessmasole Zbastiepole . . .' He went on saying it.

'Sebastopol?' Suddenly it dawned on Polson. It had fallen.

'That's it! After all this time, gloriose, gloriose—'

Fancy, thought Polson. And after all this time. For a moment he imagined the end of the siege, the blackened walls, the squeal of trumpets and the bodies of the men, ragged with shot holes, the smoke spurting from their uniforms as from fumaroles. He recalled a newspaper account describing the way 'our fellows' were dying: one fellow had survived eleven lance thrusts, had two horses killed under him, five bullets in the saddle, one or two sabre cuts in his cap and his sword bent double in its sheath by a Minié bullet, only to die inadvertently by getting in the way of one of his own cannon. Polson had felt angry then and ashamed. Now he felt only bewilderment.

Fancy. He had read the account in the *Christchurch Gazette* about May. The news must have come with the Sydney mail-boat carrying the September *Times* from London; and it was now—what was it? January. January 1856. 'Good heavens, Trotman. It happened five months since.' Polson was going.

'Wait on, wait on. There's celebratin to come, you're just in time. It goes on the week, you know. See, this day afternoon there's sports an picnic, bring vittels. This day next, tomorroa, that's the Guvunna, speeches. That's tomorroa. An a picnic an regatta put on by the Frenchies, an that's tomorroa too. An next is the gala—'

'Thank you, thank you,' said Polson. He was going. But he remembered something and called out, 'Oh—what news of Taranaki?'

Farmer Trotman looked blank. 'Tarrienakkie, where's that?'

'Never mind.' Polson told Droo to drive to the club. On the way he met a couple of acquaintances, Kidd the dentist and the Skillithorns of the Operatic Society, and asked them about the troubles in the north. They shook their heads; they too were full of the Crimea. They drove on. Polson was muttering to himself. There it was again, *Ourselves Alone*. That stupid banner. 'Purblind, Droo—these people are purblind!' Polson suddenly exploded and took the reins. 'Purblind,' he said again and whacked the horses. Then he ducked. They were crossing the bridge and urchins were throwing stones, in customary greeting to the squatter come to town. One actually bleated. Polson turned and hissed at him. 'Skinflint,' he hissed, and almost overbalanced.

'Thay it again, thir,' Droo gurgled. 'Thay it again.'

'Skinflints—they're all skinflints these people, Droo: purblind, they see nothing but their own kind. You'd think the northern island was in the moon.' A month before, Matthew Whitehouse, the Superintendent, had told Polson in a letter that the natives of the north were forming land leagues; in Taranaki they were arming themselves and preparing to drive the settlers from their farms. 'However, it will pass,' Whitehouse wrote. Polson feared trouble.

'Will there be trouble in the north Droo?' Polson said. '"Dear me no," Christchurch says.' "Why should there be that? We buy the Maoris' land for twopence and we take care not to educate them quickly so they'll grasp we sell it again for ten shillings. Look how happy they are with the new toy we've given them, we've given them Christianity! They are the most enlightened race in all Polynesia. *Charming* people. Of course some of them still walk about carrying eels. But here in Christchurch they attend receptions in stovepipe hats and feather boas, their ideas of social advancement are quite delightful." '

'That is a larf,' Droo said, hoping it was the right thing to say. The next moment he had seized the reins, 'Whoa! Boggerup, boggerup, skin-nnn-flint!' Polson was thrown forward as the cart stopped abruptly, and then he saw the grey spare figure of the Superintendent picking himself off the track. Whitehouse was waving a bundle of papers threateningly, but recognising Polson he calmed himself, tugging his beard up and down in the way that he had.

'My fault. My fault entirely, Matthew.' Polson was contrite.

'No, no. It's this confounded speech for the Governor, Amos. I was reading it. Should've heard you coming.' "

They were old friends. Polson had known Whitehouse at Charterhouse. Neither had been good at games and they had formed, during a choir practice, one of those amorous friendships for which the school was famous. Whitehouse, two years the senior, had held Polson's hand during a lightning storm and Polson had responded by teaching Whitehouse the organ. Whitehouse's people were landed and it was he who had persuaded Polson to come to New Zealand. He was urbane, shrewd, trustworthy; and the only disinterested benefactor Polson had known.

'Jump up, I'm going to the club,' Polson said. But Whitehouse declined, he had this speech to walk out; he would see Polson there.

Driving on, Polson felt better. His business at the Land Office could wait. He fell to thinking about the real reason for his visit: only Whitehouse could help him. The track followed a stream, passing the Council offices and the scrip fronts of the improvement societies, and then turned inland towards an agglomeration of Maori huts and peach groves. This was the west side. The buildings were straight slabs, and bore a conspicuous air of flatulence. They were roofed in a misalliance of tussock and snowgrass to withstand the dry heat, but already the sun of five summers had drawn the sap and withered everything to the brown musk-rat toning of the landscape. To the south, downstream, were the trim palings of the residential quarter. Everywhere flags were flying. Presently they approached a building standing a little apart from the rest, in a potato patch. Its ark-like structure appeared pasted there. The front was puddled and floated on a tray of duckboards. It had a flagpole but no flag. Gulls perched on top of the pole. This was a Pastoralists' Club. The final duckboard stopped short and members had to leap. Thus precipitated, Polson reached the verandah. He sent Droo for mail and stores.

'Oh — and Droo,' he called. 'You said something earlier about an infidel.'

'Yes, thir.'

'Why was that?'

Droo sucked his lip. 'That's what they calls you, thir.'

'Who?'

'The ones I asked you, thir, them purlblinders. Them pilgrims.'

Polson gave a cheery wave and went in.

He went about the lower rooms, tidying back numbers of *Punch* and *The Spectator* and straightening pictures as he went. The place had the air of a common room and reeked of wellingtons and vinegary cabbage. In the library he found a Kauffman he had lent hung over a notice advising that the smoking of ti-root and other rank mosses was to be encouraged. He paused a moment by an oil of Martin Gould. Gould was a romantic; in England he had eloped with an heiress and ended up in Newgate Prison. In jail he conceived a plan of the perfect Anglican settlement, a little Britain of the South. Gould was the founder of Christchurch. Polson gave him an ironic little nod and approached the window where the thin bespectacled figure of Stoddart was crouched, writing hard, in a ruby coat. Stoddart was donnish, with a mop of brass curls falling about his shoulders, and did not look up. Polson guessed he was writing one of those fiery articles proclaiming the town's independence from the eunuch policies of Auckland which so enraged the Governor there. Although the club was for squatters, people like Stoddart, editor of the *Gazette*, and Whitehouse were granted asylum whenever they chose. Polson was tiptoeing away when Stoddart said, 'Don't go, old man.'

'No, no — you're busy, Stod. I'll come back.' In the close, timbered room the young editor's face was suffused with emotion. 'I'll come back,' Polson said.

'It's the native question, you see, and this stupid new Governor.'

'Ahhh.' Polson clasped his hands behind him, rocking back and forth on the points of his toes. 'Yes that, that. I had a note from Matthew. Taranaki?'

Stoddart nodded. 'And Waikato, and all about. It's spreading. Meetings and land leagues and I don't know what. They refuse to sell any more land, the settlers are arming—six butchered, hacked down last month—and now the natives plan to set up their own King and cut themselves off from the Queen's protection.'

Polson rubbed his hands. 'It takes courage, Stod. What a splendid way of reminding us of their existence, by setting up a potentate of their own. Heaven help us if they've got a leader.'

'They have a prophet, which may be worse. Or better. It's hard to tell. These northern papers distort, distort, distort, they're full of affronts to the natives to conciliate the European settlers. But not a word about the effects of our rum, our shoddy. And the half-caste children, abandoned by—by us, running wild in the streets. Not a word, they take the side of the Government in everything. It isn't that we govern them too harshly, you see—it's that we neglect to govern at all!' Stoddart's words gushed out, thin and turbulent; he kept jabbing the desk with his pen, making the nib splash, 'And now here, you see, our Governor: ex-Fusiliers, ex-95th, ex-Everything-with-a-coat-of-arms-to-decorate-my-lady's-parlour, who should be *there*, at parley, in the thick of it, he won't see them—"naughty children, mind your manners, stop playing truant and return to Mother or we'll bang the big drum". He says. He won't see them! Instead, here he comes to Christchurch in a brig, with half a squadron, to open a bazaar and say Amen for the victims of Sebastopol who by now, poor chaps, are five months under the sod.' Polson sighed audibly. 'Shall I tell you why he's really coming, Polson? Because Christchurch has named a Square after him. It contains a pantry, a barber's shop, a perruquière, and an almshouse for Mrs. Dewhurst's Society for the Care of Distressed Needlewomen. There.'

'At all events I am reminding the Governor where *his* place is.'

'Careful,' Polson murmured, for he knew the young man's temper. He would hate to see a lively mind suppressed. The

Governor was an elderly hothead, capable of anything, and secretly envied the southern town its self-reliant prosperity. 'I have a feeling Stod — don't you think? — that the natives might arrange their salvation all the better for the Governor's absence. By the way, d'you know what *my* natives' opinion of him is?'

'I didn't know they had an opinion.'

'Oh yes. Their intelligence is remarkable. They have a mentor now.'

'Mentor?'

'Oh, a madcap. He's evangelising them and schooling them and building them a church. But — you must get on.'

'No, no, don't be vague with me. You're always vague about Odessa. What is his name?'

'Sparrow,' Polson said, in a bemused way.

'Ah. For a moment I thought it might have been Enwright — the Bishop. It was before you came. He just disappeared you know, left everything in his church and walked out; buried his wife and went. Sparrow, you say. No child with him? No. There's a rumour that the boy's still here, in Christchurch. Nasty business, Polson; nasty.'

'Very nasty.' Polson continued to rock back and forth, standing swarthy in the shadow of the window. Stoddart had tried repeatedly to enter this man's inner landscape, he always got so far and no further. A mask of bemusement came down and he was left staring at the pouched-up face, brightly smiling, imperturbable as any native's.

'What is their opinion then of the Governor?' Stoddart said.

'Oh that, yes. They call him Angry-Belly.'

He went upstairs to await Whitehouse, hearing Stoddart's chuckle echo through the scrim walls. He was hot. His fustian jacket itched at the neck. On the landing which led to some bedrooms someone had placed a wellington, in case of nightly emergency. That was new. A cadaverous man came out and went noisily downstairs, passing Polson with a desultory nod. Nathan Thomas, the grazier. Upstairs under the gables it was cool and light, and Polson walked up and down stumpily, humming to himself. The attic room commanded the town on one side, the plain on the other. At one end hung one of his own paintings. It was a view of the peaks toppling about his homestead, very early, with a great deal of crude blue and yellow in the manner of Spinola, but they had thought fit to give it a glass frame. 'That's odd,' Polson said. For stepping back he noticed that the glass by its very distortion had improved the painting, giving the peaks a brooding quality that, alone, he had persistently failed to capture. Three years before, when he arrived, he would not have noticed this. His sight then was much better.

He was of short stature. Starched almost. He had a habit of peering and strutting, though he was not yet fifty. His eyes, pale waken little things which peered and peered like buds longing to burst had been affected on the voyage out. Cholera had caught Polson's vessel, and his eyes, which had always been weak, had closed up. For the first year he was half-blind and had gone about with a gauze filter hanging from his beret. Now they were mending. 'Capital,' he said, and stepped to the window. He could recognise Whitehouse clearly, though still a quarter of a mile distant.

Whitehouse was reading aloud. Spare and grey, care-worn if you knew him, but outwardly cheerful, sanguine, the long holland blouse undone, old grey coat and old felt hat, easy, patient, generous with everyone, he never changed.

Whitehouse walked slowly along a track that defined the limit of civilisation. And for the moment Whitehouse became, for Polson, the symbol of everything that clarified and obstructed his vision. Looking down, he saw the land laid before him in natural divisions. On the one hand was the town, its life circumscribed by the stream and its fertile coastal strip undulating to the port hills and the sea. On the other, to the west, stretched the plain of Canterbury, a sheet of waving tussock. Beyond the plain rose the longitudinal spine of mountains, snow-capped, that strode the length of the horizon, unexplored and terrifying. These three areas had marked differences, of climate, of manners, of dress. This was less true of the plain dwellers, an indeterminate breed of mixed farmers: lowlanders, hard-working, predominantly Australians, who mimicked the sedate dress and speech of the town while professing the iconoclastic manners and morals of the uplanders. But at the extremities of the plain the differences were dramatic, almost Syrian in intensity, as to divide the two areas into two separate races. The townsfolk were English, middle-class, well-to-do, philistine, loyal, conservative. The squatting uplanders were scholars and shepherds, self-made and self-making, explorers, botanists, geologists, recluses, wasters, but mostly squatters, a mixture of brilliance, failure and self-seeking, a tiny mottle, of all classes. This collection, like some far-rolled lump of imperfectly scored amber, had no code save its own; it lived at one with the elements, amid sheep, and it hungered for change. Scattered among the squatters were small Maori tribes who had withdrawn from the coast at the time of ancient tribal wars and again at the coming of the white man; they were the remnants of a migration from the northern island hundreds of years before.

None of the pilgrims had taken up land in the interior. They spoke of it obscurely, through narrowed nostrils, as of a land of primeval barbarity.

Looking down in that clear southern light, Polson felt that he held all this in the cup of his hand; and he knew twinges of elation and apprehension. 'Once,' he said to himself, 'I wanted copses and country lanes, fields of wheat—' But not now. In the empty landscape was a reserve of tranquillity that did not clutter the senses and he was learning to draw on it.

The plain was dazzling in its simplicity. A few spirals where farmers were burning off, otherwise it was unrelieved, save by the criss-cross trenching of rivers and the clumps of cabbage trees marching into the mountains.

'Life is simple,' Polson's father had said to him. 'Why do you seek to complicate things?' It was the only saying of his father's that he cared to remember. 'Yes,' Polson mused, 'life is simple. Life is like that. It is bound up by the divisions and natural barriers of nature which if left alone are perfect and simple in themselves. It is only men who complicate things.'

Polson believed that beyond the mountains was a virgin place of savage beauty which had lain undisturbed since the days of the New Zealand dinosaur, the moa. He had seen this in a vision three years before, as his ship was plunging in storm towards Lyttelton; had seen, in a flash, a doorway through the peaks, and his daughter standing beside him had seen nothing. But the morning following Frances had tugged him on deck saying, 'Look, papa, you're right, the mountains *are* there.' Of course he could see nothing, his eyes all bandaged up. It could only have been a vision.

Sooner or later, he saw, the townsfolk would invade the mountains. They would smash that barrier; what lay beyond would be brought to desolation and effeteness. He saw this as clearly as he saw the distortion in the glass.

He hesitated to tell Whitehouse that he too was drawn to smash that barrier. His eyes, normally the weakest part of him, urged him on; while his character, the strong element, drew back.

Whitehouse was crossing the duckboards. Polson turned from the window, talking aloud. 'Now I hesitate, now. But why? In my mind it's all resolved—simple and clear. Yet the moment I tell Matthew the complication begins—' Polson stopped before the painting. He saw that it was already too late. The distortion was there looking at him in the glass and he was a part of it. The complication had already begun.

'How much do you want?' Whitehouse said. He had helped Polson before.

'Eight hundred pounds.' Polson looked at the other as straight as he could. He had a peculiar habit of contracting the right eyebrow and it twitched as he spoke. 'I'm perfectly sincere, Matthew.'

'I know, and that's what bothers me. For this time—' The Superintendent spread his palms in a gesture of helplessness. Then he leaned forward in his chair. 'Look, Amos, I go to the council. I say to them, let us vote eight hundred pounds for the discovery of a virgin tract. Splendid, they say, let us mount an expedition. But just a moment, Mr. Whitehouse—this will be Dewhurst, or Nathan Thomas—just a moment, pray: how do you know this tract exists? Gentlemen, I shall say, I don't know. But my friend Amos Polson has had a vision.'

Whitehouse smiled good-naturedly. Polson responded with a little acid nod. Whitehouse watched Polson tweaking the dust from his beard until it was its habitual floss of dyed cotton wool. He understood the hurt. The idealism which he had recognised at Charterhouse and which Polson pretended to have buried, later, in a Midland slum was still there.

'You're quite right,' Polson said, deflated. 'It's a preposterous idea.'

'Now wait. Stop blinking and listen. We can at least talk it out. The idea of reserving to the natives in trust a hinterland, without European interference and bounded only by their own morality and ancient tabus—good God, if it exists and if it's big enough! The idea's just. But why, Amos, why? Why bother? That is what I ask myself. Tell me your fear.'

'Very simple, Matthew: a race of helots. In the north the natives are already demoralised. They are rising. Next we shall shoot the best of them as insurgents. You say yourself the Governor has sent for troops. What is the root of their disaffection? It is land, simply that. Is the record of our land dealings any cleaner than that of the north?'

'I know, I know all that, Amos. Damme, I know it too well. And since you're concerned I shall tell you this: I have a document, left by my predecessor. It shows that by 1850 the entire south island had been bought from the natives nine times over, for sums varying from £50 to £190. I know all about the landgrabbers, the Thomases and the Banfields.'

'Then that's more than your own Land Commissioner does, since he has still not visited, not once, the land over which he is supposed to have such dictatorial control.'

Whitehouse held up his hands. 'Don't, Amos. I have enough complaints about Commander Wilson as it is. He is an old man who suffers from hallucinations and we must put up with him. Your implication is that the affair in the north will spread here. I don't for a moment consider this. I think you exaggerate the feeling of the natives. You must remember where you are, at Odessa; and that you see the worst of them.'

'And you, Matthew, living in the town see only the best of them.' Polson took some snuff and saw that his bottom waistcoat — he always wore three — was showing. He was not winning, he was sure of that. Whitehouse was too logical.

Whitehouse was saying, 'Those are poor grounds, Amos, alarmist. Shortly we shall outnumber the natives in this island.' After a pause he said, 'But the moral issue is interesting.'

Polson said, 'They have given everything. We should attempt some small restitution.'

'Why, Amos?' The Superintendent's clear eyes played about the protruding waistcoat. 'What's the real reason?'

'I suppose,' Polson said, 'to shore up our consciences.'

Whitehouse grunted, reassuringly. Polson was not normally so realistic. 'Why then a reward?' he said.

'It means volunteers. An expedition needs men and it needs a leader. They will have to be chosen and equipped here by you. By you or Burcher, not by me. I have an uncanny ability to employ the wrong men, as you know.'

'Why not lead it yourself?'

'I couldn't,' Polson said quickly. 'I'm not brave enough.' He looked away.

'Of course. It will be dangerous. I had forgotten Frances.'

'You know, Amos, the idea's so absurd. And yet—'

'You need proof.'

'Not proof, justification. Some justification. These men at council, well, you know them—their minds are safe, predictable, limited: tabula rasa. Give them a carrot and they'll follow. Give them a dream and they fall asleep.'

'Curiously enough,' Polson said, 'there is a legend. It describes a basin, teeming with life. It's said to be secreted in the sky and presided over by a demon bird without wings.' Whitehouse tapped his pipe and looked at Polson with renewed interest. Polson went on, 'I take it to be a sort of amphitheatral Valhalla beyond the alps, the entry to which is in the direction of that pinnacle of rock, the one we almost broke our necks trying to reach the day I decided to lease Odessa; in other words a forgotten or forbidden hunting ground of pre-European— possibly even pre-Maori—times, tapu, of course, possibly a resting place of ancestors, which would explain the extreme reluctance of the natives to enlarge on the legend. As to the bird: you recall that rock?'

'The one you call Seagull?'

'Yes, but it isn't a gull, that's simply a translation of the Maori name. The outline is the head of a moa.'

'You've been there?'

'I can't get across the river. But in winter when everything behind is white I can see the outline clearly with the glass. It's distinctly a moa.' Polson rummaged in a bag and brought out some tiny pebbles. 'And these,' he went on, 'are moa stones.' As he rolled them on the table, the surface radiated with a chameleon intensity.

'Cornelians, mostly,' Polson said. 'The cross-grained ones, the black fellows, may be agate, I don't know.'

'Obsidian?'

'Hardly, Matthew. They used them for digestive purposes, they're crop stones.'

Whitehouse turned the stones in his palm with something like excitement. Then he dropped them with a grunt of irritation. 'Well?' he grunted. 'So the flightless bird does exist.'

'Oh, the moa is real. And so, I believe, is the land he inhabited.'

Whitehouse's tone told Polson he was gaining. 'I have the stones from Billy, my houseboy. The boy wouldn't say where he obtained them, he simply rolled his eyes heavenward in that tragi-comic way they have.'

'That doesn't help much,' Whitehouse said.

'No,' Polson said airily, 'it doesn't. And in any case I mistrust legends. Always have done.'

The Superintendent looked at him warily. 'Nonsense. You're as excited about the story as I am.' They both relaxed then and laughed.

'Amos. Let's just suppose now. The natives flock to this Rousseau-like landscape, all is simple and untainted by European civilisation—'

Polson smirked.

'Your idyll, not mine. Let us suppose it comes to pass: there'd be a form of protectorate necessary, you say. I agree. But who would administer it?'

'I would.' Polson grinned. 'A failed squatter must do something in his dotage.'

Whitehouse stood up and touched him on the shoulder. Neither of them had illusions about Polson's practical ability with sheep. 'A failed squatter if you like, Amos, but a successful romantic in the making. I'll have coffee sent up.'

'You will keep this between ourselves.'

'Of course,' Whitehouse said and went out.

Polson was surprised at the other's ignorance of the moa, and put it down to the shrinking factor of public duties. He recalled that when he arrived Whitehouse had still read Livy and Demosthenes, and had been interested enough in natural history to open Mr. Plankton's little museum. Yet he had obviously not returned to see the moa specimens. One of the leg bones Polson had inspected was scorched as if it had been baked in liquid lava and suggested a bird larger than the ostrich. It had thrived in an era millions of years before and had run, so Polson understood, with the speed of a horse. Whereever it had come from in the north it had changed in the latitudes of the south. It had grown obese in the sun-baked valleys and had lost the desire, and then the ability to fly. Polson believed that the land he sought had contained these birds in their millions at some intermediary period between the great ice ages; and that the Maoris had hunted them for food.

Then a calamity had occurred and they had disappeared from the earth altogether. The whole subject fascinated him.

'The land's fertile too,' he mused. 'That would explain their enormous size.' Nearly all the specimens in the museum, dug from pot-holes in the coastal region, indicated a much smaller species of moa. But the scorched bone he had seen measured nearly six feet; it was labelled in Mr. Plankton's ornate hand: 'DINORNIS: Find, west hinterland; depth, of find, unknown; period, Quaternary; donor, unidentified Maori with pig-tail.' Plankton had told Polson that the native who brought it had seemed frightened and demanded rum. 'I said if he told me precisely the area of the find,' Plankton related, 'I would give him my hat instead. He seemed satisfied. I then gave him my hat. Whereupon the brute bolted.' The next day the hat was found floating on the Avon and nearby, the body of a Maori with pigtail.

That, too, it seemed to Polson, was part of the legend.

Coffee arrived and with it, Whitehouse, saying in his gruff way: 'We'd better have the chief surveyor in, Amos.'

'No, Matthew. Much as I like Burcher. It would get about. It only wants Banfield or Nathan Thomas to hear and—you know these men.'

Whitehouse took his coffee and laughed. 'We're talking now as if this land actually existed, don't you know. Do you honestly think they'd steal it?'

'I do. *Recte se possint, si non quocunque modo.* It's been their maxim for obtaining land all along. As the law stands there's nothing to stop them.'

In truth Polson would have liked the opinion of Burcher, indiscreet dodderer that he was. But he had learned restraint. What had set people against him, he recalled, was a remark he had made at the club, quite early on. Talking to a grazier about the land question, he had used the phrase 'White Squattocracy'. He had said it casually and included himself in his usual derogatory way. But the grazier, a cashiered Irish officer from India, had reddened. Squattocracy might have passed. White Squattocracy, never. The remark was soon all over the province. Polson had found himself labelled an anarchist. The implication was more complex than he at first realised. The Australian squatters took it as a slur on their efforts to discipline a new land. The English graziers took caste, offended at being lumped together with the Australians. While the coastal smallholders, squeezed together on minute plots, took from the remark a political meaning: with visions of a sheepman's league rising to suppress them, they began to agitate for the abolition of squatting altogether. The natives were offended. Some of the less patriotic chiefs, seizing on the colour implication, began to foment trouble and refused to sell more land. But this was quickly stopped. The Governor came down and distributed blankets and flour, and in their gratitude the chiefs became more conciliatory than ever. In time the phrase passed into current speech and everyone took from it what he wanted. One result of Polson's indiscretion was that he was seldom invited anywhere; and even his neighbours on Blueskins, the Hays, who were tolerant enough, tended to treat him with condescension. Altogether the pettiness and intrigue that resulted had reminded Polson of Magna Graecia; it taught him to apply at least one standard of the old world to the new. Nothing, he realised, could ever be private here. Lucidity and frankness, like intellect, heterodoxy and people who disliked beer, were suspect. He decided that in future he would keep his ideas to himself.

'Very well, Amos,' Whitehouse was saying. He was resigned to Polson's secrecy. 'No promises. But I shall carry the idea with me.'

'Ceaselessly,' he added with a twinkle. They agreed to leave it there.

But Whitehouse's mind would not leave it there; again and again in conversation he returned to it. And Polson detected in the other's frustrated desire to help a deep insecurity. The strength of Whitehouse's hold on the province had always lain in his impartiality towards the dominant elements, the squatting and the agricultural factions, who sat equal at council. On the one hand Whitehouse sought to maintain squatters' rights, a policy of token rents without which the wastelands would have remained deserted and small graziers, like Polson, would have gone bankrupt; on the other hand he was bound to maintain prices in the coastal strip as high as he dared, it being written into the charter that the acquisition of land be denied the ordinary migrant and the trades for fear this would destroy the delicate balance of classes so dear to the Anglican ideal. Besides this he was bound to promote immigration 'vigorously', pursue an enlightened policy towards the natives and cope with the changing whims of the ever-changing Governors who at any moment might overturn the whole machinery with a piece of draconian stupidity. It was an impossible task. But for six years, by employing three secretaries and engaging in a cross-fire with the Governor in Auckland and the Board in London, Whitehouse had held a fair line which worked remarkably well. Behind it all, the Superintendent confided, lurked the hidden power of the Colonial Office in London.

'But they don't control you,' Polson protested.

'No. But they control the Board and the Governor which is infinitely worse, since I see nothing of the correspondence that passes under the counter. We must, I see it now, keep this idea of yours close.'

Polson had intended to touch Whitehouse's moral sense. But he had not meant to project him towards political complication; yet Whitehouse, seeing further, had begun at once to grapple with the larger issues. It saddened Polson and Whitehouse noticed this. 'You're looking glum, Amos.'

'I was looking at that painting, I am always dissatisfied by my own work. Matthew, you mustn't compromise your own position.'

'Amos'—Whitehouse chuckled—'my position is already precarious. A little moral exercise isn't going to harm it further.'

'Perhaps not.' Yet Polson sensed that the harm was already done. With a strange foreboding he saw the simple sketch of an idea expanding like a canker out of his control, feeding on itself to satisfy the hunger of the age. All was distorted.

'My problem,' Whitehouse said, 'is how to handle our friend, the Land Commissioner.'

'I have just done it!' a voice cried. Stoddart, who had entered unheard, was suddenly upon them covered in ink and excitement, waving sheets of paper.

'You have just done *what*, Martin?' the Superintendent said.

'I've killed him off, that's what,' the editor said, thrusting the sheets before Whitehouse. 'If the Governor deserves a reprimand, Commander Wilson gets a flogging—isn't that what they got at Trafalgar? It's on the last page, sir.'

'Trafalgar?' echoed Polson. 'Is he that old?'

'He was fowling boy, or whatever the term is, on Nelson's sister vessel.'

'No, Martin, no, this is going too far,' Whitehouse said. 'You can't call him "an imbecile old backbiter".'

'Read on, sir, read on,' Stoddard said, tapping his foot. 'You see'—he turned to Polson, flinging back his hair with the pen and inadvertently stabbing himself—'Wilson sits out there at Akaroa with his manservant and his Chinese cook, having fits; won't attend Council, won't see anybody unless they go to him, writing these insulting memorandums to Auckland—'

'I am told,' Polson said, 'that he has a stock of Bacardi rum and a wonderful talking cat.'

'Yes, well it's the rum that's done for him. Dewhurst took a crew and surprised him in bed in a drunken stupor with his Chinese cook. He seized a cutlass and flung it at them, naked from the knees down. Dewhurst disarmed him—I must say it does Dewhurst credit, for one who plays the dulcimer. Then he began throwing off his upper things and tossing them on the fire, finally he rounded on the pianoforte and attempted to eat all the black notes. I had the deuce of a job writing it, I can tell you, so as to preserve some decorum.'

'Well then?' Polson said. Whitehouse was frowning and smiling despite himself.

'Brutal, Stoddart. It's brutal. But you've done for him all right.'

'The question is, sir, who shall we get next?'

'First let us turn out the old, then—'

'If only,' Stoddart went on, 'the Commissioner weren't appointed by the Governor, it's monstrous.'

'So it is, Martin, but we must put up with it. And you'd better temper your opening remarks about the Governor.'

'No sir. I won't toady.'

'Matthew's right,' Polson said. 'I hate appeasement Stod, but in your case you must appease. You want to kill off Wilson, so do we all, the land question's vital; you show the Governor his target, you may even set the sights for him, but you must allow him the honour of pressing the trigger.'

The editor snorted.

'Stod, if you force the Governor's hand too much the next man he gives us may be worse.' Polson rose. 'I leave him to your persuasion, Matthew.'

It was not going to be easy, Polson saw; Stoddart had needed a little flattery. They had been too quick with him. Now he was set. Polson was going.

Stoddart restrained him. 'You haven't forgotten that paper you promised me, on gridironing?'

'Did I promise?' Polson winked, wrenching a tumbled smile from the younger man.

'You did.'

Polson had already decided not to write the article. But the editor himself needed appeasing if only to ease matters for Whitehouse. So he changed his mind and told Stoddart he would do it.

When he had gone Stoddart said, 'That man would make a brilliant editor.'

'Perhaps. Yes, perhaps he would. Though I doubt if Amos would muster the political sense to go with it.'

'Why do you say that?'

'Because, my dear Stoddart, in the world that we're building, honesty and self-criticism are the last requirements of a public man. Though Amos is by nature a cautious man, at times his generosity and the cast of his impulses are so overwhelming as to be outrageous; and politically when it comes to one of his own ideas he can be naïve as a dispossessed Maori.' Whitehouse was thinking again of Polson's plan. 'He believes, don't you know, that by—' And then he remembered his pledge, and stopped himself. He picked up Stoddart's editorial and glanced at it. He said disarmingly, 'Naïve in everything. He believes that by taking his daughter, who is becoming by the by an exceeding interesting young woman, into the mountains, that he'll keep her safe from all the fops in Christchurch.'

Stoddart looked at the older man. 'Well, and won't he?'

Odessa Heights
9th January 1856.

Dearest Aunt Bea,

To continue, at 7 o'clock in the morning: 'No, it's this. All the spirit of adventure is here and yet there is no adventure. Only the bleat and the eternal carcase of the bleat — cold, with every meal. And the men have struck (it's Taylor again). It's no good any longer saying all is possible in the loneliest of possible worlds because the public isn't vegetarian. I am set, set on returning for Christmas. We must be out and off by winter — that is, June. But you will not have this by June! Oh dear . . .

Papa is almost convinced. Last week he nearly dismissed the hands and walked off then. There was a duststorm—our thatch and the men's hut in ruins. But then: the men forgot their strike and went out to the sheep with hoods over their eyes. 'That's something,' papa said. I was sitting under the thatch when it fell in. The whole house was shaking and the paper canvas standing out from the walls like sails. I dropped my sewing and ran out for Brandy (I needed his comfort) in time to see the tin bath starting cross country—with Brandy in it! And papa laughed, a real laugh, not the usual split smile. He does rally, you see. Won't decide. This present dash to see Mr. Whitehouse, for example—it's so irrational. He's been on the point of leaving so often recently . . . I think I'm nervy. I hesitate to grasp even the good things we have. I shuffle, edge along, as in dreams. It's true. Perhaps I share the same dreadful uncertainty about belonging. And this frustration I speak of that comes from the expectation of greatness—so constantly impending, so constantly unfulfilled.

He did try to help at shearing, by the way. The men were polite enough. But they guffawed the moment he had gone. Droo told me. Nothing helps. This is the third strike in 12 months. It began over chops, mutton chops. It's always the little things. If only he would confide in me more about the little everyday things that beset him. Yet he doesn't court failure. The fleeces are torn again. I fear we profit never if we stay a lifetime. And the practical needs of the flocks that refuse to sustain us are still as foreign to me as the turquoise parakeets perched on my window sill.

Yet the greatness *is* here. That's the frustration. Just now I'm sitting out waiting for my sun—it will lighten the desolation. There comes a moment of bare illumination that is overwhelming. And I say to myself, 'Now, now the planet will move.' Yet it doesn't. Why am I not enriched? Even when the land smiles it turns its secrets away . . . Do I bore you?

Billy says the spirits haven't left this part of the country, even yet. And there is that omnipresence: the invisible thing I keep stumbling over by the stilthouse. It is quite solid, as a stone. And *there is nothing there*. I told Billy, and he just grinned. He frightens me sometimes.

Papa will not wear the hat even if I make it, he says.
Drake-Draper has another cold.

The piece of holly did come in time for Christmas. I prick my finger to remind myself you are all there freezing in muffs, while here it is still too hot to eat meat, even at 7 o'clock in the morning.

Frances Polson put down her pen and watched the brown figure of the native before her. In the crisp transparent air everything shimmered, the muscles on the boy's back, clad in a haze of blue butterflies, the steaming pellets where the cow stamped and the spider's web that hung about the nose of a statue high over the stilthouse. The nose had a drip on the end of it. Frances was wearing the list slippers, the mauve embroidered ones. It was one of the little vanities she indulged in when her father was away. Another was letting down her hair so that it hung like dark rope. Sitting out in the wicker as big as a settle pretending to watch Billy milk the house cow — when all the time she was waiting for the sun to strike the peaks opposite, sending back the snowshine with a fierce white light, this delicious stolen half-hour — that was another.

The homestead stood on a mound. It looked upon the valley and the river, and finally upon the mountains. From afar nothing was there save the dun browns of the earth and the snows which dwarfed everything. Here the eye was committed to infinity, which was finite, for as far as it could see the infinite turned upward and outward; the alps broke their teeth upon the sky, and that was an end to it. Then the eye lowered and searched for a hut or sign of human hand; in vain. Nothing. No country was more arid. Apart from a scathed bush on a knoll, not a living tree. Closer. Then the house, hidden below the bush, Odessa homestead. Four rooms laid end to end and a dairy, stuck on behind. A horse paddock and a pocket garden and a piece of medieval nonsense, a wooden thing on stilts with a statue for a nosegay and a pagoda-like roof which some travellers noticed first and some, not at all; for the snows at this proximity were blinding and persisted even in the summer. The whata was Polson's storehouse and rose twenty feet in the air, it was Frances who said stilthouse. Billy called it the Tempul and, since he had learned the kneeling habits of the missionary at the pa, actually bowed down before it each morning before he swarmed up the rope to fetch the day's victuals. It was the statue, perched on a cathead, which gave the whata its character, an air of gallantry, faintly Greek. The statue was a snub-nosed Diana in stone, with a yellowing torso and lolling breasts. Polson had found it outside a goatherd's dwelling in southern Italy, covered in ricotta. He had scraped away the congealed cheese and bought it for a lira. Perhaps it was the Diana Billy bowed to, nobody knew; it might have been the stilts themselves which reached all the way to the platform; they were wrapped in tinfoil and glowed on wet nights.

Once Frances had climbed to the platform. Then she understood why her father had called this place Odessa. The whole buckled pattern, the glacial sea of the river, the torn valley like a bay, the fissured terraces rising on top of one another, eating back the delta like limans; and finally that immense line of peaks sealing off—what? All this had convinced her, as it had convinced Polson, that they were perched on the lip of some mysterious steppe region. So he had named his home for the Black Sea port lifted to the edge of the Ukrainian desert. It was only after the first summer when everything had shrivelled and the shepherds had struck, and the first winter when the sheep had floated down the river frozen, that she had realised how apt the name was.

'Come here, Brandy,' she called. The little terrier leaped for the cow's tail. 'Come here!' The cow twisted and turned, and the dog yelped at his game. 'Cuff him, Billy.'

'Heh?'

'Cuff him.' Part of her was like Brandy—wilful. The dog was bored with Frances and with Chesterfield the cat. Frances was bored with needles and piecrusts. The dog was forbidden to visit the flocks. Frances was forbidden to ride out alone. They shared a secret longing.

Frances sat still and elf-like, wrinkling her nose at the sun that was not yet a sun. The Diana was in the way, naked as a quill; it would warm before she did. She wondered why her father had bought it; it might have inspired Hamo Thornycroft's 'Artemis', a clumsy young woman with her hand on a hart's head—Polson's Diana was even clumsier since the hart was headless. But the nakedness puzzled her, Frances could not believe she would grow like that. One morning she would throw off her scrub gown, stays, slippers, petticoats, *everything*, and lie here on the verandah flowing and warm, like new milk, in the immensity of morning. Just to surprise the sun. She would do it now—

Too late. The sun seeped over the ridge, stirring the muscles of the boy's back at the pail. 'I could do that,' she thought. But the boy would not let her milk the cow. He was sly. One day he had brought her a bouquet from the cabbage tree. The next, he had vanished with her copper kettle. He was a fine buck Maori of sixteen, inarticulate, swaggering. His face was tattooed almost black. Each morning he woke her wailing from the stilthouse a sort of aubade; and she could not help but think it was the pagan reasserting itself. Sometimes after a restless night she woke to find the devil sitting up on the end of her bed taunting her; and Brandy, his short hairs up, cowering in a corner of the room; and later there would be Billy, his face pressed to the spotted tablecloth that did for curtains peering in and watching everything she did with a sinister attention. He would not tell her what he sang. He was sly and no authority on earth could prevent him stealing the butter which he did continually, to keep his hair toned. It was better than sheep's urine, he said.

Yet he was stupidly affectionate—the way he had stopped milking now, infuriating the cow by holding out the teat to the dog. She saw Brandy leap for the teat, teeth bared, and fall down yelping as a jet of milk caught him in the throat. Instantly he stood up and attacked Billy's arm.

The little white terrier drew blood.

'Go!' Billy said, and clouted him hard. The dog ran squealing under the stilthouse.

The rim of the sun stood up. Frances felt the hairs on her neck burn and sat quite still. Now came the moment.

The light travelled. She did not notice the valley and the columned terraces awakening out of shadow. But up there! The light travelled, and the peaks ignited. *There*. There was the snow. White ivory, tusk on tusk. The froth of the sea delivered unto the mountains.

There. Her senses swam in the red morning. But she did not feel the planet move.

The moment passed. It was quite true, what she had written; all the spirit was here and none of the adventure. The light filled the planet without wonder; the golden stubble on the ridge was only scrub and the reddened valley only scurvy grass. The wind was up, blowing her papers, bending the tussocks almost flat and carrying with it the sound of bleating. She could hear the canvas lifting from the walls inside. The flies and lizards were scattering and Brandy was trotting, chastened, towards her.

Nothing would happen. The day was normal after all. She rose and went in.

Polson walked to the Land Office in Broad Street. It would open at noon for an hour, Whitehouse had said. 'This is a petty errand,' Polson muttered to himself, hesitating at the door which was shut. The street was deserted save for some youths gathered outside a tavern. He heard the drone of a billiards marker. It was not yet twelve. He walked to the corner and back, and again to the corner. Retracing his steps, he heard hooves on the cobbles, a slow elegiac vibration which might have accompanied a hearse. Polson allowed the horse to overtake him before glancing up. 'Sparrow,' he said, unwilling to put a 'Good-day' in front of it, as the emaciated figure of the missionary met his gaze. Though Polson managed to smile and wave his crop foolishly.

The missionary turned in the saddle and bowed, slightly and stiffly, as a runner-bean might do. His eyes were half-shut and his beard reached to the saddle-bow. He wore a black choker instead of a collar and his right hand, gloved in black, hung limply. One of his trouser cuffs had fallen out with a high boot.

'The office is open,' he said, and passed on. Polson waited until he was out of sight, and ran back. The door opened with a click. He went down a corridor, nodding to a minute red head—all he could see above the counter—and came to the records book. He scrutinised it. There was the date at the top of the new page and underneath, the desiccated hand that he knew so well. '*Name:* Bernard Sparrow. *District:* Canterbury Highlands. *Locality:* Native pa adjoining Odessa Station. *Business:* Boundary Hut.' Polson turned to the clerk.

'This entry is illegal,' he said.

'Is it?' The clerk was cleaning his teeth with a pen-knife and did not look.

'It is not yet twelve noon. Officially the office is shut.'

'Yes, that's right, tis. Then again, tisn't, tisn't shut at all. See?'

Polson stood there, fingering his crop. His eyebrow was fidgeting. There was no room to insert his name before Sparrow's. The previous page was full and ruled off. He lifted the new page and considered tearing it out. But the clerk was looking now.

'People is always getting cross at me,' the clerk said.

'Please fetch Mr. Burcher.'

'Can't.'

As Polson advanced with a minatory stare, the boy unfolded himself like a spring. Polson was confronted by a grimy shirt-front that went straight up. The voice descended. 'Can't. He's gorn to the picnic. He said I was to deal with matters that prest. So'—two elbows, a red mop and a knife were suddenly level with Polson's face—'so you'll have to deal with me.'

'When does the land court sit?'

The clerk yawned and performed a minor operation with the knife. 'Not this week.'

'Tell me why you opened before hours.'

'He asked.' The clerk smiled, and slumped down to his former stance. 'Besides, I thought it might rain.'

Polson went to the book and made an entry below Sparrow's. He added the hour, 'Twelve noon, precisely', and walked out.

A flow of people was moving along the street towards the river and Polson found himself carried with it. His collar itched. He felt unwashed, peevish and stupid. He had not eaten. The sun beat down and the women's voices at his side were strident. He was walking beneath a placard, 'Save the Victims of the Crimea.' 'Go away!' he wanted to shout, and abruptly turned with his feet sticking out at right angles, wanting to find Droo and return to Odessa immediately. Now the sun was in his face. Polson walked against the flow, moodily aware that men made way for him, and felt for his snuff-box. In vain. He had left it at the club. In the square the press was greater. He seemed to be the only one not carrying a parasol, a hamper or a pigeon pie. Everyone was animated, even the piecrusts shone. The steps of St. James' Church were dappled with gaudily dressed Maoris and peaches. The peaches were overflowing into the gutters. Polson trod on one. His stick had grown heavy, his eyes smarted in the glare and the ooze underfoot made him thirsty. He turned into a public-house. Droo would be there. But in the taproom all was sepia and tobacco smoke, obstacles and abstracted inky figures. They wore wide brimmed hats with baubles on them. They were stamping and shouting slogans and there was a parakeet wiping its beak on the neck of the landlord, Mr. Boppard, who had the sort of neck only a parakeet would choose. Finding a counter, Polson leaned on it and rested his eyes. When he opened them, they encountered Boppard's. On slack days Boppard wore a hat with a black crêpe band, besides the parakeet, and would sit with his hams on the counter and his legs dangling like a salted hog, and survey the room with indifference. Now he wore a striped butcher's apron and was advancing ceremoniously, pig eyes glinting, with a crested jug in each hand, pouring the froth to left and right. Everyone was standing and drinking beer from tall pint glasses. Polson was wading in it, he knew without looking. He moved away from the counter and was accosted by three strangers, inviting him to drink. Refusing, Polson sat down at a table and accepted a glass of cognac from a man who was dressed as a jarvey. He spoke with a college accent. Polson drank the cognac and was immediately given a second glass. He repaid the compliment and tried to walk, but was shouldered down by a waiter who rushed by and mounted a table where he engaged in a struggle with a Frenchman who was beating a lamp with a broomstick. The broom carried a banner with the words, 'Victoire Glorieuse des Armées Alliées,' in tricolour. Somewhere a tuba was playing. From sepia the room had assumed a shade of crème de menthe, though Polson did not feel actually sick. Until, bending over his stick, which had fallen, vertigo possessed him. He picked up the stick and found a peach on the end of it. He gave the peach to the jarvey and watched him take it for a walk, returning empty-handed and expressionless. The tuba sounded muted. Evidently he had lodged the peach in it. A man with a slide horn approached, at which Polson's neighbour took out a flageolet and blew a welcome. Together they began to practise. Shortly they were extended by a drum, a serpent, two cornets, a long pole with a pavilion on top of it, a bassoon, the muted tuba and a nice Irish policeman who played the violin. The players stood round the table and tuned up, antiphonally. Once before, in a Belgian beer house, Polson had been subjected to a similar rite. He had burst into song and

THE STATION 43

then he had vomited. Now he rose unsteadily and made for the door. As he did so he noticed a solitary figure sitting by the window. Something about the man's posture arrested him. He had finished eating and was sitting back, half turned to Polson, observing the room with a fine detachment. One arm was crooked over the chair, the other hung down and appeared to be stroking something at his feet. The man wore patches and was bearded. His eyes glinted like speckled eggs through a rain of dust.

It was his stillness. The man created a feeling of space around him, as if fixed in lamp-flow. That was all.

Then the band started in unison, and Polson passed out into whiteness and the bump of spring carts. The tang of peaches was overpowering. Also the scent of bath salts from a man in a jane suit who was standing over him, shaking his hand, and talking opulently about a piano.

'For the Governor's lady, Polson; and my daughters are committed to play. Tomorrow, you understand—'

'Yes, yes, of course,' Polson said. 'Of course.' Recognising the modish bulk of Arthur Dewhurst and wanting to laugh. For Arthur Dewhurst breathed. He was a pendulous man with quakerish jowls and as he breathed he wobbled, like a sheep. He carried a huge bag of toffees under one arm which he patted.

'For the children,' he said. 'I have to start the bean race. Are you walking that way?'

'No,' Polson said aggressively. Something about Dewhurst roused the pug in him. He had the air less of the risen colonial than of the city father, and kept his fingernails burnished to explain the difference. But his bulk, on pointed black shoes, was impressive. He held himself braced, as if done up in a pewter harness. Polson was ashamed of his own appearance and the feeling of stupidity returned. 'That steeple,' he said, 'I wish you would tell me why that steeple is falling on top of us.'

'I believe it is cracked.'

'It is not cracked,' Polson said. 'It is because I have had drink taken. Moreover I am overcome with sympathy for a tuba which has swallowed my peach.' Dewhurst had drawn back at the first whiff of alcohol, and was studying his Geneva hunting watch.

'I tell you,' Polson added, 'I have had drink taken.'

'It is cracked nonetheless,' Dewhurst observed. 'It happened in last week's earthquake. My wife has formed a committee to repair it. Let us pray it does not cost a great deal.' He said pray with an 'e'. 'Come,' he said, patting Polson's sleeve, until he discovered it was wet. 'A walk will help.'

'A ride would be better, and since I have a cart and a driver, both of which are missing, let me drop you off.'

'You are returning to Odessa now? Like this?'

'Why not?' Polson made an L with his feet and put his stick between them. 'No, I am not. I am not, I say. We wouldn't reach the first ferry house before nightfall, would we? Therefore I am not. Where is Droo?'

'Is anything wrong?' Dewhurst said. And with such meticulous concern that Polson allowed himself to be guided towards the stream. 'Who is Droo?'

'Droo is a beetroot who has rolled away, therefore I blame him for not being here. What is wrong, my dear Dewhurst, if you will support me a little — the sleeve will dry if you hold it to the sun — what is wrong is that I've had a race with a parson and lost it by a pen-nib. Furthermore I no longer care. Therefore I shall tell you.' Dewhurst nodded solemnly. 'This missionary,' Polson said, 'has built a hut on my boundary. In it he sought permission to milk a cow. Now. I have granted permission to graze one cow on my land, that is all. Last week I wrote to him, as follows. I have a copy of the letter here. I shall read it.

' "My dear Mr. Sparrow, I find I must take steps to secure my boundary. Originally you sought to graze one cow. My manager finds there are now seven, besides a number of goats. One of the cows, which answers to the name of Molly, lately walked into my shepherds' hut while the hands were at shearing and devoured a quantity of soap. It sat upon a bunk which it broke and trod heavily upon a picture of Mr. Moffet's mother which it likewise broke. I understand the cow was reared by the tribe as a pet. It is a perfect idiot and has destroyed part of the sod hut which you abandoned on my property. Mr. Moffet says he will shoot the cow if it appears again. I intend to possess the hut, as is now my pre-emptive right, and I must ask you to remove the animals at once or I shall be obliged to impound them." '

'Quite so,' Dewhurst said. 'Does he offer to repair the hut?'

THE STATION 45

'No.'

'Does he offer to buy the hut?'

'No. For six months he has offered nothing. Until, on receipt of this letter, he has ridden down and lodged his name in the book to possess the hut.'

'Ahead of yours?'

Polson nodded. 'By five minutes. Therefore I cannot claim the hut.'

'But you can,' Dewhurst said, taking the letter. 'And I shall see to it that you do. This letter antedates the book.'

'Does it? It had not occurred to me,' Polson said. He refused to be cheerful.

'Strictly,' Dewhurst said, 'Sparrow is in the right. Nevertheless, the matter of pre-emptive rights is complicated, ahem, to one who is not versed in it.' Dewhurst gave Polson a fugitive look and patted the letter. Polson wondered whether he had suggested anything underhand. 'Pray, leave it to me,' Dewhurst said; and put the letter in his pocket. They were at the stream. 'I'm glad we met, Polson; and it is very good of you to offer to tune our pianoforte.'

'Did I?' Polson murmured, gazing downstream where revelry and punting met his eye. The whole town had assembled, en picnic. Children in frilly costumes were waving at him. Then the band marched out at his back playing 'Come where my Love lies Dreaming' and Dewhurst was moving off with his bag of toffees. Polson caught the words, '... bean race ... most important ... for the Governor's lady ... not cracked only suspended ...'

Polson gazed down at the stream. It was not the stream of life. It reflected the tranquil flesh of the flax bush and the face of a native child who stepped out shyly, fully naked, holding a kit of peaches. Polson took one absently. Then he put it back, saying to the brown eyes, 'And that is how things are. My life is a series of Pyrrhic victories, consummated by forces quite outside myself. One day, little boy, I shall be left like this powerless on a creek-bank. You'll tug this string and I shall step back, to safety. Or you'll tug that one, and I shall walk into the water and drown myself.' Here he was, committed — Whitehouse, Stoddart, now Dewhurst; committed to petty enterprises. And two days before he had told Frances that he was giving up and returning to England.

'Peach?' the child said.

He took a peach and ate it without noticing.

The band blared; children were running. Suddenly Polson was hungry. 'Why am I standing here?' he said, and walked off in the opposite direction.

Mrs. Dewhurst's mother, a dear old lady in a ruche cap looking like an Illyrian deerhound, let him in. She said it was the earthquake. The instrument had begun to play in the middle of the night of its own accord and the notes had been suspended ever since. She fed him a bap and an entire tongue and when the Dewhursts returned they found their Bach pianoforte in crumbs, but restored. Polson was in his waistcoat playing the Sanctus from the *B Minor Mass*, singing contrapuntally at the top of his voice.

Droo came to the club at six o'clock the following morning. Polson was up and dressed in a clean starched collar, waiting for him.

Odessa, 10th January

... Gilliam is sleeping on the porch until Papa's return, so I have no fears. Not even today when two men knocked and I was alone. They came on foot, bound for Christchurch from Nelson. They had hoped to make the journey in 12 days (a record) but were so much off course and so fatigued with searching for one of their party who is missing, it was not to be. I gave them tea and dark sugar and they left without delay, saying a fourth was waiting with a mob of sheep below the swamp. They seemed little concerned about the missing man. Gilliam dismissed my concern. He was angry that they had driven sheep onto our property at all.

The Maori onions and celery are dying, after all ...

11th January

You asked about the new hands. Kerr is very clever at dogs, he is the one with the satiny-coated collie I love to watch. Though the man has no manners at all. Taylor is like Droo, made of leather, but bigger, a crude hulk of a man. This morning he kicked Brandy cruelly when he wouldn't snuggle up and then I saw him flogging a cabbage tree until the whiplash parted from the handle. Afterwards he became meek and contrite as a baby. Taylor and Kerr and Gilliam are Yorkshire or thereabouts. Moffet is cockney, I think. He carries a bottle of Worcester sauce in his pocket which he drinks to take his mind off the loneliness, he says. Sometimes he adds a little red pepper to it. Laughton and Drake-Draper are still with us. Drake-Draper is doubly hyphenated, because he is ex-Dragoons. He is bone thin and holds himself very erect. I find myself listening involuntarily for the clink of the sabre when he comes to the door. He is a despairer, yet I like Mr. Draper best. (He bakes excellent bread.) On the whole they are a dogged sort.

Droo, for all his melancholy, is much sunnier. Except that he will go on about the native skeleton he uncovered by the hut. He says he replaced it carefully saving the ankle bone. I wish I hadn't told him I threw it on the refuse pit. He keeps digging for it and bringing up the subject.

The strange thing about the men is that though I speak to them every day we seem to move along parallel lines, never touching, never sharing—not even our unease. They resent me, I think; they make me feel inadequate simply because I am a woman, and this *I* resent. It is as if God had omitted this land until last, placing in it all the hewers and drawers He couldn't fit elsewhere and, having shaped us (Woman) neither to hew nor to draw, condemned us to a situation of perpetual redundancy. God really is most unfair.

Do tell Lucie that not only do we walk topsides down, but the stars also. Orion is quite topsided, like Droo's pipe.

I have *never* heard from Lionel since he reached Melbourne. 'A good mixer,' you say. Then he has changed. It must be years and years . . .

>   12th January

Of course, we might move nearer to Christchurch. But it's rather silver forky down there, they wear such muslin gowns as the ladies at home go to breakfast in.

Lionel may write, as you say. Oh, if a letter should come! You cannot imagine how one longs for news. I understand how the shepherd's dog must feel when the master is absent. They say the dog is a piner. I too am a piner.

There is one grey nursling of a cloud over Seagull Rock. It means a visitor.

She saw the body from the kitchen and ran out, though

Gilliam tried to stop her. Taylor had it across one knee and Moffet was trying to wrap the legs in a sack. 'Bring it onto the verandah,' she told them. 'Gilliam, please fetch a blanket. And a towel, there's a towel in the kitchen.'

When they had laid out the drowned man she took the towel and placed it under the head. She touched a hand, a finger. There was a ring. He was handsome. The hair was soft and sabley. There was a mark where the brim of the hat had been and a little blood about the nose. But the clothes were not disturbed and the shirtfront and wristbands were still buttoned.

'Poor boy. Horrid. But not horrible. Is it Moffet?'

Moffet had backed away. 'He's not hurt, is he, Moffet?'

'No, miss.'

'He's just—glided away.'

Taylor was making a cigarette, rolling it between his fingers.

'Washed up in a sittin position,' Taylor said.

She touched a boot. It felt soapy. Water came through the blanket onto the boards of the verandah.

'You see, Gilliam, I had always thought death was ugly. And I had to see.'

'Yes, mums.'

'It's the one they lost, isn't it?'

'Yes, mums. From Nelson. Now then.' The overseer covered the body and helped her to stand. 'Take him to hut, lads.'

'No,' she said. 'It would be fitting to bury him at the creek, where you found him.'

'Correct,' said a thin man in an old frogged coat who had appeared from the direction of the dairy. He carried a spade.

'Thank you, Mr. Draper. And I shall make tea for your return.'

She watched Taylor and Moffet pick up the body and carry it towards the stream. Drake-Draper marched behind with the spade.

The manager remained, shuffling his feet. Gilliam had a round face like a pumpkin, wadded with hairs. One felt that the hairs had been years in the making and that he had been a long time off the vine. He carried his straw hat in his hands and looked at his boots. Speech was difficult.

'It's a hard land, mums,' he said. Avoiding her tears.

'I had to see, Gilliam. If there are any articles, please keep them.'

'Yes, mums. Here is your dog.'

She watched the white fluff run down, with pricked ears.

'What's the matter?' she called. Taylor had been carrying the body one minute, the next he had dropped it and, reaching out with his leg, had hooked the dog to him. Now he was buffeting it with the back of his hand.

'That'll do, Taylor,' Gilliam growled. In a minute the dog came snuffling against her skirts. Gilliam bent and picked a tuft of wool from its mouth. 'He's been at sheep again, mums. They don't like it, hands don't like it. You can see.'

'Yes,' she said.

'Tie him up mums. Keep him by you.'

'Yes Gilliam.'

But when the overseer had gone she fondled the dog and thought about the waxen lily face, quietly resting. Her mother had lain like that. She remembered the form of the body, not the substance of the emotion. And the hand stretched out, lit by the ring. She wore the ring on her finger now and rubbed the seal on it. It was an owl seal set in a fiery blue stone, a beryl; but fiery, almost lapis lazuli. She loved her mother's ring. Her mother had died when she was seven.

It hadn't seemed tragic then.

Nor this. They had carried him off like a rag doll. 'Heartless brutes,' she complained.

She thought this again in the garden, after bringing the milk from the container sunk in the river and chasing the fowls from the pea shoots. Everything was desiccated. There was sun but no sunflowers would grow, they were husks. Even the koromiko had wilted — she looked. The flowers had gone. Last week there were three scarlet blooms. Quite gone, stolen. 'Heartless brutes.' She struck her fist in her palm and went inside to make their tea.

They were a long time in coming. They wouldn't come inside but stood with their mugs by the step, subdued; while she sat at her work-boxes making the circular hat that her father wouldn't wear.

As they were leaving Gilliam said, 'Send Billy up tomorrow mums. Early.' She looked up. 'For shearing,' he explained.

The strike had ended then.

She would never understand their minds — except perhaps

Drake-Draper's. She smiled; Draper the bookworm. He had asked for a book, and a little laudanum.

Later Frances took the telescope onto the ridge to see that no more cattle had crossed from the pa. Though forbidden to ride out alone, she might cross the creek and climb the ridge. Brandy came with her and made her hack canter. Three wekas started up, wingless gamey things on long legs, animated drum sticks, and glided into the scrub. Brandy chased all three and was left barking at a stump.

It wasn't far. She approached the ridge diagonally, from a gully, and walked Magistrate criss-cross onto a shelf. There was the pa, beyond the river. A few mud and bamboo huts grouped round the courtyard, everything tamped and baked ochre, mud ochred, in the evening light. And the smokes rising. It looked oriental, because of the palisade. Frances could see the natives walking about in coloured shifts. She had never been inside the palisade and wondered what went on in the big wooden building, stained red, at one end of the courtyard. It was the only building of size. Was that where the prophet, Hue, made sacrifice? Or was that where the women cut themselves in mourning until the blood ran? She wondered. The missionary didn't know either, apparently. 'I am not invited, my dear, to the inner sanctum,' he had said. She didn't care for Mr. Sparrow, he always looked as if he was about to sit an examination. She tried to imagine him crawling on fours into one of the huts to join his Maori concubine who would have to receive him and undress him on the ground to his gaiters, and cradle him like a limpet in the oiled folds of her person.

She shuddered. The wind was blowing the fires. They lay in wreaths along the tussocks. There were no cattle across the river. She descended with a clatter into the valley. Trotting over the floor of the valley was like dancing on tessellated cardboard. And the coracle of the moon standing up on the tops of the cabbage trees. Here was the creek again, and the mound where they had buried the young man. Brandy was sniffing. She dismounted, though she had no intention of saying a prayer. At the head of the mound they had put a cross made of driftwood, and bound it with flax. They had packed the earth with river stones and marked the oblong space with the spikes of the flax. On the cross-piece they had carved the words, 'Gladed away. 12.1.56. Traveler.'

Below the cross-piece were the scarlet tips of her missing flowers. They had placed two at the feet and one at the head. Frances fell on her knees and wept.

'Lionel is at the gold diggings!'
'Beatrice's son? Impossible. What does she say?'
'Not Bea, papa — Charlotte. Aunt Bea sends only a note with the package, the letter's from Charlotte. Lionel has sent them a long account from the diggings.'

It was the evening of Polson's return. Frances had taken the mail onto the verandah. Billy bustled out with a lamp. His owlish eyes opened at the things spread on the step: a pair of wellingtons, spices, packets of seeds, freesia bulbs and, from the toe of each boot, two tiny Staffordshire condiment pots. The cicadas were out, coughing into the warm night. Droo was lumbering about watering the horses. The smell of eel meat came from within. Polson was taking off his boots and calling for a ewer. Billy scampered.

'Well read it, girl,' Polson called.
'Charlotte says—'
'No, wait. I'm coming.' Polson emerged in a clean white blouse. 'And what does my cousin send us?'
'Seeds for you, wellingtons for me, never mind that. Charlotte says — he must have gone straight to the diggings on landing. She says, "My brother Lionel is at Mt. Alexander, after journeying five days overland from Melbourne. He writes 'I reached the mouth of the diggings a week ago and have joined a party. Already I have knocked myself up with work. I have hit on $3\frac{3}{4}$ oz of the stuff out of which there are £6 expenses. If a man can clear £15 a month he is doing tolerably well. Provisions are very dear and drinking water is scarce: we have to carry it two miles and it is fuddled. I have several acquaintances and we pass the evenings in cheerful intercourse and with music. I have so far avoided the common diseases and am in high hopes. If I do not get on I shall certainly keep travelling, and may even visit my cousin and great uncle in New Zealand. After the last drought many Australian sheepmen cleared out for there and have not returned. I imagine my uncle's pastures to be rather flat and loamy . . .' " '

'I am amazed,' Polson said.
'But Lionel couldn't be expected to know the country here.'

'Not that. What is it Horace says—or was it Carlyle? "Our works the mirror wherein the spirit sees." And a clergyman's son too.'

'You were the same. Lionel isn't so frail.'

'He was when you tipped him off the pony.'

'I don't remember.'

'You were ten and in mare's tails. Jam all over them. And your dear cousin in turkey twill. You were to instruct him to mount which you did, you hoisted him on one side and he fell flat down on the other. Then you rode off and left him in the lilies. You didn't like your cousin.'

Frances grew thoughtful. 'I liked his solos on the violin.'

'Anyway he rides now,' she said. 'He's changed.'

'Horsey perhaps.' Polson was reading the letter.

'No, changed.'

Polson looked up.

'You forget, papa. It's years and years.'

'What would he do here?' she said suddenly.

'Oh split rails? Drain swamps? Cook?'

'Many college men do. Drake-Draper, for instance.'

That's true, Polson reflected. He had found a copy of D'Aubigné's *History of the Reformation* hidden under Drake-Draper's bunk.

'Yes, Francie, they do; and most of them take to drink or finish up in billiard saloons. He might gape at the sheep. But a week would suffice for that.'

Frances pouted.

'But Francie, what *would* he do?'

'He might do nothing. He might be—a companion.'

She had that peculiar wistful expression; and her face had grown quite moist.

'Yes of course,' he said. Then: 'Did Bea send the draughts?'

'Draughts?' She was far off. Then she remembered, she had ordered a set for the men. 'No, no she didn't.'

'But you wrote nine months ago!' He stopped, realising where he was. He would never get used to the idea that it took eighteen months to get an answer from England.

Presently Frances said, 'I think you should write to him.'

'He hasn't written to me.'

'He lost the address. Look, see in the letter, Charlotte says— "In case you haven't received his letter I am sending—"'

'Then he has written?'

'Apparently.'

Later at supper—eel and mutton stew garnished with Maori cabbage (it would do for days)—Frances said, 'You will write?'

'What's the point, m'dear? You've told Bea we shall be home for Christmas.'

'I didn't say that *exactly*.'

They had reached this point before. Soon there would be an argument—their indecisions grated. The habit of knowing a place that awed them had grown strong; each wound added to the pain and, paradoxically, to the hold the land had upon them. This they couldn't see, though they felt the mystery. Polson for one, a man who professed no religion and tolerated them all, had never admitted that the land had a soul.

The land was indifferent, and it was hard to act amid indifference.

'Shall we sail then?' He could be jocund in distress. Frances was silent. He said, 'I called at Blueskins on the way, Donald Hay met me with a bottle of whisky in one hand and a fistful of rhubarb pastries in the other. Lady Suffolk has engaged a French chef, did you know? Now this is interesting: Donald offered, he actually offered, to buy me merino stock in Sydney.'

'You want to put off our sailing for ever,' she said fiercely.

'Merinos,' Polson continued. To argue was to court tears. 'I think it was intended as a bargain. He further offered, Albion was there also, to help me site my boundaries, they think I should freehold them. "Make yourself secure," they said. "Keep out the smallholders." '

'The land isn't ours, we merely rent it.'

'Precisely my words. Hay was put out.'

'You refused then—the second offer?'

'I did.'

'Good. But then you cannot in conscience claim the north boundary and the missionary's hut.'

'Quite right, I can't. And I'm angry with myself for trying. I shall write to Dewhurst and see Sparrow and make it up. Well then'—he reached across and tapped her wrist, for she was staring at a portrait over the fireplace—'what's your news?'

She was pursing her lips with sudden animosity, turning a twist of hair with her fork. At any moment, Polson thought, she's going to force a decision about sailing. She'll make a speech. First she'll rise. He pictured her risen, hair thrown back, slim body held against the table, lips parted, quivering—it was a kind of grace she had. Her mother had it too. Her mother always rose to make a speech.

But she hadn't risen. Polson followed her gaze which was on his own portrait of her mother, and the same memory rushed back. 'Yes,' he thought—for he had sketched his wife twisting a curl under a thin plaid scarf—'Mary would spend ages waving that curl and Francie couldn't stand it; she always went out when her mother was doing her hair.'

Frances touched him with the fork, all hostility gone. 'What did Mr. Whitehouse say?'

'Oh that. I think he was intrigued by the idea, as I think he was convinced of its stupidity. As I am too.'

'Papa you're not!' Polson caught the gazelle eyes dancing and wondered if this were really his daughter. Something had happened while he was away: He wouldn't say grown or matured, but—for the first time he wanted to draw her. She said, 'You care for your plan more than anything—or you would have mentioned it straight off.'

'I think,' he said firmly, 'that we should give Whitehouse a month. Yes, a month.'

So it was left, undecided.

Later Polson went outside. It had begun to rain, a warm drizzle slanting from the west. The wind was always blowing from some quarter. There was the light of the hut where the men were playing cards. Behind it, flashes of lightning stuck pins into the hills, making the hut blink in the rain.

The rain pleased Polson. He did not walk far, just enough to feel alone with the rain and his thoughts.

The men were shearing tomorrow. The strike was over, she said; good. Tomorrow he would see Sparrow and make it up. Donald Hay's offer had puzzled him; it was the first time Hay had offered anything. He would tell Gilliam. Gilliam would snort and ponder. He would say 'Now then' and pull his chin, as unenlightened as a Vorarlberger. Shepherding was such a prosaic profession. Yet they weren't bad men. But did they feel, as he felt, that the land was against them?

He should take more interest in their welfare; it was always Frances who visited, who ministered, who substituted books for their cheap periodicals.

Such a queer look she had given him as she went to bed. 'I shall stay, papa. But I can't ever love this place.' She had said that in effect. He supposed it was the drowning that had frightened her. Now Lionel. Perhaps he would help. Lionel was her mother's side, a Reardon; but further back—the same arid brilliance as Grandfather Reardon. A bit—showy. Steadiness was what counted here, steadiness and niceness. Either you had a flair for splitting posts or you were nice. Nice in the Canterbury sense meant good manners, good sense, cash in hand and *Sans Dieu Rien*. Was that Lionel?

Polson had to shelter from the rain. He walked right under the whata. A rat scurried down. The tinfoil was peeling, Droo would have to sheathe the legs again against the rats.

'A companion,' she had said.

'And what about me?' he said, peering up at the Diana. 'Don't I need a partner?' The statue regarded him distantly as if administering a snub. It had a drip on its nose. The nose was chipped where Droo had tapped it one day with a hammer, out of curiosity.

The thought of acquiring a native wife occurred then; and he considered this. 'Why not? Some are quite personable, the way they walk—a sort of wild hugging motion. As a people they're darker than the Tahitians, handsomer than the Melanesians—' Then he remembered Sparrow's concubine, a mountain, and the blubbery smell of the oil she used. 'No, no. It would be like having a blown turbot about the house.'

All the same he envied Sparrow his groping towards a new identity.

He thought of the plan. He would administer it. He had said that? But did he know anything of native customs? If the land were found, they might refuse it. Did such people want to be helped?

Walking back to the house Polson knocked against something with his foot. It had happened once before; on that occasion he had glanced down and seen nothing. He did not now connect the two instances. He hurried in through the rain. He dried himself and took down a book. It was a handbook he had picked up in London, it called the Maoris 'New Zealanders'. He did not know until he opened it that they were not the aboriginals; there had been others before them. He read until his brow twinged and fell asleep reading a chapter on the moa-hunters.

When he woke the room was bathed in light. The rain had stopped and the pain in his temple had eased. Looking round he saw that the thatch had leaked in the usual place, but was surprised to see how tidy the room was. The spade chimneypiece shone as if burnished, the iron-pots on the crane positively gleamed; his bookshelves were dusted, the paintings trim and the settle had been moved out from the wall, making a passage to his bedroom. He had grown accustomed to the idea of doing without and now, waking, he found himself bathed in unaccustomed riches. Humming a little, he went to the piano, recalling as he did so that he had once led a student debate on the significance of personal tidiness. He was humming something from *The Hailstone Chorus* and struck up an accompaniment. A sound within told him that Frances was awake and listening; and it both soothed and troubled him as he played.

MANY people noticed Mackenzie in Christchurch during Crimean Festivities week, among them Quentin Dewhurst, Matthew Whitehouse and Simon Hossack. Quentin Dewhurst remembered him for he requested, and was granted, a ride on Mackenzie's dog. Later he would reconstitute the man as a viking figure, because of the streaming yellow hair and beard. Matthew Whitehouse, who was making a speech in a velvet coat with pearl buttons, recognised him as a good shepherd for it was one of Whitehouse's maxims that only good men kept good dogs. Simon Hossack the new magistrate, glancing through his pince-nez, saw only a piece of travelling labour. But it had been useful enough. The magistrate and his family had just arrived and moved into the Keys Tavern for, as they thought, £6 a week, only to move out again when it proved to be £4 10s a day. The Hossacks (five children, governess, nurse, manservant, cook and house-maid) had moved to a cottage in Thin Street; and Hossack had tipped Mackenzie 5s to unload their belongings. But the fellow had refused the tip, saying that a glass of beer was a more acceptable payment. 'I sent the oaf off thirsty,' Hossack recalled.

One or two squatters babbled about 'the strange eyes' and

regretted not having hired them straight off; but since it was not clear if they were referring to the man or the dog and were shouting hurrah to the Governor's carriage at the time, their testimony is unimportant. Later half the population would swear to have met the Gael, such is the legend of a man's passing.

It was necessary for Mackenzie to remain in Christchurch until the celebrations ended, for he needed a new pair of Cookham boots, size ten. Ben Castle the cobbler shod what he mistook for flatirons, so hard were the feet that stepped bare onto his last. Having bought the boots and called at the Land Office, Mackenzie turned inland and walked towards the mountains.

Only one man in Canterbury could claim to have known Mackenzie, and that was Droo the bullocky. Droo would reveal that the man Mackenzie was a shepherd who stole sheep and dogs. Of sheep, this was true enough. Ever since he had been Jamie, in fact. On the peatlands where he had grown and on the tinder lands where he had matured, Jamie the shepherd had remained a shepherd. His temperament spurned a more gainful employment. His temperament was his ambition and his ambition was, they said later, a kind of revenge.

It is difficult to say in the short period of his life which concerns us if he was conscious of this ambition. Certainly it is easier to say that he was, like the sleeper in the song, a child of his race.

He had been found at the age of seven by a lowland man called Douglas who had come with his family and his sheep to pasture a glen in Wester Ross. The glen was empty. The people had been driven out. Some of the people, cotters, had not understood the coming of the sheep. They had refused the order to flit and had taken up arms. The military had come to teach them the laird's will. Then the people did understand. The Douglas had been disappointed to find the peat bare of highland cattle and the divots of the cottages burning; but he was glad to see as he rode between the smoking ruins that the peagreen grass was showing on the blackened ground. He saw an old woman by a walled-up sheiling, sitting in a hollow tree, gone cold. And walking in the runrig, by crenellated sods, he found a boy wild and staring, in a kailyard. The boy was dirty. He wore a charm and was holding a Bible.

'What's that thing on your neck?' the Douglas said.

'Father's, an he will kill you.'

'Is it bone, boy?' The boy stared at him.

'What is your name, boy?'

'Jamie the cow bairn, an I have lost my mither, an hied in caves and swillowed birds' eggs on Eagle Rock an honey too, an I have lost my Mary, an I want a doggie like yourn tha' will kill sheep, an I will kill yourn too.' As he blurted, the boy flew at the Douglas and hit him times over.

The Douglases took the boy in and taught him sense among sheep. So he became a shepherd in the house of a lowland shepherd, the servant of a servant. The Douglas was a thick kindly man and he told the boy what the factor had said to tell, namely that his mother and sister had gone to a distant land and that his father was nowhere about. The boy learned to drove the big cheviots and to pare against the murrain and mix physic against the tremblings and beware of the spring madness when the beltane dock grew, he learned sense of sheep. He forgot the Gaelic. Amid the talking stones of his boyhood he forgot many things; and he came to love the white pestilence that had poured over the land. At ten he was wiry with high cheekbones and his hair, windblasted, was the colour of amber. He shared a stone hut with two herd boys. Once they fibbed him about the lady's thing at his neck and he flew at them, banging their heads against the walls until the blood showed. He had a choice temper. At thirteen he commanded his first dog, a lowland collie; and the grey-moist eyes that never dulled except when he was telling a fiction were observant with observation, so the Douglas told the factor; and the factor promised the lad a subtenancy if Improvement (which was the sheep) continued to prosper.

'What of my father?' the boy demanded.

'Himself was a blind tall man with a face like a speckled egg,' the factor said.

'Is he newly blind?'

'Blind in the keep of the damned English,' was all the factor would say.

He had begun to dream, and his dreams were the fictions he told to his dog outside the round hut where he would sit and mouth the Bible at evening; and scrabble his long yellow hair. He always had some Scripture phrase at the tongue roots, the

Douglases said, and he forgot not everything. For when they gave him a lamb he called it Mary, after his sister. He said the lamb was blessed.

There were the days when seers came through the land and once one came whose name was Christy. Christy was a cotter's daughter. She was tall and one-eyed and remarkably plain. She took the amulet from his neck and fingered the shape that was a buck's head cabossed in stag's moss down, and said it was the crest of his forebear, Hector Roy, who had fought at Flodden.

'He was tall and auburn-haired, he was nine feet tall, Jamie. He had five hundred fighting men in these glens. He slew the Macdonalds in a bog. He was much given to fighting.'

'And what of my father?'

'He is dead, Jamie.'

'Is he newly died?'

She told him then. She shamed him. It was much vaunted by the seers, the death of this pock-pitted laird who had betrayed his people to sheep. Christy told him everything. Finally Christy blasphemed Jamie for tending rotten flesh and threw down the amulet and left him holding his belted plaid tight in his hands. When she had gone the boy dreamed dreams that he had never known before, knowing what he now knew of his father.

About a year later there was a potato famine and the seer Christy came again, crying 'GHILLE GHILLE IS MEASA NA'N DIOBHAL', the rowen of Culloden: the servant of the servant is worse than the devil. With her was a minister of the Emigration Society, and he bade Jamie join them on the road to Sutherland.

'Is my mother there?' he said.

'She is dead, Jamie.'

'Is she newly died?'

'She died on the seas, of the fever of the water they drank.'

'Is my sister there?'

'She is at Newfoundland, she is curing in a fishery,' the minister said.

'Then I mun go to her.'

'You shall, lad. But first you shall join us for Sutherland.'

'But I cannot leave the flocks of a straight. Is it mourning they are in Sutherland, Christy?'

THE STATION

'Tis evicting the Duke is. The Duke of Sutherland is making Improvement.'

'I cannot leave my ewe lamb,' Jamie told the minister.

'There has been no harvest of barley or oats. There are no taties. The people are in a state of nature.'

'We mun lift grouse and deer for their bellies.'

''Tis a hanging matter, Jamie. We can but help them to the ships. They are killing the Duke's swans for the hunger now. Tis hanging they will get.'

'We mun hurry,' Jamie said, bewildered.

'We are marching now, we are a goodly band. There is Rory the blind piper at our head and meal and taties from Edinburgh. You will find us on the Coigach road.'

The minister took the boy's plaid and laid it down with the amulet beside it, and together they knelt with the sheep around them and sang the 141st Psalm. '*Our bones are scattered at the grave's mouth, as when one cutteth and cleaveth wood upon the earth . . .*'

That night in a dream Jamie saw the tall spirits of his ancestor rise from their funeral ship and beckon him onto the waters. It was natural therefore that when he rose early and set out along the Coigach road, he should take with him the ewe lamb and five hundred members of the Douglas flock, one for each of Hector's warrior clansmen. Meat, he said to himself, was fatter than meal. Sheep lifting had never been a grave matter to his people, it was not like stealing cattle.

That was also the opinion of the judge who tried Jamie at the Edinburgh Assizes. For he was a Highland judge, he was sympathetic to the ways of his people. The Douglas gave evidence that when the flock was overtaken and the boy arrested at Strathkanaird, some fifty miles north of Coigach, the animals were not heated or winded but entire as from their native grazing. The boy was alone, he said, with one dog. The judge marvelled at the feat. He sentenced the boy to five years' transportation. Cattle, he remarked, would have been a hanging matter. The Douglas said he was sorry to lose such a good shepherd.

As for the charge of stealing dogs, this was a companionable act. After some years on Van Dieman's Land Mackenzie had been transferred to a prison farm near Melbourne and then sent, marked and ticketed, to a sheep station in the west. He had not been flogged. They had let him keep his Bible and he had taken care to read it closely whenever he was marched to the yard to witness a hanging. He had worked in a road gang. He had withstood heat and dust storms. His skin had turned hull brown and his wrists showed the diet of irons. But where other men, breaking stones, had lost stones and died, he had discovered he was built for adversity and endured. On the sheep station there were sixty convicts and some free men who commanded the flocks. In 1851 when drought sent Australian farmers to squat on the tussocks of Canterbury, Mackenzie was a free man and twenty-two. His rufous hair had bleached yellow. The Cairngorm eyes had receded against the blue haze. He had acquired the habit of patience. He walked to Melbourne and enquired a passage to Newfoundland.

'How much have you got?' said the shipping clerk through a nasal block of bandages.

'I have three pounds and ten shillings.'

The clerk laughed him out of the office.

Mackenzie worked in Melbourne; he took a bullock on the road; then he returned to the station. The manager welcomed him with £25 a year, and billet, and gave him a bitch pup with red eyes. There were nine runs on the scorched plain which extended for fourteen miles. Mackenzie worked three dogs and moved his forces with martial instinct.

'Where did you learn to mob sheep like that?' the manager said.

'On the Coigach road above Loch Broom,' Mackenzie replied.

He lumped in a short hut with a remittance man, a Cork tailor and an aborigine called Andy. The aborigine kept a parrot and taught Mackenzie birdcalls. Mackenzie taught Andy's parrot a Gaelic grace. The three of them shared a bunk. The remittance man gave him learning from a book, English learning, and this completed Mackenzie's schooling. The Irishman was a piper and when his ticket-of-leave expired he gave Mackenzie a chanter made from a wattle branch. Mackenzie taught himself to play the thing not well but with a festering sadness that made up for his lack of Gaelic. The playing soothed the flocks; also it soothed the parrot. But it did not help to exorcise his dreams.

One winter Mackenzie took a division of merinos onto the

heights above the station and watched them from a daub hut. The manager said the flock would perish and promised Mackenzie a lash for every beast that died.

But no merino died. Mackenzie decided then that of the two big sheep he had known, the lowland cheviot and the horned merino, the merino was best. 'Wild brute, comes out of Spain,' the remittance man said. 'Ugly brute too,' he added. Mackenzie grinned. He thought the ugliness expressive.

Also the merino seemed to him less tainted.

His pup at first could do nothing with the merino. She preferred pointing the parrot. She was coal-black with eyes of pictish red. She obeyed some commands and not others. Her friendliness left the sheep unmoved. She developed a habit of puffing out her cheeks and the blaze at her throat as though she were gargling. The sheep shied. She pointed with her ears pricked and they bolted, leaving her bewildered. 'Thou has a random mind,' he said.

He walked her on the hills and talked to her so she would detect the humours of his voice. He used a crook to instruct the angle of approach. He thinned her rations. He put her to run with working dogs and ignored her. In this way she befriended the entire flock and antagonised all the shepherds on the station. Invariably she returned, seeking praise. 'At least thee doesn't bark,' he said. But he condemned her all the same and sent her back to the manager. One day she trotted up and stood, regarding him. He was playing the chanter. 'Thou art wasted,' he thought, and continued blowing on the pipe. It was a threnody his mother had sung. When he had played the tune four or five times over he knew he was powerless to stop playing while the dog was still staring. He saw his own stubble reflected in two glowing almonds, coal-bright. He was tranced. But he went on playing. The dog backed down slowly, then rapidly. He followed. Slowly, then rapidly. Still playing. Andy said later that all the way down the slope the chanter never left his lips. When they reached the gully, she ran up the reverse towards a parcel of sheep, reclining. The animals scrambled up and began to stamp, looking down the hill. Two bolted. But the dog had swept under. The two halted on trembling hocks. The dog held them. The pair rejoined the group. The dog made a circle and wove them, in a pod, straight towards Mackenzie. She halted them, and regarded him with an expression of clarity.

Mackenzie did not again send her to the manager.

When he had saved £40 there was again drought, and then rains; flocks were sold, and fresh animals brought from the coast. Mackenzie was given a flock which fed poorly. He began picking up casts and rubbings of wool. He did not report this. He was woken early one morning by the dog, scratching him. She had driven up two rams. They had scaly bodies where the wool had flaked. Quickly he drove the pair across the intervening runs to the house of the manager.

'Christ,' the manager said, and called to his wife. He told Mackenzie to take the animals behind the house and slaughter them. Mackenzie did this and returned. The man's wife was there with her head in a towel, holding a broom. 'And you say you drove them pair across my whole station?'

Mackenzie nodded.

'You hear that, Milly? He drove them across *the whole station*.'

The woman screamed. 'You bloody peasant,' she said. The man hit Mackenzie with the broom. Then he sat on the step and began to weep, leaning his head on the handle. The woman went inside and closed the door.

It was some days before they obtained acids to disinfect the flocks. By then seven of the nine runs were infected with scab. More than two thousand sheep palsied and died.

Mackenzie was given notice.

'There's a ten pound of wage owing,' he told the manager.

'That's right. You'll get it when you bring the dog in. I'm keeping her.'

Mackenzie was walking back when she came to meet him. He thought it not worth returning to the hut to collect his belongings. Yes, he would need the chanter. No, he had it, in the pocket with his savings. He had the Bible in the dilly bag. 'Ay,' he said to himself. 'That'll do.'

The clerk remembered Mackenzie. His nose was still bandaged.

'Mornin,' he said. 'You look hungry.' He was eating soup from a metal dish. 'Footin it?' Mackenzie nodded.

'Wanted to go to Canada?' The clerk consulted a ledger. 'That's all right. Dependants?'

'One.'

'That's all right. Barque here, *William Jane*, leavin Tuesday,

812 tonnage, calling Siddeney, Christmas Island, Hawaii, bound Vancouver.'

'Newfoundland.'

'That's all right. Take a coach.'

'Show me Newfoundland.'

The clerk showed him. 'Deck, tarpaulin. Two blankets per body, one per minor, three pound extra each body below three years, five pounds if ovah annunder twelve, ten if ovah annunder sixteen, livestock by weight it's all accordin, inspection day of departing clearance necessary kangaroos sheep cattle foot-an-mouth, catarrh, scab, that do you? Fifty pound.'

'There is forty pound.'

'Not enough. Forty pound three years ago. Today, fifty pound.' The clerk resumed his soup. 'Lovely day,' he said to a man in a beaver hat who had come in, and hit a fly.

The man wore a cravat and adjusted his hat.

'Carry on,' the man said. 'I enjoy listening. I shall have my little flutter presently.'

'I have saved forty pound,' Mackenzie said to the clerk.

The clerk opened a copy of *Hints from the Journal of an Aborigine, by an Emigrant Mechanic*, and compressed it on a fly that was nibbling at his bandage. He opened another ledger.

'That's all right. Brig here, *Spooner Loyal*, 70 cattle, 900 sheep, 3 horses, 426 tons, cabin fifty, forecabin forty-five, steerage thirty—'

'Ay, steerage.'

'Sailing tomorrow.'

'That'll do.'

'Steerage, thirty pound. An one dependant. Age?'

'Three.'

'Sex?'

'Bitch.'

'And a very fine bitch indeed if, I might say so,' the stranger said, stroking the dog's muzzle.

'The dog is a pound. Shillin a pup if she whelps on deck.'

Mackenzie counted the money.

'There's one thing,' the clerk said, and winked at the man in the beaver hat.

'Ay?'

'*Spooner Loyal* is going to New Zealand.'

Mackenzie banged his fist. The soup lurched. 'Nothin to be

done then,' the clerk said, and closed the ledger. 'Curious noise,' he added. Mackenzie stopped clicking his fingers.

'Not you,' the clerk said.

'Ah, it is the beasties, I fear.' The man removed his hat and adjusted two white mice which appeared on his head. 'Poor dears, they are famished.' He replaced the hat.

'Gentleman-at-large?' he said to Mackenzie, noting the wrist marks where the sleeves ended.

'Shepherd.'

'Ah, yes. To each his pasture. Allow me to present myself. My name is Huntley-Shawcross but my acquaintances call me Barney. Pray resume your soup, my good fellow, and leave a tot for the beasties.' The man took out some notes and fanned the flies. 'I have been gold-digging and I have been fortunate. I have, as they say, talked with ingots in the springtime of Persephone. Do I bore you? You see, my brother who is poorly and a tradesman in Little Gaddesden would join me, he said, and to this purpose I sent him a lump of gold half as big as a saucer. A token of fraternal regard. The poor dear has sold it for £400, and got himself married. It is not the sale I mind, you understand, it is the acquisition. I know the lady. Now I am alone. In the night, I hear noises. Twice my tent has been slit. I am robbed bare. In any case the diggings are fearfully overpopulated. At night the stench—you understand, it is bad for the beasties, they are losing weight. But let me come to the point—'

'You're quitting,' said the clerk, who no longer fancied his soup.

'Precisely. For New Zealand. I shall try the northern island. Which island shall you try? No, I forgot, you want to go to Newfoundland.'

He took out more notes. 'I will give you twenty-five pounds for the dog.'

'Nay.'

'My dear fellow, you are short in the fare. I am trying to help you.'

'Why do thee want the bitch?'

'Ah.' The man wiped his spectacles on the clerk's napkin. He had small cockley eyes and, now that he was close, a smell of bird seed. 'I shall tell you. I need a companion. Not for myself, you understand. For Elsa.'

The dog stood on her toenails and sniffed the man's pockets.

'Elsa is my budgerigar.'

'Thee is crippled, man,' Mackenzie said. He turned to the clerk. 'Show me New Zealand.'

The clerk showed him New Zealand.

'What is at the bottom? The lean island.'

'Gold,' the cockley man said, and turned the islands right way up. 'Gold in the northern island.'

'And here? The fat one.'

'That is the obverse. In the lean half are the lean kine and in the fat half the fat.'

'What is in the fat part?'

'You are a tiresome fellow. Snakes, I shouldn't wonder. Snakes and elephants.'

'Bullocks and sheep,' the clerk said.

'What does the *Spooner* carry?' Mackenzie said.

'Bullocks and sheep.'

Mackenzie bought a ticket for the fat island and left.

'They often change countries like that,' the clerk said.

The man removed his hat. 'If you are quite finished? Thank you, we are most grateful.' He dropped the mice into the dish.

'I might have lent him the money if he had not been so rude to Elsa,' the man said.

When the mice had nearly finished he took a budgerigar from his pocket and sprinkled some bird seed in a corner of the dish. 'Come along, Elsa.' The bird hopped in. The mice chattered with pleasure and the bird's beak made a tinkling sound on the bottom of the dish.

'Curious noise,' the clerk said.

After leaving Christchurch, Mackenzie had greased his boots with weka oil and now that they were waterlogged they bent. He forded the rivers on bunched flax and grinned at the power of the current. The dog swam like a Turk. He was glad of that.

He crossed the plain.

He crossed swamps, jumping from nigger-head to nigger-head. The swamp eels came out onto the bogwood, inviting him to gaff them. He grilled the meat until it was golden and seasoned it with sowthistle. As the native Wiremu had taught him. By a swamp where eels dozed like pythons and grey ducks were playing prams with their young, he left the track altogether, acquiring food from the foothills with that easy instinct of the uneducated.

Sometimes at a boundary post a lone dog would rush forward barking excitedly. He would release the animal for he could not bear to see a dog chained.

Everywhere sheep grubbed in the tussock. He noticed that where the scrub displaced the veldt it was rank and of edible surprises. He recognised mikimiki, ribbonwood, akeake, holly, the holly nearly a foot in diameter. And the heaths, true ones with waxy-looking bells, growing into small trees. He cut a stick and heated it and bent it and crooked the sheep he came across. They were spiked with groundthorn and barbed Irishman. They were a sorry lot.

What puzzled him was the light. It was brittle. There was no bloom in it, no blue shadow. It made a nonsense of air and water, distilling distance, as if by its clarity it had acquired the right to bend space so that a man's gaze might leap, direct, into the mountains. They were further on than he had thought.

After four days they seemed no closer. They seemed as they had seemed when he had first sighted them from the Pacific, marvellous in the morning. But his vessel had gone on, and fetched up in a place called Otago.

As he climbed the bird life increased. There was one, greentawny, taloned, bright vermilion underwing that plundered, plundered his knife in the moonlight and ran off saying, *eeee-aaa, eeee-aaa* till it choked, that one he could mimic on the chanter. He failed to imitate the crow. By night bats invaded his camp and a tribe of ground owls perched in a druidical circle at his feet, tearing up fern root and spitting out the fibre with a deep grinding sound.

A flight of petrels passed westward and vanished behind a pinnace of rock encircled by birds. He noted the rock and he thought, 'Yes, that is what I saw in the Land Office.'

He descended a ridge and climbed another. There was the river, that great loop again. And always the white shoulders, you could camp an army of foot on that wake of shingle. But how hot, how bare the earth was! The sheep lay on the ground, gasping. Why didn't the graziers throw them higher?

Later he circled a bog and climbed an escarpment of shale and rock, everything was shale and rock and tiny flowers, flowering in the rock itself; and cabbages, rock cabbages, scrolled there. Everything, every sound was an echo, immense. You could never be lonely here, he thought. He slid onto a shelf overlooking the river. There were the clouds tearing away, throwing back the mountains.

The river ran with a soughing sound, he felt the churning under his feet. The dog sat up, sniffing. They could both smell fires rising. And the brown grass bruised by the animals' feet: the yoke of wool, unmistakable as tar. He sat still.

Evening bore down, that brief southern twilight.

Now the light melted.

You had to be quite still. As a boy he had not understood this. He had hurried through the glens, the half-light, with one hand before his face. This was because by day, on the earth moor, he had peopled his world with snow giants and talking stones, tall as the cedars of Lebanon — the giants lived by day; but with night, the first grey of night, came the turn of the little people, who would rise out of the mounds and the wheel houses to hunt in packs and pluck away travellers — he kept his hand there, hurrying home, so as not to recognise them.

Now he understood the twilight not as a time of conflict but as a time of growing: the long moment when the earth turned and he, like the plants and trees, could inhale something of that great motion. He knew exactly when it would begin. But the end, the final act of night, had always evaded him.

Even now. It was very brief.

You had to be still and contemplate it. Then when the hills lifted, the earth would turn.

Khe bird song grew, shrilling in the scree roots. In the changing light the floor of the valley crumpled into a thousand folds. Shadows darted into the river as snakes, mounted the terraces as frogs, steepled the hills in elephants' tusks. The mountains collapsed. The river sounded, hollowing out the bird song. But a thrush sang, a native thrush, out of the bubbling waters. He saw the white sheep purple with the purpling sky.

Then the river shouted and the night poured down, blackening everything.

'Let us rejoice in the bundle of life that has brought us together. Here, in this place I speak today, the day of the baptism of our new church, I speak of life. Of life together. We are together in the valley of the shadow of life and we must live in that shadow without fear. *We*, I say, mark that. I do not say we are one race, one people — though there is evidence for that too, since Maori has the same meaning as Moor and is a mixed race, while we who are of Nordic stock are also a mixed race, our blood is mingled with the dark Iberian. But today I do not say that. I say that by our differences, and only by understanding our differences, shall we know one another. For we are different. Some of us eat with forks and some with fingers; some of us hoard property and some donate it to the common fold, for the good of all. Some of us (here the preacher glanced at Lady Suffolk who was rustling her silks) some of us bathe our faces in milk and some of us bleed them and rub soot into the wounds. We are plainly different. We are today cast up as spilled fruit. Yet shall we ripen in the service of one another, for we are bound together in the bundle of life in the service of Our Father. Mark that, *Our* Father—'

A band of frost at the missionary's neck indicated that he had donned a clean collar. Even so, Frances thought, he resembles an old clothes bag.

'He's a charlatan,' Lady Suffolk said to her husband. She sat with a straight back which Donald Hay her husband always thought an achievement, for such a pillowy woman. He nodded in agreement and continued paring his nails with a pocket-knife. Albion Hay, the lame brother, studied the missionary and invoked similes. He invites similes, the brother thought. The head, bald, cod-like, an inverted pudding basin; the habit, hanging like a torn sail — clearly the man slept in it.

'It is not what you will hear preached in Christchurch. But I would have us *rejoice* in our differences! Oh yes. In Christchurch they talk of miracles, they say we have made you like ourselves. You, the Maori people. If we in this place thought that, our thoughts would be disgusting! We have understood nothing of your ways as God understands them—'

Lady Suffolk fidgeted. Her boa kept slipping, catching the light from the low windows that were not yet glassed. She can smell the oil, Frances thought, from their bodies. Frances sat with her father, just behind the Hays. They *are* a mixed race, she thought, looking round — copper, flaxen, wavy, lovely waves, some had the thick ebony mops of Ethiopians. That one was negroid. Some of the old women, sucking pipes, had the gravity of ancient Greek philosophers. Pockets of steam rose from their bodies, mingling with fern bark. The roof was moulting. There, up there! That beam. They had raised a tree. End to end, a whole tree. How they had carved it! It curved, whorled, spiralled, convoluted, circled, all those red eyes, whirling everything to a red heaven. All those red lips. All those—she felt slightly sick. It was obscene. She had not seen the other parts at first.

Polson concentrated. The Hays endured. The Hays employed no natives on principle. They had their principles.

None of the other squatters have come, he thought; only the Hays. The shepherds were there. The natives had come first; they had the right, they had carried the stones, and had filled the place an hour before the service was due to begin. They had put their babies on the window ledges and kept going outside to collect them whenever one fell down. It was difficult to concentrate.

'Is it a miracle that some of you are converted to the Christian faith? Not at all. It is belief and understanding. We, the bringers of light, we who have been cast into the desert Judea, *your* Judea, and have taken your lands (here the missionary glanced, Polson thought, at himself)—we are delighted. We trust you may learn from the Christian doctrine to forgive us. We are delighted that you contract our doctrine, delighted at your understanding. But (now the missionary lowered his voice), but I trust we are not delighted; I trust we are revolted at our ignorance that we may learn that so far the understanding has been all on one side—'

It's not, Frances thought, what I should call sacred, but as a beam it is rare. It is something different.

'What do we know of how the native lives? We see his tiny hut, see the smoke issuing, aha, we say, he cooks in it, thereby he is dirty. Let me tell you what the Maori says. The Maori says the white man is a fool. For the white man builds a big fire and sits away from it, he gets warm only by sections. Whereas the Maori makes a small fire and sits over it, and is heated through and through—'

'Amen,' said a hideous old native with green pendants in his ears. And Mackenzie walked in, wet from the river carrying a baby. He gave the baby away and bowed his head standing. He didn't see why not.

It's easy to see, thought Polson, why they hounded their

Bishop-designate from Christchurch. Heterodox, they said. Mad, he had heard that too. His sermons were not sermons but admonishments; statements of intent. Yet Polson found the intent, however obscure the motive, compelling. There was a question on his lips.

'Let us pray,' he heard. He must have dozed off. The missionary had raised his hands to a dome of prayer, revealing holes at the armpits, and a faint tearing sound was heard. One hand was gloved in black. It was an inch too long in the fingers. It was slightly sinister. Frances had gathered her petticoats into a cushion for them both to kneel. Polson heard a new voice at his back. Frances was looking at the sole of a foot. It was autumn brown, creased smooth. It was rather beautiful. There were feet all round. Lady Suffolk was inhaling, Frances had seen the little box of aromatic vinegar clasped in her glove. Impossible to pray on snowgrass!

That voice, Polson thought, is responding in Gaelic.

Those feet, she thought, have stopped praying altogether. The minister isn't praying either, he is looking.

Everybody was looking, for the responses had dwindled except for that voice; a brackish lilting voice which seemed to proclaim that the way to God was by itself. The voice continued. Lady Suffolk wanted to look, and did, she met Frances' eyes fresh from seeing, as they were bound to see, that it was only the voice of a wet plaid. 'A shepherd,' she said to her father. 'Streaming.' And nudged him. Polson nodded, but waited till the service was ended. Donald Hay did not wait that long, he turned without waiting for the collect and fairly rushed from the church.

'Really, Amos.' Lady Suffolk plucked his sleeve as he hastened after Hay. 'The Maoris sing very badly. It is just like the chanting in the Roman Catholic cathedrals.'

Lady Suffolk was on one side and Albion Hay, leaning over with his stick, blocking the other. Frances chafed on his arm. Polson sighed and waited, you couldn't shoulder past a lame man.

Albion Hay said, 'That legend on the rim is curious. Could it be oriental?'

'Which rim?' Polson said.

'The bell, the rim of the bronze bell,' Lady Suffolk said. 'Didn't you notice? It's cracked. It must be his font.'

'It is,' said Frances. 'And his little river-stoned church is *sweet*.' But it was pointless to assume finality with Lady Suffolk.

'Riverstones. Riverstones, are they? But the service. Amos: do you realise he omitted the litany *and* the communion?'

Polson shrugged. 'I hardly noticed, Lady Suffolk. I haven't communed for twenty years.' They reached the step. Yes, he should have come out when Frances urged. Unmistakable, that man.

Donald Hay was talking to him. Standing in the sun with his jacket off and his biscuit sleeves billowing like imbeciles. He was offering the man money. The man refused it. Hay was not put out. Polson could see from the expression on Hay's face when he came towards them that the man had already accepted Hay's offer of employment.

Sparrow was emerging. 'Very little, Lady Suffolk,' he was saying. 'The fact is, I care very little for the effeminacy of ritual.' Then he joined the group and invited them all to visit the pa. The Hays declined. Donald Hay apologised for withdrawing before the collection and gave the missionary two pounds to add to it.

The pa stood back from the river, overlooking the church and the valley of flocks. It was hidden behind palisades that might have commanded a fortress. They entered silently, as into a prison. The natives were squatting on the ground eating. There were a few children throwing tops. Then an old chief crossed the courtyard and welcomed them. His skin hung in folds and his face was tattooed to a blue mask. He said a few words, shaking his cheeks and making his ear-rings rattle. Then he went back to his dinner. 'I have arranged nothing,' the missionary said, and led on through a maze of huts. The huts were mud and reeds with slatted windows, like Arab tembes. Frances saw one family emerge, crawling, they kept coming and coming and still coming until, crouched at the communal pot, they covered a space twice as big as the hut. But not hovels, she discovered, stepping over a smoking midden and entering one. All quite tidy and cool, with a raised platform for sleeping. Though there was barely room for them to stand.

'I am the first white man here,' Sparrow said, entering with her father, who was smiling. Having congratulated Hay for his alacrity Polson had put the shepherd from his mind; and now pottering after the missionary he was full of curiosity. 'Then I must be the second,' he said. And winked at Frances as she went out. It was then he was given a hint of the missionary's contradictions and a tragedy different from his own.

'Abominations,' the preacher had said. He had taken down a basket hanging from what appeared to be a withered hand severed at the wrist. 'See here, Polson.'

'Yes?'

'Potted flesh.' There was a glint in the missionary's eye.

'I see,' Polson said.

'I am determined to save the souls of the heathen.'

'Yes—and to destroy their culture.'

'Perhaps, some of it.' Sparrow laughed thinly.

'And why not?' he added suddenly.

You will fail, Sparrow, thought Polson. And not in the way you imagine. But how could he tell the missionary that the reason he scorned natural man was because he was secretly attracted to him?

They followed Frances out.

At Sparrow's hut a bulldog leaped up, half mastiff, its bat ears ravaged by cats. Frances drew back. 'The chain holds him,' Sparrow said, fondling the animal with a leer that might have been touching, Polson thought, had it been granted his concubine instead.

The woman stood over them as they ate. She was pantherish, despite her bulk, and communicated with Sparrow sensually with her eyes and body. They had a curious understanding.

'But conversion isn't a simple sea change,' Polson was saying, as they sat down to a pot of rice flecked with dark blobs. They sat on a mat outside.

'You will tell me next that cannibalism is justified.' The missionary took some gristle from his teeth and fed it to the dog. Then he pointed.

Frances was hot. She was still angry with Hay; and no chance to vent her feelings with the missionary pointing out things. And that woman lolling over them all the time. She was more like a Lascar. She had a vague immutable smile. Every now and then she prodded the missionary to make him eat.

Sparrow was pointing to the palisades. 'The figures,' he said.

'Ah yes.' Polson saw now. The outer fence was thirty feet

high; it was surmounted by full length carvings painted red; there were fifty such figures. What was remarkable was not the carving but the eye sockets which were empty. He looked straight through them to the sky.

And Sparrow explained that the eyes, containing the soul force of the slain, were offered first to the chief to be eaten. In this way cannibalism contributed to the prestige of a conquering tribe.

'Oh yes,' Frances said. 'But they have outgrown all that.' Sparrow grinned and began to talk about the raised shorehouses which were, he said, Javanese in style. He was in a rare humour, taking the meat in his fingers and sucking it through loose teeth; then lying back, reclining, and continuing to talk in a metallic voice through whiskers that reached almost to his eyes. 'Eat,' the woman said, and prodded him. 'This food is special,' Sparrow said, waving an arm. 'They're eating corn — animal corn.' He didn't seem to mind the woman.

He doesn't converse, Frances thought. He makes statements.

'The bell, papa. I was to remind you about the bell.'

'Ah yes, my font.' Sparrow was off again. 'I have baptised nineteen children in that. When I came they were using it to boil up fern root. The inscription is oriental. So is — look at the weaving. Look at the features — ' Polson was staring at the woman. Her eyes were oblique and there was a remarkable depression between them. 'All their traditions point to the east. Hue thinks they are one of the lost tribes of Israel. He has set me thinking. I am writing a paper. It's all there, you see, in the Old Testament. Twenty-eight of their customs — I have made a list. Precisely those customs for which the lost tribe was driven from its inheritance. It is all there.'

'Who is Hue?' Frances said. He *would* address her father all the time.

'Oh Hue,' he said, making a sign to the woman. When she had gone he sank back. 'I have had a little setback with Hue. You see, my child, I have discouraged the tangi. Weeping and self-laceration, it is unhealthy. They use obsidian flakes and rub charcoal into the wounds to preserve them. Some of the wounds — well, never mind that. But it disturbs the planting calendar if it goes on. Last week, another death, another baby died. It was only influenza. Hue's incantations are powerless against our diseases. They brought the child to me then, I gave it a Christian burial. Since then'—the missionary's eyes became suffused, brightly marbled—'I have suppressed the tangi.'

'Yes,' Polson said, 'yes. Now there is a question—'

'Naturally Hue is annoyed, he has lost caste. So we are having a little tiff, a battle of wills. But I think, yes I think I am winning. You saw the attendance in church.'

Yes, Frances thought, he has the mind of a school-master, even if he seems not to care for the things of this world. He reminds me of Swinburne, only a little thinner and more comsumptive looking.

'This man Hue.'

'A prophet, my dear. They use another word. I would translate it as medium. He lives over there behind the carved house. His dwelling is sacred. The odd thing is that he who is the magician represents to them the real world, whereas I who teach them to read and write—I regard myself as a teacher, not a missionary—I am thought to possess supernatural powers.

'Aren't they a wretched lot?' he added, looking round. Then he said: 'Hue and I are much alike.'

'Oh?' Polson said.

'Yes. We would like to drive you and everything you represent out. We detest landtakers. I am sorry the Hays aren't here, I should like to have told them also.'

Polson had feared the man's mind was incoherent, but the actual discovery was distressing. 'They seem quite strong to me.'

Again the eyes glinted. 'When I arrived there was nothing in the houses and little out, and I had to eat fern root during the winter. You can see their plots from here. Pitiful.'

He continued inveighing, lying slack, as if the despair were in himself. Indeed, thought Polson, he swings from arrogance to torpor, and is at his most lucid when he is most despairing.

'Still,' Sparrow said, 'their Genesis is enlightening. It is the only cosmic pattern I know that denies immortality to man. I am rather fond, myself, of the fall of the demi-god Maui. Without him our Christianity would say nothing to them. I wouldn't be here; nor, my friends, would you. Maui is magical, he creates order. He was found like Moses, abandoned. He creates fire, he binds the sun and creates daylight, he is Prometheus and Herakles. He is a Sky-God, like Zeus, but in the end he is vanquished by the Earth Goddess, he is squeezed to death between her thighs. The Sky and the Earth, this is the basis of their religion. The spirit, you see, can never overcome the body.'

'I have read that,' Polson said.

'You must be the only landtaker who has.' Sparrow toyed with his long black glove. He continued to regard Polson through half-shut eyes.

We are playing a game, Polson thought. He needs my confidence but is too proud to ask for it.

'You say —' Polson stopped. He was conscious that Sparrow was feeding every second mouthful to the dog. 'You say they're demoralised. But were they not first weakened by their own wars?'

'And we have done the rest. You remember what Blunden said, the first Bishop? "I bring you glad tidings of great joy." And a great cheer went up from the assembled chiefs. We promised them fellowship —'

Polson interrupted. 'And we have dispossessed them overnight, yes. But the land was freely sold.'

'*Sold?* You do not understand. The proverb says, "More than meat alone." The land was given in a special sense. If you lend your daughter to your guardian only to discover he has bartered her for profit three times over: are you not disillusioned?'

'The land is kinship too?'

'They say, "our bones". It can never be sold or bartered in our sense. The idea of "selling" land is incomprehensible to them.'

Polson grew thoughtful.

'In that case,' he said, 'it can end only in bloodshed.'

'You are not like the others,' Sparrow said grudgingly. 'Yet you criticise me behind my back, they all do. Those who know who I am.'

'Criticise? My dear Sparrow, we all do that. You do me and I to you, it's the interpretation that counts. Criticism, I have always regarded as interpretation. Christ was the supreme critic. He interpreted the signs as he saw them. You man, your medium is a critic. So are you. This now is my criticism, my question: You spoke of awareness, of differences. Some you have abolished, slavery, polygamy —'

'Not the tapu.'

'No, not that. Slavery, polygamy, nudity, that is another. And the tangi. That's enough. You evaluate the morality of these differences according to a path you see before you. You stifle some, you promote others. I am puzzled. In a sense you are right to evaluate. Your aim is to convert. You see the natives as Israelites in the wilderness, you see the god-like element in them—the narayan, is it not?—and you will if you can give them back their inheritance, their Canaan. This I understand. You are both missionary and political agent, since the Government does not send agents into the wilderness. But the Maori sees his world as a cosmic entity—as that roof-tree in your church, for example: closely interwoven? Some parts are to our eyes gross, some ugly, some beautiful. But to him, an entity, harmonious and whole. His entity to me seems like a clock, all the parts are balanced. Are you not afraid of disturbing this balance, of creating more problems than you can solve?'

The missionary lunged across the mat. '*Destroy!* Not disturb. The destruction began long before I came!' He was bubbling at the mouth and paused to wipe it with his glove. 'All I can do is collect the pieces that remain and re-fashion them in the light of the Father.' Polson said nothing. Sparrow stared at him glassily. His belligerence vanished. 'Where is the wrong in that?' he murmured. Polson kept silence. He had always found obsession painful, whether born of imagined wrongs or a desire for self-justification. He thought of his father: he too had created an edifice made of unseen enemies and, for self-glory, self-aggrandisement, had continued to batter against wadding, what was not there. His father had preached understanding and as a result had become an autocrat.

'No, not wrong,' Polson said gently.

'Eat,' the missionary said, as the woman came out. 'It's bad manners not to finish the dish.'

When she had gone again he said intuitively, 'You think I court danger? Of course I do.' He plucked off the glove. There was a long weal on his right hand, lumpy and reddish. 'It was a tomahawk. Not, it pleases me to think, a native weapon. The native had stolen it from a sailor. He meant to strike higher. Fortunately his aim was bad.'

He reclothed the hand; rather proudly, Frances thought.

'Here?' she said.

'Oh no, my child. In Nelson. You're inquisitive about me, I see. In England I was head of a large establishment at Camberwell, a boarding establishment. I came out as Bishop-designate to Christchurch. They thought in London that I preached rather well, which I do of course. Our child died as we landed. Then my wife. Poor thing.' He touched his head. His eyes grew moist. 'They didn't like my preaching in Christchurch. They found it—disturbing. I made it known I was sailing home. In Wellington I disembarked and came south again. I crossed the straits to Nelson. I changed my name. I lived with the natives, I learned their tongue. I grew my kumara and corn as they did. They didn't like my preaching in Nelson either. So I came further south. It was God's will that I return to Canterbury. In Nelson they were not kind. Here I am tolerated, I am necessary; my God obtains in areas where their gods are powerless. I teach a few skills. I shall introduce the potato next, I think. Here they have built my church. I proceed, little by little. Only time is against me; as it is against my friend Hue.'

'What is he like?' Frances said suddenly.

'Oh, he's harmless enough. One of my pupils reads to him from the Old Testament, he can quote long passages from memory.'

'Yes, but what is he *like*?'

He stared at her wanly. 'I have no idea, my child. I have never seen him. Shall we visit the school?'

But instead of going to the school the missionary took them outside the pa onto a hill. Looking down they could see children climbing poles, sailing kites; women were washing. 'That is Hue's dwelling,' he said. It stood apart, raised up and half hidden by a wooden roof that almost touched the ground. A naked boy knelt on the platform, chanting. They could hear the chanting.

'And here—you asked about the tapu. Here is tapu.' Sparrow pointed down. It was a depression, a square of earth, partly built up with stones and railed off. 'Not long ago a visitor from another tribe squatted here and spat, there, by that pole. He was killed for it. They ate him just like pork. The ground is hallowed, it contains dead souls. They make offerings, sacrifices are offered: Rongo the vegetable god is appeased here. To approach with cooked food is forbidden, to light a fire is forbidden. To go closer, my child (for Frances was picking gentians) is forbidden. This is tapu.

'Once, travellers halted here and said prayers to exorcise Taipo, the Devil. They prayed that the earth might not be stretched lengthwise, for the Devil, they thought, was continually lengthening the distance they had to travel.'

'Look, papa,' Frances said, 'how clear Seagull is.' It was her way: to invoke that rock and give her father a look when she had had enough. The heat was stifling. And the horses, tied up, wanting water.

'Yes, m'dear. Travellers, you said Sparrow: travelling to and from where?'

'Oh there.'

'Those are the alps.'

'They know them, the older folk. Peak by peak.'

'And the route?'

'Lost, buried with them.'

'Pennyroyal,' Frances cried, stooping low. 'But what tiny little things.' She peered round. They were oblivious of her. Her father lifting himself up and down on the points of his hilows, squinting. Up, up, up, he squinted. Had the air done his eyes that much good, could he see up *there*? He was squinting beyond her rock.

She stood up. She wanted to ride. She would ride, up there. He would take her.

'Have you thought why they went there?' Polson said.

'Indeed. They plant the dead with the legs pointing that way. It is the spiritual abode of their ancestors.'

'But they do not visit?'

'They will not cross this tapu to the west.'

Sparrow smiled mysteriously.

'Strange,' Polson said. 'Because I believe that the obstacle is less spiritual than preservative. Your analogy Sparrow of the daughter: Let us suppose you have two daughters. You give one away, she is exploited. Do you not secrete the second?'

Frances lifted her head. Her horse whinnied; out of the still air a buzzing sounded; that boy by Hue's house was still chanting. And these two pecking like crows on a heath, oddly content, oblivious of everything.

'You say the natives are caught; they cannot go down and they cannot go up.'

'Will not,' the missionary corrected.

'Just so. They are between the white man's sheep and their

own superstition. Yet the superstition is comparatively recent. Could it not be that there is no obstacle at all other than a simple desire to keep the white man out?'

'Out? Out of what?'

'You have said that they resent my presence.'

'Of course.'

'Since I extend to the west I violate their tapu. Also in other ways: ponds, springs, old waterholes—'

'Droo found some old bones,' Frances said.

'One of my hands disinterred a burial ground. No doubt I desecrate their tapu all the time.'

'No doubt. But you see, my friend, where this awareness leads? It leads to the wonder and mystery of the Christian God —since He is all-powerful and appears to condone these sins.'

'I am not mystified, though perhaps they are.' Polson paused. 'Once I believed that if you solved a people's material problems, you solved half their problems. I no longer hold with that. Nor do I hold with proselitising, however enlightened the biblical repairs. The one induces torpor; the other is less venal and the results, I fear, may be more surprising—violence after all is only another word for spiritual confusion.'

'What do you believe then?'

'I believe in responding to a demand,' Polson said. 'Sometimes I think it is not the natives that need reforming but we, the reformers. You say it would please you to evict me. My dear Sparrow—I would go willingly, if you would only come with me.'

The missionary's teeth parted in an ugly smile. If only, Frances thought, he were a little bit cleaner, I might be on his side. How could you leave the natives alone to their fate? Her father was as contradictory as Sparrow. Conversion was such a difficult business.

Polson said, 'I wonder what they would say if I proposed giving them *back* an inheritance?'

He said things so pompously at times it was no wonder people laughed, she thought. Sparrow had tilted his head— all his unswept teeth were there, and the shirt parting from the collar. The missionary's laughter crackled out like snapping twigs.

'You must ask Hue that!' he said, wiping the saliva from his mouth. His hand fell away then and was suddenly white against the rusted garment. He gave a cry. It was then that the incident occurred. They turned, Polson turned, as running feet and a sound of hot pitched voices shrilled below them. Though it couldn't have happened just like that. The figures passed below them. Yet moving with astonishing speed. It was moaning not wailing, the wailing came later. A hunting party, Polson thought, seeing dogs and spears.

'A hunting party returning,' he told Frances, turning her so that she wouldn't see what they had already seen: the man in front, chested, spattered with blood, running hard—he did not moan—carrying a child. He carried the child in a shirt.

'It is nothing,' the missionary said, and stumbled down the track. And indeed it might have been nothing, simply a race, but for the red stumps protruding from the shirt.

Gored, he thought.

The women were there, in their coloured shifts, their wet hands. They had left the washing. The elders were there, all the old men. And the children, pulling in their kites and running. They had grouped themselves in a ring before the carved house the way peasants gather at the coming of a stranger; and they drew apart, hugging their shifts and blankets as the silent man ran through and stopped before the open doorway. Then he turned and faced the throng, displaying the shift, and a woman ran screaming from one of the huts. Even as she threw herself at his feet she had changed and become what she was not, an animal, rending and tearing. She clawed her hair, her face, her armpits, her clothes. Not one person alone now but fifty; all clawing; then a hundred. Then the stamping. So this, thought Polson, is how a tangi begins; though afterwards he remembered nothing but the sound. It broke first from one side, then from the other, a lamentation that pitted the air and shook the earth, joining onlooker to onlooker, voice to voice, body to naked body, as that great grief poured like a tide across the courtyard. Whether the man and child were raised bodily or borne mesmerically on the tide, into the carved house, he did not see; nor the passing of that tide. He saw the door close. He saw the bare court, the coloured shifts lying trampled in the sunlight, he saw the sunlight on the ground; and the missionary standing there alone, a few feet from the door, excluded.

Only once in the days that followed did Frances mention the events of that Sunday. She said, 'I didn't like that man.'

'No,' her father said. 'Yet his rashness is a form of courage.'

Polson was on the verandah sketching. He put down his brush. He had called on Sparrow the day before, alone, only to find him ill, ill and green on a mat of rushes, staring glassily before him. Yes, he was ill. No, not very ill. The woman was treating him. He was alright. Yes, the child had died. No, there had not been a Christian burial. Sparrow coughed a lot. The natives were angry, he said, that Droo had disturbed that skeleton by the men's hut. It was a sacred burial ground. Had everything been put back? Good. It was a highly tapu spot. How did the natives know? Oh, they knew, they knew. No, he was alright, the woman had a physic. No, not Hue's physic, one of her own. Thank you. He waved Polson out.

Polson had been thinking about the missionary a great deal. Now — he was mixing the paints with a nail — he recalled his meal with Sparrow, the rice and the meat. He compared his thoughts to the grains of rice and the other's to the pieces of meat. The meat was harder to digest but without it the dish had no flavour. Also he recalled the allegory of the child's death: the mourners within and the strange god rejected at the door of the temple. Hector mourning Hecuba, and the watchers without. Polson saw himself as the watcher and in a sly sort of way found that he had come to admire the missionary, the man without who would not be turned away.

'I admire his willpower, Francie. He is a man — I think, Francie, he is a man whose natural way is to remain aloof yet who is bold enough to involve himself in forces that are beyond him; and he knows it. He won't let go. And that, since we are involved in a similar way, is somehow comforting.'

'Nonsense, we're not involved with him.'

No, he thought; and I did not mean that.

'And you're not to pity him, papa. He isn't compassionate. He hates too much.'

'It isn't hatred at all, Francie. It's love—'

'Love?'

'In disguise. That's what frightens me. I'm afraid one day he'll abandon Christianity altogether and cross right over.'

'Pah,' he heard her mutter.

'*Not* to pity him,' she said. She was in the kitchen, rolling dough with a vinaigrette bottle. 'Do I disturb you? I have to talk to roll it flat. He isn't truthful either. He said he lost one child. There were two, there were distinctly two, Droo says. There's a boy still living somewhere.'

'In any case, papa'—she had to keep stopping to push her hair back—'I didn't mean Sparrow, I meant the other man. The shepherd.'

Polson was painting again. He wasn't listening.

Later he called out, 'It's no good!'

'What, papa?'

'This landscape. I can't capture it. Oh the sketches are alright, but every time I use the paints it's English grasses, English mosses, English *tones* all over.'

'Let me see, don't tear it.'

He came in and put the canvas against the kitchen window. She glanced at it and turned to the fire. She dug at it and peered into the camp oven—the oven was big enough for a loaf or ten scones but not both—and wondered why whenever she baked the kitchen smelled of fermented jam. She turned to the painting again. 'Still,' she said, tying up her hair in twists, 'you'll grow out of it, papa.'

Sometimes, he thought, she can be quite brutal. He took the painting away and broke it on his knee.

But he kept to painting, as he kept to thinking about the land, what Sparrow had said. 'More than meat alone.' He would catching himself riding out to muster or to seek new pasture (always seeking)—nuzzling the cat that travelled on the saddle-bow, thinking aloud. 'Perhaps he's right; perhaps it isn't indifferent or hostile—perhaps the hostility is in ourselves.' It didn't solve anything, this thinking. But it reminded him of the plan. Though he heard nothing from Whitehouse (how should he, so soon?), still his mind half-dreaming half-waking would leap into domey places and pilasters of light, and the gateway was always those mountains.

Yet still they talked of sailing, still in the evenings he conversed with Frances, now in Italian, now in French. He kept up these mock ties with Europe as he kept up the London *Times*, which he read not haphazardly when it arrived in bundles months late but precisely in sequence, issue by issue. He even cut an opening in the door; and sometimes he would fold a copy and put it in the opening, to see how it looked.

Nothing was decided.

* * *

Days passed.

Once Donald Hay rode over. He wore a purple hunting jacket and looked very mighty on a white horse. Polson was at the shearing. Hay laughed ebulliently when he saw the way they did it. He had come for no particular reason; except that he heard the Polsons might be sailing and if so, why, it was just a thought, but he knew people, friends, who would buy handsomely, buy Odessa up to the hilt, so that Polson wouldn't sustain too much of a loss.

'And these friends — they would freehold?'

'Of course. Fence the boundaries and freehold them, as I am doing — as you are not doing. We've talked about this before. It isn't only to keep farming trash out, I detest trespassing. Always have done. The natives, these beggars across the river, they used to come on my property. They think twice now when they see my fences. You *are* sailing then?'

'Perhaps,' Polson said. 'It really rests with Frances.'

Hay gave Polson a pitying look. Not having himself been enlightened by the therapeutic floggings of a Christian father in his youth, Hay could not understand the freedom Polson allowed his daughter. He regarded this laxity as symptomatic of a diseased nature. Hay was childless and a traditionalist; self-made; the son of a Nottingham hide merchant and the second husband of Lady Suffolk. They were known as Lady Suffolk and Mr. Hay.

'Lady Suffolk is well?' Polson said.

'Yes. She sends you this.' Hay gave Polson a book and the latter made a face. It was a copy of *The Imitation of Christ*. Apparently Lady Suffolk had not forgiven him for trying to convert her cook to atheism.

Hay was in high spirits. He said, rubbing the pommel of his crop over his maroon beard, freshly dyed, he was about to change some sheep with the Emperor Louis Napoleon and by God, Polson, one lamb, it would fetch ninety pounds.

By God, thought Polson, you are a lucky man. And what of the new shepherd, he asked.

'Unruly,' Hay said. 'Coarse. He has ellipsis of the mind.'

'Oh. And what is that?'

'Never mind. He has it, and it isn't straight.'

'It sounds,' Polson said jocularly, 'like one of Lady Suffolk's judgments.'

'Never mind. You saw the marks on his wrists? Once I decide to engage a hand it's the only question I ask, I asked him if he had served time. "Oh ay," he said gaily, "they lock you away right enough for stealing sheep." '

'And what did you say to that?'

'I told him to mind his tongue. I am sorry I bought him.'

Polson bit his lip but said nothing.

Hay said nothing more about the merinos he had offered to buy in Sydney.

'And what about the new flock?' Frances said to her father when Hay had gone.

'A thousand,' Polson said evasively. 'I need a thousand, don't I?'

'I suppose so. But where will you put them?' His temerity baffled her. 'There's nowhere, is there?'

'Not really, m'dear.' He fell silent. 'I wonder—'

'Yes let's! Let's ride up to Seagull and look.'

He'll funk it, she thought; heights terrify him. To her surprise, however, he agreed.

They rode out next day.

On the way Polson visited the shearing. He had three thousand sheep and went most mornings to check the previous day's tallies with Gilliam. He was of little use since he couldn't shear, but he liked to sharpen the blades for the men and keep an eye on Taylor whose petty mutinies were as apt to break a sheep's back as Gilliam's temper. The men were shearing out of doors. It was early but the sandflies were already massing. And the gulls wheeling overhead, waiting to drop at evening for the red ends. They made Frances shudder. As they arrived she saw Taylor kick a ewe aside half shorn and collapse by the creek, not a word of greeting as they passed, and there begin picking his teeth with a bowie knife, bouche bée, like a besotted cow. Her father had a word with Gilliam. They rode out then to the west. They had been climbing for an hour when he said: 'Gilliam doubts there will be a profit.'

'That means another loss.'

'He doubts that too.'

'Then splendid, papa.'

'Why?'

'Last year he wouldn't commit himself at all.'

'That's so.'

'What did Mr. Hay say about the shearing, you said you'd tell me.'

'He said the system is ludicrous.'

'It's amazing, isn't it, how he can appear cheerful and generous and disdainful all at the same time? The Hays are bad for your morale.'

'Donald is, certainly.'

'And Lady Suffolk is bad for mine. I sent her some baking. She gave it to the ducks. She said so.'

'But the system, Francie, the actual system of shearing, it works.'

'Of course it works!'

'It's unorthodox but it's theirs. The men would resent it if I hired professionals.'

'We couldn't afford them anyway.'

It was a bad system, he knew; his wool was dirty, always burred and sewn into bales anyhow. His bales looked like badly baked bricks. But in this one month the men earned their year's wage twice over; and he was grateful to them.

They descended into a basin. It was wide and stony, pitted by faults and dry creekbeds. Here and there the moraine stood up, scorified, in cairns. There was a little pasture. Then the ridges began again. They lost the river for a time and turned north, then west again; once, crossing a saddle, Frances looked down and saw the river as a green needle rushing uphill. She tried to canter; but the wind pasting the dust to her lips made her gasp and slow the grey hack. So she was glad when Magistrate shied, the dunce, and plunged off a ledge—a little drop, but it shook her—glad they were proceeding only by plod and by zig-zag. Magistrate was old; he kept turning; and grinning at her. Her father hadn't noticed. He was ahead talking to himself or the cat, that cat. Chesterfield. How she loathed that cat. It sneezed. It wouldn't purr or grin or mew it would only sneeze. Lying motionless across the saddle-bow. It had oily deciduous whiskers. It would regard her with disdain. Then it would sneeze. It was as much as you could expect from a cat.

The sun, slanting through the blown clouds, spread a diaphanous haze. They could not see the mountains. The haze softened the ridges to a maney texture, but when they got up the ridges were darted with Irishman thorn. And the barbed Spaniard growing invisible in the crevices. The horses plunged and reared, bloodied to the knees. Now the scrub receded. They were at the limit of the foothills.

'Wait, Francie.' She had started down a terrace. The way was down. The foothills were transformed, falling abruptly to a tabled moraine; below was a chasm; water was about them and thin mist; and somewhere a lost sheep, bleating; the wind was alpine and the shelf they had been following, nowhere. Instead there were the ranges, clammy, lunar ribs rising from the moraine.

Polson had reined in from giddiness. The clouds, mountebanked, were suddenly blown from their eyes, racing eastward like torn cloaks and leaving gaps, shreds of sky and arid walls, superimposed on a kaleidoscope of soaring peaks. The change was overpowering.

'It's no use, Francie, there's nowhere to put merinos here.' She looked at his face, her horse tugging and his, Hector, standing stiff in the wind. His face had somehow failed. 'You see, up here—no sheep can endure here without ten acres to himself. A thousand merinos is ten thousand acres. Where are they?'

'Over there—across the river.'

'A shepherd, Francie—after six months here he would drink sheep's urine. He'd go mad.'

It was panic, she saw. The panic of heights. His eyebrow was twitching.

'You need the merinos, papa.'

'I don't,' he said.

'Yes. Your flock's too small. And you do want to put a man here. You want him to find a way—up, up, up and over to the other side.'

'No, Francie. Not "a man"—myself.'

He was stroking the cat. Then suddenly Chesterfield had walked away and was sitting up, between Hector's ears, and he was stroking her hair. She had ridden up and laid her head on his saddle.

'The trouble is,' he murmured, 'I'm no good at it.'

She wrinkled her nose, making him look. 'That famous Egyptian nose,' he said. But he wouldn't smile.

'I'm sorry, Francie, I can't even manage Seagull.' He glanced away. 'Not today.'

'Shall we go back,' he said. It was not a question.

'Oh papa—back where? England? Odessa? You sit here

between one land and the next and you screw yourself up because you won't cross the border. You have done this all your life.' She smiled, to show it was not a fault. 'You want to accomplish everything yourself, you're greedy. No, not greedy. You're afraid of ridicule. But so are all men, all men are the same. All men dissemble, cheat, deceive, say the opposite of what they're thinking in order to know what they cannot possibly know or what they cannot possibly do. You told me once that the soul is a force within and a curse which we must accept as a birthmark—as our limitation. I have my limitation, it is being a woman. I accept that. I do, I think. You must accept yours.'

He said, 'Francie, I like you when you're being intense.'

'Don't pat me like that, that's what Mr. Dewhurst does.'

He was silent.

'Papa, it is your job to think of expeditions, not lead them.'

'There's no one else,' he said bleakly. He shrugged. 'Tomorrow I think—'

'Tomorrow, papa, you may think what you like. Today you listen to me. We are going to Seagull.'

'You forget,' she added. 'You've been there. I haven't.'

'No. I didn't pass the rivers.'

'There are two?'

'They have eaten under the terrace, you can't see them.'

'Well?' she said. She was starting down but he caught the bridle.

'Francie—' he began. Then he said, 'My eyes are better now.' He gave a short laugh and dismounted. 'We must walk the horses.'

It took them half an hour to descend the terrace. Rocks fell with every step. Once Polson glanced back as if he would return; petulantly he kicked a boulder which crumbled and dropped sheer into the waters. Now she saw the current tearing the bank, exposing the roots like tentacles on the bright veined rock that under-pinned them, and cried: 'I tell you what frightens me.'

'What?' He was below, shrunken in the mist.

'Not this. Odessa. That tapu, all that talk of tapu. I never told you. Droo's corpse: he didn't put all the bones back. I kept one. I used it to stir the porridge, until Billy found out. Then I hid it. Then I threw it out by the temple. Now I'm afraid to walk there—something rises up and kicks me. You're not listening.'

'Yes.' He would not tell her the same had happened to him.

'Yes,' he said, stopping on a parapet. 'Well, we shall find the bone and give it a decent burial.'

'That's the point, papa—' He was looking down, filmed in spray; she was wringing her hair and watching the horses drink from the seeping rock. 'I did bury it, I put weeds on top and I have dug and dug and now there's nothing there.'

'Is there not? Leave the horses and look here.'

She joined him on the edge. Twenty feet below the rivers merged in a tongue of rapids and milk rock. The spray rose in flights, drenching them. As they watched the mist began to lift and the sun, high now, found them at last. They ate some biscuits. Polson began pacing up and down.

'You're not to brood, papa.' He was staring over the parapet, transfixed. 'Something else I wanted to tell you. That man—'

'I'm not brooding, my dear. And I know what is in your mind. That man Sparrow. You say we are not involved with him.' He pointed down. 'You see that stream. I tried to cross.'

'What happened?'

'That doesn't matter. Oh very well. I turned Hector's head without thinking and he stepped off a ledge into deep water. He tried to bottom with his hind legs and we were swept under. Whitehouse was with me, he saved us. But—it was a good lesson. The point is this. I tried to cross it negligently as I would cross a field. I dismissed its presence and the next moment was up to my neck in it. I was suddenly very much involved. It's the same with people—with Sparrow. You find him odious, but I—I can't dismiss him. Just as we cannot dismiss this river. We cannot walk away and close the door and pretend he isn't there.'

'Why are you telling me this?'

'I don't know, my dear, it simply occurred to me.' He gave her a wry smile. 'Life is a series of episodes—today is one of them. I want to go on, yet somehow I can't. That for me is an episode, it costs a decision. I believe that life exacts different decisions at different times, each more difficult than the last. Life in this sense is like a mythology and as you graduate so you perceive. If you live long enough and pass your examinations, you may perceive a whole pantheon. Perceive, not attain. I doubt if we're granted that. And perhaps something is revealed; perhaps it is simply that we find our identity. Odessa is something of the kind. These mountains are a kind of Jacob's Ladder. Sparrow in bringing light to the heathen is attempting to climb it. I, too, with my plan, I fancy we are both on the same rung.

'You want to dash across the river. I was the same. Never mind. Do you know it's taken me all my life, fifty-three years, to become aware of the tasks we set ourselves? In the towns it was not the same, my perception was only half formed, and if there was a ladder to climb it was a different sort of ladder.'

'Papa, I can't *hear* you. Do come away from the edge and stop talking to yourself.'

He turned towards her, his eyes feverish. 'People say "How I envy you your solitude," they say. Or else, "How simple your life must be." Such fools they are, Francie. They perceive nothing. They are deprived of wonder. I am a child to think it, but it is the sense of wonder that is so awful here. Wonder and savagery, the sort of savagery that has gone from European mountains. Yet that's what makes living here so difficult.'

'You want to understand everything, don't you?'

'Yes,' he said.

'So you can,' she said lightly and led him off the ledge.

He followed now, still talking. She seemed to be leading a little old man to the workhouse. They descended onto the riverbank and rode upstream, slewing the horses through neck-high vegetation. The banks kept subsiding where the river had taken ravenous bites, it was like soap. Eventually they got onto the flats proper, a shingled place. The river had split into five channels. Magistrate baulked, Frances could feel him sweating through her own chapped thighs. Polson shook his head and she saw that if before he had been afraid, now he was terrified.

'It's no good, Francie.'

He threw a stick and watched it swirl away to the left. She could see boulders on the bottom. A tree floated past.

'I can't allow it.' He was grey.

'In that case—' She wheeled her horse savagely. 'I shall go alone.' But he caught the bridle a second time.

'Don't be stupid, girl.' Her lips quivered. When her jaw announced itself like that he loved her very much.

'Look.' She pointed to the table that rose up in a V from the other side. 'There are your ten thousand acres.'

'How can you tell? Everything is distorted.'

'If everything is distorted, how can you not tell?'

He gave in at last. He tied the stirrups across the saddle flaps and motioned her to do the same. He put the cat in a wicker bag that hung from one side and tied his watch in a kerchief about his neck. By the time he had given her instructions and gone forward, he had succeeded in thoroughly frightening her.

She did as he said, tucked her riding-habit and petticoat high on the saddle and straddled it, like a man. She watched his sorrel, Hector, stumble away. Already he was in the main stream. Hector had lost his tail. She rode her grey into the current, and saw her father kneeling on the saddle. 'Did he say for me to kneel?' The sedge on the far bank was moving upstream, horse and rider were away to the left hand. She put Magistrate into the water and he turned and looked at her, gone waspish. She urged him, thank God for the stick, she was chattering, all the time chattering to herself. And there— Magistrate had stepped into a hole and stopped, she was on his neck—there was her father, clambering out, waving to her, a tiny speck. Waving her across. Magistrate was crossing, he was plodding on. 'I am, I am,' she said, and the horse slid. He would slide, steady and bottom. He was plunging in and out of holes. Her knees were cold. Her father had ridden upstream, he was there opposite waving a handkerchief. Yes, yes, she would steer for that. 'This is awful,' she said, gasping at the boulders that swirled by. Something had happened. Magistrate was stepping up and down in the one place. She could not see the bottom. Yes, keep the reins low and the head up when swimming. But the din drove out all reason. The current was pulling her knees. They were not moving. 'Wait!' she cried to the river, and flung herself on the mane. 'While I get his head up!' She had lost the reins and fumbled. 'Wait!' She had them all the time. She tugged. The head jerked one way and the rump another, they were spinning. Something floated by. She saw a log borne over rapids. It rose slowly into the air, through a cauldron of milk and flies, and the flies were coloured puce. It was a whirlpool then. Magistrate was steering alone. He had four ears. It occurred to her then that Brandy had not been fed, he would be eaten by Maoris if she didn't return. Her arms ached, ached intolerably. Something hit her in the chest, and she sat up. 'Dear God,' she prayed. Then the bumping started again. She opened her eyes and there was Magistrate's hog-mane coming to view in its natural jaunty position. And her father, sabled from ear to ear, running down in a grin to meet her. In his socks. 'I am so glad,' she said, and slid forward into his arms.

'But I was not frightened,' she protested a little later when they had rested and were riding up between the rivers. 'I loved it.' (Oh God, she thought, and we have to go back the same way.)

'You know,' he said. 'I had to unclench your fingers. You had the reins in a vice.'

'Why did you remove your boots?'

'Oh, that.' He laughed at his precaution.

Now the rivers left them on either side and it was a relief to canter after the intolerable slowness of the morning. Tilted, the table rose in tiers of washed gravel, rose for miles, then expelled itself frontally about the bluffs of Seagull. The ground was clumped with ti-palm; they raced on paths of gravel, bright with flinted stones; past sudden pillars of driftwood petrified and baked to an ochreish yellow; and a sedge, stiff and reddish with barbed fruits, prolific, that stung the horses' fetlocks and sang in the air like wire. The wind had dropped.

'There are several ways up,' she said, as they passed from glare into the shadow of bluffs. 'What are those foxholes?'

'Defiles,' Polson said. He had banded his kerchief over his eyes which had never served him so lucidly. He had never felt better in his life.

Presently the ring of hooves changed to a sharp swishing sound. They had entered a zone of bluish pasture. It grew thickly, twining above the horses' knees. He shouted to her and galloped towards the left hand ravine, the cat clinging on for life. They entered a tunnel of beech and lianes. The birds were deafening. She burst through, brushing karamu berries aside and staring up, up at the club mosses, growing shades of shellac green fifty feet high out of the forest floor. 'Bush,' she murmured. The air was draped with mosses and tree ferns and slow-flying parakeets, flopping about their faces in waves of dark blue nightshade. 'Real bush.' Then she remembered that the brow of Seagull lay above.

But they could not get up. Once they were halted by a fall of water and once by a chasm where Frances saw her reflection in a pool forty feet below; a third time they found the sun and looked up a blue gorge onto the shoulder of the rock, but the gorge was impenetrable.

They rode away in silence.

'Strange,' she said at length, 'how much has happened today; yet really nothing's happened at all.' Polson nodded in a bemused way. He kept rubbing his beret and looking back at the mountain as if expecting it to speak. His sorrel had sweat caked to the saddle flaps. That was the river line, she realised. She laughed. 'Do you remember what Mrs. Dewhurst said when we arrived? "My deerr, you're not going up there alone? Without a chaperone? My deerr, you will become semi-burburous. My advice to you is to set up the lay figure of a lady, carefully draped, in your sitting room, and always behave before it with the utmost decorum as if it were your mother." Arid. Arid, arid, arid woman. Look at me. I've never been more filthy in my life and yet I feel somehow *cleansed*.'

Polson gave his daughter a special look that he reserved for puppies and candid women. He hated being uplifted by failure. 'The fact is that if everybody felt as you do, Francie, life would be an intolerable strain. Up here the sky is higher and life appears enormously simplified. But simple things—the sort of simplicity you speak of, the sort that's about us is a privilege, and it carries a penalty. You have to know your job. It takes a lifetime to adapt to such simplicity. A man is a fool to try.'

'That's what I have been telling you all day, papa.'

'Why are you stopping?' she said. 'Who are you waving to?' She wheeled and stood in the stirrups. A man was approaching. Only the head was visible. That shepherd, Polson thought, nobody else has yellow hair. He marched rapidly towards them with a bundle and a dog, he was chewing something. He greeted them quizzically, with his head on one side. He was chewing a loaf and said 'thee'.

'Thee went up the wrong crack,' he said. His eyes jingled.

'You were *up there*?' Frances said. 'This isn't your land.'

He gave her a laugh, a throbbly sound that emphasised the boyishness of his person. His eyes were queerly sunken, jingly bright. They looked straight down the aquiline nose, jesting and insolent. She thought him insolent. He might have been thirty or forty from the wheat husks under the chin, or from his clothes. He wore a jerkin over a patched coat, buff trousers, no socks, they were just clothes.

He dropped the bag and leaned comfortably on his stick. 'I saw thee. Thee went up the wrong crack.'

'I saw none better,' Polson said.

'Tis the valley on the right what is better. There, where the birds is feeding on the berry. Where the traveller is buried.'

'Traveller?' Polson had taken his glass and was scanning the plateau.

'There is an cairn and a name scratched.'

'What is the name?' said Frances.

'The name is Drowned. Tis carved in rock. An so it should be. The traveller crossed at the wrong place. An so did thee. I see thee from the brow.'

'I see no cairn,' Polson said.

'Thee need spectacles then, tis an crack wide as oast stack. Tis only sapwood choking up the hole.' He tilted Polson's telescope to the right. 'An passage for flocks too.'

Polson lowered the glass. 'Flocks?'

'Ay.'

'Why do you say that?'

'If thee looked thee would see. Where the beak is—that wall, scarped. See? That is wallface, that. Behind is three ridges an valley, but the valley is bush, bush an ridge. Then a saddle with a nick an a wall, hard by. But that wall is off the saddle by an mile, tis half an hour's walk steep and that is an mile; yon blue space that I can see and thee cannot, that is pasture. All pasture. Tis the belly of an moor for sheep.'

He looked from one to the other. His eyes were grey fallow moons, exultant. His eyes were piercing.

'Sheep?' Polson said again.

'Ay.'

'I see.' Polson's cheeks were flushed. It was all too sudden, too simple. All he could say was, 'I see.'

The man threw a crust to the dog. 'Well then good, if thee can see without looking. Will thee put sheep up?'

His voice had a flutish sound. 'Tell me what thee sees then.' He persisted.

'I see that you are a shepherd and that you have a good eye.'

'Some say I am an scholar.'

'Really?' Frances wheeled her horse almost on top of him. He looked up, scarcely moving. Both man and dog. Their stillness irritated her.

'What's your name?' she said.

'Mackenzie.' He turned to Polson. 'Ay, that man down there, the Donald, he said it. He said I am a sort of scholar. "A compliment," he said. But I didn't like the way he said it. So I walked up here. Twas nay a compliment, was it?'

'I cannot tell,' Polson said. Hay was right. The man had an oval cast of mind.

'I can tell,' Mackenzie said. 'He told me ride out on the boundaries, feed yon boundary dogs; an I said Nay, I walk. He grew hot and said take the horses or he would whip me. Twould take a week to walk, he said. It did near, it took three days. He has eight boundary dogs, an it were three days' walking to find them. Tis the biggest walk ever I seen for sheep. Tis four rivers, thirteen streams, ten minor mountains an twenty thousand sheep, tis two hundred thousand acres, he said, how much is that of miles? Tis three days' walk, I know that. I told the Donald I would loose the dogs if they was chained, but he didna believe me, I think. They was chained and I did loose them, I took them back. I fed them first. They was wasted. One had been chained so long it had lost the art of running. Then they come, the Donald and the crippled brother, the Albion, an I showed them my wrists and I said, Did they know what it felt to be chained? I told them a dog is not a convik to be ranked to a stake, I said it was want of sense. Then the Donald said the scholar words and raised his whip, which I took and broke, I was frightened he might strike one of the animals.'

Polson was breathing quickly. 'Do I take it that you have left the Hays and do not intend to return?'

'Thee speaks mannered like they do, I thought thee would,' Mackenzie said. He took more bread and chewed it, gazing slowly about him. 'All this? Thee have all this?'

Polson nodded, a half smile playing on his lips. The man was smiling also but in a different way.

'Ay, twill do,' he said and picked up his bundle. 'I will not cost thee much for the keep.'

'Well,' he went on, oblivious of the effect he was producing, 'the Donald said tha' flocks was thin and tha' pasture thin an the men that worked it bawbaws. So I thought I would come. An I am come.'

'Are you finished?' Frances said. She wanted to shake her father for not hitting him. But her father sat content.

'The wee girl is cold,' Mackenzie said. 'I will come to the house.' And he left them as abruptly as he had come.

'Papa what have you done? What *have* you done?'

'Why, my dear, what have I done?'

'Everything, oh everything! And you didn't even question him. Oh, why are you so weak with men?'

'But my dear, I haven't engaged him.'

'But you will, you will!' She burst into sobs.

Polson gave her his kerchief. 'You're quite right Francie. I should have questioned him. I should at least have asked him where the proper ford is.'

They found the ford nonetheless. The river at this point was a mile across but beached and easily fordable. Of the man himself there was no sign. He appeared to have been swallowed up.

'We must search,' Polson insisted. They spent an hour riding up and down without success and rode home sulkily.

At the homestead they found Donald Hay waiting. As he heard Hay's version, Polson realised that Hay was simply annoyed that the shepherd had not waited long enough for Hay to discharge him. It was the first time Polson had seen his neighbour put out.

'We think he is drowned,' Frances said.

Polson described the search at the ford.

He found himself describing a raging torrent that was entirely imaginary. Frances' eyes opened but she did not contradict him; and Hay appeared satisfied.

'Good riddance then,' Hay said. 'He's a scoundrel, he stole a bag of flour. I came to warn you.'

Mackenzie did not come that night. Nor did he come the following day. Neither Polson nor Frances believed him drowned, each in his way believed he would appear again. As indeed he did.

MACKENZIE reached Odessa after nine days. Polson found him before the verandah one morning whistling. He did not apologise for his lateness, he merely asked for a tumbler of water. When he had drunk it he took a turf from his bag and put it in Polson's hands.

'There,' he said. ''Tis all that in they places uppat what they call Seagull.'

'They?'

'The ones at the pa. I cooped there last night.'

Polson examined the tussock casually, as if it were a turnip.

'Taste it,' the man said.

Polson said, 'You mean this, the blueish stubble at the base?'

'Ay, the whisker. 'Tis sweet. Taste it.'

Polson declined. He stood, weighing the sod absently, first in one hand then in the other.

'The whisker, man, that is the stamina.'

'If,' Polson said, choosing his words, 'if I decide to hire you, you would have me graze sheep there on this, I take it. How many would this tussock support?'

'Fifty. Five hundred. 'Tis no matter. There is passage.'

'And you—if I take your word that there is passage—you would lead them up?'

'Ay. Who else? Thee cannot. Them in the hut cannot. Though there is the dwarfey one that is good with dogs. I put my hair inside. The paunchy one that is the Gilliam, he is kindly. The others did not fancy me.'

Polson smiled ironically. 'And did you by chance ask if there was a bunk?'

'Ay I did that. There was not. But I shall coop on t'floor.'

As he was talking Droo crossed the valley behind him, leading his bullocks to the river. Seeing Mackenzie, the old man stopped short. He remained a moment motionless, then continued his way.

'Tis all arranged,' Mackenzie said.

'So it seems.' Polson could not bring himself to be angry; he felt instead that a responsibility had been taken from him. He was amused, chiefly on Donald Hay's account. He looked closely at the man. His stillness and tawny clothes, merging with the landscape, gave the eyes undue prominence. They were startlingly grey. The dog too was part of it; crouched, immobile; lifting her muzzle with a dead stare whenever confirmation was required.

'I must tell you,' Polson said, 'that I have with sheep the reputation of a Jonah. I am something of a failure. I've had all the diseases and my wool clip is disastrous. People of these parts, they don't like to see an amateur prosper, therefore they would have me fail. I tell you also that I have no experience of country that high, nor has Gilliam. You would be alone.'

'Well?' Mackenzie said to the dog, rasping his fingers as if crushing a tiny leaf. The dog raised her head for scrutiny and Polson found himself nodding into two coaly eyes that were almost human.

'Good,' Mackenzie said. He raised the pendant at his throat and to Polson's surprise touched it to his lips.

'What is that?'

'My own father's, he is dead. He is dead out of a cannon. Before that it was his own father's. He died in a battle. He was made short by the head. Tis an charm that leads me.'

His voice had become intimate.

Yes, Polson thought, slightly embarrassed, perhaps I trust you. The man seemed to chuckle.

'I shall talk it over with Gilliam,' Polson said.

'And with tha' daughter?'

'Why not?'

'Thee needs to know tha' own mind first. Tis nay an girl's mind that will trust me.'

'That's right, Mackenzie, not the mind of a girl. This is a woman's mind.' For some reason, he would explain himself before the idiot.

'An woman, ay. Thee needs that about thee.'

'And why do you say that?'

Mackenzie suddenly reached out and took Polson's wrists. Polson did not withdraw but allowed the other to turn his palms upward. The hands that held him reminded him of barnacles.

'I will tell thee why. Because thee is soft.' He dropped the palms. 'An because tis lucky to have an woman.'

Polson looked at his palms and he looked at the sod which he was still holding. As the other was walking away he held up the sod, symbol of the only topic that mattered, and said:

'And if, if it were possible to lead a flock onto this: what would you put?'

'Oh the merino. They big one out of Spain. What else?'

Frances spoke to the man a few days later as she was returning from the pa.

She had gone to see Sparrow, she had meant to go earlier; and the sight of those stained and crooked teeth coming to meet her at the gates had filled her with dismay.

'You were ill,' she said.

'I was, I was very ill; and now I am well again.' The missionary seemed excited.

'I have made you some scones.'

'Indeed, willingly my child. Thank you.' He said it sing-song, as if she were a child, grasping the cloth bag she carried and tying it about the rope he wore as a belt. He insisted on taking her to the schoolroom. 'The children saw you coming — they want you to hear them recite. Only for a minute, mind.'

He walked on.

It had rained in the night and strong odours rose from the earth: of ointments, of pounded herbs, of taramea musk and the stench of smoking refuse pits; children were defecating behind the dwellings and pigs chewing the ends of bracken fern. She passed storehouses, mildewed with dried shark hanging from the platforms; and then crossing the courtyard she was facing the ranks of distorted carvings, and stopped. Some of the bad impressions returned and she half-listened for the screams of a maimed child. Some men whetting implements gazed at her through closed lids, as if the bottom half of their faces were frozen. Sparrow walked quickly. Once he ran to chase a young truant, who was flying a kite; but the lad got away and the missionary was jeered at by old women.

'The natives are friendlier on the coast,' she said.

'Of course. Their bellies are full.' He did not quite snap at her.

'Mr. Sparrow, there is something you said the last time which puzzled me and I'm sure you did not mean to. I mean — Thank you. It is easier if you walk more slowly. Thank you. It's simply that you said you lost one child. Were there not two?'

'Yes, there were two. The boy is well. He is being cared for, in Christchurch.' He spoke the words laboriously.

'I am sorry if I've upset you,' she said. 'It is just, I would like—'

'You are not sorry at all, you are inquisitive like everybody else.' He looked at her from what seemed a great distance. 'Only, perhaps you aren't so ashamed of me as others might be. You are not afraid of frank speaking. You would like — what, my child?'

'I thought I might visit him for you, that's all. Since you must find it difficult to do so unobserved.'

He smiled in a deprecating way and walked on. 'Perhaps,' he said dreamily.

He entered the schoolroom, forgetting to let her pass in first. The air was fetid. Children grimed with mud were sitting on bedplaces; some sat by a fire scooped out of the earth, writing with a nail on blades of flax. 'Creatures of darkness,' Frances thought, recalling the missionary's own phrase, as one by one they stood up and recited their catechisms by rote. Somehow the pictures on the walls, the mildewed prints and exhortations taken from missionary society journals, made the degradation seem worse. Behind the desk, scrawled in charcoal, were the words *Ko te atua to tatou piringa — GOD IS OUR REFUGE*. The inscription crossed the wall. The lower half was vacant save for a funereal presence in hoops, pasted up from a newspaper and identified with difficulty as Queen Victoria. A boy in European trousers with his hair smarmed down and eyes that never left the missionary's stood and recited Psalm 22 from memory. Sparrow held up his hand to silence the hum; then he squatted down like the rest and led a hymn. All the time, children kept coming to him with nails and boards and cracked slates; some unpicked his laces, some rubbed charcoal on his legs through the holes in his socks. Sparrow returned them to their places with such natural affection that Frances wondered if she had not misjudged him. He has a heart after all, she thought. In the end she stayed two hours; and as she was leaving said to him, lightly: 'But it was you who wanted me to come, not they. Wasn't it?' For an instant his eyes softened, but he said nothing.

'I suppose you cannot persuade the older folk to attend.'

'No,' he said. 'But at least I can try and convince them there is good in what I teach their children.'

They parted almost formally.

Riding back she felt curiously jaded. And yet everything about the school had heartened her—so many little savages crammed together, so alive, so avid, so captive to the mysteries of learning. She couldn't explain it. She crossed the ford and instead of cantering straight down the valley decided to follow the arc of the riverflats. Here halfway round she came upon Mackenzie. He was bending over a sheep.

'Is there no shearing today?' she said, intending to stop if he looked up.

Mackenzie shook his head and continued to examine the sheep. She stopped nonetheless.

'Is it ill?'

'Tis the footrot.'

'I see nothing wrong.' She leaned over. 'Where? Show me.'

'Tis the wee dent, a nick only that is rotted.' He did something with a knife and released the animal. Then he stood up. 'Thee will lose that,' he said.

'Thank you, I hadn't noticed.' He took the crop she was holding and, in what seemed a short time, some twine and a needle from his bag and began to stitch the leather thong where it had frayed. She saw that his wrists were scarred but deft; while the fingers, reddish and covered with tiny white hairs, were awkward. His dog trotted up.

'Where did you learn about sheep?' she said after a pause.
He mumbled Australia.
'Yes. Tell me about Australia.'
'My kinsman is there. He is an official in Victoria. He found me a billet an rations.'
'Then why did you leave?'
'Thee asks a lot, thee asks as much as Mary.'
'That's not an answer. And who is Mary?'
'Ay an tis. Mary is my own sister, she is somewhere else. I mun seek her in the land that is newly found.'

He handed her the crop, mended. She thanked him and said, 'In Australia I also have a kinsman.' The word sounded rare. She tried to picture Lionel's sensual mouth and aesthetic hands but Mackenzie distracted her. He kept looking at her sideways, as if she were on the end of a fork. 'Tell me more,' she said directly; and, dismounting, sat on a hummock and faced him with her skirts spread over a cotton plant. 'About Australia, I mean.'

Now he was tongue-tied.

She stretched her hand to the dog. The dog turned and sat facing the other way. 'Your dog doesn't like me.'

He grinned at her.

'It is the colour of a fox in shadow,' she said.

'She is black an tan.'

'The colour of a black and tan fox in shadow then. Where is there tan?'

'Nay, not a mite. But they called her black an tan when I got her, an they were wrong.'

'You need a hat against the sun,' she said petulantly, and rose to go. But her grey had wandered. Mackenzie laughed then and rubbed his fingers, and the dog brought the horse.

'In Australia they give a man umbrella against the sun,' he said. ''Tis deserts an waterholes. A desert is an station an tis black with flying insects, lass. An they give a man umbrella against the sun.'

She sat down again.

'We put soda in the tea for the thirst. An the sheep is ravening from the dry beds, thin as mortals. Thee can put tha' finger in the fleece an part it.'

She sighed. 'I thought you would tell stories, the way Droo does.'

'Ay,' he said, as if remembering something. 'He would tell stories, that one.'

'Did he tell you how he got his scar? He got it in a fire. The whole prairie was aflame, and he had a pink mule with a sore foot. He drove it in Latin, he said, though I don't believe that. It had a drum on each side of the neck which he beat with a wooden spoon as he went along, he was selling things. If he didn't beat the drum the mule wouldn't go. When the fire came the people ran out of the houses and raced to the river. There was no time to take anything but themselves. One woman whose husband was sick tried to put him on Droo's mule, but the mule wouldn't have him and so the woman snatched up the wooden spoon and chased her husband to the river. And Droo was left with the mule in the main street—it wouldn't budge you see without the wooden spoon. Droo went into a saloon and drank half of everything he could find. When he came out he felt better. But the mule wouldn't budge. The fire was a little way off yet so he went back into the tavern and drank the remainder. The snakes had come into the town looking for water, and when he came out again the fire was as close as they were. Then Droo knelt down and promised the mule he would buy it a spoon of pure gold if only it would get up and lead him to the river. The mule was lying on its stomach, it was fearfully hot; it saw the snakes lolloping through the fire and it tried to get up, but it couldn't. It was the snakes that decided Droo. He took a last drink from the very last bottle. It was whisky, I think, he said it went down like molten lava. Then he picked up the mule and carried it through the flames to the river. And everyone cheered.'

'Why?'

'Because it was a miracle.'

'Then what happened?'

'I knew you'd like it. Nothing happened. They lived in the river for four days. Food was provided, goats and cattle, they took them from the river ready roasted as they floated past. Done to a turn, Droo said.'

'After four days the meat would be cold. Thee is a child to believe that.'

'You say that now. Yet you listened.'

'An how did he get the scar?'

'I don't remember. I suppose he got it in the fire.'

Mackenzie was silent. Then he said, 'Tha' father should burn the hillsides.'

'He hates fires,' she said. The dog yawned and put its red tongue to her. Suddenly she jumped up and clapped her hands. 'Yes, yes! Then all the shoots would come. They're burning on Blueskins. Look.'

Far off over the stilthouse rose blueish spirals, tinting the sky.

''Tis late for burning, the time is December,' he said. 'The cottonplant would come and the peagreen grass.'

'And anise? I would love a fire. I've never seen a real fire. Papa should burn the terraces, the scrub, the raupo—' She stopped. 'Why are you grinning like that? We all have conceits. Peagreen ground, you said. That's a conceit. Why not just green?'

'I've seen it, lass. The peagreen shoots on the black ground.'

'You must tell my father to burn in December.'

'I am gone in December.'

'Of course, to fetch your sister. But first you have to find her land.'

'I was meaning that,' he said.

He was gazing out. He seemed to be rubbing his eyes, though his hands were at his sides. She had seen pictures of men like that, faces that stopped the wind and communicated a sense of aboriginal wonder and private, almost physical pain.

'Will you go up there?' Her gaze followed his into the mountains.

He had become strange.

'Is there a way?' she said.

How far-away he was. Why didn't he confide? He was as bad as Sparrow—what was it they were afraid of, all these men?

'In Australia,' she said, arranging the cotton plant under her skirts. 'What about the flowers?'

'I never saw a wild flower,' he said.

'No gentians?'

'The land is against it.'

'Lionel writes of flowers.'

'What man is that?'

Frances smiled. 'Once I tipped him off my pony.' When she smiles, he thought, her face becomes an apple. A red crispin apple, he thought, with a bite out of it.

'Lionel's the cousin I spoke of. He is at the diggings.'

'Ay. Then he would see flowers. There is an red weed about the creeks.'

'You were there?'

'Ay, I took stores on the road. I came to a diggings.'

'Lionel says there are bushrangers.'

'Oh ay. I found one man, hanging. I cut him down. He was bare in the pockets but his boots were clean. I had a month inside them after I cut him down. He was no longer a man. I thought it a wicked thing to do.'

'Why do you tell me this?'

'It were the flowers. I dug him a grave. When I came by later there was flowers growing on the mound. Is tha' man one of them what "has"?'

'I suppose so. He's taking orders in the school of adversity, as we say. But he isn't fitted to it.'

'Then he shall come to thee.'

'Lionel simply wants to get on. He is not a farmer.'

'Then he shall come an make speech and go back to his society in England.'

'You know nothing about it, nothing whatever.' She glared at him. 'You haven't said what you did along the road.'

'People came an slept under the dray for protection. Because of the dog. We was once troubled at night, in a gully.'

'They say "Bale up", don't they?'

'There was two, an they said nothing till the dog was chewing them. One was clumsy; she took him at the lip and chewed it till he gave up the weapon. We found his nag, saddled with pots and pans. We made a raft an floated the man down a creek. We put stones pon the man's chest to stop him sitting up in an comfortable position. I thought he would be little damaged.'

'What was his name?' she said.

'An I were right, it did not damage him at all. He floated down a brae barking he had been horse-whipped. His name were Bridie. We was conviks together but he was nor good nor Christ-loving. He swore to kill me, an he never did. He kilt his wife instead. He took the wee thing an broke her with a sandbag, I thought it a criminal thing to do.'

So saying, Mackenzie took some bread from his pocket and destroyed it at a mouthful.

'Your stories are horrible,' she said.

He grinned at her. 'Did you ever think,' he said suddenly, 'how queer the stars are fastened in these parts?'

'All the time,' she mused, 'we are inverted.'

'I do wonder sometimes if Himself sees us that way.'

'Perhaps,' she said, 'perhaps we are upright and it is the Lord who is upside down.'

'And why not?' she said. He was peering at her. He never looks, she thought; he peers. And it struck her what an aquiline nose he had.

But he was shocked. His eyes flashed. 'Tis an wicked thing to say!'

'Good,' she said, and laughed. 'Good, good; I wanted to see you flush and it's all over your face.'

He left her without a word.

The man is a boor after all, she thought. She rode home in a temper.

That evening Frances completed the straw wide-awake she was making for her father. When it was finished she put it on his head. Polson was reading under the library lamp.

'It's too big,' he said. 'But it's very nice. Thank you.'

'It is especially nice,' he said, 'for reading.'

Frances pouted. 'It needs some ribbon yet.'

'No, it's perfect, my dear.' He gave her a kiss and continued reading, with the hat on.

'I spoke with Mackenzie today, papa.'

'Capital. What about?'

'Sheep, Australia, Lionel—You will write to Lionel?'

He grunted.

'Nicely?'

After a little she said, 'You know that chant of Billy's?'

'Which one?'

'The one that goes shriek at the end. The one about a stranger leading them to the land of their fathers.'

She added, 'I think this is the man.'

Polson looked up. 'It must have been a long conversation.'

'Quite long. He mended my crop. He will journey into the mountains.'

'That is what they all say at first.' Polson sighed. 'I'm reading, my dear.'

'You're always reading, papa. Or painting.

'You know what he said to me? He said, "What is thy father, gentleman farmer or gentleman painter?"—and it struck me that if you painted less and went about the flocks more you'd— are you listening? I mean, the hands wouldn't be so surly with you. Perhaps. Papa?' He wasn't listening.

Then she said, 'He has found a pass.'

Polson dropped the book. 'Did he say that?'

'No, papa. I said it.'

'Why on earth did you say that?'

'I don't know. To make you drop the book, I suppose.'

He studied her a moment from beneath the hat. Once they had been staying at the rectory at Melton Constable (when she was fifteen and quite striking, it was when she first grew her hair down). And she had said, speaking of a house carpenter who was mending the roof, 'He has found a lapwing's nest'—in just that tone of voice. She had become infatuated with the house carpenter. Now—No, I wouldn't say striking now, he thought. Except— Now she was again growing her hair to the waist and taking it straight off the brow it—yes, it did something for her.

'Then he has not found a pass?' Polson said.

'Silly, of course not. He hasn't looked yet.'

'Thank you,' he said, as she handed him the book. 'It's late, m'dear.'

'I was to remind you to write to Mr. Hay,' she said. Going out.

He nodded. And fell to musing about the matter.

It occurred to Polson that he should not write to Hay about Mackenzie at all, he should send the fellow back. And it was time he wrote to Lionel.

He found his place and continued reading.

A few minutes later Frances returned for the hat and stood beside him, looping her hair. 'Shepherds are so superstitious, aren't they?' She sighed. 'About God, I mean.'

'Hm,' Polson said. Her hair smelled of birchwater. Now she was twirling the hat, throwing shapes on the print.

'Papa' (she stopped). 'When will you burn the hillsides?'

'Dear me. Never perhaps. The soil's too steep, it would fall away. Besides it is nearly autumn. December is the best month.'

'Oh,' she said. 'Then you know about that.'

When Mackenzie had left Polson and Frances on the plateau he had doubled back along an earth fault to the traveller's grave; he had gained the summit of Seagull and camped in a fern whare. The whare was abandoned and full of grey rats. He did not know the rats were vegetarian and therefore edible, so he set the dog onto them, fetching them from the roof trees with the crook of his stick. He used the whare as a base and each morning explored the valley that led into the upper range. Everywhere he found gorges and tracks of uprooted plants where wild pigs had passed. On all sides terraces, hidden from below, spread upwards tier on tier like fortifications. The symmetry was however deceptive. Some of the terraces were perpendicular; others unfolded to reveal miniature plateaus. Many were pitted with caves, their entrances encrusted with lime and rocks which had fallen from the roof. In one cave, hidden behind blocks of limestone, he found an arsenal of stone weapons scattered about an airy room a hundred feet wide. The weapons were covered in silt. The floor was porous and rocked slightly. Arms led off and in one there was a sound of water running. The room was beaded with glow-worms. At first he recoiled, for the domed walls were peopled by dragons; then he saw that they were drawings scraped directly on the rock in vivid colours. The creatures had long necks and upturned feet, half bird, half dragon. They went up both walls and across the ceiling. They were magical, he knew that. So that when the dog disappeared into a great eggshell, expelling strings of beetles with long antennae which floated hopping up the walls, bringing the dragons to life, he fled that phantasmagoria. But on emerging no evil befell him; so he went into other caves and even slept there, like an anchorite; and in the end he grew quite fond with the dragon-birds. He decided that if flocks were to shelter in the caves the birds would not harm them much.

As he went higher the vegetation increased. In the cliffs he noted a base of quartz and marled limestone, and some hard stuff which he took for granite. Quartz again in the faults along the riverbeds, bright shingle wastes full of crystals and hard flints. He followed one river to the ice level: a glacier had come down, bending its course. He thought the level of ice was descending, for the river was both above and below the glacier. 'Thou art major,' he said, contemplating the current which, in order to circumvent the glacier face, had eaten fifty feet out of a precipice. He named it the Major River.

In these days he lived on birds and insects. There was a grub with a brown shell that fell off, obligingly, to indicate when it was cooked; and the blue lovebirds flew so close to his face that he plucked them from the air.

On the fourth day he woke to find ice coating the tea-leaves in his billy. He took another river and walked all day, continually climbing onto spurs and descending into watercourses. He came to a place where the river narrowed. Here the spurs drew in to form a saddle over the river and opened again on the other side. From the saddle he looked over Seagull onto the cardboard plains of Canterbury. Eagles came about him and hovered in the air currents.

Already he had found country. Everywhere there was cover for grazing. Yet he was puzzled. The range that should have led directly into the alps had become a false range.

Northwards the ground spread out in a fan for miles until it was stopped by a rampart whose reddish crags sprang upward like an unclenched fist. That, he decided, was the beginning of another province. Leftwards, the river swung west towards a low range whence it issued. He followed its course until dark and camped under a ledge. In the morning he saw that the ledge marked a passage. He crawled along it and stood up. Instantly he dropped to his knees as the dog started and a great swishing engulfed them. Laughing, he rose again. 'Spiders, lass,' he murmured. His voice echoed. They were in a vault. 'Spiders, lass. They canna be crabs.' His voice floated back from a high cupola from which hung pendulous turrets, thin and greenish-white with a whiteness that took his breath away; they were draped in a lichenous moss that hung in folds — and where they stopped just above floor level the floor rose to meet them, thick with human bones. Mackenzie backed out of the vault on hands and knees in a clumsy obeisance. Once he paused to grasp an object that cut his knee. Outside he found himself holding a jade pendant. The design on it, pricked into the felted fibres, was the figure of a man with a pot belly. It was familiar. He grasped the charm at his throat, Wiremu's pendant, and compared the two. The patterns were identical.

He would certainly go higher.

Again he followed the river. Before noon it had forked, and forked again, but he kept to the western arm looking down now on boulders, now on whirlpools, now on the face of smoking lignite seams which he was forced to go round. He crossed an open space where leatherwood and flowering broom blew in his face. It grew cold. Presently he entered a narrow gorge. The walls drew in. As he went higher they pressed upon him, and a mist came down. It grew dark. In that narrow street he felt both sightless and weightless. No light penetrated. He walked in pitch, tapping with his stick. He passed under a waterfall, with the dog held to him. He seemed to be holding an icy rag. A greyish vapour returned and the street reappeared, shrouded in dripping precipices. Here were bog pines. Above and below, the waters. He looked up and for an instant saw a cleft, a tiny blue needle. He turned a shoulder clinging to scree plants and saw the sky again, blue and oblong. It went blank, then reappeared as a lighted window. The frame was a chimney, projecting into the sky; and on either side, as if sundered by that needle of light, the walls of the range parted and opened out. He knew the chimney marked the summit, even without the stream that hung gushing from its foot.

'Tis the way!' he called to the dog. As the mist returned, blotting out the needle in the sky.

He left that awful street and went down, rejoicing.

After thinking the matter over Polson decided he had no intention of releasing Mackenzie. He was sitting out one morning painting when the shepherd appeared.

'The Gilliam wants thee,' Mackenzie said.

'Where is he?'

'There, pon Loaf. Waving the hat.'

Polson squinted. He had been painting that very hill.

Mackenzie turned to go. Polson restrained him. 'Mackenzie —something I've been meaning to ask you. About seeing. I have a problem. How is it you see so far so quickly, and always the right thing so that you seem to go straight towards it?'

'I dinna know what thee means, except I never see too much.'

'You mean you see everything, everything at once and instinctively select? Unconscious selection?'

'Eh?'

'Oh nothing. Thank you, Mackenzie.'

'Why? I have done nothing.'

'No. But you have taught me something. Thank you.'

'Oh, and Mackenzie,' he called out. 'I have another problem.'

'Ay?'

'I don't know what to do with you. You see, strictly, I should send you back to Hay.'

Mackenzie waited.

'But I don't want to. I should like to keep you.'

'Thankee.'

'Why?' Polson said quickly. 'I have done nothing.'

They laughed together then, and Mackenzie went off with a wave.

Polson's decision to send Mackenzie at the head of an expedition did not reach him all at once, it was not a sudden conversion. Nor did it altogether relieve his uncertainty, a foreboding that the plan would fail. Yet there was this about it; it seemed predestined.

Also, the man gave him confidence.

As his confidence grew, Polson's dilemma — which was simply a desire to escape the fear of his environment — was sublimated more and more by his vision. He saw the plan now as a moral necessity; and his Canaan as an instrument to purify the spirit of the age, could he but possess it. Mackenzie's arrival — he saw this not as something fortuitous but as the incarnation of his desires. And the artist in him was roused, he saw the god-like element in the man. Thus his belief, which was a metaphysical belief, in the man's ability to cross the barrier for him became invincible.

Two things influenced his decision. One was Frances' quiet statement about the pass. The other, which was perhaps the supernatural element, occurred some days later when Polson was woken as usual by the sound of Billy's chanting. He had heard this particular chant so often that he took it for granted, but this morning he sat up and wrote it down. Then he made a translation. Sparrow provided a second version and from the two translations Polson concocted a third. He showed it to Frances.

'The men of Kahiki have climbed up the backbone of Heaven
They have climbed up and returned

Only one kind of man has arrived
Has reached the other side:
The Haole.
He is like a God, they are like men
A God, indeed. Wandering about
The only man who arrived.'

'It's rather stilted,' Frances said. 'But it's plain enough. What's the Haole?'
'I don't know. There are several possibilities. One is a "stranger". But it could mean "white man".'
'Well that's plain too.'
'You're very complacent, my girl.'
'I've told you all along, papa. This is the man.'

Polson sent a note to Donald Hay informing him that Mackenzie had turned up safe, but weak from exposure; he had therefore set him to recuperate. Hay was leaving for Sydney and on return would be occupied with his new stock and the matter forgotten; so Polson calculated. He thanked Hay for the offer to purchase a new flock for Odessa. He had decided to take advantage of the offer. He would hazard a thousand merino ewes. Droo would go down with a note to Polson's agent in Christchurch and the money would be waiting when Hay returned.

'But papa, how are you to raise the money?' Frances said.
'I haven't the smallest idea. Something will turn up. Why, girl, whatever is the matter?'
She had flung herself on his neck, wetting his collar. 'You! You're the matter papa; it takes courage and I love you for it.'
He was overcome. He went to his room, thinking what a skittish child she was. 'I suppose I see her still as a child. Eh Chesterfield?' The cat was curled up in one of his waders. 'But emotionally she still is.' Now he'd forgotten what he had to do next.

Lionel, that was it.

Dear Lionel (he wrote),
I am instructed to write to you nicely about your prospects in New Zealand, should you decide to visit us. Let me say at

once that we are in the wilds of the southern island and the prospects are contained in a single word—work.

It is no good, as you seem to intend turning up with a portmanteau of recommendations. That might do for the Society of Melbourne, but it won't do here. This is not a land for favours, and recommendations are as little welcome as a tribe of Cherokee Indians. Rather less so, for the Indians might join the Maoris in road gangs; and we badly need roads.

Money would help, certainly. But I understand you have little of that. Digging for gold seems to be an expensive pastime.

I have before me a document issued by the Canterbury Board in London. It would have you believe that Christchurch, some fifty miles away, and Port Lyttelton, nine miles beyond, will become the Cambridge and Liverpool of the South. The one is all match-boxes and dram-houses with rather less architectural distinction than Battersea; the other is all water and very little port. Christchurch has one or two pretty churches and a grammar school, but its streets are paved with officials who are either corrupt or else ambitious which, in a society where land-grabbing is the principal occupation, amounts to the same thing. Land is a disease here, and all men contract it sooner or later.

I say this in case you imagine there is a city as well as a country occupation. There is not. There is only the land.

This brings me to the issue. Odessa is near Maoris. A small tribe which came south about the year 1500 and was once nearly extinct, has settled not two miles from this homestead. Now the Maori, you know, is a proud nomadic barbarian who has established out of chaos a system of cosmic order which rivals Genesis. In this system he attributes a divine potency to the land which, not unnaturally, he loves. It is his strongest article of faith. We have overturned his faith; in three decades we have overturned it completely. We have done it by Christianity. And we have done it by Treaty: we gave the chiefs a pound of nails and a blanket each and they in return made over the governor-ship of their lands. Know that Auckland, the capital, was bought by your Queen for the equivalent of a chain of hardware shops in the Old Kent Road, rather less than your father paid for his town house in

Hanover Square. Now, having got what we wanted (the best arable land) we are withdrawing the missionaries and indeed are so intent on *not* upsetting the Maoris further that we neglect to govern them at all. You cannot teach a child to swim in a bath tub and leave it to find its own way out to sea. It will raise wrath. In the north the natives have rebelled: first by violence and second by setting up an independent King of their own. The King territory is vast. No more land can be bought and Europeans travel at peril. What is significant is that by a primitive government, self-created, the natives are now doing more for themselves than we have ever done. More chiefs are joining the monarch's cause; Auckland quavers on his doorstep; the Governor is forced to acknowledge the Maori King (which he will not do) or go to war. It means war. Not a tribal affray but war full scale, since as well as fancy dress we have also given the natives muskets.

There will be repercussions. Here the injustices to the natives outnumber those of the north tenfold. The Government's agreed price to the natives was 6d an acre (sold to the colonists at 10s). But in Canterbury it paid less than a farthing an acre. True, we have left the Maoris a few lakes and preserves; but my neighbours, Lionel, are biters not nibblers, and these areas are constantly being eaten down. (The most hated man is the surveyor and the most hated animal, the sheep; and if you seek a parallel you need not look further than the Scottish Clearances.)

The Maori is nomadic. Alienate him from his hunting grounds and he becomes indrawn, selfish, lazy and despicable. This describes the natives at Odessa pa.

I mean to take a hand. It is a gesture, rather a grand gesture for your grand-uncle. I propose laying title to a vast tract and making it over to the natives in gift. It will be a case of land-grabbing in reverse.

I have said enough. Except to say that this idea is the fruit of a private need which you may understand. We have something in common: we both tried for the ministry and failed. I threw it over, you were thrown over. The difference is slight. We both preferred self to the discomfort of giving. But life, my boy, is a cycle, and old pains return as new wounds. Committal is pain. Therefore I do this thing.

I had better add that my hopes lie in a dumb giant who walks these hills like a god. But the plan wants managing. I shall not be here for ever. It wants an astute brain, an understanding of native lore and may mean entering politics. I say no more, except to request that you do not lose this address a second time.

A word about our circumstances: We are seven hands and 42,000 acres. Perhaps a twentieth part is genuine pasture. We go in dread of disease—among the animals, I mean, for our sheep are our true masters. For them we exist body and soul. Our founders thought to peg us down in numbered lots, to transplant us in social classes about a Lilliput London. But some of us—*nous avons changé tout cela*. Tradesmen roam the sheepwalks on equal terms with their masters, and one day they will buy us out. Either that or we shall all be the same. God forbid. And yet, it is better. I sense this change. Exploration is the national pastime as drowning is the national death. The rivers run with Promethean power and after a fresh can mount fifty feet in an hour. Thus, to your idyll of a bowered cottage set in arcadian simplicity, you may add the exquisite sensation of daily risking your neck. We are great improvers. We add to our dwelling stick by stick, as a bird builds its nest. It is as elemental as that. This is an empty infuriating land. There are no pigsties, but there are no palaces either. The tendency is puritan and prosaic. Clever, you may be. Intellectual, never. I did once find a man reading Machiavelli's *Discourses upon the First Decades of Livy*. He was baking at the time. I noticed that he hid the book under his bunk when his mates entered. The truth is that there is no inducement to get on beyond one's own private vision. I have mine. You are welcome to share in it. To Frances, living here is still a shock and an adventure. To me, indeed to any man who comes out seriously inclined, carrying on becomes an everyday effort of will.

Ever your affectionate uncle,

The clock was striking twelve, he had been writing all morning. Polson pushed the letter away and went into the big room. 'Chesterfield,' he said, lifting the cat and the *Times* from under it, 'I am among the cursed. In that I think at all, I am among the cursed.' Polson stared dully at the personal column.

Something with nasty hindlegs, a weta, was advancing towards him by way of the deaths. He recoiled; called to Frances. Where was she? The cat was demanding lunch. He wrote her a note, 'Chesterfield not fed,' put it under a vase and went out.

He walked down to the river and sat on the shingle. He told himself that the letter was false. It was presumptuous; so was the plan. He found himself questioning what he had always taken for granted: his own identity. 'The natives are not my brothers nor I their keeper.' Then what was he? He had burned his boats with England, his family, his inheritance — the new flock would see to the final reversion owing him. What else could he do but respond to his environment in the only way that seemed morally justifiable? He turned back. Just now the air had a peculiar lightness that foretold the changes of autumn; the mountain caps stood up clearly, like antlers; men were whistling dogs. Yes, just now it was idyllic. And tomorrow he would hate it all. 'It's this terrible gulf between the land and the book. Where do I belong? That letter: it means a committal for life. And I involve not only myself but two others, have I the right?

'No, no, it isn't that; I'm simply frightened of ridicule. I dream a noble dream, a turkey dream, and I'm terrified lest it turn out to be colonial goose.'

Yet perhaps life was like that: the dream and the doubt. Cocooned in your dream, your hopes and illusions, you took it as a blessing, like a prayer, and remained snug until the doubt crept in. Then you did battle. At this point it was important to defeat the dream with open eyes and make it a reality.

'To defeat the dream,' Polson muttered, and went inside. There was the cat sitting on the table, sniffing the vase which had flowers in it now. The note had been amended. 'Chesterfield _still_ not fed,' it said. Polson took some bones onto the verandah and began to chew them until he remembered and set them down for the cat; then he went to his desk and sealed the letter.

Looking out, he saw a man and a dog crawling up the terrace. The man's hair brindled in the sun. There were clouds on the caps now. According to the legend, the bird spirits created the mountains, as Tane the forests, Tangaroa the sea and Tawhiri the winds and storms. But who was the god of the mountains? He was in one of the chants, but Polson could not remember his name, he could recall only what happened to him. He was buried alive.

'Good Lord,' thought Polson, 'if men drown in the rivers they'll certainly die up there.' He was suddenly grateful to Mackenzie.

Days passed. The hills grew sharp with early frost and a blessed cool invigorated the land. Sparrow came to dinner. He discussed the troubles in the north, but was more concerned with hunger at the pa. Rats had eaten the kumara, it was the second year in succession the crop had failed; families were already debating which of their dogs they would fatten for the coming winter. He inspected Polson's paintings and pronounced them arid, like the landscape, a remark which pleased their owner. He departed bearing a copper urn, explaining that his baptismal font was grown small. Polson concluded that the affairs of the missionary were progressing.

The shearing ended. The next few days were the busiest of the year. Polson stopped whetting shears and honed knives instead. The men pared footrot. For three days the men pared feet. Gilliam went about with a long face checking tallies of ewes and hoggets, writing everything down with a nail on a trap-door; there was branding and ear-marking; wethers killed for the salting pit; the flocks turned out; the wool pressed, sewn up and stacked to be sent down. Finally all was done. On the morning that Droo loaded his dray, the men sat down at a trestle table out of doors, wine and cheese provided by Polson, and drew lots for their holidays. Polson sat down with them. He paid partial wages only. He had not forgotten his first year when three shepherds had failed to return and Droo had reappeared a month late, still drunk, and attempting to hang himself on the gallows in mistake for a sheep. For work done Polson now paid in part; the rest on return in a tapered-off condition; and a bonus for cold sobriety. To his surprise all anounced their intention of returning. Polson added his own surprise, the news that the expected loss on the wool clip had not materialised.

'It is profit then lads,' Gilliam said. And Frances, sitting next to her father, smiled at him in a special way.

Then Polson called, as was his custom, for the complaints. But nobody spoke. The silence was broken by the sound of Frances' dog skirmishing under the table. The men shifted uneasily and looked to Gilliam. Finally Laughton who was called the Professor and seldom spoke at all said, 'They're chary to talk before the Missus, Miss Polson, sir. It's on account of the little dog.'

'This little beggar,' Kerr said, tearing his straw hat from Brandy's teeth. The dog leaped for the hat, then made at Kerr's laces. Kerr picked up the terrier on his boot and almost threw him into Frances' lap.

'Well Kerr,' Frances said, trying to quieten the dog, 'now that the shearing is done he won't be such a nuisance. Will he Gilliam?'

Gilliam cleared his throat and put his thumbs into his waistcoat. The men were looking at him.

'Now then: I am fond of little fellow, sir. But it do act guilty, like, amongst flocks.'

'What do you suggest, Gilliam?'

'You understand, sir—'

'Take the animal in, Francie,' Polson said. 'We can't hear ourselves.'

When she had done so, Kerr stood up. He was a jutty little man, about forty-five, with a cast in one eye. He had a tight whipcord voice which he addressed to his working dogs with a certain flair.

'Sit down man,' Gilliam said. 'Pour yourself tipple and sit down.'

'Yes, Kerr?' Polson said.

'I say this: that dog is for whipping.' Kerr remained standing. Polson leaned forward and crossed his hands. 'Mr. Draper?'

'Dishonourable discharge, sir. I would post him to another unit.'

'Whelpin,' Taylor said. 'I would whelp vice out of im.'

Laughton and Moffet nodded in agreement.

Mackenzie spoke. 'Whelpin is ay the fool's cure. The thing is but a wee canny mite that does mischief for want of training. Want of training an want of loving.'

'If you talk any o that bluidy religious nonsense,' Kerr said, 'I'll brak your face.' Then, to Polson, 'I'd whip tripes off im, the young bugger killed lamb last week.'

'Sit down and mind your tongue,' Gilliam said. 'It may have been gull that did it, sir.'

'Are you sure of this, Kerr?' Polson said.

'Ask Taylor.'

'See it twice,' Taylor said. 'In the distance, like. Tore neck out an left lamb for bleeding, second dead this month. Both torn. An Gilliam knows it.'

'Now then, Taylor.' The overseer's face sagged. He turned to Polson. 'Like. Little fellow, being white sir, runs up, an before they sees it for dog he's in amongst them.'

'In that case Brandy will have to go,' Polson said. 'You may sit down, Kerr.' Kerr sat down and nothing more was said.

It was then that Polson told them he would depasture merinos onto Seagull. 'Gilliam is against it, I should have you know, he thinks me foolish. And so, if I'm to judge by your expressions, do you all.'

'Animals won't succour two weeks in winter,' Taylor said.

'Precisely Gilliam's words,' Polson said. He smiled at them and passed round the wine.

'I'm not goin uppit,' Kerr said. 'Nor's Taylor. Nor's Moffet.'

'Of course not,' Polson said. 'Nobody has suggested it. You have told me what I wished to know. Mackenzie will go.' He paused, savouring the wine and letting his smile linger. 'Alone.'

Slack grins spread round the table. Presently they rose, to speed the wool run.

Droo was waiting with his team. There were seven bullocks. Their line extended along the face of the homestead. Droo was leaning on the yoke of the white leader that he called the Apostle, his belly distended like a bag, cleaning his pipe with a hen's feather. The animals were lying down, plundering the bottom of their feed bags. The dray itself was loaded to the roof; there was just space for Taylor, first in the holiday ballot, to squeeze up behind the driver. Frances and Billy had come onto the verandah. The men put on their wide-awake hats and stood in the sun, smoking. As Polson came up, Droo stumbled along the line, a pillar of white smoke and a crimson shirt tail flapping loosing feed bags and checking the harness.

'Team present and correct, thir, Athtral, Castor, Veenth . . .' Droo reeled off the names of the team, after his conception of the heavenly bodies. 'An I was to remind you, thir, to check the stores.'

'What's that you're smoking?' Polson said.

'Turnip top, thir. Must 'n turnip top. But won't smoke on the road, not with the fleethes up, and tell mums I won't forget the braid. I've got her sample wired to me vest.'

Polson checked the list of provisions and ran his hand along the kowhai yokes. They gleamed like dense gold. It was a moment he enjoyed. He gave the old man a mock salute and watched Droo clamber up and don his satanic canvas hood. His face was a leer of awful pride and moist moustaches. Soberly, as if drawing a sabre from a corpse, he raised the whip from its holster and gripped the handle. He held it a moment poised; then he cranked and fired the whip three times. As the lash uncurled over the ear of the foremost bullock, Droo braced himself, tightening the reins with his left hand, and the Apostle rose unwillingly to his feet. Slowly the others followed. The driver lunged a fourth time. 'G-G-Gerrrrr-upp-p!' The animals seemed to crouch an instant, winnowing the chaff from their nostrils and raking the ground with a queer dishing motion. Then with a sudden pawing and snorting the white leader was moving and they were all together with the lumbering gait of their kind. Frances waved, Taylor over-balanced, the men shouted and threw their hats and as the dray reached the corner of the homestead a ball of fluff darted out, matching the energy of Droo's tongue with a last snapping farewell. The little dog almost collided with the leaders and sprang back. The men laughed. The dray lurched, bumped, straightened, rounded the house and was gone.

Dearest Aunt Bea,

We are cooped up, rubbing our joints, lighting fires, preserving eggs, fingering our patience until we go down to stay with the Dewhursts. She is zestful, and has an Adam's apple. She keeps a sort of open house for gentlemen (there are five daughters) and makes it a point of honour never to serve mutton—and after eight years, apparently, has never done so. He is rich and plays the dulcimer; although papa says it should be the hurdy-gurdy, in accordance with his shape.

Mr. Whitehouse presses the plan and papa is very bright. I think it is the coming of the Gael; as you say, he has wanted someone. He has taught Billy to starch collars. He is not the least distressed that the natives predict a disaster this winter.

Mr. Sparrow scorns the prediction. (Hue's work.) He is baptising and stamping out superstition wherever possible. I think he is wrong. Repression is surely more dangerous than freedom of utterance, however misguided. He says the Maoris are an apostate people, a remnant of the lost tribes of Israel, and is writing a book about it. He says we *must* find that bone.

Yet I pity him. He is somehow desperate. And makes me ask myself—since we, not society, are the author of our pains (are we not?)—why is it always the rejected ones who try to perform the most good?

Brandy is reprieved. I pleaded with Papa and won.

A delightful puzzle: a pukako. (A pukako is a sort of grandfatherly grouse—a most forbidding mien; just like papa when I disturb him at reading.) This morning I visited Drake-Draper and solved the mystery. I found D-D wrapped in a blanket and an old Wykehamist scarf, stirring that great iron pot. I gave him some drops and he fished out for me a portion of the most delicious boiled fowl. He said the Lizard brought it. So our mysterious donor is the Gael. They call him the Lizard because he is always about crawling up hills. He is a strange reluctant man with bright yellow hair and has the immunity of a steer. He seems quite untroubled by the little discontents that bother others. Just now in driving rain he is turning onto the Gut a division of sheep that normally requires two horsemen and three dogs: he has one coally dog, and walks. Perhaps the Gael will teach us all our business. Yet the men mistrust him and Droo cannot speak of him without choking. I can't remember speaking two words to him. Therefore: why give us presents? A native subservience, papa says. He is a victim of the Troubles, whichever they may be.

There is nothing fresh from Lionel. Brandy sends a considerate yawn from my dresser leg. He is quite accustomed to the leash now and his behaviour *impeccable* . . .

The rain that followed Droo's departure brought thunder and drizzle that pervaded the valley and the house with a dreary malodorous tint. The men sat about the hut half-dressed playing cards or reading the literature Frances had sent up. Only Mackenzie went out. From the house she watched him. Even through the shuffle of the rain he was clean on the hills, for he walked bareheaded, with an oiled sheet about him as a plaid. The ends billowing, and the dog behind.

'What is that you're knitting?' her father said to her one morning.

'A comforter.'

'Oh. And for whom?'

'I don't know. I hadn't really thought.' She flushed slightly. He looked at her sideways, and went on playing the piano. He was composing a fugue.

Now where, she thought, looking at a bare finger, have I put mamma's ring? She went into the kitchen to look for it.

Presently she called out, 'What do you think they talk about in the hut?'

'Us,' he said. 'They would like to be as we are, and then they'd be the unhappiest dogs alive.'

'But they'd hate to talk as we do.'

'It's curious, that.' Polson struck a chord. 'Their language is monosyllabic, like dry music; full of silences and innuendo. It is a language of the spaces—as if there were so much around them, so much to contain them there's no room for thought or words. Sometimes—haven't you noticed?—they simply say "Hm" or "Ah-hh" for minutes at a time, and they understand one another perfectly.'

'Like Brandy and Chesterfield,' she said, coming in again. 'It isn't there.'

'What?'

'You know,' she went on unheeding, 'men here are much less fond of animals than in England. That reminds me: Droo's terrified of Mackenzie's dog. He's becoming senile, papa.'

'Who?'

'Droo. The other day he insulted Mackenzie by asking him if he had a Bible.'

Polson said, 'Your thoughts are very strange lately. Who did you say you were knitting that for?'

'Why you, of course. Silly thing.'

Polson grunted and went on playing.

The rain continued, warm and grey, and the men grew restless in the hut. It was a draughty place, cob and appleboxes, much warped. Only Droo, who slept apart in a shed off the dairy, did not use it. One afternoon Kerr brought his dog inside and had it dance, tip-tapping on the skin of a home-made drum. Kerr had trained his satin beast to leap over the backs of sheep and block them with its flank as a wall; now, gripping a stick with its front paws, it performed a slow waltz on hind legs, bowed twice, and then repeated the dance in double time with a distinct yodelling sound. The men applauded and fed the dog cheese. Mackenzie sat by the stove making tallow candles. His own dog sat up with an air of amused tolerance.

'Can she do that, laddie?' Kerr said.

'Yon bitch? Ay she could, but she is nay musical.'

'Then she could not do it.'

'Oh ay, she could if I learned her to it.'

'How would you learn her, if she be not musical?'

'I would learn her by example.'

'You should learn her then.'

'Oh ay.' Mackenzie gave the dog the wick he was teasing. She held it in her teeth while he straightened the length. 'Oh ay, I should. But I havna the inclination. Besides, she is stone deaf.'

Kerr stared, squinting through his good eye, first at Mackenzie and then at the dog.

'You mean tone deaf,' the Professor said. Laughton and Gilliam began to fling darts at an uncooked potato.

'Does she not hear, laddie?' Kerr said, with the dullness of his middle years.

Mackenzie was intent on the wick. 'She likes sacred music best,' he said at length.

Kerr said, 'But is she *deaf*?'

'Ay, deaf,' Mackenzie said 'Deaf as Draper.' Kerr frowned and retired from the conversation.

It was growing dark when a thudding on the roof caused everyone to look up. 'The washing!' Gilliam said, and the Professor sprang outside.

'Insurrection?' Drake-Draper sat up in the top bunk, his frame exposed against the rafters. He was wearing braces, he had lain there three days.

'Keas, man,' Gilliam said, throwing a dart.

'Steers?'

'Kee-as.'

Taylor took a pole and banged it against the rafters. The thudding increased. More keas arrived. The birds were whooping and glissading down the iron roof.

'Too late,' Laughton said, entering and throwing down a sodden bundle.

'Torn?' Moffet said.

Laughton held up vests and shirts, already in shreds. 'There's clouds of them.'

'Shoot the buggers,' Kerr said.

'Good luck,' Drake-Draper said, as Taylor and Kerr went out with guns. Drake-Draper recalled a previous visitation. The birds had perched on his very barrel and he had shot the ramrod out of his musket.

Some shots were heard. Silence followed and the men returned. Two minutes later the noise began again.

Soon they could no longer hear the rain.

'D'you hear them, Draper?' Gilliam said.

'No, Gilliam. I have fires in my belly.'

'Do you *hear* them, Draper? They're dancing for supper, an so are we. Get up man. Get up and cook. Now then.'

Drake-Draper groaned and pulled the blanket over his head. It was one of his periodic attacks of gastric influenza.

Mackenzie rose and donned his oil.

'Are you going then?' Gilliam said.

'Is it too much for you, laddie?' Kerr said.

'Ay. I will draw the birds off.' Mackenzie went out followed by the dog.

Now a wailing sound was heard, more piercing than the grating of talons. The men went to the window, craning their necks. Kerr put his head out the door. The draught made the lamp spurt, flinging shadows over the forms at the window.

'D'you see, Kerr?' Moffet said. 'What is it?'

'A bluidy bosun's whistle.'

Gilliam said, 'Now then Draper: the Scot is playing his pipe.'

'Eerie, isn't it?' Moffet said.

'Listen,' the Professor said.

Presently the birds stopped drumming and began to mimic the cry of the pipe. Drake-Draper sat up, rubbing his half-moon beard. His bony face was pervaded by an expression of joy. 'I say, Gilliam.'

'What is it?'

'I believe I can hear an instrument.'

Drake-Draper pulled himself upright by a rafter. 'I can distinctly hear a musical instrument.'

'They are begun singing,' Moffet said.

Drake-Draper lay prone and began moving his arms stiffly up and down, under the blanket. 'Gilliam, I have it.'

'Have what, man?'

'It's a pibroch. It is a pibroch in the area of E minor, and the beggar has the beat all wrong.'

'He's marching round the hut,' Laughton said.

The note swelled. Slowly it circumnavigated the building. The men followed the sound, the whites of their eyes turning to the voice that had persuaded birds to sing in chorus and Kerr to stand in the open doorway sucking a thumb and getting wet. Three times the note turned the hut. Then it receded into the night.

There was silence then.

'I say,' Drake-Draper raised himself. 'I say. The blighters have gone.'

The men looked at one another. 'Well I'll be married,' Gilliam said.

In the morning when light entered the hut Kerr and Mackenzie woke first. Kerr was below Drake-Draper, his features protruding from a grimy blanket. Mackenzie lay on a palliasse on the ground, breathing audibly through his long roman nose which he stroked pensively between thumb and forefinger as if some distant part of the anatomy had lodged there in error. He lay under his patched coat; at one end two feet emerged from a tatter of sage green like slabs of driftwood; the dog shared his pillow. The wind blew in gusts, lugging the door on its chain with a knocking sound.

The two men regarded each other without speaking; until Gilliam sneezed and Drake-Draper opened an eye and began with his palm sedulously to iron his beard until it lay like a raven's wing on the blanket before him; and the hut awoke. Then Kerr said, 'Did you come late, laddie?'

'Ay.'

'An is it a sort of pipe you have?'

'A sort of pipe, a chaunter.'

'An does it play dances?'

'Ay dances, dances and reels and the psalms of the Sabbath.'

'Give us a ditty then.'

'I am busy with the wick, Kerr.'

'Put up wick an be busy with pipe.'

Mackenzie continued to roll the wick into twists, gazing up at Kerr with an indolent smile. His ears pointed, like a fawn's.

Kerr pulled on his trousers. 'Show it me.'

'Nay. Thee would blow spittle and wake the dog.'

Kerr said, 'Why do you bring bitch indoors, laddie? Is it a soft thing?'

'Ay soft, soft for my company.'

Softly and insinuously Moffet began to sing a song about a moll.

'What I want to know is,' Kerr said, 'is, how does bitch dance to sacred music if she be deaf?'

'I didna say dance. I said she likes the air of it. Sacred music affects her most.'

'Very foxy your bitch, laddie. Foxy nose. Very pretty too.' Kerr sniggered. 'I say, laddie?'

'Ay.'

'Have you ever had moll?' Mackenzie ignored the question.

Kerr gave a loud guffaw. 'Course you have. Course he has lads. There she be! He sleeps with silent woman every night.'

Very quickly, before Kerr's laugh had died or the chuckles of the hut had become audible, Mackenzie had crossed the floor and had the smaller man out of bed. He lifted him by the shirt and propelled him, face forward, to the wall. Kerr turned, crouched and ferrety as if to spring, while his hand sought to unfasten a blade at his belt. Mackenzie walked forward, put his elbow against Kerr's neck and delivered a blow, low down, which left the older man fastened to the wall in a state of leaning and intense pain. A sucking noise escaped from his lips and his arms hung to his sides like planks.

Gilliam bustled across, very Grampians, and laid Kerr on a duckboard in a horizontal position with some of the previous night's washing under his head; and Mackenzie put on his boots and went outside.

He walked away to the mound above the house and watched the sky dawn, orange and unimpeded. He saw the form of Billy swarm up the rope and then the chant of Billy came to him. He watched the big house come alive and heard Frances calling to the hens in a low voice.

Walking down he found a ram salivering, rolling on its back in a thicket. Instantly he knelt and set his fingers to the itch. As he pressed on the sore spot the ram ground its teeth. He took his knife and cut the beast's throat. He took the news to Polson, running.

'*Can* you, Droo?' Polson was saying. 'Can you turn about and be back here again in four days?'

The old man had returned from Christchurch. He was white with river salt and his body appeared to have succumbed to a sort of ague. All the grog blossom had gone from his cheeks. Polson saw none of this.

'Can you do it?' he repeated. The old man held a notebook and his eyes kept straying to the line of bullocks before him. When he did not reply Polson shook him. 'Droo, it's scab. Scab man—scab. *Can* you?'

Droo shook his head. After a long time he appeared to notice the carcases rigged to the gallows and he mumbled 'Scab, eh? Well who'd a-knowed it for scab?'

'Never mind that. Mackenzie isolated it. We owe him our thanks, he knew it in Australia.'

'An shipped it here like as not in is boots.'

'Droo, my sheep are dying—this is no time for petty feuds. I've told you before, I'm not interested in your private lives—'

'Oh shut up,' Droo said, and Polson blinked. Then he saw the tears in the old man's eyes.

'Is something wrong?'

'Count them, count the blathted things! I got seven, ain't I? Now there's only thix.'

It dawned on Polson then that one of the bullocks was missing.

'Castor, thir. Gorn. Yusterday night at the Dane's house, accommodation house; an this mornin e gets up an gallops out of the traces an dies. I wept thir, I blubbered like a kid.'

'I quite believe it Droo, at forty pounds apiece.' The bullocks were Droo's.

'Happened this mornin, thir.'

'Castor, you said.' Polson could not remember which was Castor.

'This ballock, thir, could take a eyelash out of its eye with its hindfoot.'

Polson could not think of what to say. Droo was blubbering again.

'Castor was me favourite.'

'Tutu?' Polson inquired.

'We opened is stomik an there was the weed lying like clover.'

'Tooted. I'm sorry, Droo.'

'An I told im the weed was poison! I *told* im about the toot. I told im of all the poisons I knew—' Droo broke wind then and began to wheeze.

'Beg pardon, thir.' Polson waited for the wheezing to subside. 'Did you say scab, thir?'

'I did, Droo. Time's short. You're three days late already.'

'Thir. You does not know what it is to have two animals goin on the open plain in oppothite directions.'

'No, Droo.'

All the other misfortunes came then. Polson listened with deference. When they were extinguished he took Droo's notebook.

'It's all there, thir.'

'Thank you.'

'Scab is it? They as it in Nelson, thir. You'll want boilers.'

'Precisely, Droo.'

'Three boilers. Annacid.'

'Yes, Droo.'

'Boilers. Acid. Anna dip.'

'The men are building a dip now.' Polson turned at the sound of voices. 'Four days, Droo. Can you do it?'

But the old man was again looking at the gap where Castor had stood. He took a shirt tail and appeared to blow his nose on it. He opened his mouth to say something. Then seeing Mackenzie approach with Gilliam and Frances he closed it again and walked away.

Frances said, 'Will he go?'

Polson groaned. 'Humour the old devil,' he said. And went in.

Polson stood in the kitchen with his back to the window and tried to recollect something Droo had said. He drank some water. Sighing, he opened the notebook, and read what Droo had written:

3 march Little dog upseting hands. Ditto master. Sheerin
        endid. Depart. 20 bales. Rain
4 march Taylor drunk. Rain

5 march River up. Slept at Billings. ful of gotes and peopl. All sexes, also a curit. Taylor drunk The curit has lost both his horses. taylor as I expected lost ½ his munny. Rain

6 march Town. Taylor drunk Off loded wool. also Taylor. Stores Rememburd brade forgot colur Also legings. Trowzer gone Rain

7 march Mail. xmas box Ful of mothers noshuns. She is a deer. Saw Mowray prinsess nisely tattood. hamster Hotel. Bopard is meen to bulockees. rain.

8 march depart. River up nothin but sprey & schreeming guls mail whet. Billings. no legings and a spare suit only in bed

9 march Waited al day Billings. ful of bridle party. A cross bride in the best bedroom shaming sick the husband sicker a horse trod on the botom of his stomik. They were splised only last Wensday.

10 march waiting for river. met Ostraylien mate Have whip kontest He kan cut a rat in 2 from galoping horse so kan I
Lost bulocks

11 march looking for bulocks

12 march looking for bulocks

13 march found bulocks . . .

Presently Frances ran in to say that Droo had watered the team and was preparing to leave. Polson bustled out. Mackenzie was unloading the last of the stores. Droo was sitting up, eating a vast sandwich.

'Four days, Droo?'

'He says he can't do it in four, papa. But he might manage it in three.'

Droo's neck, grizzled like that of the foremost bullock, glowed an instant. 'Thir. One item.'

'Never mind the item,' Polson said, 'something's just come to me. Did you say they had the disease in Nelson?'

'Goodanpropa thir.'

'Then—I see now. Francie, you remember? That passing flock in January. The disease was incubated then. You remember? Good God, Droo. You must inform every station on the way down, it will infect the entire province. And *hurry*, man.'

'Very good, thir. Thir. One item.'

'Yes?'

'Your hat. The braid mums wanted. I lotht the sample. The wire was not effiekayshus. Was it green or blue mums?'

'Blue.'

'Then I'm wrong again. I'll remember thith time, thir.'

'Oh, damn the braid.'

It seemed to Frances that she did nothing but make soup—mutton soup for the men, mutton bones for the dogs; and salt mutton; and hang mutton; and carve joints of mutton; and count the carcases Billy rigged to the gallows; and curb Brandy from disturbing her father sitting in his cone cap at the piano, in the days following Droo's return. Death itself did not move her, except ethereally; she gathered her strength as if recognising that the disease that had come among them were but the symptom of a stigma more general, more terrible still to come.

The men were surly or rageful, broiling slabs of sheep's body whole, cutting at the newly dead with pocket knives and offering her to feast with the oafish hospitality of their kind. But she understood that. Her father's moods—a self-indulgence that overcame him, so that he played the piano hours on end and barely noticed her—she was used to them. Only Billy upset her. He became abominably cheerful. His stained grin at the window seemed to mock her in a manner profound and incalculable. Which was nonsense, she told herself. Yet she found it hard to look on those grinning white teeth without a shudder.

In his thoroughness Gilliam insisted that the men scour the entire flock. They had built a trough by the riverbank and began washing under a windless March sky. The heat was oppressive. The stench of the boiled juices, acid and saltpetre and tobacco leaf, was intolerable. Drake-Draper retired with an eye scalded. Moffet, lifting a ram, collapsed over the side of the trough. All the men were sick. Frances begged Gilliam to wait until the wind blew. It would blow by morning, Gilliam said, as indeed it did. In the night the south wind came in gusts and the barometer soared. In the morning it was blowing hard from the north. By noon it had backed south again, gusting and cold, as if to chide the mercury for its precocity. Hail and sleet came in squalls, followed by thunder. In the night the sheep were scattered. Next morning mist enveloped the valley and the keas came down in hordes. The birds sat on the trough in a tribal wall, and jeered. Taylor seized a lamb and flung it at them. The birds jumped up to let the missile pass, and the lamb fell down with its back broken. The men were clawed and bitten. Frances was pecked on the neck bending over the tomatoes. Mackenzie, mustering strays, reported that the birds were pecking sheep above the small of the back in such a way that the animals were unable to dislodge them. The squalls continued. The men hung over the trough, adumbrated shapes indivisible from the driving rain. Scuds of lightning drove the keas indoors. The birds penetrated the chimneys, robbing Moffet's watch and breaking the clock on Frances' dresser. Grey rats broached the storage platform. Billy caught one and devoured it raw, smacking his lips. The rats ate the cheese and turned the flour sacks into colanders. They stayed just long enough for Polson to sketch one. 'For Mr. Plankton,' he told Frances, since that ornithologist had declared that the native species of rat was extinct. The humidity increased. The sky, between grey and purple, mounted plumes of orange at evening which suffused the rain pools of the valley with an eerie glow. By day dark-edged cumuli hung low, open-bottomed, like vast strainers into which the mists towards noon dissolved and out of which the rain descended horizontally, gusting over the land. The storms disturbed all living things. Flies vanished altogether. Likewise the smaller birds, bush robins, minas, black and pied fantails. Plagues of locusts fell from the sky, darkening the pastures in clattering flights and beating themselves insensible against the windowpanes. They died in thousands upon the floors. Each day petrels flew inland, ringing the hills with hollow laughter. From the steppes behind the pa wild dogs appeared. The prick-eared beasts encircled the valley, howling through the mists, and fell with an unwonted rapacity upon the sheep. Many died even as they were lifted into the trough. Frances sent broth every two hours and worked with linaments and anodyne to rally the inert Drake-Draper who seemed convinced that he, too, was about to die. Polson played Pergolese. During a hailstorm he composed a cantata.

Sometimes he wrote, looking up with jaded eyes as the carcases were trundled past the window to the gallows. But mostly he played. Rocking himself in his flushing jacket, singing softly and hugging his thoughts, evoking sweetness as if to assuage the canker that clung to his house. It was a strength he had, this mental abstraction, and Frances took comfort from it since from the men she gained none. Her kitchen stank. She burned incense to cure the air and fretted for the open, like Brandy. The little terrier was forever fretting on his chain. At night she would release the chain and smoothe his white socks and the oysterish growth about his ears and tell him, 'You're the only living thing who prefers a gown lap to cord breeches.' She took him into the little stand of bush above the house and let him chase weka about the trees.

Mackenzie surprised her one afternoon. He appeared, pressing the black trunks aside, walking quickly towards her.

'You startled me,' she exclaimed.

'Ay. An with reason. Where is tha' dog?'

'Why here of course.' She looked down. The leash was empty. 'Then he's slipped the collar, he does that.'

'Call him.'

Frances called Brandy and he came almost at once. Mackenzie replaced the collar and shook himself. Brandy did the same.

'You're wet through,' she said. 'You should wear a coat. Is anything wrong?'

'Tis tha' dog is wrong, he is worrying sheep in the night. He is out tha' window an back again before thee wakes.'

Frances fidgeted. 'But he does no harm.'

'Thee *knows*?'

'You can't blame him. Have you been spying on me?'

'Get thee another collar lass. An fix it.'

'Very well, if you say so. There is another collar. And that's what you came to tell me?'

'Ay, tis.'

'Very well, thank you.'

She walked towards the house. It was raining again, a thin straight rain. It was very still. She could hear the sap running into the ground. She felt unspeakably sad. She turned. He was still there, illumined by moisture, silvered under the trees. She said, 'But you're *not* to spy on me.'

'Very well, if thee say so.'

'Says so.'

'Says so.'

'That's better. I can't see you. Come closer.'

He did so.

'Say after me,' she said. ' "I say." '

'I say.'

' "You say" — no, that's wrong. "Thee says." I'm sorry, it sounds quaint. I promise not to laugh again. "Thee says." '

'Thee says.'

' "He, she or it says." '

'Thee is daft, lass.'

'Say it. "He says, she says, it says." '

'He says, she says, it says,' he repeated.

'That's right. "Say, says, says." '

'Ay.'

'Now you are laughing.' Frances pushed back her cape. 'Mackenzie, I think you're the first person to cheer me for days. When you smile your ears point. They're leprechaun's ears.'

'What is leprechaun?'

'Oh — a spirit.'

'Thee is touched by spirits, lass.'

'Why do you say thee?'

'I was taught it.'

'There, he's done it again.'

Brandy had slipped the leash, but it was only to scent a tree. Mackenzie lifted the dog and cradled it. He said nothing. Frances noted how quickly the dog was soothed as he stroked it; the terrier was licking his fingers.

'Now Droo,' she said. 'Droo's touched by spirits, he says.'

'Ay. He's makutu. For lifting they bones.'

'What does it mean?'

'It means, makutu.'

'But what does it mean?'

'Perhaps he will die.'

'Now it's you who are daft. Daft. I can't say it as you do. I don't believe a word of it; and anyway there's too much talk of death. But I'm sorry for the sheep. How many have died?'

'There's eighty gone.'

'And you'll save the rest?' He nodded. 'Then papa's right, it isn't a calamity.' She threw the rain from her hair. 'Everybody is too serious.'

'Tha' father is not, an he should be.'

'No. He is worried to death, only he doesn't wish to show it. That is why he plays the piano. It's a trick he has.'

'Then tis an mean trick. Tis lying.'

She saw that he meant it and teased him with her mouth. She could make a cat's mouth when she wanted to. 'Have you never told a lie, Mackenzie?'

'Ay, I can tell a fiction.'

'Tell me a fiction then.' She took the dog from him and watched him wipe the rain from his face under the trees.

'If thee says so,' he said, and did not notice her smile. 'In my homeland there is an crag, an tis Eagle Crag. An here in this place there is an crag, which is called Seagull Crag, an tis similar. Tis similar because of the birds, look. Tis still on yon crag. Tis so still, lass, thee can hear they nest eggs crack. An I was dreaming. Twas on the day thee mounted with tha' father. There was eagles flowing. An white moss food growing, the birds was picking it out of the air. An one bird came by; an some said twas bird and some said twas person. An all agreed that it lived on air. Its name was Moah. It was brown green with the face of a man an it grew legs like horses. As it run it trampled the ground: trees an birds an reptiles—everything it trampled. Then it run into the gorges and I followed. It mounted a cliff like an street, look. An there it entered a cave.'

She was watching his hands, not to look at his eyes. When he looked at her like that he made her head churn.

'Now at the cave is an masted rock, an tis guarded by great lizards. The lizards keep watch an the monster sleeps. I couldna pass for they lizards. I knew the beast would nay eat me since it fed on air, but I feared it might trample me. So I sent the dog an told her bind the legs with flax while Moah slept; an this she did. Then I slew the lizards an passed into the next country. When I returned no one would believe what I had seen. Then I give them Moah's egg which I took from the cave an I give them greenstone which I took from the next country. Then they believe me.'

'An that is the fiction,' he said to her.

'Lovely,' she said: and gave one of her coppery laughs. She had been watching his hands. His hands moved in the rain. They seemed to caress the rain in the gathering dark. And now he was looking at her again in the way that made her head churn.

'You have good hands,' she said. 'You have the hands of a storyteller.' It wasn't what she felt, but it was all she could say.

'Tis a fiction, lass.'

Suddenly she caught his arm. 'Mackenzie, you *will* journey into the mountains?'

'Oh ay, I shall journey.'

'You must promise.'

'An I tell thee, lass. The way is clear.'

'And I will find the other collar.' She left him. Then she called back: 'Why did you come to warn me?'

'The men would be for shooting him.'

'Brandy! I don't believe it.'

'But you wouldn't,' she added.

'I would na shoot a dog.'

Frances ran down to the house. Her head was filled with strange thoughts and premonitions. 'One thing's certain, Brandy,' she said, hugging the dog — 'and that is, one of us is touched by spirits.'

At the dairy she stopped, hearing words. 'Blatht,' she heard. And there was Droo white-faced and wheezing, scrabbling at the compost heap in the spitting rain. 'That bone will be the death of him,' she thought. From the dairy she took a spade and joined him. Together they dug until it was too dark to see. But they didn't find what he was looking for. Nor did Frances find the collar. She remembered, going to the cupboard where she kept it, that she had given it away.

There came a day towards the end of March when the flocks were clean of scab. The dead had not risen above ninety and the men no longer feared the symptomatic sores on the living.

Droo noticed the gulls first. They came from the direction of the coast. 'Thtorms at sea,' he declared. But the gulls remained even when the wind had died, wheeling and dropping over the western pastures. They seemed loth to leave the station.

It was Moffet who discovered the torn lamb, guided to a low cliff by the dropping gulls. It lay panting a little way up the rock. It was torn at the throat. Moffet called to Mackenzie who was near. They searched along the wall and found two more lambs, in clefts. These two were dead. They had been bitten at the throat and then savaged by gulls. The gulls had nipped off the tongues and torn the bellies from below, plucking out the intestines. 'Wild dog,' Moffet said. They sat up that night with guns, also Kerr, stationed along the cliff. They saw nothing. They watched for three nights. On the third night shortly before dawn Mackenzie was roused by a light shape driving sheep in the shadow of the wall. He fired into the air and the dog disappeared. When Kerr and Moffet ran up he told them it was a Maori dog.

'An you missed,' Kerr said, 'you bluidy missed?'

'Ay I missed, I missed in the dark, look,' Mackenzie said. And set off for the homestead.

When he arrived Taylor was lolling on the verandah rubbing his back on a post. He was smiling to himself, enjoying the scene within. Behind the door Mackenzie heard sobs, then raised voices. Presently Polson came out, in his nightshift. He was white.

'Where is Gilliam?' he said.

Taylor shrugged.

Droo came, followed by Moffet and Kerr. Nobody spoke, though Taylor nodded vigorously to Kerr. Fresh whimpering sounded. A door banged. Then Gilliam arrived, half dressed and all in a bustle. 'An blessed row is brewing if there be no culprit this time. Who fired? Kerr? You Jock? Well, where is it? I see no dead dog. Now then—' Recognising Polson, Gilliam stopped and touched his hat. 'I heard shot, sir.'

'Gilliam. The culprit's here. Taylor was on the verandah when the gun fired. He saw the dog return and enter my daughter's bedroom. I've seen it; there is no doubt. I am sorry I relented before. The dog must be shot.'

'See?' Taylor could not resist saying to the overseer.

'Well there is an end to it, Gilliam,' Polson said. 'This morning then. You have a gun.'

'No sir. Not like that,' Gilliam said.

Kerr snarled and threw his cap down. Taylor stood over Gilliam malevolently.

'Not like that,' the overseer said. 'Jock, you fired. Did you see Miss Polson's dog?'

'Nay. I saw nowt in the dark.'

'One man's word for another, sir. I would see little fellow at it first, myself. And so would you, sir. Now then.'

After an argument, Polson agreed to that.

He rode out next morning before light. Frances came, she

refused to be left. At the place the others were waiting. Laughton took the horses a little way off.

They crouched down in a hollow Kerr indicated, and waited. Taylor knelt with a gun across his thighs, Kerr next to him. Then Mackenzie, Gilliam and Polson; and finally Frances, muffled and upright on her knees, and very still. The cliff was before them.

'In a few moments,' Polson said, 'Droo will slip the collar.'

For a long time Frances could see nothing. Then shapes loomed on her right hand and began moving out from the cliff face, quietly stirring. Taylor did something to the gun. Frances glanced along the line. She felt no pain. The wilful mood of the scene with her father twenty-four hours earlier was still with her. She was stronger than they, these men who stood against her; the men who opposed frivolity and therefore femininity; and therefore herself. 'Beasts,' she thought, catching the glint of Kerr's pig eyes. They were not able to touch her — her mind. Therefore they would destroy something. They would destroy her dog. 'But,' she thought, 'I won't let them. Even if Brandy is at fault I won't let them; something will happen.' Something would happen and she would defeat these men who crouched and waited.

She said something.

'What was that?' Polson said.

'I was quoting, papa. No one has more followers than a thief to the gallows.'

Polson said nothing.

'He will nay come,' Mackenzie said.

'You see, papa. I was right.' Frances stood up. 'He's not the guilty one.'

Taylor hissed.

'It is unpleasant waiting, I know,' Polson said. 'But wait we must.' He drew her down by the wrist.

The cliff was lightening when febrile sounds began to travel along the face. The sheep that were cropping looked up and moved off in a line. Frances saw then. Away to her right, a parcel of shapes moving towards her; and behind, a small bounding form. At a certain point almost opposite it stopped the sheep and began with nimble steps to trot before, turning their heads this way and that. The animals bunched, compressing themselves to the wall until it seemed the innermost ones must be crushed. Frances saw the terrier crouch, motionless. She would have cried out in admiration, had not her father tightened his grip upon her wrist.

'Don't fire, Taylor,' he said.

As he spoke the terrier leaped. It seemed to rise into the air and bury itself in the smother. The sheep stampeded. Some — ten or a dozen—ran up the cliff, followed after a moment's pause by the dog. Two lambs had run together higher than the rest. How nimble he was! Quarrying them from under with grim little snaps. She guessed his mind now; he would select the bigger and slower of the two. This he did. He forced it even higher and then quietly paraded it onto an overhanging ledge. There it stood. It stood in a state of doubtful tranquillity until the terrier came. She saw the dog tumble it by a leg and secure it at the throat so quickly that she was amazed, and did what her mother had advised her to do if the world should ever bruise her, she bit something. Her father cried out, and let go her wrist. But already Mackenzie was scrambling and cooeeing 'Ho ho ho', up and running, and flinging stones as he ran. She saw the animals separate—the one struggle and totter, and slowly sink again; the other stand a moment, lop-tongued and detached, with its tail stiffly moving. Then it ran down, sniffing, and trotted back the way it had come.

Frances had to be lifted back onto her horse.

Mackenzie and Gilliam came to the house later.

'Is there a remedy?' Polson said.

'Break his teeth,' Mackenzie said.

'No,' the girl said.

'The four main teeth. Thee breaks the teeth in half, look. The dog can mouthe food but the pain leaves it unwilling to mouthe sheep.'

'No! No, no, no.'

Now Polson could not say it. Now, with the terrier frisking at his laces, and Gilliam looking at his boots, and Droo mooning about his daughter mothering her like a hen, and Frances weeping—now Polson could not bring himself to say it.

'Give me tha' gun,' Mackenzie said. 'I will do it.'

Frances turned, speechless. She saw now what she wished to see: the mildewed stubble, the proud nose, the half-smile crisping in the sunken eyes, the arrogance and obsequiousness of his race.

'Thank you,' Polson said. 'Frances, you had best go.'

'*Where?* Where shall I go?'

She continued to stare at Mackenzie.

Polson went to his room and fetched his fowling piece. It stood by the bedstool in one of his waders. He gave the gun to Mackenzie and two cartridges. Mackenzie examined the gun first. She saw the hairs on the back of his hands stand up, and shuddered. He took the dog and went out.

Frances was in the kitchen when the shots sounded. For a long time she stood at the window, fingering a porcelain mug with some seeds in it. She told herself that she was waiting for the kettle. When the window had steamed over she turned and found that the kettle had boiled dry. Later she made tea and brought a cup to her father with one of her bran biscuits. He was playing the piano and did not look up.

April 3rd

My dear Matthew,
I think that you may now safely tell Burcher, since I shall want his advice on arrival, about the expedition—size, choice of men, etc. The shepherd I spoke of will do our bidding. His knowledge of country is peerless, God grant his quality of leadership likewise.

The reward is handsomer than I feared. Five hundred pounds is a charitable sum. I say feared lest the purpose be known. I hide my plan as Abraham his wife, and for the same reason. Advertise the expedition as boldly, as benevolently, as you see fit.

We shall be late. Frances has taken a turn. But it is nothing a few days cannot mend. Until then,
Ever your affectionate,
Amos

But Frances' 'illness of the spirit', as Polson termed it, was protracted; then Whitehouse was called away on business; in the end they did not visit Christchurch until the late autumn, nearly May. The two men met finally at the club and talked late into the night. The council's offer of £500 for the discovery of 'A tract of new sheep country behind the alps' had stirred the province, Whitehouse said; men came to the Land Office every day seeking directions; some were planning to start before winter.

'So shall we, Matthew,' Polson said.

'No. We prepare for the spring.'

'But in spring the rivers flood. My man is ready now.'

'Nevertheless.' The Superintendent tapped his pipe and leaned across the table. He put a hand on Polson's shoulder. 'It will be alright, Amos. It will be alright. And we shall have the pick of the men, never fear.'

Whitehouse suggested a game of whist. They drank a good sherry and played, and Polson won £3; and drank another sherry and became jovial. Polson left reassured.

But in the morning when they met again Whitehouse questioned him closely.

'Amos—if the land is found and I cannot have it gazetted exclusively for the natives, what then? Had you thought of that?'

'I had thought, Matthew, that no such doubt was possible.'

'So had I when I wrote. But the vote wasn't easy. The town members like Dewhurst want money for a railway. Three abstained. The small holders are delighted, of course. But the squatters are suspicious. They see themselves being pushed back, they are terrified of a change in land rents.'

'But they virtually control their rents; they have a majority.'

'A slight majority, Amos; very slight. At all events the graziers are suspicious. They want the money reserved for the discovery of a payable gold field. In the event, we might have to make concessions.'

The council had met in secret session. Whitehouse did not tell Polson that in order to carry the vote he had made concessions privately already. 'Now tell me,' he went on, 'about this man of yours.'

'I trust him.'

'Of course, Amos. Nevertheless—tell me again what he said to you.'

'Why, he said nothing denoting fear or surprise. He said he would go, that was all.'

Whitehouse sat back watching Polson, his hands pointed to

his chin like a mitre. Until recently the sensation of power, the power to intimidate at council, had not touched him. But now that his own tenure as Superintendent was in the balance, he had to rely less on personal conviction and more on mesmeric charm: what his opponents were pleased to call 'that antic concentration'. He still had power over men and, being of an age where nothing in politics was novel any more, he had begun to enjoy the sensation of influencing men for its own sake; a tendency which sometimes served for the influence itself. He had even begun to practise it on friends, as he did now with Polson, rolling the stem of his pipe about the roof of his mouth and watching the younger man feel for his words.

'Go on,' Whitehouse said.

'He said he would do it. And take half a dozen sheep.'

'Too rigorous for sheep, Amos. They would founder.'

'That's his point. If sheep can go men will follow.'

'Men will follow, you know. Even though they may vote in the first instance in favour of native ownership.'

'Does Hay know anything?'

Whitehouse shook his head. 'But he raised a question about this new flock of yours.'

'Ah.' Polson gave a long sigh. 'I see.'

'I confess, Amos, I don't. What have these sheep to do with your plan to coddle the natives?'

Whitehouse corrected himself. '*Our* plan, I should say.'

'Nothing at all. I simply want to prove something to myself.' Polson smiled. 'Another foolish venture, Matthew.'

'Tell me,' Polson said, 'did Hay mention Mackenzie?'

'Yes. He said he was no good. I'd like to meet the man myself. Amos, when you spoke to him what else did he say?'

'Nothing else, he said he would do it. It was curious—' Polson stopped. Whitehouse was leaning forward, wreathed in smoke.

'Go on.'

But Polson could not go on, he could not explain what was curious about the encounter. He had met Mackenzie, walking down from the pa, swinging kits of flax. And without ado had told him: the rudiments of the plan, the debt to the natives, that there would be a party and a reward, that Mackenzie himself would lead—'Ay, I will go,' he had said. Like that. Rubbing the hemp of his beard, looking at the dog whose

Roman nose pointed wetly towards the peaks. The dog's eyes glinted and together they faced the peaks, man and dog, as if to accept and confirm. And all the while Polson was exposing his warrant, the motive and honour of it, so the man might grasp it was an enterprise with greatness in it. But the fellow stood there, booted and hairy, unconfounded by all that prose. 'Well, good,' he said. Clicking his fingers. And again, 'Good.' Blowing out one nostril, sidelong. So that Polson felt witless sitting on his horse, talking to the air, when the fellow had agreed in the first place. Until the white teeth bared in the yellow beard and the two men looked and discovered each other. Polson saw two pools of moss, ponds of innocence, he saw the child and safety of the man. Mackenzie saw two black stones, crimpled with anxiety, and he chuckled. He had chuckled. That was the curious thing and Polson could not explain it to Whitehouse; could not tell him of the ungovernable depths lurking in those eyes or the hint of mockery behind the chuckle. For with Matthew Whitehouse, his benefactor and inquisitor, Polson was for the first time having to justify himself and appear what he was not: undoubting and masterful. Therefore he said:

'He won't march on Sundays, he said that. We laughed about it.'

'Hmn.'

'He is a very simple fellow, Matthew.'

'Oh well—' Whitehouse got up as Burcher the chief surveyor entered. 'Perhaps I am getting old and suspicious, like everyone else in this place. He shall lead us in the spring, never fear—the first week of October, eh Burcher?'

But Polson could not rid himself of the thought, especially after Burcher had joined them, that Whitehouse no longer took him seriously.

'Indeed why should he?' he said to Frances as they drove out that afternoon in the Dewhursts' spare gig. 'You know, Francie, I had the feeling when I asked Mackenzie to make the journey—I had the feeling that all the time he had been waiting for me to ask him. What d'you think?'

'I think—this.'

Polson winced, swerving the pony round two Maori women bearing kits of peaches and forcing one of them into the ditch. The woman fell over and roared with laughter.

'Yes?'

'This: he can hardly run off with the reward until he's got it, can he?'

Polson gave a wry smile. 'Yes, yes of course. That is so.'

'Nonetheless, papa.' She added soberly. 'When you meet Mr. Hay—if he claims Mackenzie you must give him back.'

'Of course,' he said. To please her.

'Good,' she said, looking about as if seeing the town for the first time.

He would not have said that she looked bitter.

In fact, though she still suffered occasional chimerical fits, Frances had recovered remarkably from her collapse. She had begun to talk of another dog to replace Brandy. With her mother's capacity for generosity and none of her father's instinct for self-torture, she had stopped hating Mackenzie; she could not hate for long. And the plan—Polson had managed to involve her in that—the plan had helped; had saved her from brooding. She saw an epic. The men departing, climbing into the void; then returning hoar-frosted and blasted with the wonder of what they had seen. She saw it brilliantly and prismatically, she saw the nobility in it. Even going about Christchurch in a big Scotch maud with ruff, and her hair up, and ankle boots—for it was foggy when they arrived—she saw and she wondered. So that the glances of the young men in holly-coloured shirts smoking cigars at the street corners fell from her unheeded.

But now the sun was shining and they saw the town in all its vulgarity, forgetting they had been hidden and were sensitive. The town had doubled in size. Where before all had seemed a limitless waving brown, now everything was built up. Swamps and piles of timber obtruded everywhere. The air rang with the knocking of axes. Driving along they passed men tearing out native shrubs, firing bulrushes, building bridges. Polson drove over one that was not finished and got sworn at by the workmen. There was the cathedral sited; and the piggeries and jail had been banished to Lyttelton, thus improving the prospect from the Embankment. Creek really.

'Shall you send the merinos straight up, papa?'

'*If* Hay's got them, certainly.' Why Polson doubted Hay he could not say, except that the man was successful.

He was making for the barber's. He needed a shave and

new brushes, Polson was rather hard on hairbrushes. He turned up Thin Street whirling mud and making the duckboards clatter. 'Damn.' He reined in, blocked by drays and bullock trains, juddering and backing at the toll gate. The entrance was alpined with loose wool — a dray had upset. Polson watched the farmer pick up his fleeces in armfuls and throw them onto the cart only to see them blown off again into the mud. The bystanders jeered. Frances jumped down, skirted a ditch and shaking out her hair ran into a mealy place.

'I would like the *London Illustrated News*,' she said, entering the shop.

'Yes, Ma'm. It is the latest.'

'And the *Times*.'

'Exzorsted, Ma'm.'

'I would like then something by Jane Porter or Anne Radcliffe.'

'Next time,' the man said.

'When is that please?'

'Next boat, Ma'm.'

'And when is that to be?'

'Next month.'

'Are you quite certain of that?'

'No, Ma'm.'

'Could you tell me where I might discover a quilted cloth hat?'

'No, Ma'm.'

Frances paid for the journal and then saw that it was two years old. She turned away tartly, slipped and almost fell down a hole. The drainage was frightful. Later Mrs. Dewhurst showed her how to put screws in the soles, a great help, and lent her a nice wide-brimmed leghorn.

They drove on then through the market, a dark little lane of trees that flowered and flowered and yet were budless; the flowers were dry crepe. There were no townspeople about, only servants. The vendors hung sloven on their hand carts in the manner of a painting by De Groux. There was a smallholder tugging a cow to the tail of which was attached a goat on a string. Every few yards he stopped to milk them, one and the other, into a greasy pail. They passed travellers bent double from the weight of their wickerback houses buying cauliflowers, wizened blue cauliflowers, reminding Frances of the dried heads in Mr. Plankton's museum. The travellers looked up as they passed. As a market it was flaccid, Polson thought. Only the Maoris redeemed it, sitting under the warped trees and slapping at their children with their broken stovepipe hats. The women sat stripping flax, their babies lashed behind with rugs; they had bantams in their laps and some had peaches which they sorted aimlessly, eating the bad ones and spitting out the stones. Polson was depressed, he could not say why. But it was Frances who pronounced, 'I shall *never* want to live here, papa.' As if impatient already to return to that desolation he wanted for the moment so ardently to forget.

'After all,' she said, 'Odessa is home.'

Before her simple clarity he was budless, like the trees, and was jealous of a generation that accepted without question all things new and indifferent in this new land. He looked at the crooked trees struggling to withstand and drove on without a word.

At the barber's he bought two new hairbrushes and sat on a bench with farmers. He sat between an ormulu beard and a chippendale beard. Humming a bit of a tune to the scissors, with one leg folded over his paunch. The objects prickling the walls made him nervous and he began with deliberate strokes to brush his hair, ten strokes this side and ten strokes that, until he had reached a hundred. He observed the beards. Those that did not have beards had moustaches and those without moustaches had sore lips and great blisters running over their noses and onto their chins. Of his own black fuzz Polson saw no peer and therefore agreed with the man who stepped down newly shaven and deemed it exclusive.

'Donald Hay! I knew you were back.'

'Yes, we landed yesterday. We called at Wellington, boarded Hossack and one or two others and came on straight, shocking vessel. The Lieutenant-Governor's eloped, did you know? I'll tell you about it at the Dewhursts on Friday. Hossack will be there, I'm told.'

'Yes,' said Polson, who had not met the new magistrate.

'He's a friend of the Governor, very promising. Jolly little fellow. You'll see. We can talk there; I want to hear from you about this scab. I hope to God I'm clean.'

'You are.'

'I want to see for myself. I shall wash anyway.' Hay stood

there pink-lipped and prosperous, testing his adam's apple against the pin of his cravat, conscious that he dwarfed everybody who was listening. He continued craning over Polson and talking in the loud way he had caught from Lady Suffolk.
'Terrible crossing, Amos. Gales.'
'Lady Suffolk is well?'
'Never better. She came down to meet me. And so are the stock. My dear man, the stock!'

Polson could not take his eyes off the other's kangaroo-skin gaiters which were kicking themselves with the energy of the man, scattering the underbrush into islands.

'Strong meat, Amos. Horned as the devil. Wool to here, all pea, no pod. But—' Hay paused, lowering his voice. 'They were rather expensive, Amos. So I halved the quantity.'

'You mean I have five hundred merinos instead of a thousand?'

'Yes. I telegraphed to your agent and he, replying that your not being—quite—flush, in the circumstances I thought—well. Five hundred was perhaps expedient.' Hay twirled his cane. 'You are not displeased?'

'I am rather,' Polson replied. 'But I owe you my thanks all the same.' And he excused himself and got into the chair knowing that he had not so much as dented that bland and patronising countenance.

Still, Polson swallowed his hurt and fell to thinking about these five hundred beasts for which he had mortgaged himself, every penny, including the small Norfolk property which was the reversion of his father's estate. He longed to see them, satin on the hills, and Mackenzie droving. Preoccupied, he got down feeling rudderless and went out leaving his hairbrushes behind.

'He's made your ears stick out,' Frances said as he rejoined her.

'It was a barber from Wopping,' Polson said. 'And we go back on Friday, straight after the function.'

Frances pouted a little. 'It was Mr. Hay, wasn't it? He came out looking very cross. Did you upset him about Mackenzie?'

'No, my dear. I forgot to mention it.'

'I have been thinking, papa. You really have taken the man falsely; and it worries me.'

'Why does it worry you?'

'It is Mr. Hay that worries me, Mr. Hay and the other

graziers that covet the hinterland. That's what papa Dewhurst says. He was talking last night when you were out. Mr. Hay won't be brooked. He mistrusts you somehow, he will do something. He will take Mackenzie back or he will try to stop the expedition. *Therefore*, papa—are you listening?' She lifted the leghorn and leaning forward dabbed the spots of blood on his cheek. 'Therefore you must act: you must either give Mackenzie back to him or start the expedition with Mackenzie now, alone.'

A little high-pitched, like her colour, Polson thought.

'Alone, he would perish.'

She was amusing. But he couldn't break faith with Whitehouse; Whitehouse would not be amused.

'Very well!' Polson suddenly seized the whip and drove off, for all the world was teasing him, just as all the world was watching the process of dabbing. 'Hay can have him. I'll send him back the moment we return.'

Frances sat back with an air of defiance. 'Don't,' she said flatly.

That night the Dewhursts took them to a got-up ball for the families of the victims of the Crimea. The ball was held at the Mechanics' Institute, with supper available through a hole in the wall at the Fotheringay next door. Between sittings a policeman played alternately on a flageolet and a violin and glees were sung. All the aristocracy was there besides the five Misses Dewhurst, and no frights. Lady Suffolk confided to Frances that the floor was rather shabby. Mrs. Dewhurst, a thin bird-like woman with watery eyes, held court on a small stage and received donations to the cause without prying, clasping the crisp envelopes to her bosom and fluttering her lashes in the manner of a munificent nereid. As befitted the instigator of the Sebastopol Salvationary Committee. Beside her sat her husband, in weepers, attentive to her every want. Together they embodied the text, printed on a card between two pots of geraniums, 'We are the Givers'. And when the bishop made a speech alluding to the magnanimity of certain givers ('whose righteousness endureth forever'), the pair clasped hands publicly in a manner that would have been outrageous had it not been sincere.

Polson talked with Whitehouse and with Hay from whom he

learned that the merinos had already been sent up. He also had a conversation with a young Maori chief who wore goldlaced trousers and tried to shock him. The chief spoke impeccable English and told Polson he was returning north after a fruitless attempt to secure tribesmen to fight against the Queen.

'Why fruitless?' Polson inquired.

'The natives here will not fight,' the young chief said sourly. 'There is too much Christianity.'

'I quite agree. I am surprised that you have not taken the vow yourself.'

'Tonight I have made a different vow,' the native said, politely fingering the chain to which Polson's watch was attached. 'Tonight I have met twenty sheep men like yourself and I have vowed to shoot no more soliders.'

'Oh, and why is that?'

'It is not worth it, sir. My powder costs me 10s a pound and the Queen can obtain another solider for a shilling. Now I have observed that it costs a very great deal to make a land-thief like yourself; and in future it is people like you I intend to shoot.'

Such honest intention impressed Polson. He introduced Frances. The young chief bowed, bending his black ringed curls so low that Frances felt she ought to knight him. She thought he would ask her to dance, but he only drew himself up, clicked his heels together and left them with a smile of scorn.

'He has fine teeth,' she thought, watching him stalk away. And then she was picked from her reverie by Rose Dewhurst, the plainest and most dramatic of the five sisters. Rose was miserable. She had been censored for dancing with a post-hole borer. Frances danced with everyone, from the Superintendent to a despairing Viennese Catholic called Veitch who claimed to have instigated a chapel of one. Mr. Veitch had difficulties both temporal and spiritual. He was, he told Frances, being driven from his mind by the dogs of the parish. Frances advised red pepper but he said he had tried that and had taken to throwing chairs at them. He added that either he would go mad or he would be forced to return to Europe since his furniture was nearly used up. For some reason all the men Frances danced with confided their troubles to her. Except for one. He was very freckled and carroty on top and he waddled.

THE STATION

He wore a candid shirt and he came and went from the Dewhurst circle repeatedly. Rose claimed him.

'Are you going to marry that young man?' Frances said to her.

Rose Dewhurst moved her head in such a way that it appeared full of water for it made a gurgling sound. She had a big milky face and heaving breasts tightly corseted; and was most dramatic when most sad, thought Frances, noting her eyes. Her eyes were remarkably cow-like.

'Should I?' Rose said in her gurgling way.

'Well. I should have thought that anybody who attends a ball in green socks deserves some consideration.'

'Are you?' Frances persisted, discerning a hopelessness behind all that bovine moisture.

'No. He dislikes me and mamma dislikes his class and I—I detest mamma.' With that Rose Dewhurst burst into sobs.

The young man confronted Frances during a Sir Roger. He told Frances his name which was Dick, owned to having bored post-holes in the colonial service but was now a surveyor, he said, taking sheep on thirds. Apart from that he was entirely silent. He jigged, holding her at arm's length with a playful fixity that she found impudent and somehow disturbing.

Frances returned to the Dewhursts at four a.m. with her hair all danced down.

The Dewhursts lived close by the town. It was a residence: seven bedrooms and an etna in each, and some of Minton's loveliest vases. The drawing room, like the garden, was palatial and contained a straw fan slung from the ceiling in the manner of a punkah. The Dewhursts were gentle rich people with a horror of dirt, one of two factors which endeared the household to Polson, the other being the Bach pianoforte. On the morning after the ball Polson was sitting playing it when his host walked in looking pink and magisterial in a bathrobe and stood beneath the fan rubbing himself. Each morning—as Arthur Dewhurst explained—he plunged in the stream and then with Isaac the houseboy ran across to the lake where Isaac gave him hot mud packs.

'It's called the allopathic,' Dewhurst said. 'For the gout. I haven't got the gout yet, but pater had it and our curate's just got it. You should try it, Amos. The stuff comes out of the ground cooked, like junket. Nothing like it in Norfolk.'

Polson declined—he had a horror of revealing his body, as he had had a horror of undressing before his wife. It struck Polson then that he and this opulent vegetarian had nothing whatever in common and he said so. 'Nor can I think why you have invited me,' he added.

Arthur Dewhurst tut-tutted and stroked his chins, a habit he had caught from the bishop. Even in the mornings he was grave. 'You can help me, Polson. Indeed you have already by inviting Rose to Odessa. It only wants my wife's consent and— really, it will be a great help.'

'And,' he went on, 'I believe I can help you.'

'How is that?' Polson said.

'I deal in land,' Arthur Dewhurst said, inhaling as if he owned the whole of Canterbury. His glance, like his person, contained promise of secret reserves. In England Dewhurst had been a poor church solicitor: until the day the Canterbury Fathers had retained him. Before leaving England he had bought up four times the amount of land to which each migrating family was entitled. Dewhurst did this on behalf of his three brothers. None of the brothers had any intention of leaving England; and indeed, as he subsequently explained to disembarking migrants in Canterbury, none of the brothers had. When values rose Dewhurst was able to sell the fraternal property, piece by fractional piece, at eight times the sum he had paid for it. He had been profiting by such jobbery ever since. Naturally he did not tell Polson this.

'Land,' he said, 'of all kinds. Land here is influence, Polson.'

Land, thought Polson, is the new English vice. It has no soul and therefore inspires no conscience. It is something to be tossed about, like wards in chancery or the motto of a preparatory school. Land from the natives because it is cheap. In return for Christianity because it is convenient. Polson was on the point of blurting out his plan. But he did not know Dewhurst yet and so said nothing.

'Land,' the other repeated. 'It pays, Polson. And that reminds me—Friday. I want you to meet someone.' He paused, mopping his face on the towel. 'I see you are puzzled by my pastimes. I have two pastimes. One is helping people, and the other is—'

'Land,' Polson interpolated.

'Land,' Dewhurst intoned drily.

Soon, thought Polson, we shall begin dancing a minuet.

'Believe me, it pays, Amos. Furthermore it gives me leisure to guide some of Emma's committees. However else would we build our cathedral, for instance? Somebody has to do these things.'

'You are quite right, somebody has to,' Polson conceded, and remained puzzled by the ambivalence of goodness.

All their conversations were like this, baroque and elliptical, and Polson began to wonder whether it would be possible ever to communicate with anybody in this land of self-advancement where lucidity and frank speaking were despised and everybody withheld, not because of hypocrisy which was something subtler but because of niceness which was somehow more malignant.

Arthur Dewhurst continued to intrigue him. The way he had erected a private system which in a few years had become a colonial ideal. 'Fear God, loan at twelve per cent and disinherit the natives'—such appeared the Dewhurst System. Also the way he managed to look about him without malice. At fifty-two, he was town councillor, proctor of the college, ex-officio deacon in charge of congregational affairs. On questions of land rent, levées and lapses of religious zeal, Arthur Dewhurst was always consulted. Also, Polson noted, the way he was devoted to his family. He had provided his wife with bird's-eye maple (luxuries and needfuls) and held wool for her in the evenings. He played a mild dulcimer to his daughters' still milder violins; and on occasion would hum a motet with them, in dog-Latin. He was fond for their pleasure of acrostics. His accomplishments were many. Yet they were not remarkable. Polson could not help noticing that Arthur Dewhurst was hampered by a lurking deference to his wife. Emma Dewhurst was a woman held together entirely by prayer and good works. Frances had a word for her—zestful. She was not merely thin and bird-like but very tall, with unfortunate ears. But the frailty of her appearance and the delicacy of her utterances— she was inclined to say pāth, and grāss—were deceptive. In the little ruche cap she wore, even under her bonnet, she was indestructible; and she flew like a fair-skinned kite over the women of Canterbury. The committees of her making trailed obediently behind: the Committee for the Recovery of Distressed Needlewomen, the Committee for the Baptism of

Maori Infants, the Committee for the Banishment of Profligates. In the evenings when the young men who paid court to her daughters had gone Mrs. Dewhurst would sit and ponder her affairs supported by the unfailing bulk of her husband. Seated before the samplers their daughters had embroidered which decorated the privacy of their lives. One enveloped the piano, its luminous text backing to the floor. Then Mrs. Dewhurst would ask Polson to play for her. She would compose herself by the marble chimney-piece in her pointed slippers and her pointed hair and sit with her long hands folded, looking exactly like a prayerbook marker. At such moments, Polson thought, she had a thin regal beauty.

He regarded the Dewhursts as a small bridge club who played together on the surface of life in that state of well-bred ease which was the acme of colonial idealism. But he was forced continually by their efforts to convert him to compare them with his father, who had been a rector, and whose ideas of redemption and immortality had consisted in cudgelling his sons and the sins of others in order that his deeds might live after him. For his father Polson reserved a special category. In it he placed most of the devout Christians he had known.

Mrs. Dewhurst turned to him one evening and said, 'You play beautifully, Amos. I may call you that, mayn't I? Doesn't he, Frances? You must both come again.'

And her husband said, 'Yes, Amos. You must. Emma is devising a committee to keep this country from the pollution of convict immigration. We cannot afford to be unvigilant. We could, you see, arrange the meetings to coincide with your visits. We thought you might rather like to *serve*.'

'Thank you,' Polson said, smoothing the sampler. 'I would if I could, but I'm afraid that I can't. It would mean breaking faith, since I already employ two of them.'

Mrs. Dewhurst tittered slightly. Arthur Dewhurst mopped his brow and consulted Frances.

'Yes, two convicts,' Frances said, putting down her book. 'One is called Droo.'

'Droo is my bullock driver, Arthur. A hearty radish.'

'He murdered somebody,' Frances said. 'And the other one is called Mackenzie.'

'And what did Mackenzie do?' said Mrs. Dewhurst warily.

'He shot my dog,' Frances said, and faced those long courtly lashes which, for the moment, neither Polson nor Arthur Dewhurst cared to do. 'And what is more, of all the men on our station those two are the best.'

Mrs. Dewhurst sighed. A sound of simpering caused her to glance at the rocking chair where her mother sat knitting. Having assured herself that the latter was nodding and free from the danger of contamination, Mrs. Dewhurst composed her hands. 'Gentlemen-at-large, I believe they are called,' she said through her nose.

'Capital, capital,' Arthur Dewhurst had caught Polson's grin; his cheeks wobbled and he prepared to laugh. Then seeing his wife's face, he recalled himself and stood up. Whenever he deferred to his wife like this, Arthur Dewhurst appeared to bend slightly at the ankles.

'Never mind, Arthur,' Mrs. Dewhurst's look told him, 'we shall try something else tomorrow.'

Aloud she said, 'I think we should all like some tea Arthur.'

'Of course, my dear,' Arthur Dewhurst said, and went to find the maid.

An hour later as Mrs. Dewhurst lay down under her nainsook quilt, which remained miraculously undisturbed by that thin form, Arthur Dewhurst stood at the window in his nightshift gathering a last gasp of air before plunging into the fumes of violet powder with which Mrs. Dewhurst nightly surrounded her person. Etched against the window and a distant steeple (his wife's favourite prospect) he was seen as a padded white form, rather tufty, with tiny pink hands and tapering feet. His ears which were also tiny had fled his cheeks and in the light of the taper he held appeared to lengthen, pendulous and palpitating, as if they would overtake his shoulder blades.

'Come away from the window, you will catch cold, Arthur.'

'I was thinking, Emma.'

Mrs. Dewhurst smoothed her cap and waited.

'About Rose,' he said.

'I dread it,' his wife said, 'I dread it, and I forbid it, Arthur.'

'No, it is quite in order,' Arthur Dewhurst said, for he had determined to make a stand. 'Rose will go to Odessa in the spring. She and Frances will get along famously. I have talked to Polson and it will be quite in order.'

Slowly, like a monk performing hidden offices, he paraded before the window with the taper, ever watchful for his wife's tears. When they came he set down the taper and advanced to the bedside. Taking his wife's hand he soothed it, sitting on the edge of the bed, and talked to her for a considerable time. For the Dewhursts had a problem. There were five daughters; and ever since the eldest had become engaged three years previously, it had been their concern to ration off the spares. Mrs. Dewhurst believed in sudden love, *Sans Dieu Rien* and correct links. To this end she promoted gatherings. The first had settled Charlotte. Another had eased Sarah. Harriet, the middle one, was nearly promised to a conchologist called Gideon Pringle; while Caroline, the youngest, was being drawn surely if intractably towards the purse of a rich grazier's son, Adrian Banfield. All solid dependable matches which would never cost her a penny. But Rose, who was twenty-one, had rebelled. Rose had become taken with a surveyor who doubted God. She had begun to dress like a hoyden and to read Homer. Whenever the young man called she would read Homer. Or she would read tracts. The tracts, supplied by Mr. Veitch. She became deliberately unhappy. Her mother pitied her and the more she pitied her, the unhappier Rose became. For a time she spoke only French and declared her intention, like Charlotte Brontë, of going to Brussels. Then she fasted and became ill. Recovering, she burned the subscribers' lists of her mother's 'hateful committees', as well as all the novels of Charlotte M. Yonge. She declared she would never marry, since marriage was degrading, and had demanded to be sent away or she would become a Roman Catholic. At which point Arthur Dewhurst acted for the first time in his life against his wife's wishes and invited the Polsons. Arthur Dewhurst was a great believer in fresh air. If fresh air could turn normal people like the Polsons into infidels, there was every chance it could restore sanity to abnormal ones like Rose.

So he reasoned, stroking his wife's hand along the coverlet. 'They are not bad people, Emma. Just odd. I am sure Frances in the country is a sensible girl. She says these things merely to shock. Why, the first time I met Polson he asked me if I believed in God. Just to shock, d'you see. It is their way.'

'It's because Rose limps that she does not like me,' said Mrs. Dewhurst.

'Come, my dear, she doesn't hold that against you.'

'After all I have done for her.'

'I know, Emma.'

Mrs. Dewhurst dried her eyes and lay very still until the bones at her neck, fine and white in the light of the taper, were still. Then she said, 'What was he?'

'His people were invincible. Two bishops and a headmaster in the family; his father was a rector, I believe. He used to be a solicitor.'

'Then he has slid, Arthur.'

'I believe he was meant for the ministry but took up painting or some such.'

'And then God left him, I see.'

'But as a person — as people — they are not uninteresting, Emma. Just odd. Country dwellers are, especially the converts.'

'Your kerchief once more, Arthur.' Mrs. Dewhurst dabbed her eyes and gripped the silk as if in spasm. In reality she was not wrestling with infidels or Rose's happiness. She was somewhere deeper. Now that her biological function was complete Emma Dewhurst was not conscious of her debt to the colony which had permitted, in its place, the seed of archetypal matriarchy to grow. But sometimes beneath the layers of her subconscious, somewhere further in, she felt an infinite pain and was afraid of giving in. At length her grip relaxed and she said:

'Very well. Rose may go.'

Arthur Dewhurst took the kerchief and mopped his cheeks.

'But only for a week,' Mrs. Dewhurst added. 'A month would be dangerous, Arthur.'

Arthur Dewhurst was really very tired. He acquiesced silently and blew out the taper. As he settled down onto his side, staring out at his wife's favourite prospect, he consoled himself with the thought that if Emma was archetypal at least four of his daughters would consolidate the stamp, and humble greater men than he.

Lying on the same side of the house in the little French room that Rose had given up to her, Frances woke from a dream. The bed hung short, she was choking. Fleeing from a man, or men, they were all about her. One was Taylor, another was Kerr, a third was Billy with a bone between his teeth. Her father stood there reasoning with Brandy, and did not look up when Droo fled shrieking across the ceiling in a chariot pursued by avenging angels. The little dog was convulsed on a bed of straw. At the window stood Mackenzie, looking in. She cried out to him and as Taylor and Kerr and Billy advanced on the dog she flung straw in their eyes and beat them with the broom. Then Sparrow came and read the burial service. Then the dog died. Just before it died a lamb was born. The men jeered to see her, naked like the lamb. She had taken off her clothes. She made Mackenzie cover the dead dog with her dress while she wrapped the lamb in her petticoats. She was running then with the lamb, to save it; but she kept bumping Mackenzie's legs which were not hard but pliant and covered with white hairs. And suddenly she was lying on the floor wide awake entangled in valences and her face down and her teeth knitting up the opossum rug. She pulled herself back onto the bed, coughing up pelt, and found that her nightshift was rucked and messy. Shadows startled her. She looked round guiltily and lit the lamp and discovered only the dimity curtains blowing.

The sun was streaming in and something was bending over her with a string of lettuce on its lips saying, 'France, France,'—like Hans. And, 'The lamp's still burning.'

'Why?' Frances murmured, lying bathed in the plumpness that was Rose Dewhurst. There was something bovine about her, about those big doleful eyes. 'You smell of earth,' Frances said. 'No—cows.'

'Gillyflower water. Mamma's. I've stolen it. Here.' And she sprinkled them both from a bottle.

'Let's be devils,' she said suddenly; and Frances sat up, feeling awake and conspiratorial. Now the other, the younger girl, was embracing her like a vibrant plum and they were together in private smelling of gillyflower water.

'How?' Frances said.

'That tree.'

There was a solitary cabbage tree through the dimity curtains.

Rose said, 'Could we see Odessa from there?'

'It looks dangerous. Lovely!'

'Mamma wants to cut it down.'

'Let's climb it.'

'We can't, that's the trouble. Mamma forbids it.'

'Then let's!'

Rose nodded and gurgled. 'I'm so glad you've come, France.'

Then: 'You know, you were calling out in your sleep. I came in twice.' Taking her hand which was clenched tight. 'What are you holding?'

'This.' Frances smiled and opened her palm. It was empty. Then she said enigmatically, 'Mackenzie.'

'Is that the shepherd?'

'Yes.'

'The one that frightens you?'

'Yes.'

'What is he like?'

'I don't know. He is a man who cannot parse. He is a man —no. He is a creature—that's not right either.' Frances lifted her eyes an instant. 'He is what, Rose, each of us would wish to be if only God hadn't fashioned us otherwise, there.'

Suddenly Rose said, 'That's it. That's the name you were calling out. France?'

'Yes.'

'Why mustn't he go alone?'

'Is that what I was saying?'

'Over and over. Why, whatever's the matter?'

'Nothing, Rose. I cannot understand myself, I thought I'd been dreaming about a dog.'

Of all the beings in that house—there was also Quentin who was four and two mushroom maids and the sonsy Maori boy Isaac whom Frances called Thirteen, since he was the thirteenth and a zinc bath which was brought in and actually used and seemed an additional member—only Rose had outgrown the superstition that a child unless baptised goes to the wrong place. Only Rose was vulnerable. So Polson noted when that morning at breakfast she was put upon as usual for coming late with a book in her hand and retaliated by suddenly stating that Mrs. Abigail, the late rector's wife, was mad. 'True, true. She sits out in her brocade dress with a spotted kerchief on her head talking to nobody,' Rose said. 'The maddest little body in town.' For some reason the news upset Mrs. Dewhurst and there followed such a display of taunting on the part of the sisters that Rose was brought to tears. Finally Charlotte said 'You are always hurting others. You know Mrs. Abigail is mamma's dearest friend.' And Arthur Dewhurst observed, 'Old ladies do sit out on autumn evenings alone.'

'Oh yes,' Frances rejoined, for Rose's tears if not championed were terrible to behold. 'But not eating snails.'

In the debate that followed Frances took Rose's part so vehemently that Polson half expected his daughter and the sisters to come to blows; and it struck him then that Frances and Rose were very much alike. Rather, the different isolations they suffered—the one geographical, the other spiritual—produced in them the same frustrations, the same smarting aggressions: hot-tongued little outbursts, callow, rude (Rose had a bawdy tongue) but for all that not unhealthy. Still, watching the pair escape later from that rectitudinous house into the cabbage tree, he did tremble to think what sort of escapades they might be plotting together for Odessa. Rose (one stocking twisted and hair in her face) swarming up like a wild bat; Frances in a cream frock with flounces at the ankles sliding behind, gazelle-like, swaying, fifty feet high, then stopping, cajoling, whispering, tugging Rose round towards Odessa where the wind was blowing—they could tell the wind from the fires, burning off. Frances had the leghorn thrown back and her face branching into the wind, though the wind was fifty miles off, as if she would fly to it. Polson need not have worried. Inside, though the two girls might share like pariahs the thought of committing outrage, once out of it they did nothing of the sort. They discussed men.

Rose said, 'What will you do, France, if Lionel has furze to the chops like them?' They were looking on the streets and the overweening young men in holly-coloured shirts, smoking cigars. 'Would you marry him?'

'I'd send him to the Zoological. No—no, I wouldn't. I'd give him to you.'

'Do!'

'But you're against marriage, Rosie.'

'Only to spite mamma.'

'Then would you like him?'

Rose considered that, wiping her treacly hair from the branches. 'No thanks. But from your description he sounds as if he needs some mucking about.'

Which was an expression Frances had never heard before. She supposed Rose had caught it from that young surveyor, Dick.

It was a misshapen tree, bunching and unbunching like a

collation of ostriches. And a treehouse in it which Thirteen had built. Thirteen came too and showed them the loft: then he showed them the town which was just below them, while Frances kilted up her skirts and climbed even higher among the earwigs and saw a red flower like an agave spilling above the lawn. 'Very pwetty,' Thirteen said, meaning the town. It was pretty, Frances thought, with the rivery bathwater of the Avon dawdling down from Dewhursts through flowered plots and white-trimmed gables. Yet the town seemed curiously inert, as one of Quentin's drawings. The houses so neat, so diligently raised, shrank inwards; also the people, statues at the flowery gates, pleading grace for their town, so neat, so diligently raised. 'Look,' they seemed to say, leaning on the gates, 'we have planted the brown earth. But the earth mourns, it has no chest to it. We have planted a town with no nerves.'

Then the flower caught her. 'Look,' she said. 'What is that?' For the crimson panicles, borne on black sticks, were printed on the sky.

'Harakeke,' the boy said.

It was a common thing. But the petals, suppliant. Trembling and lifting their palms. She saw hands spilled on the sky out of the earth's mourning, and remembered the communion in the stillness. It was almost still enough for prayer.

'Harakeke?' Frances climbed down and ran through the garden until she came to the fans that thrust the crimson thorns.

'Why,' she called, 'it's only flax. We have that at Odessa.'

'Only flax,' the treehouse called.

'Good for baskits.' The voices floated down.

And yet the flower born out of the wild basket leaf made her proud. Clustered on the strong black loins, spreading nectar out of season. When everyone knew that autumn was a time for dying. And round about all the little new planted English things waning into the ground, resenting.

Later Frances lit the tapers by the ormulu card tray and knelt to Mrs. Dewhurst's favourite prospect, and prayed God for the strength to see goodness in all the common things that grew in this land.

Gilliam stood looking across the creek to the long hill. His straw hat was pulled down and he held a watch. 'Now then,' he said to Kerr who was on one side of him, and Mackenzie who was on the other. For he had decided to settle the difference that was between them, with dogs. The two dogs sat up, their ears laid. The men were behind on the stiff ground.

There was the shingled creek and then the first hill rose for perhaps a mile where it ridged and flattened; then it rose again to a crust which was called the Loaf. The sun was not yet on it, only a man; and a small flock on the lower hill.

'Now then. You see Professor, pon Loaf? He has thirty them new merinos behind him, in two bins. When I wave he sends fifteen. They will bolt down behind Loaf, out of mind. Just here, that shingle, is point of arrival. Agreed, we are. You first laddie. Now then.'

Gilliam nudged Kerr and shook his hat at the summit where another object was seen to shake in reply, on a stick. Kerr's satin dog was already in the creek, swimming. It ran up the first hill, scattering the sheep that grazed there to the margins, and disappeared over the ridge. It was seen again, somewhat slowed, as a thin furrow gliding up the crust. And then nothing.

'Long time on manœuvres,' Drake-Draper said.

'Shut up.' Taylor spat.

'The silenter the better bhoys.' Droo was there also, lighting up.

'They're coming,' Moffet said.

A parcel of straw had appeared on the crest and was moving down the Loaf. The dog was behind, invisible.

'Five minutes,' Gilliam said.

'Home in ten.' Kerr squatted, shading his eyes. He wore a sort of knitted pancake folded over his ears which jutted, like everything else.

'Comin clean,' he said.

Taylor nodded. 'Very clean, Alec.'

The animals came on, unbroken.

Mackenzie watched intently as Kerr's satined dog, brightly weaving, drove the bubble of horns down onto the shingle.

'Held!' Kerr said. And stood up.

'Nine minutes and forty seconds.' Gilliam tapped his watch.

'Nine minutes un forty,' Moffet echoed.

'Now then, Jock.' The overseer waved again and a shred of pebbles knocked his gaiters as Mackenzie's bitch went forward.

'Good charge, gentlemen,' Drake-Draper said. 'Cavalry trained, you can see that. Strong in the water.'

THE STATION 163

'Slow on the hill.' Kerr looked pleased.

'Very slow, Alec.' Taylor clasped his braces under the jacket, imitating Kerr, who had knelt on one knee. Everyone was kneeling to the sun with his hat tipped forward. The sun had begun to gild the Loaf and rain deep shadows onto the smaller darting one. Mackenzie was still looking at the shingle where Kerr's dog held quarry—as if doubting that quarry. Then he knelt also, shading his eyes, and saw his bitch fling herself over the crest into the orb of the sun.

'Five minutes,' Gilliam said.

Droo's pipe made a sucking sound.

'Six minutes.'

Kerr stood up then and eased himself, making a sluice. The runnels steamed and dried, leaving a tracery in the stones. 'Of what use,' he said, 'is working dog that mislays quarry?'

'Enemy approaching.' Drake-Draper was stooping on bent knees and appeared abstracted there in a firm riding position. He had a pound on Mackenzie's dog, against everyone.

'Where?' Kerr said.

'Flanking movement, gentlemen.'

Drake-Draper pointed not to the top but to the side where the sheep had appeared. They wheeled and straightened, plunging down. The dust showed.

'Now then. Eight minutes.'

'Still slow.' Kerr had omitted to fasten his trousers.

'Very slow, Alec.'

Mackenzie had a clod in his throat.

'Beautiful charge, gentlemen.'

'Nine minutes.'

There was silence, except for the drumming of hocks on the moving ground.

When the animals were down and the two forces of merinos camped together on the shingle, a little apart, with the wet dogs crouching into their eyes; and Mackenzie had said 'Held', and Gilliam had looked at his watch and said 'Nine minutes and *fifty* seconds'; and Kerr had laughed with victory as the men came and hit him on the shoulders, they heard a shout. They looked up to see Laughton running down, waving his hat all over the Loaf, while before him bolting this way and that was a solitary sheep.

'Ha!' said Drake-Draper, upright at last. 'Deserter.'

Gilliam walked into the creek and gazed at the sheep opposite. 'Kerr, laddie,' he said. 'Your satin cannot count.'

'Why, what's wrong?'

'Mine hath fifteen,' Mackenzie said.

'Well?' Kerr said stupidly.

'Take a roll call, man. Step in and count your troops.' Drake-Draper was also in the creek.

Kerr waded a few steps and began to count. When he had reached fourteen, he stopped. Then he turned to Mackenzie, rather sallow. 'I suppose you'll play your bluidy pipe now,' he said.

But Mackenzie was thinking.

'I rule no contest,' Gilliam said. 'We must make it again.'

'Nay.'

'Why nay, Jock?'

'I can show you.' Mackenzie motioned his bitch across and told Kerr to do the same. And marched off with his back to the creek, bidding the others follow. Which they did, with the dogs proud and dripping in their midst. After a bit Mackenzie stopped and faced about.

'Now then,' Gilliam said, coming up.

'We will bide,' Mackenzie said, 'an watch.' So they watched. The merinos left untended on the shingle had begun to wander, some to leap, back onto the long hill which the other flock, of crossbreds, was beginning to recover. 'Un hell's job we shall have no separatin big brutes from others,' Taylor said, recognising that the two breeds would shortly merge. As they watched, the breeds did merge, The merino was swallowed by the greater numbers of the cross. Indistinguishable, at that distance.

'Now then.' The overseer was getting short, and no breakfast. 'Tell us your mind.'

'That is the task,' Mackenzie said, glancing at Kerr. The man had a ferrety look, with a sticky beret and a confusion of sheep. 'We mun separate yon merinos from the cross.'

'Pretty,' Drake-Draper said. He had taken a long pipe and was scratching an armpit. 'A pretty tactic, gentlemen.'

Gilliam said: 'Can your satin do that, Kerr? Now then.' Kerr threw back his neck and laughed. A gristled laugh that was not a laugh. The others heard it out, since it was not an answer either.

'No, Gilliam. I have trained dog for runnin and for headin and for drawin, but not for jugglin.'

'Well Jock, can yours?'

'Oy ay. She will do her best.' Mackenzie moved his fingers and the bitch left his side.

Shortly they saw her on the hill, the white-tipped tail dressing the shadows. They saw the animals look up and edge together. They saw the tip begin to revolve, concentrically, and the bunches of white open and close. They saw this happen many times, hands on chins. Saw the animals trot a bit and stop a bit, and finally become rooted in the companionship of the magnetic spiral; until the men themselves had become fascinated by the circle of fire ringing the hillside. They saw this without speaking and were disappointed when that moving tip merged in the throng and disappeared. It reappeared however, splitting asunder the block, driving a number of sheep all of a piece. They came on.

Moffet blew his nose. 'It's unnacherill,' he said. 'Like I said, the dog is unnacherill.'

They went forward, a wambly little group, and counted thirty merinos on the shingle. After that they chuckled and talked and hit Mackenzie on the shoulder pins, and Moffet said it wasn't natural again. Drake-Draper drew on the pipe and notched his winnings on the stem. Kerr recovered his spleen and shook hands.

'What I want is to know, Jock,' Gilliam said, 'is where did you learn to learn dogs like that? Now then.'

And Mackenzie replied, 'On the Coigach Road above Loch Broom.'

When the men had gone to their breakfast he went to the sheep. They were gathered before the dog blowing their slavonic cheekbones, fit to charge. He admired their strength, more than ever he admired this. The warmth of their hostility to the dog that held them.

He sent them off and walked along the creek to the ti groves where they had shorn. All along the creek grew flax bushes and he noticed that the ground was verdant. Only here. While elsewhere, even where Gilliam had sown grasses, only blunt tussock showed. He walked about examining the places where the pasture appeared and could be called pasture. Those were the places where the flax grew.

He sat a moment to empty the water from his boots. Now if the plant did thrive—there, where he was going for Polson, he pondered. Then, he thought, Polson's land would indeed be fertile. The stiff fans of the flax rasped his ears. He lay back until the red keel carried on the stalk was directly overhead. He thought no more, for he fell asleep looking at it.

'And now, my dear.' Lady Suffolk drew Frances aside, smoothing her ostrich plumes. 'Tell me. Has Christchurch been good to you?'

'Well I do think our shepherds are more civil than the shopkeepers,' Frances said.

'So do I, so do I. They assume the independence of grandees and express it in the accents of the Tilbury docks. Horrid, horrid.'

'Aha. Millicent,' said Mrs. Dewhurst, appearing with a plate of coddled ices. Very stately in a silk morning gown. 'Doing us down again?'

'Some people,' she added, turning to Mr. Hay, 'do object to the independence of their manner.'

'As usual,' Hay said. 'As usual Millicent has forgotten that everybody here is well off. Damned well off.'

'But Donald, gracious! I *like* to see it. Everybody is tolerably well off, I like to see it. I enchoy the upright gait. It is infinitely preferable, Mrs. Dewhurst, to the servility of English people at home. The mass, you understand.' Mrs. Dewhurst nodded and went to the door, people were arriving all the time; and Lady Suffolk smiled inwardly, both from the ice and the knowledge that she had as usual persuaded both sides while agreeing with neither. Frances smiled also. She had been seeking a word for Lady Suffolk and now she found it—*embonpoint*. Noting the full cherry gown adorned by pink roses which she wore with the assurance of a four-poster. In that drawing room of biscuit cambrics and autumnal chintz Lady Suffolk basked with an air of voluptuous disdain, as accorded the fitness of her station. Whenever somebody was introduced to her she would close her eyes for an instant, as if passing their lineage through the medium of an invisible crystal, and then adjust her behaviour to the message she received.

'I loved the ball,' Frances said.

'Which one?' said Lady Suffolk, staring past her. 'Who's that bumpkin?' she said, indicating a rubicond face talking to Polson.

'Oh that's Farmer Trotman. His wife has just died.'

'How unfortunate. Well *I* wouldn't have had him in.'

Mrs. Dewhurst at least isn't a snob, Frances reflected. 'What on earth are you talking about?' she said to her father as he approached with Trotman.

'Mook,' Polson replied pleasantly, and passed on.

Mrs. Dewhurst's 'morning' had begun well, for she knew the art of receiving roundly. As of dressing. Her figure on such occasions assumed a fullness which showed her fine bones to advantage. Half the aristocracy of the plains was there and she noted with satisfaction that the flowered waistcoat, which distinguished the rising young colonial, was distributed equably about her daughters. So she had planned it.

The Hays had just come, and the Skillithorns of the Operatic Society. And Trotman the farmer had come. Mr. Trotman had merely called, bearing a bag of French beans and some rhubarb. Unabashed, Mrs. Dewhurst had given him straight over to Polson. 'A stray, Amos. But of the land. Quite superior to the younger brother, and *far* more steady.' Polson had been delighted to discover that Trotman was expert in the procreation of artificial manures. It was remarkable, Frances said to her neighbour, how the men secluded themselves from their wives. 'You will learn, my dear,' Lady Suffolk said, observing her husband walk off to join Nathan Thomas and Murdo Banfield. The three graziers sat down in a corner and Frances could not help feeling that they were discussing her father.

More people arrived, clad in the prevailing colour of straw; and Lady Suffolk knew she had been right to wear red. These were followed by Quentin Dewhurst in a nankeen suit, blowing soap bubbles. 'Such a hot little face,' observed Lady Suffolk, and then lost her colour. Behind Quentin had appeared Miss Le Loup, fully caged, wearing bright cerise: a creation fortuitously enhanced by the soap bubbles through which she was perceived by all.

'She looks radiant, doesn't she?' Frances said.

'*Doesn't* she?' echoed Lady Suffolk, with a thundering stare.

Miss Le Loup sang.

'Green socks, extraordinary.'

'I beg your pardon, Lady Suffolk.'

'That young man, talking to your father.'

'Oh yes, he's a surveyor. Rose's young man.'

'That explains everything. That girl—' Lady Suffolk's eye swept to a chaise longue from whence Rose was gazing languorously in the same direction. 'That girl will kill us all. That girl—!' And she swept off. Her skirts made a swishing noise on the Axminster, as a weka moving through pampas.

Tea was served. Polson appeared with a Sally Lunn and some damson cheese and took Frances aside. 'That young man has been talking about the expedition. He knows, Francie.'

'But everyone knows, papa. It's advertised.'

'My hand in it is not. Have you discussed it with Rose?'

Frances reddened. 'Is it so very bad that he knows?'

'Hm,' Polson said. 'Alright m'dear, don't be upset. For a young man and a spotty young man, he is very circumspect. He wants to go. No, I don't suppose he knows any more than Nathan Thomas who keeps sniffing around the subject as if— you'd think, Francie, I were plotting to overthrow the government. Just look at the three of them. If rumour is all these people have to worry about, God help New Zealand! I wish Whitehouse were here. I wish it weren't postponed till spring. I wish—never mind. Enjoy yourself, my dear. I'm going out for air.'

Just then the Hossacks came. 'This is the man, Amos,' Arthur Dewhurst said, brushing by. Polson continued walking towards the French doors.

Maids in gimped smocks were bringing the tea on trolleys. Frances joined Rose behind the piano. 'Dear Rosie,' she said, linking arms. 'Is it Dick?' Rose nodded but said nothing. She wore a black delaine that was too tight for her and was tugging at a bangle fit to snap it. Her eyes were red and her cheeks blotched as if she had scratched them. 'Men,' she muttered; and then turned to her sister beside her. 'Caroline, leave Isaac alone; he's doing his best.' For Caroline was complaining that the houseboy had omitted the slop basin *again*. Frances turned and was met by the gaunt face of Adrian Banfield, Caroline's companion. An acid stare and not a hair on his chin. What a cold face, she thought, and confided this to Rose. 'Yes,' Rose said. 'And that's just how Dick's been looking at me. He won't come near.'

'I don't believe it,' Frances said, taking her tea and seeking to distract Rose.

'Yes, he's jilted me. He has two barometers, France, and one is aneroid inlaid with—something or other. It's famous. It came to him from George Stephenson, the families are related. He promised it to me and now he's changed his mind. It's all over.'

Such a little thing, thought Frances; Rose is truly smitten. At this moment her eye fell on the petit-point draping the back of the piano. She had not read the sampler before. '*LOST between daylight and darkness,*' it said. '*One GOLDEN HOUR, set with Sixty Diamond Minutes. No reward is given for once lost they are GONE FOR EVER. Work while the day is young for Night Cometh where no man works. PEREUNT ET IMPUTANTUR.*'

'Who did that?' she said. But it was the wrong thing to say. Rose was in sobs.

'Mamma made me. It was an anniversary present.'

Happily at that moment an Irish water terrier, belonging to Mr. Trotman, bounded in and leaped upon the piano where it proceeded to shake itself. Rose's sobs turned to hysterics for the company at the piano was dripping. The dog had been in the stream. 'Hurrah for Hossack!' Rose said, sitting up with new animus. The new magistrate was drenched.

The Hossacks were removed to a window overlooking the garden. They were dried, cosseted, given a settee, revictualled; and presently the magistrate's voice was shrilling like a cricket's. 'Lady Suffolk: the Lieutenant-Governor's elopement is disgraceful. But you'll see, you'll see. The Governor may be in your opinion, ah, temperamental (ha, ha), but at heart he is a patient man and a generous man, and in the end all will be calmed without opprobrium. So I judge. You see, the Governor is not vindictive. Were he so he would have sent troops ere this to quell this—this King fellow who has set himself up to rule in the north. "What's his foreign policy?" I said to the Governor. "That's just it, he hasn't got one." "Fie," I said, "his policy is disobedience. It is agitation, defiance and disobedience from beginning to end." "Oh no," the Governor told me. "It is true he treats my officers with disdain and won't allow them to pass his territory without risk of being shot at. But I am sure he is well meant, as I am sure he is misled; as I am sure I am right to ignore him. I have withdrawn the missionaries. I have withdrawn the magistrates. I have withdrawn the school-teachers.

He will acquiesce. It would be foolish to be precipitate and quell what may not be there to be quelled." You see how reasonable, how patient . . .?'

Frances could not see very much; just a plain Mrs. Hossack accompanied by a praying mantis in spectacles and patent leather shoes. The voice continued amid placatory gusts of approval. For Christchurch, however much it detested sycophantic officials, feared them as worms: whatever information was introduced at one end bore no relation to what was distributed at the other, into the ear-trumpet of the Governor. The fortunes of Christchurch rested on this channel of communication.

'Tell me about him,' Frances said to Rose.

'Hossack's a spy. He has seven children and a cruel set of maids. He came out with letters of introduction to everybody and immediately struck up with the Governor who listened to everything he said, through his trumpet. His appointment was pressed on us. Mr. Whitehouse was furious. He stayed a week and said nasty things about Mr. Whitehouse and the land muddle, he blames everything on Mr. Whitehouse. Then he went away. Now he's back again, boding something.'

'Yes, papa?' Rose looked up as the form of Arthur Dewhurst towered above them.

'Frances,' Arthur Dewhurst said. 'I cannot find your father anywhere.'

Polson walked into the garden. There was an incipient softness. It swept down like the Bath dales, laurel and hawthorn and a tiny wych-elm, the first in the settlement. There was a plaque saying so. The native things had been uprooted as if by act of faith. The cabbage tree would go next. Mrs. Dewhurst had said. As he passed down the knapweed towards the stream, that prayerful jaw accompanied him. Here was her holly and there, a quince; that would be a fernery and there a greenhouse, awned, for light teas. Here was a sacred place. Each member had taken a trowel and raised the import of his choice: pinks and crocuses for Charlotte and Sarah, primula for Harriet, wood violets for Caroline; a laurel at one end for Arthur Dewhurst, a laburnum for Emma at the other. The harmony of this lineage was spoiled only by Rose's plot which was mysteriously bare. But Polson knew, for Rose had told Frances, that into it she had spat the stone of a Maori peach. Good for Rose, he thought. Polson plunged into the wild things overhanging the stream. Everywhere the scarlet flowers of montane fuchsia carpeted the ground. The eggy fruit, black on the scarlet ground, gave off whiffs of tannin as he stepped on it. Behind, the long paper stems of manuka, screening the water, held out their white arms like bead necklaces, each flower pinned up processionally by a small greyish-brown marble. After the cabbage tree, this wilderness; all would go; they would raise a brick wall. He mused. Standing and sniffing. He was invisible, even to himself. Those marbles had something of the eternity of the olive. 'Brave little proletariat, aren't you?' Something was calling. He listened, assailed by sounds he had not noticed at Odessa.

'Ah, there you are,' said Arthur Dewhurst, bearing through the flax.

Polson, half hidden, regarded his host quizzically, one ear cocked.

'Native thrush,' he said. Standing on the lobes of the scarlet flowers.

A gush of warbling sounded. From somewhere downstream came an answer. In trills, ending in triplets. Then the warbler again.

'Almost,' Polson said.

Dewhurst blundered forward. 'Terrible mess, terrible—'

'Shhh.' Polson put a finger to his lips.

'Almost,' he said again. 'But not quite.'

'Amos, tell me the truth,' Dewhurst began.

Again. Tonic, mediant and dominant. And the fluted echo.

'Very nearly,' Polson said.

'Very nearly what?'

'Very nearly the opening bars of a Handel oratorio. But the second voice, down there, is sharp.' Polson stepped clear. A lobe of fuchsia had caught in his beard. He looked refreshed. 'Just contemplating the life upstairs, Arthur. I sometimes think that the birds lead a superior existence to ours. Morally I mean.'

'I don't see that they have much to be dishonest about.'

'Oh but they have—considering the degeneracy of their line. The Ancients didn't exalt them for their looks but for their moral perfection. Aristotle tells us that. Furthermore their manners are impeccable. What they feel, they express publicly. Why, they even listen to one another. Now we, stupid mortals, don't listen; we harken to rumour. The first sign, Arthur, of a debased intelligence.'

'Now,' Polson continued, steering his host along the bank. 'You have been listening to rumour. And you would like to know what I am up to.'

'Why do you say that?'

'The garden, my dear Arthur, affords a prospect of the drawing room. After you announced Hossack—I take him to be that little man who resembles a pawnbroker—you were accosted by Messrs. Hay, Banfield and Thomas. And they have sent you out to discover my mind.'

'Not entirely. But continue.'

'I shall. They are puzzled and you are puzzled. Donald Hay offers me a hundred merinos on trial. No thank you, I say. Suddenly I accept his offer and order a thousand. Equally suddenly, up pops this damnable expedition. It's on everyone's lips—in the streets, in the cafés, in the hostelries, is it not? "Aha," they say, putting one and one into one, "this is Polson's hand, Polson is behind this. Only Polson is a failed squatter, only Polson's land is arid. Only Polson must expand to save his life. But," they say, "*we* are the expanders—we, not Polson. An amateur! Just look. He plays the piano. He paints. Anyone can see he isn't fitted to expand." ' Polson chuckled merrily. ' "A thousand merinos, dear me." '

'They are enough as the law stands to stake an area as large as Wales,' Arthur Dewhurst said drily. 'Tell me this then. Is it true, as I have just heard, that you refuse to gridiron Odessa?'

'Absolutely. I regard the system as iniquitous, you know that. I intimated as much when I wrote advising you to let the boundary hut lapse.'

'As a matter of fact, Amos, I didn't take the letter seriously. So I did not let it lapse.'

Polson was aghast. 'Do you mean that I *own* it?'

'Of course.'

'But I have paid nothing for the freehold.'

'No. I have paid it.' Dewhurst waved his hands, pink and manicured, to convey that the sum was a trifle.

'Why in heaven's name did you do that?'

'Let us say: a gesture. Returning to my question. You realise that by not sealing on your boundaries you run the risk of being bought up?'

'Perfectly.'

'Your belief in the benevolence of your neighbours is incredible. On the other hand such a course enables you at any time, does it not, to strike camp and move on without sustaining loss of capital, since you have expended nothing?'

'Perfectly true.'

'I should tell you that your neighbours hold to the second interpretation. Moreover they are no longer disposed to be benevolent. They distrust you, Amos.'

'Go on!' said Polson, in his best colloquial.

Dewhurst attempted to maintain gravity, and also to snap his fingers which were not made for the exercise. 'Amos, they can crush you, like *that*.'

'I suppose they might upset the law relating to cheap lands,' Polson said thoughtfully. 'They are powerful enough. Yes, that might hurt.' He was silent for a moment. 'A new Land Commissioner is to be appointed, isn't he? Yes, yes, I am beginning to see. No, I'm wrong, they must maintain the rents at all cost. If, as you say, their appetites are fired by this land, any change in the law would be bound to hurt them as it would hurt me. I believe, Arthur, they fear two things. One is a flood of new settlers, small farmers; the other is an unsympathetic Commissioner. A combination of the two would be fatal. By coercing me to lock up my land, as they have done, I strengthen their camp; and ipso facto their case for maintaining the status quo. Yes?'

Dewhurst was stroking his cheeks the way he did when waiting for his wife. 'I cannot deny that it would be in your interests to join them.'

'No! I won't do it.'

The vehemence of this statement had a strange effect on Arthur Dewhurst. Something, a flicker, a fleeting smile ran like a sparrow through his weepers.

With sudden insight, Polson said: 'What is it you want from me?'

'I also,' Dewhurst said, choosing his words. 'I also incline to the second interpretation. Observe carefully. Alone you may act: as the law stands you may find a new Wales, stock it and lease it for a sum so small as to be ludicrous. If you act at once. But I believe you cannot do this, I believe your expedition cannot start before the spring. This will be too late for one whose means are as slender as yours. Now Amos. Look about you. The town is built up. My activities here, though interesting, are limited. Soon the plains will be dotted with farms, with townships, there will be a railway. That is more interesting. The railway will enter the mountains; the wastelands will be transformed. More interesting still. But beyond the mountains, which lies there? Gold? A new city? Another California? That, to a financier, is *fascinating*.'

Dewhurst paused. His eyes, milk blue, like talismans, stood out on stalks. He went on:

'Who made our Empire: men of vision or financiers? Dreamers or entrepreneurs? I will tell you. Not the one nor the other, but a combination of the two. They are, if I may use the term, blood brothers. You are amused, Amos. Those gluttons in there are not amused, they are in earnest. You have upset Hay. Hay says you have stolen one of his shepherds and for some reason the matter has assumed grotesque proportions in his mind. Let me be frank with you. I care nothing for petty dishonesties. But that is the basis of Hay's passion, of everything. I say again, gluttons. These men are boors, gluttonous boors.

'I have watched you, Amos,' Dewhurst continued, his voice assuming an opulent tone. 'And you are not like that. You are not as we say "sheepy enough". You are governed not by passion but by reason. Wise men are. I believe you are a wise man, Amos; as I believe you have had a vision. I would like to help you. Let me strengthen that: I *intend* to help you, and I offer my partnership.'

'It wouldn't do, Arthur. It would be against your principles.'

'I don't understand.'

'The man, the shepherd in question: he will lead the expedition.'

'Well?'

'He is a convict.'

Arthur Dewhurst's reply was not at first audible. His jowls had begun to tremble and the tulips in his cheeks seemed to descend through his body like jelly, making him wobble inside his clothes. His hands clenched and unclenched spasmodically. He looked into Polson's eyes and his patience broke.

'Dammit, man, haven't I made myself clear? I am above such pettiness! I am offering—let me be specific. I am offering you my name and my support: five thousand pounds to guard against any contingency or change in the law which may upset you. In cash.'

'You would like, forgive my obtuseness — you would like to share the fruits of my vision?' Polson emphasised the word share.

'Fruits there will be, Amos — though perhaps you cannot see this as clearly as I. Amos. God has chosen to give you a vision. If he chooses also to give you the unbounded pastures, what else will you do with them? Bequeath them to the gluttons? Give them back to the Maoris? My dear man—' And Dewhurst, misinterpreting the other's grin, put his hand on Polson's shoulder. 'Fruits, Amos! Prosperity for all — all men, all Englishmen. Come, come. I haven't been a speculator all my life without learning something of the risk you run. Alone, you are lost. Alone — no, no, Amos.'

'And I need hardly add,' he said, glancing up at the house, 'that we would do the thing *decently*.'

Dewhurst watched Polson stir the ground into a mound with the toe of his boot, then stoop and pick it up.

'I am sure you would, Arthur, according to your lights. The trouble is we stand at opposite ends of the spectrum. No — I cannot accept your offer.'

'Tell me the truth: what are you planning?'

'A gesture,' Polson said, shaking the dead flowers and letting them fall back onto the earth.

'It is not — nothing dishonest?'

'I am sorry, Arthur. More than that I can't say.'

Dewhurst fell silent and Polson saw that he was hurt. From the drawing room came the sounds of a glee.

At length Dewhurst said, 'You think we are playing at life?'

'Either that or are bored with it. It comes to the same. What makes me intolerant is that the only issues of importance such as the native question, we ignore or leave to idiots like the Governor. I seem to remember, Arthur, that in England life was a muddy horsepond. I was through no fault of my own born into a family whose fortunes rested on the three pillars of English society: nepotism, hypocrisy and public piety. I had a murky childhood. I was brought up by a man whose life was illuminated by the amount he could put away at dinner and the number of beatings he could give to his children. The beatings were accompanied by an appropriate text from the

Bible. He was, needless to say, a rector of the Anglican Church. For forty years his precepts dominated me, until one day I landed here. Only then did I see my life for what it was—an empty hollow. Shall I tell you what I did? I had a trunk full of my grandfather's writings, all annotated in my father's hand, I had all my father's books, tracts, treatises, family photographs, Bibles, catechisms, I had all my own writings, my testaments in the original Greek: a precious store, a forest of piety. My father had charged me with the task of writing my grandfather's life. I had already begun it on the voyage. As we came in sight of Lyttelton Rock—you are quite right, Arthur, about the vision—a flock of cormorants flew out of the clouds across the wake of the vessel, and through a break in the clouds I saw what I can only say I was destined to see. I had been unwell. My eyes were affected and I feared blindness. At that moment I saw a glimmer of—of truth, if you like. Anyway I took the trunk and with the help of the ship's carpenter I dropped it into the sea. As it dropped I felt a great weight off my mind. Since that day I have had nothing to do with the kingdom of cant and humbug and have followed instead the dictates of my own conscience. I am much the better for it.'

Arthur Dewhurst drew himself up. 'The late Bishop-designate, as I recall, committed a similar heresy when he abandoned his station and walked into the wilderness.'

'Perhaps he also found the burden of piety too great. I am not proud of losing that trunk, Arthur. It was the hardest thing I ever did. I had only to write what was in it, to perpetuate what was there to be perpetuated, praise what everyone said was there to be praised, and my name was made—my grandfather was a very great man. Before we threw the trunk overboard we rested it on the rail. "D'you know what's in here?" I shouted to the carpenter above the waves. "My life's work," I said. And I described the contents. The carpenter was Scandinavian. He had an ascetic's face and a beard like Jesus. He laughed. "Ants' droppings," he cried, and together we heaved. He was quite right. They made but a very small splash.'

'Why are you telling me this?' Dewhurst said with a movement of disgust.

'To explain my position: I decided that if I were going to live in the new world I would first have to abandon the old.'

'So you threw away the best part of you.'

'As you will, Arthur. But I believe that God—if there is a God—does not only create; he also destroys. And sometimes he destroys in order that he may create. In a similar way man, if he is to evolve, must challenge the assumptions of the past. If he fails to do this he withers.

'Just now you invited me to look about me. I did. I saw a stream of running water. That stream. If you bend over you can see your own reflection. When we talk of a Better Land what in fact we mean is an Easy Life. No muddy horse-pond here, Arthur. Morality, crime, lust, outrage, terror, injustice— where is that? I look about, I cannot see it. "Of course not," you say, "we have banished all that." But Arthur: stir a little in the stream and see what rises. Oh yes, the mud is there all the time, it is always there. Here is the paradox. This is not that Better Land. If it were men would grumble less and work more —to some moral purpose. It is not that Utopia.

'I am almost done,' Polson said with a little bow. 'Really your attitude to the land question is not so very different from that of Messrs. Banfield, Thomas and Hay. It is, I admit, more refined. But the difference is only of degree, which is why I reject it. Agreed—we both serve an empire. But give two men a pot of clay: one will make an image in his own likeness and sell it for profit; the other will fashion a rose and present it to the first beggar he sees. We are all entitled to make our own shapes with life. I am afraid that I don't equate Empire-building with land-grabbing, however decently it is done; nor do I hold that we are in some curious way members of a master race. I am sorry, Arthur—'

Dewhurst appeared not to have heard. 'How can you say nothing is being created?' he blurted. 'Look round—look!'

'I do, Arthur; and have done; and shall do. This also I see: that already we are reducing a proud race to a congregation of helots. Slavery—it is slavery, Arthur.' Polson chuckled. 'But mind you, very nicely done.'

They had regained the lawn and paused by a statue surmounted with oleander. Arthur Dewhurst looked about him. Looked at the stabled field beside the stream, at the garden and the house he had raised, at the carriages and dogcarts drawn up on the gravel path. What these conveyed to him was not immediately clear for he was shaking again. Summoning himself, he became solid and planted, interpreting his vision which was now also solid before his eyes; and therefore right. And doubly right, he thought, since I have made the effort of leaning towards you. You are quite right, Polson, we stand on opposite sides of the spectrum—with the difference that yours is the more friendless of the two.

Aloud he said, 'I must go in.' Yet he remained a moment longer, pondering the swarthy little man whose eyes—not a stye, not a cast but a tiny blemish nonetheless—had never ceased to twinkle. Arthur Dewhurst would genuinely have liked to become friends, and was moved instead to pity. The goodness in him prevailed and he said: 'At all events I would see Hossack.'

'Why?' Polson said.

'Like yourself he is ambitious; but unlike yourself he is open to suggestion. You know, don't you, that the jail has been removed?'

'I have seen the gap where it stood.'

'And that the courthouse is falling down? You see. There's nothing here for a magistrate, nothing. I don't particularly care for Hossack myself, but I make a point of having him to my house. It is wise. Now I say this in confidence. It is very probable Hossack will be the next Land Commissioner.'

Dewhurst allowed his words to sink in and then said, 'I would see him. Oh I don't suggest that you ingratiate yourself—'

Polson raised his eyebrows. 'Why else should I meet him?'

'When you meet him,' Dewhurst insisted in a vexed tone, 'it would be wise to suggest a further talk. Say, tomorrow. He is free tomorrow.'

'Impossible. We're leaving in the morning.'

'Amos. So long as we remain a colony without representational government the office of Commissioner will continue to discharge immense power. You understand? Stay another day, nothing simpler.'

Polson said, 'Hm.'

'Hossack is not a fool. Like yourself he is ambitious. Like yourself he is also in an Ishmaelitish position. At the moment he is making soundings. He will follow the current fairest to his purpose. I rather think that you could make a worse ally.'

'You surprise me,' Polson said.

'For offering advice? It is one of the few things I am equipped to give'—Arthur Dewhurst smiled frostily—'beyond these little gatherings.' He shook himself and strode off. Only to turn back. 'I want to say this; and it is meant cordially. We are none of us what we appear. And I, while I may give the impression of sitting down to life, I do not do so quite as to a feast; just as you, Amos, I am sure, do not engage it quite so bitterly as a battle-ground.'

Polson watched the pleated back of Arthur Dewhurst cross the lawn and disappear into the house. A good but not a moral man, Polson thought. The trouble was, he rather liked him.

Damn Dewhurst! Whitehouse was right. There was no escape from the minds and laws of men.

He went in.

That night Polson lay in his room under the mapled ceiling smoking a cigar. 'Yes,' he told himself, 'I am ambitious. But for what? For the respect of people like the Dewhursts?' For it was the Dewhursts who would triumph, he realised, they would rule this land as they ruled England.

He watched the smoke from the cigar rise in layers. There were two bands, one rising and one falling. Now the one that rose descended and the other began to rise. In a moment, he saw, they would cross over. They did. As they crossed they hung a moment together, in symmetry. Then they continued their separate ways. This happened four times. Polson watched fascinated. It would be, he thought—now let's suppose one layer my ideals and the other my actions. They issue from the same source, my brain, but they coincide—how often? Hardly at all my dear Polson, hardly at all . . . If *only* he could empty himself, could throw out this stupid craving for self-respect, he might attain that. That moment in peace. Might even prolong it. Mightn't he?

Mightn't he?

His cigar had gone out. Polson jumped up. How stupid. As if I don't know my own mind! He opened the window and let the smoke out.

In the morning very early he left with Frances on the return to Odessa.

Odessa Heights
12th May

... BILLY was baptised yesterday. Afterwards we went to the pa and ate washtubs of rice. Mr. Sparrow talks of miracles, his baptisms; but there are almost as many deaths from sickness, he seems not to care about that. His wife kept mothering me with her slit eyes, and saying guri, guri, which is their word for dog. I felt most uncomfortable.

The butter churner is broken again. Droo has made me a desk, a sort of scholar's thing. He said he employed 'thixty nails'. I can tell them all. He is grown rheumy and says he will lie down this winter, as if it were meant to happen.

Papa is writing a paper about gridironing. I shall try and explain it. It is what people like the Hays and Thomases are doing. They burn and then sow; then they fence the land in blocks which is called Improvement and this allows them to buy tiny strips of freehold along the boundaries and so keep out the agriculturalists. They call the latter farming trash. The whole process is called 'locking up your land'. As you say, in the colonies anything goes. In Christchurch we learned that the Hay brothers have leased a further 50,000 acres.

When I say leased: they claim to have bought it from a chief, now dead, and litigation had been going on for months when, in February, the Land Commissioner was relieved of his post. In the absence of a new Commissioner the Hays have simply taken the land over and posted guards to keep the natives off. They are burning it now, despite the season, as fast as they can. When the smoke is up papa sits with his back to the window and will not look.

Lionel is coming but does not say when. He said the strings of his violin were stolen and that shortly after this a man was found hanged. Do you think he is boasting? The Bishop came. I was learning to milk at the time. He is a brave old thing with budding cheeks and, so we thought, quite harmless. Then from his saddlebags he drew a wild pig he had shot riding along, and numerous botanical genus. He stayed two days, made no conversions and I have been finding his 'darling specimens' among the blankets ever since. His visit was really an excuse to discover the whereabouts of Enright (our missionary Sparrow) and prohibit his preaching. He asked papa for directions. Papa offered to convey him to the place (pointing in the wrong direction) if the old gentleman was prepared to catch typhoid. The old gentleman gave us his blessing and said he was not prepared. The cow, by the way, is a frightful beast. Droo gave it the stick and an emetic, and it is better now.

Frosts are here. An early winter means an early expedition; it is our great hope. The Gael will lead. Meantime he is four miles high, having mounted the new merinos. Papa instructed him to take a dozen on trial and we returned to find he had gone off with a bag of oatmeal and two hundred of the beasts. He really has the most wonderful nerve . . .

At Odessa no leaf fell. Nothing mellow nor fruitful. 'Yairs, the dull time,' Droo said, swinging the pail where the blue cow stamped and he was teaching Frances to milk. Droo aged and talked of death. They enlarged the house. Gilliam received a quilted hat by post from Yorkshire and talked of retirement. They deepened the well. Mists came and white ants nibbled the thatch. The flocks grew heavy with wool and the pellets lay undigested on the hard umbry ground. No leaf fell. But the birds moulted. The parakeets that drowsed on the peach tree that was leaning into Frances' bedroom, the Dorking hens in the yard, the rails and wekas and yellow runted riflemen that sat along the verandah. They moulted. The birds were the trees of autumn. No leaf fell. Yet the air was redolent of no other season but itself and it affected them all. It was a necessary season. For Polson writing his paper: he saw now waking each morning less the imperturbable hills and more the refractions of light that produced their ale-like quality. He laid aside the paper and took up his paints, feeling a new growth. For Laughton, called the Professor: Walking over the flats one morning he perceived, as he wrote to his father who was a beadle somewhere in Kent, not the usual discolourings of swamp but 'fields of waving copper, blazing after a night of rain'. For Taylor: Who was thrown by the Spaniard plant and took the trouble to inspect the bayonet ends he landed on. The yucca-like tips exuded a wax smelling of aniseed and he lit one, causing the plant to ignite with a rush of flame, firing its neighbours, until the whole thicket was carried off for a distance of fifty yards and he was able to walk through kicking the charred heaps aside with a grim satisfaction. Even for Droo: Who, observing the flight of dottrels high up, was moved to commit an act of poetry. He pronounced them 'balls of thithledown on two legs'. This remark was overheard by the bishop in the course of his pastoral visit and it caused the bishop a moment of doubt. 'Perhaps, who knows?' he wondered, 'perhaps even a bullock driver has a soul to be saved.' So each in his way was able to reconcile a little of himself to the land; and in that treeless autumn the strange newness that was around them became a little less strange.

There were no more frosts. Nothing blossomed or sickened or died. Yet the land, lying slack under its dun cloak, was not deserted. For that autumn there were the seekers. They came seeking the infinite for the measure of five hundred pounds. They came from the direction of Hays, passing behind and above, sometimes across the station. Some had pack-horses and some did not and Frances, seeing their camp fires flickering in the mountains, laughed at their ridiculous hopes. Polson frowned. But Frances could afford to wish them well, knowing that they would fail. They would not find that place. As the last kumara was reaped late, and floury, it should have been yellow inside, she watched the fires mount and descend; and as the seekers returned she knew a quickening, for failure was printed on the skin of their faces. Some returned and stopped, bleeding from face and hands. They were mostly smallholders and tenant farmers from the immigration barracks, their wives had driven them; two were brothers, market gardeners, called Erk—they had acquired three acres in Christchurch from a man called Dewhurst and it was all bog. Frances gave them hot gin and mollasses and a little sympathy.

'What prevented you then?' she would say, drawing sap from their wounds with a vicarious excitement for that other man who *knew*, and who was above petty chronicles.

'It is the rivers, miss. They dismantle a horse's legs, the way is choked by rivers.'

Or Polson would say, lifting his brush: 'The land has no rest then?'

'No, sir. It is impenetrable.'

Some did not return until they were washed down in rags. While others returned and did not stop. They walked down head high. Yet though their pride absolved, it did not hide. There was failure in their legs, in the lifted arm that was no more than that, in the dog that limped and the horse that had to be led.

So autumn protected the Polsons. The infinite was still eternal, at least until the spring.

On Seagull Mackenzie waited and grew afraid.

It was the change from scrub to forest, from fuchsia to mountain gentian. Every morning when the edgeless mists had lifted he looked clear across eighty miles of hill and plain to the coast. He could see the ships. He imagined the Christians walking down below, tiny insignificant creatures, pygmies, and he boasted to the dog: 'Likely today Himself will give us a sign'—for he thought God would appear as unto Moses in a fiery bush and tell them to go up. But then, walking up to the sheep with his face pointed to the mountains, he trembled. Beneath their plutonic caps everything buckled to impotence. He, most of all. The first snows had come. Everywhere the rivers ran rime. At night he heard them rumbling. Low sounds came down the gorges. He trembled.

Now after a month on Seagull he was growing impatient. He sat one afternoon outside the whare roasting a diseased sheep and pouring off the fat for candles. He sat bare on a log, a rug on his knees. His trousers were drying, ballooning in the wind. Through the vent in the legs he could see the merinos pouring off the slopes; and behind, the mountains running south; repeating themselves. 'Like gods,' he muttered, turning the wicks with a long-bladed knife. The fire spat and the dog blinked. 'Like wee gods,' he boasted. For he would discover the mountains only once, in this he would not repeat himself. In this however he would be greater than a god. He watched the eagles slide from the yawning mass that was Seagull with an ease that infuriated him. Waiting. Seagull was like that. Seagull was the place where spirit and dream fused and would not wait; and yet he was forced to hang in a borderland between dream and action under the loom of that enigmatic rock, waiting.

Two things had decided him to wait. One was an old woman he found. She was a woman of great antiquity and the last of an extinct tribe who had attempted to cross the mountains; the Maoris had told him. The tribe had been trampled by the Moah, except for this woman who had fled back towards the pa. At Seagull the Moah had overtaken her, but Tane the forest god had secreted her in a hollow tree. Here she had lived until death. Her hair had grown below her waist and was quite white. Her skin was like the papyrus plant and when Mackenzie touched her forehead it fell away, leaving a grinning mask. The other was a seeker who came upon him in the moonlight. Mackenzie had gone out—for no reason except that he liked to lie in a place with his face in the stars. He was walking back to the whare when he felt the temperature drop; the next moment he felt a bang on the ears out of the south. He began to run and was running when he received a second more palpable blow in the chest and the next moment was grasping something sodden, a jacket or other garment which tore in his hands; and the man reeled off. Only to close again, but so slowly that the whites of his knuckles holding a raised knife could be counted. Mackenzie felled him with a rock and dragged the man inside. He was sorry later he had not carried him. The firelight showed a frame hideous with exposure. And it had been a man once like himself, he was of those proportions. He breathed breath into the lips, meeting teeth, for the lips had fled. He blew hard, then he sucked and blew rapidly as with a sick lamb, spitting frequently. At length he staunched the fire and went out. For the man would recover. He had begun to mouth the word 'hunger', only to say when Mackenzie brought hot gruel, 'No, no—I am too cold'; and then to writhe, drawing up his knees. He would scream before he recovered. So Mackenzie went out. Then it was that he understood the visitor, as he had understood the old woman, for an omen and a warning, and he knew he was meant to undergo a deeper preparation. He picked up the long-bladed knife where it lay in the moonlight and when two days later the man departed he kept the knife, remindingly.

Suddenly the dog leaped in the air and spun full circle. Part of the sheep he was roasting had exploded. He laughed at the dog and she, signifying her understanding by licking the fat from her jowls, crouched lower on her bone, liplidded. Mackenzie refilled a pannikin and poured tallow into the mould on his lap, twisting the wicks clear of the rim with the long-bladed knife. He stuck his feet out and yawned. Everybody, he had thought once, wanted to live like this with their soles basting and ravenberries dropping from the trees in the sight of a logical white heaven. But not so. Not so, the girl told him. Down there they lived in houses. All their days. *Christians*, the girl had told him. But what sort of Christian was that that faced the sea which was hidden and did not aspire to this which was revealed? Some would come, more seekers. After him Christians would come. But would they be content with the natural order of things? He did not reach a conclusion for just then the mould ran over and scalded his foot.

The dog laughed at him.

He thought about the girl. He had a memory of discovering her brightly gartered bending over the well and of the way her lips had parted when she turned and saw him. They parted easily. 'Like a red crispin apple with a bite out of it,' he thought. But he would not make the journey for her, he would make it for himself. He would use nature. Once, nature had used him; now he would use it. Since use was discovery and discovery was joy. He would make it for himself out of the passion of his dreams. Every night his father came in a dream and told him to lead his clansmen up—and his father had loved him once, until he had lost his soul in the hire of the damned English. He would make the journey for himself and his birthright and if they gave him the reward of five hundred pounds he would fetch his sister Mary and all his clansmen too and they would live there. He had no doubts.

Such thoughts are dangerous in the eyes of society. Society calls them outrageous. Mackenzie did not see that the knife he held was a symbol of that society's expansion. Yet it is probable had he done so that he would have accepted the penalty of his birthright just the same.

'A little kail will grow nicely, lass,' he told the dog, 'when we fetch Mary up.'

Or should he fetch the girl instead?

He had some lumps of greenstone in his bag. He took one out and began to polish it, idly at first and then with concentration. He would give it to the girl since she had looked at him like that. He chuckled. 'If we fetch that one up, lass, she'll keep us both warm in the nights.' His father wouldn't have had her, such a milk thing. The lairds had straddled cotter's girls, girls of iron, as his father had straddled his mother. His father's father, the same. His ancestor Hector had sown half the glen and a spotted ewe besides, Hector was much given to straddling. The girls took it as a bounty and a respect. But what was this one, girl or woman? She was something unbranded, he knew that. He thought of sporting with her, he knew a way—since she had looked at him like that. But he was afraid.

The sun went in. He continued polishing beside the embers until he could see the fibres felted in the jade like the crazing in his fingers. When finally he stood up and fetched his trousers they were quite stiff.

Autumn drew out intolerably and Frances waited for Mackenzie to come down. As he would, Gilliam said, to change the sheep and for branding.

One morning as she was passing Droo's shack he called to her and she went in. There was a table with some pipes on it and an armchair he had fashioned from half a barrel. There was just room to squeeze between the door and the table without falling over his whips and the end of the bed. The old man was lying limp on the bed holding something white before his face. His breath reeked of methylated spirit.

'See this?' he said—and she saw that it was the missing bone—'Now this is how they do you. This is the curth, see. That black savage Billy ad it, he been laughing at us all the time. And youse afraid and trippin ova things cause the bone was cryin to go back to its ancestors—o it's very effiekayshus this curthing. The little savage ad it all the time. He come in ere jus now an give it me. I'm boned, mums, boned, that's what. I seen it in Australia. He ad no right to do this, did he?' Tears rolled down the old man's cheeks onto his beard and apron. His eyes were saucered, incarnadine with fear; he kept turning the bone over and over. 'I keep lookin at it an thinkin, I'm thinkin if I only knew the answer. But I don't.' Suddenly he sat up, 'I'll break is blathted neck!'

He was all hunched and furtive.

Frances did not know what it was about this lugubrious scarred old man. But she liked him. She liked him in the same way she had liked a ghastly cracked brown chamber pot she had had as a child; she didn't know where it had come from but she had cried for days when it was gone. She put out a hand. 'Give it to me, Droo.' But he lay back revolving the bone with a manic fascination.

Before he could stop her she snatched it up and ran outside. She found Billy with the horses and told him to remove the bone in such a voice that he obeyed instantly.

When she returned Droo seemed, even in the short time she had been absent, to have entered on more dying days.

'It's gone, Droo.'

'Thank you mums. But it makes no differenth. I'm done. I'm thinkin now it is the curth for sinnin with my missus. I ad a little girl jus like you and one day when it were two months old — Did I told you this story?'

'Yes, Droo.' It always began, 'I ad a little girl jus like you,' and it always ended 'An I hit the mother with a sandbag God-restersoul an the bag never burst.'

'Did I told you why I did it? Cause the girl died through her negligenth. A man come an slept with er, they was frolikin like rabbits—'

'Yes, Droo.' She had heard the story so many times she had come to believe that he had in fact killed his wife. But she did not accept the motive: that the child, left unattended, had crawled into a pit and been gnawed alive by rats.

There was a hammer behind the bed and nailed beside it a notice which said, 'DROO IS WIZE BUT NOT SO WIZE HE NOES THE ANSWER'.

'Tell me about the fire,' she said, for he still wore a furtive look and had a need to talk.

'No.'

He lay with his hands clasped under the cord of his apron. They were big hands, empty hands. 'I want to talk about the missus.'

'The moa,' she said. 'Tell me about the day you saw a moa.'

He felt for his pipe and filled it and put it in his mouth. He struck a match. 'In Australia. I lassooed it, I told you that.'

'No, Droo,' she said. And made him tell it again.

The match burned down. He threw it on the floor and struck another. Thereafter he struck match after match without succeeding in lighting the pipe, until the box was empty.

'It was bendin its neck uppan down the way a swan does,' he began; and he told it right through.

'It's a lovely story,' Frances said when he had finished.

'Yairs.' Suddenly he sat up, throwing off dead matches, choking and coughing as if his mouth were full of needles. 'But I wanted to tell you about the missus,' he said.

She touched him, she was determined to raise a smile. 'Do they *have* moas in Australia, Droo?'

'Never mind,' Droo said.

His breath had staled. He lay like a rumpled bolster. His eyes closed. Frances stole out, carrying the marks of the barrel where she had been sitting.

'Soon it will be winter,' Frances said to nobody in particular, poking round the beetroot with a little fork she carried in her apron.

'So it will,' said a voice in the morning. And there was a milk face with freckles on it at the fence. 'Got a cup, miss?'

She did not take him in then, in these days there were always strangers on the fence. Another seeker, she thought, and went to the kitchen and boiled the kettle. 'But not a failure,' she mused, watching him pace the verandah with a bright waddling motion; he was too fresh and his ears were clean. He wore a sort of zouave jacket and green socks.

'I've remembered. Dick Hollis,' she said, taking the tea out.

'Yes, and you're Frances. I'm behind you.' So he was, perched on her father's cane-bottomed chair. 'Is that your mother?'

'That portrait, yes. I thought you were on the verandah.'

'I took the liberty.' He had risen and taken the tray as well. His glance played over her. His blue eyes shone under the carroty hair; small round features and a tiny chin, he was almost cherubic. 'Would your mother mind?' he said.

'I beg your pardon?'

'If we took tea together.'

'I—I suppose not.'

'Your father will be along presently.'

'She's quite striking,' he said as Frances went out for another cup.

Yes, and now he's comparing me, she thought. Feeling like a maidservant. There was no butter for the scones, it was in the river. And the pocket of her apron torn. She had heard of young men like this; they imposed because they wanted something.

That must be his room, he thought, seeing the books and a gun in a wader. Odd place this. Outside apart from the garden everything bald as an egg. Here, the opposite. There was a gallipot hanging. More books. A flax punnet with berries in it, gourds for ornaments, a potsherd (splendid) beside the Amsterdam clock, canvases, a Maori adze, collections of stones, crop stones probably . . . They were right about old Polson then: he aped the squatter and dressed up as a college undergraduate. Except for the cat. And there was the piano.

Where was she?

She came from behind the piano and settled herself on the bolster at the fire, facing him. She stroked the cat.

'Nine drownings since this search began,' he said.

'This river—I've been up there. They wash down preserved, poor devils. So cold, you see.'

'Why are you here?' she said, feeling the glow at her back and making the cup last.

'Ah-hh.' He had a sing-song voice and a habit of perching with his elbows out. 'I came to see this dumb Goliath who will lead us. Shepherd?'

'He isn't here.'

'So your father says.' He crooked a finger. 'Frances—I don't believe that he exists. Nor does Mr. Whitehouse.'

'Does the land exist?'

'You ask *me*?'

'Yes.'

'I don't know,' he said. 'Perhaps that's a squatter's dream also.'

'Then why would papa engage men like you and go to all this trouble?'

'That is what everybody is asking.'

She would not tell him. He was silent. She saw through the open door that her father was coming down with Gilliam.

He was eating. Not the way others did, but licking the ends of his fingers, casually. His freckles stood out in the firelight and spoiled his nose, she thought. And one of hers is a dimple, he was thinking.

'The trouble is,' he said, 'your father hasn't engaged me. And I want him to.'

'What will you do if you find the land?'

'Cut it up.'

'Because that is your job? D'you think the land has no soul?'

'Good heavens! I wouldn't be a surveyor if I didn't believe in thrashing nature. Why else are we here? Frances, my girl, you've a lot to learn. Nature's disorganised, chaotic, cruel, we must thrash it. You live here and you don't see that? What does your father imagine? — he can't keep the land to himself.'

'You must ask him, he's coming now.'

But he saw from his chair that Polson had stopped to talk.

'Frances, don't talk about souls. Please. Whitehouse won't have me, I'm too green he says. He's worried by the drownings, he wants to cancel the whole business. But I want to *go*. It will help if you tell your father that. Will you?'

She wrinkled her nose at him. 'Very well. I shall say, "Papa, young Mr. Hollis wants to go." '

He saw that she would help and relaxed, putting his elbows behind his head. They were jigging up and down. His ears protruded too. They were waggling. He was doing it deliberately. 'You're just as I pictured,' he said. 'At Dewhursts you were a lady, very artful. I watched you. When I knew I was coming here I pictured you: "She'll be trussed in an old scrub gown all cat like and won't show me her shepherd," I told myself. "That means either he's a figment of her dreams — because strange things happen to young women who live alone — or else he's real and she's smitten and wants to hide him from me. In either case she'll be remote as a cat and I shall become even more curious about her." And this, you see, has happened. Are you smitten with him, Frances?'

'Don't be a goose.'

'There, you see—he exists. Good. And I've got your temper up. I had to do that to see if you're worth—'

'Worth what?'

'Coming back for.' He said it looking straight at her.

She was drugged. The warmth at her back, the sunlight filtering into the room—she was drugged by the tea or the fire-glow between them. Was it possible to be drawn into a circle of light and live there? she thought; and wondered why he had begun by talking of dying.

'When I come again we shall go riding,' he said. 'No, we'll dance.'

'Do you play that?' He pointed to the piano.

'No,' she lied.

'As well as you dance?'

'Oh—tosh.'

'But you do play it. You play it when you're tired of housework and when you think of your shepherd.'

'How do you know?'

'I pictured it.'

Suddenly he was perched forward almost in her lap; freckling all over; talking. Talking greedily and inviting her into the pool of warmth. She clung to the cat, it was solid enough. He had taken out a flat pencil and was drawing with it shapes, people and shapes they both knew. Drawing in the air. He was not eloquent. But he offered something—himself, his own pose for her to accept or destroy if she cared. He drew Mrs. Dewhurst, her glide. Miss Le Loup's bosom. Arthur Dewhurst, taking mud packs. And then she laughed. At last she rocked with laughter. The cat screamed, she had dug her nails to the bone. And her father was there, on the step, admiring the visitor's piebald, entering and taking charge.

It would not happen again, she told herself when they had gone out. Walking and talking, it was a man's habit. He was quite right, she was still wary of strangers. Yet they had laughed; they had laughed. For how long? Five seconds? Fifty? But her world was intact; happiness was never so fleeting as that.

He had given her goosebumps.

It would not happen again.

But it did—or very nearly—an hour or so later. She had taken up the drugget and swept, and swallowed dust; and boiled up the jam which had fermented; and was playing the piano instead of dusting it when he put his head in to say goodbye; and the next moment they were dancing, duster and all. It was so quick. He was singing—a terrible tenor. Jigging and waltzing and bumping things, and the cat sneezing at them behind the trivet. Then she stopped and pointed down. Men did not usually say goodbye, she said, with their boots already off.

'Family failing, Rose,' he said. And all the milk left his face.

'Yes,' she said, on straight knees. 'And you have two aneroids, one of which is famous and inlaid with something or other.'

'That's right, I do. Mother-of-pearl. Here—let me get it for you.'

'No. Give it to Rose.' She could be very prim. Even for a lost cause.

He pushed a hand through his hair and said: 'You must be very lonely. You should get a dog.' And so he went.

Mackenzie descended the mountainside and saw the girl riding out from the homestead. Well, an it was a cold evening to meet her. And Gilliam, standing at the hut, trying to count; Gilliam would not believe that two hundred had gone up and two hundred come down, the fool. Thriving, the fleeces were. You could lose an arm to the elbow in they fleeces, it was like donning a coat.

Through the glass Polson watched Mackenzie fall out of the sun, his flock smoking with the translucent fire of evening. Polson was elated. Gilliam had talked of smothering in the ravines, had said only the half would come back. Well for once he, Polson, was right. How should Gilliam know the merino? It was the same horned beast of the Egyptian friezes, it had this lineage. It had wandered the desert places of Arabia and half the alps of Europe. It had appeared first at Moriah, unto Abraham; at Cyrenaica, at Numidia; at the end of the first millennium it had appeared in Spain. When the Moors were expelled it had multiplied in the Sierras and wandered to the Pyrenees. Napoleon drove a flock across the alps after a campaign. George III kept a flock at Kew. Now it crossed the world from the royal studs of Europe. Why should it not inherit the mists of Odessa?

Thin notes of music reached him, high and sibilant. Good God, the man was playing an instrument; walking in front and blowing his cheeks out. Well, he had a right to boast. The merinos came on more recklessly than any animals Polson had seen. 'He gives them a challenge: to die in the high places. And he harasses them as little as possible, that's his way,' Polson thought. 'And the dog, of course; they have a partnership that's almost holy.' Polson watched him turn them from the staircase into the Gut, a frightful drop; soon they would be on the terrace and he would lose sight of them until the ford when they would plunge back into view through the neck of the valley—but by then it would be dark.

Frances crossed the ford and cantered down the riverbank under the terrace. That piping had stopped. Above her the drumming of hocks sounded on the caps of rock. The terrace projected over her like a roof, garlanded with scree roots that made her crouch in the saddle. She turned a bend and there they were down in a company, bruiting about the flats. She was cantering, almost on them, when Mackenzie ran out with raised crook to stop her; she stopped abruptly and Magistrate reared. And there suddenly, directly overhead, was the matter. The dog, darting upwards; and a ram that had somehow missed the descent poised on the lip of a bulge. It stood queerly, head up, a spiral of horns and a satyr's face, pawing the lip. Ruinous, that ledge. And Magistrate reared a second time, almost throwing her, and neighed. At the sound the ram drew itself up and plunged forty feet to its death. It lay at her feet without moving, a stream of blood at the nostril.

Even in death it was beautiful.

She saw his face crumple; and then almost at once right itself, as if he had digested the emotion whole. This man took no comfort from the sensual pleasure of death.

'Tis the back broken,' he said. He walked over and kicked the animal to make sure it was dead. He called to her. He lifted the carcase and threw it over the saddle. The warm head hung at her thigh and blood ran in her lap. 'Tis lucky there is the horse,' he said, rubbing an elbow across the spurting nostril, 'nor thee would have carried it thaself.' He tied it down, herself included, and strode off driving the sheep, leaving her to follow like a herdsman's wife. They went in silence. It was a strange burden, widening her lap; and yet so warm. She held to the fleece and felt the sog of it escape to her legs. *His* legs seemed barely to touch the ground. She noticed them, a swinging of calf and thong that made it seem she had been walking in his steps all her life. 'They're only a pair of legs,' she told herself. Yet she went on noticing them. She might be driving the flock herself if he but knew it. The flock was snug, all of a piece, in the space between Magistrate's ears. 'Perhaps the journey will be like this,' she thought. Twilight overtook them, walking up the bed of the river. Everything aureoled and brightly noted on the blue pebbles: the moving flock, the brawling waters and the first stars breaking in the cold night sky. As if answering her thought, he stopped and greeted them, turning his head in an arc from north to south. So all men need to worship orderliness, she thought. He continued. The hound star, first in the procession of Orion, shone in their way and the black objects of the pa came in view. The cabbage trees slid into the void. At the ford he stopped, betraying concern, and led her grey across.

'You are not angry with me still?' she said.

'Ay.' He gave a wintry smile. He wore a headband and continued walking at her side.

'It was a natural way to die,' she said.

'Why does thee say that?'

He was cross again. She fumbled. 'It was like — like plunging in sleep. As natural as drowning.' He looked up sharply. 'Let the living put out the dead,' he said. She went on unheeding. 'I saw a young man once, drowned. He smiled even in sleep. Drownings are so common here, papa says, they should be counted as natural deaths.' She added, 'Can you swim?'

'Nay, lass.'

She was sorry she had spoken. 'Then tell me — what is a natural death?'

'Natural? My own people was put in an barge an burnt. Twas like the blister of creation. But not natural. Or they lays thee in a pit an goodnight, six squares of sod an four pennies for the pastor an ten years after thee is not four bones, that is an mean death. Natural is dying in nature. And then floating up there to coop with the kelpies an God's lamps. Every lamp is an soul, lass. The big lamps is the big souls an the wee ones the mites.'

'You did not learn that in the Bible.'

'The Book is for commanding an the singing of David.'

'Mackenzie: do we die?'

'Ay. When tha' lamp goes out.'

She laughed. 'I love the way you think about nature, as if it were orderly and logical. Yet somehow it doesn't make it easier to live in it. By the way, there's a young man coming on the journey who will argue with you. All is chaos, he says. He doesn't believe the land has a soul.

'Ay, an there's some don't believe as the earth is flat, nor a man can walk with a woman without straddling of her.'

'Is that what they say in the hut?'

'Ay.'

They passed behind the hut and he slung the carcase down saying, 'That'll do,' as if he were dismissing her.

She felt unequal to the situation. 'An thy father is an muckle moraled man if he thinks the same,' he said. Turning to her with a hot stare.

A man came from the hut and gazed at the sky. Then went in again. The sheep went by in a rush.

'Is that all a woman is to them: something to lie with?' She had to say it; for she had thought about it, often, and there was nobody else. But he was throwing something to the dog, ignoring her; rummaging in his bag. 'Here,' he said. He held up a hand. He was very close. She took his hand, preparing to dismount, then felt something smooth pressed into hers. 'Oh,' she said. It was cold. It was a stone of some sort.

'Tis the fiction I was telling thee of.' He stood askance in the half dark.

'I can't tell the colour,' she said.

'Green. Tis an polished green stone.'

She gave a short laugh. 'Ah, the fiction, your piece of treasure. I had forgotten about that. Thank you.'

It was not what she had expected. She smiled at his simplicity, his awkwardness and he turned from her disgusted.

Now he was going to put the animals across the creek. 'I am coming,' she said, and led the way since she knew it.

He was easier there away from the hut. But it was not the same, with the sheep rasping the flax in their ears—did he suppose that sheep couldn't see?—and the dog standing on tip-toe, sniffing the distance between them. The night was cold with a lurid cold and there was a distance between them.

'I want to ask you something,' she said. She had dismounted.

'Ay.' He had spread the contents of his bag—a rat trap, meat bones, a Bible, a long-bladed knife. He was undoing a brown paper parcel and throwing scraps to the dog. 'Here,' he said, throwing a shirt, 'wipe thaself.' But the blood in her lap had caked. She shivered. 'Here,' he said again, and threw an old comforter. But it was more holes than comfort. His attentions annoyed her. She wanted to say something. Now he was rummaging again.

'Mackenzie—I want another dog.'

'Oh ay.' He continued searching and having found what he wanted lay back on an elbow and, 'So,' he said. Very sly. 'Tha wants another dog?'

'Please.' She was twitching the crop in her fingers. 'One of *hers*.'

He sat up hugging his knees and peered at her, his brows raised impishly and a great grin spreading, turning his head from side to side. His ears pricked like a fawn's. He began to laugh and jig cross-stitched in a sitting position. His shanks began knocking together with mirth, and with that he set the pipe to his lips and blew.

She stood over him in amazement, lifting her crop. But he only blew the harder.

'One of hers?' he said, breaking off. 'Did thee not love thy own?'

'Stop, are you mad? Stop playing that thing!' She brought the crop down. He chuckled and rolled over on his side, clapping his heels and piping still, for the blow had glanced off. Maddened, she hit him again and again without succeeding in dislodging either the instrument or that ogling expression. He rolled about kicking up his heels and gasping 'eee' and 'aaah' between breaths, as she rained blow after blow until she no longer knew if he cried in pain or if she had the will to stop. Finally he sat up and scratched his neck. She hit him then where she intended, on the mouth, causing him to foam and shake his beard. He hung forward defenceless and she was calm enough to do it again, striking him across the eye. He cried out at last in abomination and threw her floundering in a thicket, wresting the crop and throwing his body across her body, face and hair and breasts, all at once. They lay a moment stubbled in each other's arms. And she imagined rather than felt an exquisite moment of terror, holding him, half holding him, as comets and orbs spun slowly about her. He mumbled something. 'Twouldna work, lass, thee an me,' was what she thought he mumbled. As the hairiness departed and the shadow of the dog that had been crouched by her throat melted with it into the darkness. She sat up. 'Mackenzie,' she called. He came readily enough. Then he knelt and began methodically to repack his gunny. 'See?' he said, wiping his cuts. He was holding up the rat trap. 'If I hadna wrestled thee, she would have closed up thy throat—like that!' He sprang the trap. He put the trap away on top of the Bible and the meat bones last.

'Here is tha' crop,' he said. 'Now get thee up.' He lifted her roughly and marvelled at the lightness of her form, the slimness and the stubborn white throat. She began to cry. She could see the weals. 'An pay mind, lass, else I'm thinking thee be born of jackanapes and wild beasts. Tha little fellow isna died, only taken.'

'Brandy!'

'Ay, the stupid bawbaw. I took it away from flocks. Twas natural enough.'

Her lips parted.

'I told thee I wouldna shoot the wee whore.'

She could only smile at him through parted lips. 'Alive?' She repeated it to herself over and over until that word alone mouthed in tears was all that was between them, her and his slow disfigured grin.

'Alive an curing. An I shall bring him thee after the journey, not before.'

Everything was turning again, mirrors within mirrors—and it was useless to run or ask questions or fall down or sing his name or sob halloween out of her being, as she wanted to do, because he had picked up his bag and was gone.

The night was full.

'Dear God—' she said. She would never rub away these tears —this moment. 'Alive?' But how easy it was now to love the land. This valley, these hills. And the mountains, sharp and clear, crowding their tops to her feet. A star fell, a soul. The southern sky came down in companies of white and the valley was filled with souls. She heard music, a soft piping. 'Dear God,' she whispered, looking up. As all desire, all fear left her and a great tranquillity filled her senses.

There was a lantern swinging under the house, under the Clouds of Magellan. Forgetting the horse she ran towards it.

WINTER came.

> Christchurch Gazette
> 8th July.
>
> My dear Polson,
> I have received yours by special messenger. Thank you, and thank you. The articles are not ponderous at all. They are exactly right. I understand perfectly your desire for anonymity and shall follow your suggestion that the Superintendent read them before publication.
> The news from the north is not good. There are more deaths in Taranaki, land sales blocked, troops drilling. In Waikato the tribes are seething, awaiting a sign. The Governor is away collecting native myths. Affairs of state are carried on by a Land Department and a Native Department each of which countermands the actions of the other. Your paper is timely. 'Things heard stir the imagination far less than things seen.'
> Ever your respectful servant,
>
> Martin Stoddart,
> Editor

In the event, the editor did not consult with Whitehouse until the first article had already appeared.

'It is fashionable nowadays (Polson had written) to decry the Governor either as a moral coward, for not putting troops to quell the native "rebellion"; or as a moral delinquent, for announcing his mind so to do and refraining from doing it. It is generally forgotten that the Governor is *elderly*, and that he cannot thus always be held responsible for the inanity of his utterances any more than for his (fortunate) restraint in not carrying them into effect. While not wishing to appear his *censor morum*, I trust that His Excellency's sin may long continue that of omission. It is significant that in other respects our ruling class, which is to say the Squattocracy, has nothing but praise for the Governor's actions; indeed my fellow squatters praise his cheap rents policy to the clouds. Yet have I seen it charged upon the Governor that this policy is a deliberate concession to the speculators of the north in order to finance his own popularity among them. It is possible, since the Governor has issued no public denial, that this is so. Be that as it may. The cheap land policy for the south, benefiting the few, was hated by the *people* of Auckland and Wellington when it was promulgated just as much as it was hated by the small farmers and agriculturalists of Canterbury, whom it was designed to benefit not at all. What has this to do with the Maori rebellion? Readers may ask. The Maori rebellion is about land; it is about dispossession. When all the natives of the north have been dispossessed, where will they turn? They cannot turn to Canterbury, for in Canterbury there is the Governor's cheap land policy . . .

'I do not denounce the system out of hand. A man has the right to secure his house—his castle, his shed and sufficient acres to earn a living. This was the purpose of the act. But the act is now abused. If gridironing is not abolished, an entire province —half a country—an area as large as Bavaria—will in a short time be vested in the hands of not more than twelve men. What *is* gridironing? If any man doubts what gridironing is, let him not doubt what it leads to. Three of these twelve men have families of four, three and three—ten souls in all. Their land covers 700,000 acres. This means 70,000 acres per person, excluding water-courses. In a few years these twelve apostles will possess the heights of Canterbury for the price of a few niminy-piminy huts and a few coils of wire which the law, as it stands, is pleased to call Improvements. Possess, not rent. Proprietors, not squatters. I am a squatter. I count it a privilege. I rent my acres for the sum of one farthing an acre. I am content to remain a squatter. If I exploit my privilege, the privilege of arriving first before Mr. Smith or Mr. Jones who are now landless, I become not merely a proprietor. I become a feudalist. We are already establishing a feudal landscape, the very thing we sought to leave behind us. The Cheap Lands Act was promoted to people this land, not to create a dominion of lairds by a process of artificial stimulation.

'In his official correspondence to London the Governor is pleased to enumerate the numbers of sheep which graze the pastures of Canterbury. Nearly two millions, we are told, more than the flocks of England and Scotland put together. So is His Grace, the Earl of Sutherland, pleased to speak of Improvements on his Highland pastures in Scotland. The two systems are not dissimilar. In each case men are landless. In each a sheep ranks higher than a man. The Governor has heard of the Highland Clearances. I understand that he condemns them. In which case he incriminates himself, since he, no less than the Duke of Sutherland, is guilty of sinning against mankind. I ask him: Where will the natives turn? Where will Mr. Smith and Mr. Jones turn? For the cry is, "No More Land". The truth is that the land is here, in abundance, and it is being locked up by twelve men.

'May I remind the Governor, also the Fathers of Canterbury, that a sheep does not rank higher than a man. Nor do fifty sheep. Nor fifty thousand . . .'

It was unfortunate that Polson's first article appeared under the title, 'THE GOVERNOR AND THE DUKE OF SUTHERLAND—TWO OF A KIND', and not, as Polson had suggested, 'The Twelve Apostles of Gridironing'. Also that Whitehouse did not see it before publication, for he would perhaps have deleted the word 'inanity', a word which particularly upset the town magistrate. Mr. Hossack read the articles. In the circumstances it was inevitable that he should infer from them less a desire to reform the land system than an attack on the Governor himself with the aim of belittling him in the eyes of the Colonial Office in London. In July Mr. Hossack travelled to Auckland to see the Governor. Shortly after his return to Christchurch in August he was promoted Land Commissioner.

But the Polsons knew nothing of this when Frances wrote to her aunt towards the end of that winter.

> Odessa Heights
> 21st August
>
> ... Papa's paper is all over the land. In Auckland the *Independent* has devoted an entire issue to it. Papa is pleased, I think, but worries now about the expedition. He hopes for September, but Mr. Whitehouse says October and will doubtless prevail. It is strange how an attitude formed in schooldays, admirer to admired, persists. Papa has never succeeded, he says, in throwing off the yoke of a father figure. At his age!
>
> We are left wondering who will manage the merinos left behind when the expedition does start. None of the men can control them; the beasts are half wild. The Gael has now taken them *all* onto Seagull and absolutely refuses to bring them down. His will be done ...
>
> Strange doings at the pa. Some distant natives (Europeanised) arrived on a pilgrimage, bringing with them common measles. Hue commanded the child who took ill first, since it was the guilty one, to be buried alive. And this, it appears, was done. The visitors thought it quite in order. By a coincidence Hue's action seemed to inflame the disease which spread through the pa with many deaths—it seems with them a terrible and exotic sickness. Sparrow told the natives that God was punishing their pagan sins. Hue gave the victims over to Sparrow—'a Christian burial for a Christian disease'. Again, more prestige to Sparrow's arm. It seems that suffering, ignorance and genuine medical enlightenment count for nought in the battle for souls. 'Only faith informs,' the missionary says, as if to explain matters to the Maoris were a kind of heresy. Papa says (he really was incensed) that Sparrow is perfectly right; that this is why the missions are very close to logical Catholicism, which also explains nothing—and remains, does it not, the strongest power in the world? Meantime Sparrow exults and the war of attrition goes on. It now turns to comedy. Since the measles Hue, nothing if not crafty, has changed tactics and come down from his Mount and now fulminates on the marae in the gravest mock-Christian way. It appears he has been studying the Old Testament. He has

'had a vision' and declares himself a second Abraham. Last Sunday he took for his text, 'And I will bring the land into desolation'—he seems obsessed by the plagues in the Third Book—and this, interspersed with mumbo-jumbo and god stick waving and those little charms of human bone he wears at the neck, gave to his harangue a genuine mystical air. All this from Mr. Sparrow, you understand. On the same day in church Mr. Sparrow preached the Millennium. They came in hordes.

The missionary is forever on our doorstep. Nothing, he says, can dim his gratitude to papa for defending his mission. It is ironic to think that by diverting a Bishop papa has been the means of saving souls. Papa is again in conflict with himself. It is so hard for him to do what is right. 'Are you now against christianising savages?' I asked him. 'Yes,' he said outright. 'At this stage of their growth, yes; for it disrupts the tribal way and there is no natural transition.' I reminded him of his plan as the solution to his dilemma and he replied that its very sanity caused him to fear more than ever for its outcome. 'Only the insane shall inherit,' he muttered . . .

It was a mild winter. The snows did not lie. The ewes, brought to the sheltered flats, dropped their young in the creviced places, immaculately and invisibly; and overnight the valley was full with the bleatings of their increase, heard to be seen at last. The men made their rounds mustering the newborn, blowing proud breath as if they and not the rams had performed office; and counted more than 1800 lambs. The visiting natives left for the coast, canoeing down the river with a skull for a baler and carrying with them the news of a second Abraham. A message reached Polson from the lowlands to inquire if there was any truth in the rumour that a heretic called Hooay had arisen prophesying disaster for the white man's flocks. Polson replied that no legend foretold such an occurrence. On Blueskins the Hays, ever watchful of the mercury, turned their flocks onto the spring pastures. Polson did the same. He also arranged for Sparrow to conduct a small thanksgiving service in the homestead to mark the fourth anniversary of his arrival in the colony. It would be held on the last day in August. Not to be outdone, the Hays announced a celebration spring ball for the week following, 'on the occasion of ten years' residence in the uplands'.

They sent down cards, adorned with a tuft of that year's wool clip; and no sooner had the plainsmen said they would make the sacrifice of crossing fourteen rivers than the pilgrims accepted the invitation as well, after first drawing up their wills.

Towards the end of August the sticks of hoar frost lacing up the cap of bush snapped and the peach tree at Frances' window burst prematurely into blossom. Spirits rose. That Sunday, Hue's predicted calamity having failed to eventuate, Sparrow again preached the Millennium, a doctrine less chiliastic than apocalyptic, for in his favour was not merely the promise of an abundant spring but the Lord's hand itself which had appeared as a meteor in the western sky two nights previously. In his sermon the missionary made much of the revelation and those unconverted natives in the congregation did not doubt that God had come among them. 'In our midst,' the missionary said, 'has arisen one who says he is a prophet. I do not call him that. I call him the Antichrist! He has set himself against me, therefore he is against God. He has called down death and destruction on us all. But where is this prophet of vengeance? Hue, where are you? Come forth and repeat your prophecy in the eye of the Lord. Mark, my children: he does not come. Yesterday on the marae he blasphemed in the name of Abraham. But he does not raise wrath in the house of the Lord. He dare not. He is afraid of the white man's God who is an *all powerful God*. Mark, my children, God's blessing. I called on Him to bless you in the sowing time—and lo, He promises you great fruits. "No more winters, no more white nights and the rivers running full with honey and milk.' Now mark his anger. For there are those among you who, like Hue, shall be punished for your sins, for worshipping false idols. I shall walk among you and set my face against you.' So saying, he stood down among the congregation. The missionary stood with bent head defenceless in the throng; and Polson was uneasy. Now is the moment, Polson thought, when martyrs are made. But in that hush, no hand was lifted. The missionary opened his eyes. 'Out, out!' he called. 'Into eternal damnation! All ye who sing my psalms and despise my laws. Who sit in my House and praise false prophets. Ye it is who will sow your seed in vain. Out, I say. Get ye gone into eternal darkness. Lest ye come forward and receive my blessing. For he that believes shall be *saved*.' One or two natives threw off their blankets and stood up. Others shuffled on the snowgrass or glanced at the door. Sparrow had already gained the door as a precautionary measure. He raised the index finger of his gloved hand. At the altar a native helper began intoning the 96th Psalm. The congregation rose and took up the chant. 'For all the gods of the nations are idols: but the Lord made the heavens . . .' As the chant swelled the missionary, pallid but smiling, walked slowly forward, palms outstretched, through the aisle that had been made for him. By the time he had reached the font half the congregation was at his back, jostling to be first to receive the sacrament.

The Polsons left then.

Later Sparrow came to the house. He showed the strain of a long crusade. But his eyes, filmed with excitement, betrayed the light of victory. The pa had fallen to him at a sweep. He had baptised until the water in the font turned grey; many had come forward to be baptised for the third and fourth time. 'Now my real work can begin,' he said.

'And what of Hue?' Frances said. 'If he fails will he too go into decline, like Droo?'

'But, my dear, he has failed.'

'Perhaps he will simply go away,' Polson said. 'I am sorry not to have met him. Toothless, you say?'

The missionary nodded. He appeared to have something on his mind and would not sit down.

'And how does he take this latest coup?'

'As ever, Amos. We greet each other with disdain. He is busy now chanting his karakie with his few followers. There is talk of sacrifice.'

'Sacrifice?' Polson said. The other nodded. 'Cataclysmic as ever. Fire, sword, tooth and nail, he will have us all in the pit.'

Polson nodded to himself. He did not believe that the two men were so very different.

'He has a flag now,' Sparrow said. 'And he has had another vision.'

'Perhaps he also saw the comet,' Frances said.

The missionary's thin lips parted and remained in that position; he seemed unable to muster the strength to complete the smile and sank wearily into a chair. 'I am sorry,' he said. 'But I have lost interest in the conversation.'

'Bernard,' Polson said—it was the first time he had used that name. 'I want you to do something for me.'

'What is it?' the missionary said; and then added with surprising coarseness, 'The only thing I want to do is drink myself into a stupor.'

'Bernard, I want you, after our service on Wednesday, to go away and have a complete rest.'

Polson's tone was kindly. He knew now that the missionary was prone to a hallucinatory melancholia and the only thing to do was treat him as he would a ward.

'Go to your child,' he said. 'You have talked of it so often lately.'

'You should,' Frances said, 'you really should.'

Sparrow had taken off his glove and was wiping his face with it. He began to hum a psalm. Then he stopped. 'Shall I tell you something? The child was so young when I left Christchurch — you know, I cannot remember if it is male or female.'

'That is nonsense,' Frances said.

'No, I cannot. I cannot do it.' Polson waited for an explanation, as he had waited so often of late; but as usual no explanation was given. Instead the missionary stood up, twisting his comforter in his hands, grimacing. 'Blast you, Polson. You want me to go away, don't you? You have always wanted me to get out.' He stared at one and the other, white-lipped. Then he began to mouth words which his lips could not reproduce above a whisper. Saliva came from the edges of his mouth. Polson feared a fit and returned the other's look of hatred with one of intense pain. It was over in a moment. The missionary's face went slack and the bulbous eyes dimmed. Frances brought glasses and brandy.

'Forgive me,' the missionary said. Seeing the brandy, he shuddered and turned away.

Frances half filled a glass and took it to him. 'This time,' she said, 'you will please *me*.' Sparrow demurred. Then his teeth parted crookedly. 'Trapped,' he said. 'And the strange thing is, Amos, it is always a woman.' With that he swallowed the glass.

'Did you know, Amos, that I wanted to be a famous headmaster? And that I failed because of this?' — he held out the glass for more. 'I collapsed one morning before seven hundred students, dead drunk. I put on this garb by default and became Bishop-designate by an oversight. They are quite right, you know, those who say that the colonies are shabby little stages fit only for critics: we are staffed by an elite of all the failed performers of the world. Well? And now I am a missionary by deceit.'

'That is the one thing I am sorry to say you are not,' Polson said. 'You pick up souls as a sheep does biddybids.'

'They come,' Sparrow said.

'They cling. You see them. A bishop would see only coriander seed. Conversion is in your blood. The spirit is misguided but the will is sound; with me it is the other way about. We're a pretty pair, Bernard. Would to God your mission were less successful, our differences would be as pennies instead of pounds.' Polson raised his glass with an ironic smile. 'To Victory,' he said.

They drank with heart and proceeded to finish the bottle.

'The curious thing about this reforming business,' Polson said, 'is that the purer the inspiration — and we pride ourselves our motive is more or less spotless, don't we? — the more malignant the progress. It is like a tumour. So many little growths, so many varieties of reform, we end up by competing against one another. Sooner or later we defeat ourselves. Those of us who don't see common reason and give up fighting the age we live in, commit suicide. Those who don't commit suicide get married — there is always compromise. Those who don't get married are devoured by self — self-loathing in your case, self-doubt in mine. Self, or ourselves. Sooner or later we become lower than the objects we are seeking to raise. Like Ovid, we approve the better way and sink to the worse — of fighting one another. There are seven different missions in this country, and all fighting tooth and claw for the soul of the Maori. It's no wonder he is confused in the north. I met a northerner at a ball, he was highly intelligent. He became a Christian and then reverted. 'Why?' I asked. 'I prayed,' he said. 'I prayed to the Good Lord for a whole week. I asked Him to send me muskets. But the Good Lord did not answer my prayers.' When all the missions are extinct there will be left in the antipodes a new species: he will have a brown skin and a tubercular face, he will be dressed in a top hat and a loin cloth, and he will exhibit the mentality of a pagan, the manners of a mestizo and walk about singing 'God is Love' in the accents of Wardour Street. My dear Bernard, the cognac has made me cynical; and I'd intended to pay you a compliment. I had forgotten that here prayers are being answered. For there is an eighth mission, is there not? Yours.'

'Mine,' the missionary agreed. The missionary had grown accustomed to Polson's repartee.

'You, Bernard, are in a separate category. Now this is what I mean. We do defeat ourselves. God save your uniqueness! For if the other missions are but half as victorious, you will end all of you by making my plan obsolescent.'

'Oh that!' The missionary raised his glass — he was tipsy. 'Let us drink, shall we, to the decay of christianity in the north?' They drank.

'Papa is jealous,' Frances said.

'Well, my child, we shan't argue about that.'

Frances stood at the window, looking out. Droo was sitting against the whata under a brass sky, carving something: he would not say what. He had been sitting there in the cold for days, with his knife and his block of wood. He was waiting for the sun, he said; but she knew he was waiting to die. He was quite content and they scarcely noticed him any more. She turned to Sparrow. 'No,' she said. 'Let's argue about your health instead.' The missionary was far away. He was reading the portrait of her mother above the hearth, his eyes preternaturally moist, and she caught an expression that was almost serene.

'What is the name of your child?' she said.

'Mervyn,' he answered. 'Thank you.'

'Thank you,' he said again. 'But I tell you both, I cannot afford to rest. There is too much to do.' As he was leaving he said: 'You see, Frances. I cannot go away, if I did who would succour your little dog?'

'Have you seen him today? I have been wanting to ask — How is he?'

Sparrow gave a convulsive tug to his collar. 'Well now, when did I see him last? This morning. And look, look where he bit me. He still snaps. But the teeth are healing, and he's much better. *Much* better. To tell the truth, I am grown quite fond of the little chap.'

'And you won't tell me where he is kept?'

'No,' Sparrow said, catching her father's eye. 'No, my child. Not yet. Patience.'

When he came to the neck of the valley in sight again of his stone church Sparrow sank onto a rock and hugged his cassock.

It was not cold. The sky was opaque and seemed to cast a shadow, although it was quite light. Across the river a flag waved: Hue's red blanket. He could hear feet stamping and the low mesmeric chanting of the madman's disciples. They would work themselves up before the flag till they fell down exhausted. Then they would sacrifice a bird or frog to it, perhaps that was what they were doing now. The missionary drew his cassock close, winding it round his legs like a toga, as if to steel himself in order to continue the journey. The sounds sickened him. Yet as he sat alone in the valley those very sounds seemed to revive him, his giddiness passed and his strength returned; it was as if the Lord had placed a bar at his back and straightened him. 'Strange,' he thought, 'and I did not so much as offer a prayer. And yet, but a few moments ago, I was on the point of giving in.' He had gazed on the portrait of Polson's wife. A loving face, a face of beauty and torment that pleaded forgiveness for transgression. 'Did she deceive Polson too?' he wondered. Looking on the portrait, he had been weak. He had thought of abandoning the pa, this stinking pa, and of running to his own abandoned son, Mervyn—the son that was not his son. The thought had come to him suddenly. Why hadn't he given in to it? He knew now why, rising and going towards the pa. Yet he stopped and put his hand out, and sat down again. He was uneasy. Again the thought of escape presented itself. He had known self-loathing before, but not, not for a long time this terrible self-doubt. 'O Lord, why dost Thou taste bitterly in the moment of Thy triumph?' He looked on the vacant sky and saw that no meteor would aid him today.

And now, the dog.

He had lied to the girl. Her frankness, her trust worried him. There had been no chance to draw Polson aside and tell him. For weeks now, ever since the Scot had brought the animal to him, Sparrow had been visiting the yard where it was hidden, feeding it and walking it as the Scot had instructed. Already the broken teeth were healing. The final cure, that of tethering it to a wild ram and setting the ram galloping until the dog knew a lasting and sickening antipathy to sheep, would follow. To all this Sparrow had agreed with a will; he loved dogs. The natives, with their love of secrecy, had entered the game; parading blank smiles in answer to Frances' persistent inquiries. Billy came regularly to play with the animal, even Hue threw it an occasional bone. Yesterday Sparrow had seen the old prophet fondling it, like a child. This morning, however, when he had gone to the yard to feed Brandy, the dog was no longer there.

The missionary accused himself. He should have taken Brandy right away. He sat for a long time. He believed that he dozed.

He entered the pa testily and began to interrogate every native in sight. But as he drew near the yard, behind Hue's dwelling, an excited yapping told him that his anxiety was groundless.

Snow began to fall on the following day, Monday, a fine powdery snow, mantling the valley. It did not disturb Droo, sitting out whittling his block of wood, or the lambs who gambolled about his feet wrapped in sacking. It fell again on the Tuesday. On Wednesday the day of the thanksgiving service, the sun shone clear; but towards two o'clock as the service was beginning the sky clouded over again. They were singing the hymn, 'We see a new, a better home', the Halleluias given out by a native monitor with a bell-like voice, when Frances looked out and saw Droo creeping from the whata driven by flurries of snow. The snow was driving onto the verandah, making the Maoris who stood there, unable to get in, edge forward. The room was already crowded. Only Droo had stayed away. Droo did not hold with varnishing his sins save once a twelvemonth; he had been kirked at Easter, he said, and lain up his stock of divinity for the year. The snow was falling thickly. Polson had not noticed. He was singing lustily. It was only in the last verse when with a final push those outside squeezed right in that the hymn faltered and Polson looked up. He gave out two or three Halleluias and began to conduct, resuming the opening verse. Throats opened, white teeth showed and the hymn took up. It was a proud service. There had been on proselytising. Polson had insisted. A simple lesson, a thanksgiving; hymns and psalms by the bushel. He loved to hear the natives sing; their pitch was good and their harmony, learned from the white man, was better than the white man's, for they had no inhibitions. They made the roof lift. 'Do they accept me?' he wondered. Huddled at his feet, responding to his conducting—he had picked up the poker and was using that—they were no longer the suspicious savages he saw at the pa, but intent beings glorying Him and the heavenly anchorites, their fathers. It was easy to see why Sparrow looked on them as his children, his flock. The missionary sang with a crusted smile. During the 23rd Psalm Frances had wept. So many changeling faces shining in their wet green eyes, so much rapture—she had wept. Now as they knelt in their blankets to say the Lord's Prayer she looked over their heads to the shepherds bowed in the doorway, their dogs crouched patiently in the falling snow, and wept again. 'Never since the dawn of creation have these sounds been heard in this valley,' she thought. She caught her father's eye and saw it moisten; her own were so brimful she forgot the guests and remained with her back to the Hays throughout. Only Droo hasn't come, she thought. And Mackenzie.

They stood, and the room seemed suddenly to grow dark. It was uncanny. It was not that the figures blotted out the window panes, for the door stood open. The firelight appeared to flicker, throwing out pale wheaten shafts. The snow was falling in columns; the faces that saw it and returned to the preacher had blanched; and the preacher, rising to lead the 105th Psalm, appeared to sink instead. His voice quavered. His hands made the pages of the Bible fly. But in that light nothing could be seen to be read. The dogs were coming in. Some Maoris were forced into the kitchen; on the other side Polson's door gave with a snap and those leaning against it were flung onto the bed. 'Please sit,' the missionary said. Polson could no longer distinguish the doorway. Outside was a turgid greyness, like fog. The odd thing was that there was no wind. The Hays exchanged looks. The missionary was using a reading desk propped on a barrel. He had abandoned the psalm and begun to extemporise. The natives stared fixedly at their service books.

'For God is our refuge and our strength,' Sparrow was saying. 'And lo! He spake to them in a cloudy pillar. Though the hills melt and the mountains topple—'

'Psalm 105,' Polson interposed. And spoke the opening line.

The missionary extended his arms. They began the psalm.

The singing helped, certainly. Twice they faltered. Polson, leaning back, was able to intone the text from the firelight. The air grew close. Some of the natives began removing their outer garments. The singing was thin and quiescent. It was not the same.

'And gave them the lands of the heathen: and they inherited the labour of the people . . .'

The psalm ended there, as all heads turned to a door giving onto the dairy. Something small and aged had entered and was approaching the fire—Frances caught the gleam of Billy's hamitic smile in the background. Small and lithe, seemingly cloaked in dark wine, the figure bowed to the two European women and spoke not to Sparrow, cast spectrally in the gloom, but to Polson. 'I am Hue. God is with me. I wish to speak.' He held out a hand and a boy of ten or eleven who had been sitting near the front joined him. The lad was pitiable: his cheeks were wasted with consumption and beneath his shift were the ravages of scrofula which had torn holes in his neck and armpits and chest. By contrast Hue appeared the younger of the two. His face was spherical and intricately chiselled with the tattoo of the high born, emphasising his clear skin. He reminded Frances of a gargoyle. A single feather was tipped over one eye. This eye was half closed; the other, lurking under a corner of the brow, was abnormally large and whimsical. So deep was the line dividing his nose and running onto the chin that he appeared to have two faces. He wore a scarlet rug caught up to his ears like a ruff, and shrugged it.

'I will speak for three minutes,' he said.

'Oh, do let him speak,' Lady Suffolk said. 'He is *amusing*.'

'It is the Word!' voices cried, and Polson felt powerless to refuse.

'I *am* the Word,' the prophet said, with a sardonic bow to Polson. 'I am the Voice of my ancestors. I am the Voice of the wind, of hail, of fire and tempest and the froth of the sea which is white as the tip of the huia feather. Look: wind is with me.' As he spoke a flurry of snow descended the chimney. 'Where is wind?' He drew forth a small red flag and held it up. It hung limp. As they watched it began to flutter. 'Here is wind. Wind is with me, o Rakamaomao. Where is tempest? Where is hail? Where is fire? Tomorrow, o tomorrow, is tempest, is hail, is fire. O tomorrow. And what of yesterday? O yesterday is the time of your God. What of today? O today is the time of my gods. Amen.'

The Hays were chuckling and the face of the missionary smirked a little. Polson was struck less by the rehearsed patter than by the soft voice. Here was no gasconading madman but a gentle demagogue whose mystical derangement had left his mental processes quite sound. The audience had begun to sway, as in lull. It seemed to hear in the soft gloating voice what it wanted to hear, and in that subtly changing atmosphere Polson's judgment was suspended. He felt instinctively something embryonic and sinister, yet the more he felt this the more he seemed to succumb to what was, by general consent, only an influence for good. The prophet lapsed into Maori. He walked forward, displaying a tiny object between thumb and forefinger. The voice induced a quickening and something, some expression, less fawning and more aboriginal, was restored to the onlookers.

The prophet turned. 'Where is fable?' he said, and drew a small paper bundle from under his rug. Solemnly he placed it on the desk before the missionary. 'There is fable.' Again he held out thumb and forefinger, this time with a sprinkling action copied from the sacrament of baptism. 'And here is fable.' Very quickly the old man placed his fingers in his mouth and swallowed what they held. Neither Frances nor the Hays could see distinctly. But Polson heard the low moan that escaped from Sparrow's lips. The sound was muffled by the din as the natives stood up, alive and reverent. Hue's face was suffused with pleasure. The mellifluous voice resumed. 'O my people, come. You wanted strength—here is the strength of the white man. Come. Where is forest, where is lake, where is the shining white fish of your fathers? Come, o my people, the land is before thee and I will take thee up, in the name of the God of the white man. For I am the Word. It is written in the Book of the white man, "I will rid evil beasts out of the land". Come. *I am the Word.* O God, O Io, O Jezebel, O sin. Where is sin? Here is sin. Sickness is sin. Come . . .' His hand placed firmly on the head of the sick boy, Hue stepped forward and went out into the night. The word 'Come' floated after him. So cleverly was it done and so strong was the impression of night that descended that Polson started when the Amsterdam clock struck three. He stared angrily about him. What were all these people doing in his house? Throwing prayer books into the rafters? He saw his choker walk into the night and Frances pick a baby from a large saucepan which had appeared under an old woman's blanket; Moffet was speaking in one ear and Lady Suffolk in the other; and here was Mackenzie striding through the open door like some patriarch from a passion play, bearded from head to foot in snow and carrying a lamb under each arm. 'Come . . .' The word sang in his brain, and all he could think to say were the words of the pious poet: 'A painful passage o'er a restless flood, a vain pursuit of fugitive false good—'

'Amos, you really must do something.'

'Do *what*, Lady Suffolk? Very well, Moffet. Well pick him up if he's fainted. Droo, you here? Why are you wearing pyjamas? Taylor, please help Moffet. Yes, Draper. Mr. Draper, somebody is ringing the toby bell in Frances' bedroom, and stop that ragamuffin walking up and down my piano.' *Nil mirar, nil mirar* . . . he kept saying to himself, thinking that even Horace would have screamed. He saw Taylor and Moffet bending over a black form. Now Mackenzie was bending over it. Mackenzie was kicking the slumped missionary and saying, 'Where is the dog, man? Where is the little fellow?' Lady Suffolk was quietly donning her cape. 'So this is my man, is it?' Donald Hay said, and strode towards Mackenzie. Mackenzie had sent Frances to the kitchen with the lambs, telling her to heat things, and was shaking the missionary with both hands as if he would break him in pieces. He flung him down and, ignoring Hay, approached the fire. Sparrow suddenly started up, seized the parcel from the reading desk and made off bareheaded into the snow, Droo hard at his heels. 'Damned niggers, damned looting niggers,' Hay was saying. The last of the natives departed clad in a counterpane. 'I do beg your pardon,' Polson said, turning to Lady Suffolk.' I have been rather rude, I think. I am a little confused.'

'There is nothing broken, Amos?'

'I really—really, I cannot say.' Polson gave a weak little smile and escorted Lady Suffolk to the door.

'Good God man, you can't do that here!' At the sound of Donald Hay's voice Polson turned to see Mackenzie peel off his garments and then fling himself, naked to the waist, against the chimney where he remained breathing deeply. Steam covered his body in clouds; at his feet a small lake formed. 'Don't be silly, of course he can; he's come a long way.' Frances appeared and bore off the sodden clothes to the kitchen, from whence came a sound of bleating. Certain events began to reform in Polson's mind and, abandoning Lady Suffolk, he came to the shepherd. At length Mackenzie faced him. Frances entering the room again stopped, noticing the bare torso. That, and the man's vulnerability. She saw the pockmarks on the neck and breast, the small depressed scars on the wrists and the rough but tapering hands numb with cold. How white his skin is, she thought. White as a boy's. She found herself staring at Mackenzie as if she had not seen him before. And listening to his voice which had a brackish melody in it, listening and biting her lip.

'Is it bad there?' Polson was saying.

'Ay, an twill be worus here,' Mackenzie said. Snow was melting on his face, running free. He slapped himself, neck and armpits, and then, seeing Polson's starched dress, said with a kind of breathless fire: 'Boots, man. Boots.' 'Of course,' Polson said, and wondered why Donald Hay was beside him, drumming a crop on his palm.

'I want an explanation from this man,' Hay said.

Taylor, Moffet and the hands stood by; awkward and buttoned up, in black shoes.

'Boots!' Mackenzie roared at them, hitting his own. 'An fetch yon dray.' He began throwing wood on the fire. The men turned and went out.

'I thought Gilliam was your manager?' Hay remarked, and signalled to his wife at the door. Lady Suffolk indicated that the trap stood ready. She was talking to Frances. Lady Suffolk had already decided to devote the few minutes remaining to her first by ignoring the weather, second by rearranging her collar and muff, and third by preventing Frances from gazing with such enormous eyes at the monster by the fire. All this she contrived to do while maintaining an alarming conversation with her husband behind the girl's back.

'I believe Gilliam has the gout,' Polson said to Hay. He was staring at the reading desk, trying to remember. Everything had two faces, two tones, two shapes, as if he were looking at things from the bottom of a tumbler. At the same time he was mildly fascinated by Mackenzie's actions; the latter was rolling back the drugget. Hay said something. Polson did not reply and Hay turned on the shepherd. The sight of this immaculate figure, in beaver cloak and astrakhan cap, prodding Mackenzie's bare back struck Polson as absurdly comical.

'I want an explanation from you,' Hay said.

'Ay. An the Deel will give it thee if tha doesna shift tha

legs.' Mackenzie pushed Hay away and began clearing chairs and tables, kicking the carpet aside. 'Why are you doing that?' Polson mumbled.

'Lambs,' Mackenzie said. 'Lambs in tha house or lambs is dying. *Boots*, man.'

Moffet entered. 'Near a foot on the ground, sir.' Polson allowed Moffet to help him on with his waders. 'We'll need you, sir.'

'May I remind you, Amos, that that man is still theoretically in my employ.'

Polson smiled glassily. Hay was forever standing over him. Why didn't he go? He felt he was taking part in a deathly charade; he was alone in a room full of people, and nobody knew he was there.

'Buckets, lass,' he heard Mackenzie say. 'Buckets of vittels. Hot broth an rum, buckets an work. Work is for all.'

'Polson.' Hay spoke sharply.

'Not now, Donald. Not now.' Lady Suffolk took her husband's arm. 'You can discuss it when the storm is over.'

'Storm?' Polson sat up. 'Who said anything about a storm?'

For the first time Hay looked out and noticed. His features darkened.

'Yon valley last,' Mackenzie was saying to the men. 'Start pon Gut an cross ravine. Then the Basin an work down. We have nay time to gather the Forks. But the Quarry, the Swamp, Mt. Maggie, Broken Ailsa, all that, Pudding, Dipper, Lizard, all. Loaf an valley last. Together, an work together. All men, all dogs. An bullocks. We mun keep the night.'

'Mackenzie. I want your prediction.' Hay's voice was no longer querulous.

'Where is tha' flocks, up or down?'

'My flocks are where they should be, down.'

'Then tis the luck fellow an the second prophet ye are, for ours are up.'

'Come, man. Advice. I want a civil answer.'

'Thee have heard of the Thirteen Drifty Days?'

'Donald, he is reciting book titles. You can see the man is a boor. We shall manage. Albion will have the men out already.'

'The Thirteen Drifty Days,' Mackenzie repeated.

'No,' Hay said. 'I have not heard.'

'It was in Scotland before thee was babed. It was in a book, a seer showed me. I dinna tell which book but it was the one of them. Well, that is the drifts we shall be getting here. Of the same greatness.'

Hay burst out laughing.

'Come along, Donald. He wants to frighten us.'

Mackenzie was donning Polson's old clothes. Nothing would fit. Frances went for more.

'Before we leave,' Hay said, 'I should like an answer, Amos.' Hay persisted.

'Of course.' Polson stood up. He had remembered what Mackenzie had said to Sparrow before the missionary ran out. He forced himself to go to the reading desk. For a moment he knew relief. The desk was bare. He touched it. He withdrew his fingers hurriedly and wiped them.

'Dammit, Polson. It's no use posing—' Something about Polson's expression made Hay pause. His head, jutting forward, was bathed in perspiration.

'Donald,' he said, speaking very deliberately. 'That old Maori. What did he swallow?'

'Oh damn the old Maori. I don't know. Ask Millicent.'

'Boiled sweets, Amos, those round things, brownballs. They're always sucking them. You know.'

'Thank you,' Polson said.

'Good God, are you ill?'

Polson went quickly outside. There he vomited, leaning over the verandah rail. Out of the whiteness a series of images flashed before him: faces, figures and the small bounding form of Brandy. Last of all there appeared a row of totems, no longer human but canine, the heads socketless and open to the sky.

Sparrow had not gone fifty yards when he ran from the house before he was lost. He had one thought, to bury what was left of the dog and rid the house of Hue's curse. But Sparrow had never seen snow before, thick blinding snow, and he was bewildered. He turned to the left where the ground should have fallen to the river, but instead it rose and blew in his face. Stumbling, he fell; and rose again. He was being pursued. He went a few steps and found he no longer had the brown paper parcel. He began to weep and bite his hand, going on his knees. 'O my God, Why hast Thou forsaken me? . . . Look, I may tell

all my bones, see how they rise and stare upon me . . .' He was
in this condition when Droo blundered up and pinioned him at
the throat. 'Where is it, what you stole?'

'Dead, Droo, dead and desecrated.'

'What you *stole*?'

Having worked himself into a rage, Droo beat the missionary
about the head. Sparrow offered no resistance, nor did he
reply, since Droo's knee rested upon his windpipe; and, as
Droo's anger was slower to cool than his brain, he went on
beating his man. He had come in from the stilthouse when the
snow began to fall. He had undressed and gone to bed. Each
day he did this, hoping never to wake; and each day he woke
again, in his misfortune, deserted even by death. Ever since he
had believed himself cursed Droo had wanted to die; for, only
by dying, could he prevent the spirit of his curse from being
reborn in the house. He had lived with this melancholy too long
to resist. Also he knew — he had seen it happen to a black in
Australia — that to resist was useless. Resistance brought pain
and Droo wished to die content, without pain, having performed
one good action in his life. For weeks he had felt no pain. He
felt nothing except a melancholy desire to die. But the more he
desired it, the more he seemed to live; until finally on this day,
seized with an impotent fury, he had gone to bed at half past
two, a little earlier than usual. Lying on his bunk holding a
piece of twine, he had heard the service through the wall. He
was knotting the twine. He would make one knot for every
creek he had crossed with his bullocks. Then if he was still alive
when he awoke he would get dressed for the last time and cut
his throat. He willed this to happen, lying there knotting the
twine. He was woken by noises in the dairy. Billy's voice, and
another's. It was dark and Droo was frightened now to get up.
At length he crept out and passed through the dairy. As he
entered the big room he was seized by an indefinable presence
of evil, and at the same time by a suffocating desire to live — by
killing the author of that presence. He stumbled about in his
pyjamas. *Somebody* was responsible. It was at this moment that
he saw Sparrow, his face eroded with guilt, snatch up something and run from the room. It could only be Sparrow. But
now in the snow Droo had grown tired of pummelling that unresisting shape, and stood up. He felt no remorse, only a weariness and a disappointment that it was over. He stood up and

considered who he should kill next. He decided on Billy. After a while he heard his name spoken. The missionary sat up. He complained of his throat. 'Help me up,' he said. To Droo's surprise he did as he was told. Presently the missionary began groping about the snow. 'The girl, Droo. It will kill her if she finds the parcel. Help me . . .' He crawled away. Droo crawled behind and caught him by the leg. 'Is mums safe?'

'Mums? Yes Droo. *No*, Droo, no. She is not safe. Help me to find it.' Droo was blubbering. 'I wish you was Billy,' he said.

'Why, Droo?'

'If you was, I could have kilt you easy.'

'Droo, do you wish to be saved?'

'Don't know.'

'I see tears, Droo, but no remorse. If you wish to be saved and keep your mistress safe, you must help me.' Sparrow continued searching.

Gradually it came to Droo that more imperative than the need to commit crime was the need to find whatever it was the missionary was seeking. As the urge to kill left him, he looked into the night and felt a hand of contentment settle on his brow. It occurred to him then that instead of performing one good action he might perform two.

'Lissen,' he said. Crawling forward. 'I want to pray.'

'Let us pray,' the missionary said.

'I pray,' Droo began; and then he said, 'What is we findin?'

'A parcel.'

It had been on Droo's mind to demand to die while the good in him prevailed, lest the bad should reassert itself. He found this difficult to express in words. So he said, 'I pray to find the parsil first an die second, an both tonight for the love of God, an mums amen.'

Together on hands and knees they searched.

The Hays were lost to view before they had driven twenty yards.

'Damned insolence,' Hay muttered. 'Damned insolent snivelling little backbiter.'

'What *was* that bundle, dear?'

'I don't know. It was a bloody mess whatever it was.'

'Donald, I wish you wouldn't whip the horses. That was a hole.'

'As for that shepherd: I will have him, Millicent. I *will* have him. You remember Polson's letter? He made out the man to be debilitated for life.'

'Yes, that was regrettable.'

'Debilitated!'

'He is well made, I admit. But Donald, he's so uncouth. And you don't need him.'

'Never mind. Without him Polson is done, his expedition's done and so is his spirit. He's sinking anyway. His houseboy wants to leave; two of his men have approached me. Something's wrong, they say. Well there is something wrong, you felt it.'

'Polson is a fool,' Lady Suffolk said. 'But a rather grand fool.'

'What's that you say?'

'Donald!'

'I can't help it, Millicent. I can't see a thing. If I don't whip them, we flounder.'

'Donald, you said that our flocks were down.'

'So I *did*.' Hay spoke with such bitterness that when a minute later the trap swayed and almost overbalanced Lady Suffolk declined to grasp his arm for support. His acrimony had been smouldering for weeks. Now it seemed to have reached insensate proportion. For the first time Lady Suffolk paused to wonder what it was that moved this man, her husband, to whom she had been married for fifteen years. She admired his spirit, his dash and zest for life, his loyalty to his own kind, his practical flair, she was thankful for his little kindnesses, all this. But she found in his attitude to Polson a want of—what was it? Whatever it was it wasn't moral. 'Amoral.' She said the word aloud. She had remarked the trait in Donald's friends, but she had not suspected it in him. Or had she simply ignored it? For all her worldliness Lady Suffolk was a little frightened of her husband. Yet she herself was part of this attitude. It was founded on the need to retain mastery, to appear right when one was not, to keep up appearances. Self-respect demanded it. But it was Donald's way of *going about things* that bothered her. It was somehow base and done deliberately; with a deliberate pride. As for Polson—'that frosty little man of principles' she had once called him. In a country where practicality was God she found his conceits, his little hesitancies rather fetching. She disliked him, of course. Yet she saw no need to harm him, since he did not harm others.

'Donald, why must you fight him?' Lady Suffolk said.

'He's the wrong sort. And I detest his principles.'

'You can't fight his principles.'

'No, but I can fight the effects of them. Those articles—scurrilous. A scurrilous attempt to make a mockery of honest endeavour. High-minded little pimp! How I detest clever little men. He can go elsewhere with his clever notions, we don't want him.' Hay gave an ironic laugh. 'In any case he's put a noose round his own throat.'

'You have no proof, Donald, that Polson wrote the articles.' Hay continued chuckling. 'Have you?' she said.

'I was in his room. There was a letter from Stoddart thanking him.'

'You found the letter, I trust, by chance.'

Hay laughed. Lady Suffolk looked at her husband. She could not bring herself to say what was on her mind, that his want of scruple was demeaning. It no longer seemed true. He was frightened now and worried for his flocks which were not down but high in the back hills, scattered and exposed. Half blinded by snow, tearing at the reins; yet proud, debonair; a little smug yet taut; yet all the time coaxing the horses, whispering to the horses, masterful with the horses, in control—he never lost his head. She found that compelling. Despite the hurt to his vanity, the fear of being ridiculed by a weaker man, he was still *sound*. She was grateful for that. Anything less ruthless at her side in this primitive land and she would have found it difficult to cope.

'Why then,' she wondered, 'do I have this feeling for Polson?'

They had entered a gully and were pulling out of it when the horses stuck, floundering to their bellies. Without a word Hay jumped down and with patience and cajoling got them out. This happened three times before they reached the top.

'When we arrive,' Lady Suffolk said, 'I shall put on my mac and come out with you. I may not have been able to bring you children, Donald, but I can still bear a lamb or two.' Hay nodded. Tight-lipped, he drove on into swathes of white.

'Oh dear,' Lady Suffolk said. 'I do hope Albion has had the sense to stir the men.'

'My brother Albion will be either practising his pidgin French on your chef or else he will be sitting up in that observatory of his cursing because he can't see the eclipse. Good God in heaven, *that* is why it's so dark!'

'Then that is all right. If it is only an eclipse.' Lady Suffolk touched her husband's arm.

'Donald?'

'Yes, Millicent.'

'That was another hole.'

Presently they stopped. Hay got down and walked in front. 'Can you see me? I'm waving.'

'No,' his wife said.

'It's getting worse,' Hay said, and started off again.

Now there was only Frances in the house, and the falling snow. She stood in the middle of the room and listened. The snow fell silently, straight up and down in steeples, hurrying down as if to bleach out the other elements for delaying its coming.

It was beautiful.

Strange, there was no wind. 'What a beautiful night to die,' Frances thought.

The clock struck the half hour. Only half past three. It seemed to her that an age had passed since she had risen and begun tidying the room for the service. And now, look at it.

Yet she laughed. A sliding coppery laugh that seemed to mock the men who had departed into the snow. During the last half hour Frances alone had been herself. She had watched the scene: a fretfulness, a petulance, a childish urgency of men, she had likened it to childishness. Even Mackenzie, though his arrival was exciting, had failed to excite her in the way Lady Suffolk had imagined. She alone had remained alien and herself, both woman and mother. So she laughed, for she was above criticism. Her children had gone out in the snow to play.

She went onto the verandah. The snow hid everything. Unseen eddies blew in her face, mouthfuls of powder. Gasping a little she went in and closed the door, leaning against it.

On the other hand there was now this. 'Vittels, buckets of vittels, hot tea and broth . . .' he had said. Yes. This event, this quickening. Her heart was beating. She had waited for this. It was hers as much as theirs.

She began doing what had to be done.

Droo came. She had changed into a scrub gown, had built up the fires, had pots simmering and was replacing the paintings that had been torn down when she turned and saw him. He was blue with snow. He was standing inside the door, standing queer. She did not recognise him at first. She ran to make tea.

'A lantern, mums.'

She could tell he was in a hurry. But when she had brought him the lantern he remained there, looking at her. Perhaps they talked, she did not remember. She continued doing things, taking his mooning presence for granted. It was the look she remembered afterwards.

He said, 'I am jus looking at you, mums.'

She gave him a heel of pie. 'Let me get you a coat,' she said.

He seemed to draw himself up. He had grown younger. She thought he looked rather fine.

'Give me my thtick,' he said.

'But Droo—' For Droo never carried a stick. He means his whip, she thought. As she was going to fetch it something occurred to her and she turned to him. But the old man was no longer there.

'Come along, papa. Drink this. It's ten o'clock.'

Polson took the glass of hot milk and tried to sit up. The bed was strange. Everything was strange. He appeared to be half dressed. There was a buzzing in his temple; bangings and bleatings; a terrible stench.

'This isn't my room.'

'No, there are lambs there, papa. Mackenzie will put them on the verandah later. They are boarding up the verandah now.'

'They're making a pen on the verandah,' she said. He hadn't understood.

He said, 'Who is that moving about?'

'Mr. Sparrow, he's sleeping here. In the other bed.' She had put them both in the new room beside the dairy. 'He is raking the snow from the paddock.'

'Sparrow is raking the snow from my paddock.' He repeated.

'For the lambs, papa.' She made him sip the milk, then drew the curtain. But little light penetrated. 'I can just see them,' she said. 'D'you know you rescued three hundred lambs last night?; and the men say they will save another three hundred today.'

'Yes,' he said, without expression. 'What time is it?'

'Ten o'clock.'

'I must get up Francie. The Hays will be here for the service.'
He tried to get up and failed. He lay back, feeling his face.

'I am bruised,' he said. The buzzing in his temple had increased.

'Did you sleep well?' he added.

'Yes,' she said, and had to sit down. Her hair, parted of itself, hung over her cheeks in damp shawls. She had not been to bed at all. Yet her will was strong. His—She watched him sipping the milk, not noticing the brandy or the drops in it. He was chuckling to himself and humming a snatch of a Charterhouse song. Soon he would give in; it had happened before; it always happened when he sang *Carmen Carthusianum*.

'Francie?'

'Yes.'

'Sing the top line with me.'

'Mackenzie's waiting, papa. I have to mix meal.'

You mixed the meal with milk and filled bottles for the strongest; you put your lips to the weakest and breathed and rubbed, and fed them from a teapot. Sometimes the lambs revived. Her lips were raw from reviving. But he had praised her for it, he had called her Mary by mistake. She would never have believed a man so primitive could be so gentle with living creatures. His face had lit up when Moffet came in saying there was a parcel of two hundred safe under Broken Ailsa, safe till morning. And praised her again for staying up raking the paddock when the others had gone to their beds. They had been together all night. She had made him a chop. He had said a Gaelic grace—and Sparrow coming in, discovering them sitting down together, had begun a Latin one at the door and been asleep on his feet before he had reached the table.

'You have some sort of shock, papa.' It was better this way; the men found his presence a responsibility.

'The men say you worked very well last night.'

'Do they? That is kind of them.'

Polson remembered now. Trying to reach The Gut, Mackenzie in front. Polson could not keep up. He had sat down and they had kicked him, actually kicked him. To keep him going. Was that before or after they loaded the cart and dragged it, like a tumbril, full of lambs? The lambs were strong, they had punched him. Punched his chest as he fell about trying to hold them. Scuffling and grappling. 'Why am I doing this?' he cried.

And Mackenzie had guffawed at him, lying there. A mob passed over him, one trod on his mouth. That must have been when he lost a tooth. But why, why did they need to carry him over creeks when he, he alone, was wearing waders . . .?

Polson smiled at his daughter. 'You must not believe what you see,' he said. 'I am perfectly well.'

'Of course,' she said.

'Is it still snowing?'

'Yes.'

'I thought so,' Polson said; and fell into a deep sleep.

That day the men brought in a further four hundred lambs. But the following morning they managed fewer than a hundred and fifty, the snow lay deep. By nightfall they had managed barely twenty more and were confined to a radius of half a mile from the homestead. All that day, the third, the snow continued to fall straight up and down. Sounds faded; voices, footfalls, bleatings, her father's knocking, all was muted. That night the wind rose a little and the first drifts came. In the morning when Frances went to dig out wood and Mackenzie appeared, he found her cast to the armpits. 'Thee is the prettiest lamb I hae saved yet,' he said, pulling her up. She coloured and waited for him to hug her, as he had done the day before, but he only drubbed the snow from her back and looked meditatively at the sky.

'Speech was given man to show his thoughts, not hide them.' she said.

'Tis boxed in, they are, at the hut,' he said at length.

'You mean the men won't come?'

'The Moffet is trying,' he said.

'We are short of utensils. There's no milk. There is a bag of meal left.'

He chapped her hands and blew a little breath into them, sending her inside, and swarmed up to the storehouse in the patched coat she had mended for him.

Only Moffet and Laughton came that morning. They took spades and went off with Mackenzie. They were gone more than an hour. She knew they were looking for Droo and said nothing when they returned and began with buckets and pots and her father's debating trophy, everything there was, to feed the brawling lambs. To conceal, to pretend. Not to reveal. No fear, no pride, no emotion, but simply carry on, it was the only way. He had taught her that. She was learning. Standing in the dark kitchen behind the slatted pen, eking the meal for the lambs, with the library lamp steaming above her.

In the afternoon Taylor and Moffet carried in a few more. Then they went again. She fed the lambs from a bottle. They seemed thinner than the rest.

'Well, what with yon pen an yon paddock, tis eight hundred mites in their beds beside thee,' Mackenzie said to her as he went off. 'Tis what we have done, lass.'

In bed she looked out and saw a glimmer of sky.

Droo died that night.

As he died he was granted the blessing of lucidity. He told himself, 'I have jus lain down'; although he had been lying for three days. He looked up into the falling sky and it seemed to him that he saw steps. He saw the hand of Orion hanging down. He looked up into the night and everything was blue, a deep transparent blue, and behind that blue again; and he climbed into the hollow of the hand that hung down the sky, and understood.

Before he died Droo did curse.

The next morning without waiting to dress properly Frances rushed onto the verandah. She came in dejected and kicked off her wellingtons. They appeared to float. The floor was a lake. There was a prayer book lying, with a cake on it. She did not bother to pick it up.

That morning only Moffet came with Mackenzie. For the first time she was frightened. Whether he sensed this or not, Mackenzie spent the day about the house. He was never far from her. He made her a pair of clogs, rafts really, that she might walk outside without sinking. He cleared walks, no longer walks but underground passages—to the stilthouse, to the well, to the fowls; and a tunnel round the house to the paddock where Sparrow bent beneath his cassock, like a mushroom, clearing a space where the lambs might peer for the earth they could not see. He set Moffet to massage the bullocks with turpentine; and discovered the cow, licking the cob from the wall where the peach tree drowned, lifting a pale bud on the end of a spike, all that it could. He came towards her driving the cow, just a beard parting the snow, and settled her down to milk. She laid her cheek against the warm flank, feeling the vibration, pulling the springy taps, and wondered if it was necessary to be ill in order to be in love. Though she was merely counting the patches on his coat. If this is illness, she thought, I should like never to recover. She smiled up at him. 'Tonight,' she said, in what she hoped was a commanding tone, 'you sleep here.' He looked so startled that she did not add what she felt, that each morning now she woke crying in case he he would not come. 'It is not what you're thinking,' she said; and added to cover her embarrassment, 'The teats have shrunk, the beast's dry.' ' I have never cooped in an house in my life,' he said. Over his shoulder, moving away. But he found the goat, there was a goat, and brought her milk. He moved through the showers like a Trappist, half hooded, his coat held across with twine, the sacking over his boots thonged to the knees. He took his food standing, with Moffet, reaching out and flavouring everything from the bottle of Worcester sauce that Moffet carried in his pocket.

The next day Moffet did not come. But he continued to come, each morning a little later than the last, as the snow mounted and the first lambs died on the verandah. 'I mun stretch a wire,' he said on the morning of the sixth day. 'I found tha' father's nag eating the thatch.' They exchanged statements. He was preoccupied. He refused intimacy. He seemed to be living not for her nor even her wants, but for something bigger. She no longer cared. So long as he gentled her for what was to come. Whatever it was, he imparted the feeling that while he remained she was inviolable.

Each morning Sparrow went into the paddock with a spade and nibbled at the indifferent banks of snow; and again in the afternoon. He had taken on a blueish tint. 'It is my hands,' he would say, coming in. He would come in and warm them at the fire and wait until the blueness passed. Then he would go out again. Each day he dug down two banks and each night the snow covered them again. But the lambs came out in the morning alive.

'You are a stoic,' she would say, bringing him beef tea. 'Why do you keep saying, "I may tell all my bones" —?'

'To remind me, my child.' With a gruesome smile.

'Do you think Brandy is safe?'

'Of course,' he would say. Putting snow in the tea and drinking it quickly and lifting the spade again as if he were lifting fathoms.

'It is only my hands, child.'

'Please stop,' she would say. Seeing the irregular dark blotches like the spots on a plaice. Yet she knew, from the pain, that he would keep on at the indifferent bank until it melted. He would wear nothing over his cassock. Yet he did not hide his pain, as Mackenzie did. Was suffering harder then for him, she wondered. And if harder, was it greater? Or nobler? Watching him, with his hacking cough, his pained and angular motions, she could not believe that suffering ennobled.

Yet there was also this — if this were possible: she remembered the victory of her tears when they had sung the 23rd Psalm. It was Sparrow's victory too as much as hers. Now it had been taken from him as it had been taken from them all. So now he suffered, as Christ suffered, not only for himself but for them all. Was that possible?

He would eat little. At meal times he sat with her father and read to him; sometimes they sang motets. They had established a strange intimacy.

Polson kept to his bed. On the third or fourth day he noticed that the bleating of the lambs was becoming fainter, and after that he did not want to get up. He was not ill, he was simply incapable. He was not cold; the snow entombed and Frances had given him a lap brasier. But his eyes were bad, there was a swelling behind the sockets; and the buzzing in his temple was searing. On the seventh day — the day he decided his flocks were doomed — he asked Frances to apply homeopathic doses of tincture of laudanum. This brought him out in boils, but it eased his shame and left him lightheaded. His flocks, his inevitable failure became as unreal as the falling snow and he was able to reason quietly to himself, without remorse.

Occasionally Polson thought of the journey. 'But if my flocks are done for I needn't think of that any more, need I?' He smiled with relief.

He was not heroic. He did not pretend to understand the workings of heroism or stoicism or even the currents of passion that he saw kindling his daughter whenever she spoke of that man: the man who could not save him from ruin. That man was like the Bible, a desolation and an astonishment. It was not heroism. There was a fire in him that would not go out. 'I have done without all my life,' Mackenzie had told Polson. He had amassed nothing, not civilisation, not books, not property—it must be true. 'Blessed are the poor in spirit,' Polson murmured to himself, 'for they have everything to give.' His father had made him learn that in Latin at the age of three; he had never understood it until now, at the age of fifty-three. For the first time he found it possible to believe that goodness was close to godliness.

Every time Polson got up he fell over. The buzzing would not go away. 'My noises,' he would say to Sparrow, waking in the darkened room. They would lie there talking and recalling student days, as others recall wars; until Frances brought them breakfast. Sparrow would barely touch his. He would dress and go out like a ghost. Polson would brush his hair and eat two breakfasts, reflecting on the missionary's exertions. He was intrigued by that willpower. Polson's own was nothing—like his body: thickset above, it fell away to nothing like a prow rotting beneath the waterline. His willpower always deserted him in a crisis. Once at Charterhouse he had tried to harness it by willing himself to learn by heart all three volumes of Ovid's *Ars Amatoria* and in the end had only partially succeeded, by shaving his head so that he was forced to stay in his room. Sparrow would kill himself, digging. He was doing it because of the dog, he said. Polson had cut him short, to no avail. The missionary continued to dig in expiation. Sometimes Polson thought of his wife whom he had loved and who had died of an incurable disease. He loved her still, for giving him Frances and for relieving a morbid hatred of his father whose early bullyings had convinced him that he was both perverted and impotent.

He liked this room. It was neutral. His bed was in one corner, Sparrow's in the other. It was like a cell. He liked the closeted feeling, the solitude; and it was comforting to hear Sparrow's cough outside and the scratching of the spade.

On the eighth day he woke feeling almost lucid. He remembered a student friend who had encouraged him to paint. After lunch when Frances took in his Warburg's drops she found him sitting up in his Phrygian cap, knitting. The sight of his squarish head, hunched slightly forward under the woollen cap, the knitting and the smell of Sanatogen took her suddenly back to his bouts at the rectory; and she remembered the flavour of castor oil which her grandfather used to mix regularly with his son's potatoes at dinner.

Polson held up the knitting. 'For Miss Peebles,' he explained. 'I don't know yet if it will be socks or a kettle holder. What do you think?'

'Why my dear, whatever's the matter?'

'It has stopped snowing,' she said. 'It has begun to freeze.'

Frances dozed fitfully, turning with the cold. She wore a gown over her nightshift. She kept rising and going to the fire, and back to bed again. She woke to hail and sleet and the howl of wind. The whole house was turning. There was a soughing in the rafters, '*aah-h-h-me, aah-h-h-me*', as of keas crying or Droo intoning an unaccustomed grace. Once she woke to a fill of blue lightning and the walls shaking; snow was flying onto the bed. In the big room she found three feet of snow at the entrance, the door rocking on one hinge, paintings down and the gallipot hitting the rafters, glee gashing against a rusty hook. The house shook with crashes. She could not close the door though she broke her arms against it. She heard a wild laugh and screamed. A figure was there in the sky, a shroud, white as bone, looking down. The laugh was repeated. It seemed to come from behind her. She whirled round as the kitchen fell. '*Aah-h-h-me, aah-h-hhh-me*', the rafters cried. She looked again. The figure was gone. Streaks of hail descended jaggedly, firing the porch, and what she saw now terrified her far more. On either side of the door, where once had been a walk, was a yawning gully. The snowbanks lining it were higher than the house. She dragged the table against the door and turned away. In the kitchen everything was down, broken. There was an old porcelain mug on the bench, whole. She went to the fire and remained there, sobbing and cursing Mackenzie for deserting her when she needed him most. Though he could do nothing, she complained, flinging the things that were in the mug into the fire: seeds, a brooch, a needle, something else, ribbon or galon, that roll of blue galon Droo had bought for the hat she had never finished. She thought of running through the dairy to her father, but fear of the dairy walls collapsing and crushing her made her stay where she was. A flash lit her mother's portrait. She saw the brush strokes on her mother's brow. She prayed for catastrophe—now, swiftly; for the roof to cave; to be swallowed painlessly by snow, since snow was such a painless killer. She *willed* him to come. 'Coward!' she cried, flinging the galon in the fire. She did not realise she was holding the mug until she came to something that was small and round. It fitted her finger. It was her mother's signet ring with the owl seal. She slipped it on. Her fingers were stiff, but she could tell the seal; and was calmed by it. She remained by the fire until the shaking stopped and fell asleep by the bolster with the sound of the pot glee gashing in her ears.

Sparrow slept.

Polson sat up in bed wearing three waistcoats. He heard the thunder. He felt the roof shift and the weight of snow that was crushing his flocks. 'So I am doomed,' he murmured, without trace of pity. 'But not an ordinary failure, Polson, this will be a disaster!' He was in a mood to continue knitting. But the candle kept blowing out. 'At least,' he thought, 'I can try one on'; for he had finished one sock for Miss Peebles. He tried the sock and it fitted. Then he lay back and cried, he was so cold.

Outside Mackenzie laughed at the storm. He was high, higher than the roof, snow-gabled high; and he walked on the rooftop of the world laughing at the storm as it plucked and railed at him. He held it for a moment, and it held him. He struggled silently to regain his power, and with each fresh gain he would shout his mastery over it. Only to be knocked down and struggle afresh, and shout. His voice frightened him, the sound of it. He was afraid to cry Victory.

Yet this was the sign: these elements. And laughter was but a condition of his acknowledgment.

He looked down once and saw the vision of Mary. He was near enough to touch her. The face pressed upward, the gazelle eyes, lit precariously by a single candle that died even as he was toppled from his perch. But for an instant the eyes remained with the expression of a wounded animal, staring intently at him. It seemed that they had been granted solely for his illumination. He rose up then with all his strength, his pride overcame him and he shouted the word: Victory.

Angry at himself, he descended into the cutting that divided the pens and set about clearing it. Otherwise, he told himself, the Christians within will be girt like moles, an that was no mortal way to die.

Frances woke to the crackle of ice. The fire had died. There was a sound, as of heavy weights being dragged across the porch. She reached for the poker, and cringed. She felt the presence of an intruder. She took a step, stumbled and fell headlong.

'It's *you*!' she cried.

Mackenzie sat up.

'Mary?'

'Thank heaven,' she said, and flung herself into his arms with relief. But he was nothing but a board of rime, and she recoiled.

Mackenzie mumbled something. He was curled round the bolster like an animal.

'Have you been keeping watch? I knew you would come. But you've let the fire down.' She coaxed the fire until there was a glow. The dog laid its muzzle across his ribs, sniffing the hearth. 'Exactly what Brandy used to do,' she thought. The gallipot had stopped creaking. Apart from the dragging noise, the house was still.

He wore a tender expression. His ears point, even in sleep, she thought. There was a pinkness under the ears and about the lips and nose, a delicate veining, that she had not seen before in men. He was quite young really.

'I was dreaming,' she said. 'I dreamed that St. Bernard descended in a shroud and stood in the sky mocking me. Do saints mock?'

He opened his eyes and laughed softly. She knew that sound. '*That* was you?'

'Ay. Thee will nay have the rid of me till the storm is done.'

Now what did he mean by that?

'I thought thee was the Holy Virgin,' he murmured. He kept waking and dropping off. She would have liked to cradle him, but his head was away from her. His ankles enfolded her own rubbing her slippers. She could feel him thawing, the moisture seeping through.

'And I dreamed about—strange, it is all muddled. This ring, you see: I gave it to him and he was tugging at it. It wouldn't come off his finger.'

'That were a canny dream, lass.' He was on an elbow closeted beside her so that she found it difficult to breathe. It was only for an instant, he lay back unexpectedly passing a hand across his head as if gripped by sudden nausea.

'How long will you be away?' she said. Breathing again.

'You see,' she found herself saying when he did not reply, 'I know it is important to leave, to open doors. But it is more important to return.' She thought he grunted. 'You were dreaming. You were dreaming when I woke you.'

'Who?' he said, in such a small voice. 'Who was my dream?'

'You said Mary.' How strange, she thought, that he should say Who.

'Then Mary is dead,' he said. He said it quite simply, staring at some point inside her; he lay there dazed, knotted about the eyes. Then he was beside himself, convulsed. She believed him. She could tell by the way his legs were behaving. They were jerking up and down against her slippers unnaturally. She held them. It seemed to her that his legs were the best part of him and she would not allow some other woman to drain their power. She held them, on her knees, tighter than she had held anything in her life. She calmed them. Rubbing and chafing them with her breasts and cheeks and lips. While he lay there making thick runic sounds she did not understand.

'Mary is dead, lass.'

'I know.'

The things holding the sacking to his legs were crusted with ice and cut her lips. For a second she told herself she was behaving like a character in a novel. Then she tasted blood. Smiling, she pressed her mouth until she was biting on the thongs. And the ice melted in her mouth, turning the blood to water, and she gave it back the way he had taught her of lambs, with her lips, breathing life into life. So they mingled. And they remained like that for a very long time.

Dawn came unseen. As the elements ceased to struggle and resumed their separate entities.

Polson woke. His beard was solid. 'Bad news, Bernard,' he said. The other's bed was empty. Frances woke to find the missionary standing there in a temperament. 'We are entombed,' he said. Frances ran to the door. The opening was a wall of ice. Mackenzie woke and saw stalactites hanging from the thatch. He heard Frances' cry from the door and remembered the purpose of his incubation. He flew at the wall of ice with his bare hands. Nothing happened. A few splinters fell down.

'Tis solid,' he said in amazement.

'You are bleeding,' Frances said.

The missionary apologised for leaving the axe and the spade outside.

Polson crossed the room leaning on a stick.

'Tis an berg,' Mackenzie said. 'Tis an iceberg.' His voice retained a sensation of wonder. Polson ran his nail over the surface in a bemused sort of way.

'It's the same in all the rooms,' Sparrow said. The missionary knelt to pray. Polson turned and hit him with the stick. 'Stop whining, Bernard, and help me back to bed. Get up.'

'Nay! Keep tha' back straight.' Mackenzie stepped on the missionary's back and swung himself up by a divot. He crawled along to the icicles and lay back on a rafter. He began kicking the roof. 'Stop that. Stop that, I say.' Polson reached the bookcase and began to hurl books at him. Mackenzie laughed. Frances looked up. The roof caved. Showers of ice and snow fell about her. When she opened her eyes the room was full of blue dust and a fine rock flour was settling. An echo of Mackenzie's laughter floated down. She shook her father and pointed. She had to wipe his eyes before he could see: a patch of china blue. He stared at it without blinking.

'Is it thawing yet?' Polson said.

'No, papa.'

'What time is it?'

'The pendulum has stopped, you know that. Everything has stopped.'

'Yes, you told me that. Very well. My gruel is cold.'

'You have finished it, papa.'

'Oh very well. So I have. Are they coming?'

Frances crossed the room and put her ear to the wall. 'No,' she said. Polson pulled his cap and his rugs about him and turned to Sparrow who was holding a copy of *Idylls of the King*. Frances had persuaded the missionary to wear her father's old hunting jacket. The two men were huddled together in that odd harmony which misfortune occasionally provides. 'Go on,' Polson said. The missionary lifted the book and continued reading. From time to time Polson would say 'Stop' and turn, his eyes forlorn and watery. Frances would rest her book and go to the door, pretending she could hear the sound of tunnelling. She would return to the fire and take up her book. She believed she had read the same page twenty times. Sometimes looking up at the thatch where it hung in daggers she would see again a tiny patch of sky, and be reassured. 'He won't come,' her father kept saying, making her glower. He would *always* come. As the day wore on her trips to the door increased. The slightest sound would set her running. Polson would start. Or Sparrow would wet his finger and hold it up, making the silence even more uncanny. He had this peculiar habit of wetting his finger and displaying it. She had ceased to notice what they were saying or doing. At the door she would rest. She would lay her cheek against that delicious wetness and sink into a tunnel. Only the weeping wetness prevented her from falling asleep. She would climb slowly out of the tunnel with hyacinths stranding her hair and return to the fire, her ear singing with the cold. She made cups of hot chocolate.

So they waited.

At length Polson tired of Tennyson. He began to teach Sparrow 'John Barleycorn'. When Sparrow had learned it they sang a duet, in parts. 'It is a mummer's song, Bernard. Pre-Saxon. You reminded me of it. You and Hue. I think the idea of the corn spirit must be universal. In the song John Barleycorn is symbolised by a human representative who is flailed and crushed to death by the grinder's stones. They used sacrifice in England also, you know. It was to do with the fertility of the soil and the crops. It is the same with Hue's ritual incantations to the kumara god. We are fortunate, I suppose, that he chose to sacrifice a dog and not one of us instead.' Polson looked to see that Frances was not listening. 'The mental process is the same. Brandy — a worshipful animal — is chosen as our representative, as the repository of a superior power, and after sacrifice is displayed before the congregation to release this power for human aid.

'There. It was not your neglect, Bernard. You needn't stare at your hands any more. There's no stain.' The missionary replaced his glove. He looked up as Polson said, 'I shall miss you — when this is over.'

'You know,' Polson went on, 'if I were not frozen into idiocy, I would write to Miss Peebles.'

'Miss Peebles?'

'The lady who will receive the socks. An old student friend; she writes books. She is creating a character who is to die in a state of arctic cold and she wishes to know his innermost thoughts as he does so. If the mercury hadn't fallen out of the bottom of the glass I would at least be able to tell her the exact temperature at which such thoughts appear.'

'Strange,' Polson added.

'What is strange?'

'The verb "to die". It won't conjugate. You cannot say, "I have died".'

Sparrow opened his mouth to say something but Polson interrupted. 'Frances, my girl, it's no good looking up there. I tell you, he won't come.'

'It has gone,' she said.

'What has gone?'

'The sky. Either it has gone or night has come.'

'Then night has come. It always does.' Polson lapsed into the *Messiah*. He despised his mind. It always did this. It came beastly alive just when he most needed to despair. In a very real way he hoped never to emerge. 'Come,' he sang, to the *Messiah*, 'He will not come, they will not come, tum-te-tum, *we* will not come . . . Sparrow?'

'Yes.'

'Have you ever seen a frozen sheep?'

'No.'

'I have. It is beastly.'

Frances went into the kitchen. The two men stared moodily at the fire.

'I shall miss you, Bernard. I mean that.'

Sparrow appeared to return from a long way off. 'Did your wife ever deceive you?' he said.

Polson looked round. Then he replied, cautiously, 'No.'

'Mine did. She did it once. It was enough. I never forgave her for it, nor the child; not even when she died. They say I drove her to it. She took her life. There was a scandal. I lost my post.' He smiled bitterly. 'You know—' He broke off. There were tears in his eyes. He went on, 'Of all the good women in that city, there was only one I could find to care for the child. And that was a native woman.'

'That was why you became a missionary?'

'Perhaps. Mervyn, the boy—I didn't want him. I wanted never to see him again. Until—until that service. That other boy, standing up, consumptive—'

'Reminded you. Of course. I have said, Bernard: your mission is not a failure.'

'Oh no, nothing is ever a failure. Therefore I shall do this thing.'

Polson raised an eyebrow. 'What will you do?'

'I am not going back to the pa, Amos.'

Polson said nothing.

'You see, it is not enough to teach that one Maori should love another Maori. Our age will never be regenerated until there is goodness among all men.'

'Of all the statements you have made, Bernard, that seems to me the most fatuous.'

'Unless one proposes to act on it. I shall begin with myself. I shall go to Christchurch, to Mervyn. I need his forgiveness. Then I shall start again.'

'Another pa?'

'Of course. St. Paul didn't preach only to the Galicians. But I shall grind more slowly next time.'

'No, Bernard.' Polson spoke gently. 'You see, there will always be a Hue, there will always be a malicious man. Goethe says, "Why deride your enemies, those to whom your way of being is a constant threat?" No mission has ever prospered by simply replacing one ethic with another. Conversion of itself is a form of derision. This is where Christianity falls down. Unless—Tell me: When you came to Odessa, how many able-bodied Maoris were there?'

'Sixty. Or seventy.'

'And there have been various epidemics: scarlet fever, diphtheria, cholera—?'

'Not cholera, measles. Mostly measles.'

'And how many able-bodied souls are left?'

The missionary hesitated. 'About twenty,' he said.

'I venture to suggest that if you returned as a tanner or a toolmaker displaying the skills of a surgeon-general, your influence might be more lasting.' Sparrow was twisting his glove. He might have been smirking. 'Since you talk of neighbourly love,' Polson said. 'Why are you so blind? Why evade the issue? All missionaries do—as did the early Christians. The early Christians were not sympathetic to medicine. It *is* a form of blindness; Paul would say of sin. You're a godless beggar, Bernard. So long as you shun sickness and misery you are as godless as the catholics. The good bishop when he was here thought that my Scots shepherd had as little religion in him as an old cat. That man — that man, Bernard, has more religion in him than all your missions put together. Shall I tell you why? Because he has a compassion for life. He is a healer. Just think. Religion, *persuasive* religion is not so very different from medicine: the aim is always to heal. The Hues of this world, what are they? They are not prophets. They may well be saints, but they are not prophets, despite their prophecies. Yet theirs isn't religion. At one level they are nothing more than primitive men of medicine. Hue's influence is almost exclusively herbal. Had you thought of that? But at a deeper level — have you noticed his hands? They are the hands of a healer. So with all tribal priests. They call themselves priests, but they are healers; some good, some bad. Hue isn't all bad, his hands tell you that. Therefore why fight him? You will only cancel each other out. You must work *with* him.

'Bernard, don't you see? The idea of sin, which is your specialty, is outmoded. The Maori didn't have it before you came; he doesn't want it now. It confuses him. Throw it away.'

Polson could not tell what effect his words were having. 'True faith — if you will forgive the expression from a free-thinker — is possible only if there's true understanding. The great difference between us, Bernard, is this: you believe and hope to understand; while I, like Abelard and the heretics, I try to understand in order to believe. Surgery, Bernard! Surgery is what you need. Amputate your preconceptions and save the world!'

Polson stood up, chuckling at his own frivolity, although he was deadly serious. He tried to kick his feet together, but he was too cold. He could tell from the way Sparrow had stiffened that his words had had little effect.

'No, no, I was too quick,' the missionary was saying. 'Next time I must work more slowly.' Suddenly he turned on Polson: 'Why do you despise the faith?'

'Once it was because my father was a rector. But I have outgrown that. Now — I do not any longer believe in solutions.'

The missionary laughed, a tiny laugh of triumph. 'And what of your plan? Is not that a solution?'

Polson was silent.

'That is so,' he said at length. It was as if all the problems from which his illness had protected him had congealed in his head at once. The jauntiness went right out of him.

He happened to glance round and see Frances by the door. 'What are you doing over there?' For a moment he could not remember where he was. Gradually it came to him. Something about her attitude arrested him. He went to her. Frances, with her ear laid flat, held out a hand. She did not speak. Her eyes were shining. She cupped his head against the cliff beside her own, watching him. He gave no sign. Then an eyebrow began to contract, his face puckered. There! Polson called Sparrow. They listened. A tiny scratching reached them. A stratching. Soon it changed to a cawing note. Polson began kicking the wall. The sound faded. Then it began again in another key, louder. Suddenly their ears were filled with a deep gonging note. They fell back.

A thud sounded behind them. An axe was lying on the floor. A long form dropped through the roof. Mackenzie stood there, holding the axe, icicles hanging from his beard and nostrils. He managed a drenched sort of grin, nodding and sucking his breath. They stood back as he began to chip with the axe. They could hear voices now. He swung the axe. Ice flew. They retreated to the fire. A rumbling filled the house. Polson had taken Sparrow's arm. The missionary had linked arms with Frances. 'If we're so happy, why are we cowering?' she thought. But her blood was singing. Mackenzie called out. Voices answered. He was swinging and shouting like a fool. He threw the axe aside. 'Tis moving,' he said. 'Tis thin an tis moving. Bring me an object.' She brought him the swill bucket which was frozen solid. 'Ay', he said. He led her back. 'Ay,' he said again, and ran forward. Before he reached the wall he flung the bucket.

'Good God,' Polson said. The wall had simply collapsed. The force of Mackenzie's run had carried him through. He lay full length, ensharded in rubble, the soles of his boots towards them; while beyond, slithering up a long corridor into a pale, pale heaven, was the solid cone from the bucket. They were all there: men of rime, holding implements. Polson stood up. For some reason he had been bending. 'Is it—?' he began. Everything was subdued and strange. His ears were popping. So this is what it is like to rise again, he thought.

'It is a mercy.' Frances gasped.

'Is it—are we late?' Polson said.

The men, who had been standing back deferentially, their eyes full of interest, scrambled forward. Then something happened that Polson would never forget. Taylor called for three cheers. As the men cheered they picked up Polson and bore him into the tunnel. 'Come on mums,' Gilliam said. His gouty hands were wrapped in socks. 'Now then.' He hoisted her behind her father. They crawled along, Polson in front. Wind sang in the tunnel and a grey light bore him upwards. He did not notice the projections tearing his hands.

They emerged at last. 'But—' Frances said. And that was all. For there was no sound; only a singing in their ears, as of tumblers hitting together. There were no stars. It was not night. Before them earth and sky clung together in a sheet of white. All landmarks had disappeared.

As they stood there, tranced, their hair seemed to clot and freeze. For a moment Frances was intoxicated with the scene. She saw clouds detach themselves from a vault of slightest blue; a hanging saucer; and over the trough of the land a haze of moondust—insects, dancing the marmoreal sea.

Suddenly she gripped her father's arm. 'But—but where are all the flocks?'

Polson turned away. 'Come along,' he said. 'There is nothing for us here.'

They counted three hundred and twenty dead ewes in the valley alone. Frances discovered one group of lambs frozen, just as they had lain down. The living were pressed upon the dead and had to be dragged apart.

At first their hopes were high. Along the creeks ewes clad in fine wool walked out of the drifts alive. They had lived in chambers. The snow had drifted over their steaming bodies and insulated them; they had breathed through tiny chimneys formed by the breath of their nostrils. They came out thin but warm. It thawed by day and froze again at night. Each night the stars shone with a cruel radiance, the moon's saucer grew into the springtime, and in the morning the ground was hard with frost. The men walked on the black ice, poking and prodding, uppermost beings raised to a new vision; for the hills appeared to the height of a man and the gullies had filled in to meet them.

Each day brought fresh horrors. Taylor's dog, crushed by the weight of ice when the kennel collapsed, its mouth bent on a bone; sheep tearing out their own wool for sustenance. Polson saw one eating the fleece from her own lamb while the ewe herself was torn from behind by a ram, dividing the living pelt into strips. Small birds had perished and great boars alike, drawn together in the lee of the creeks; in places instead of climbing banks the sheep had plunged into the flowing carpet and drowned, or had made their own graves, turning in circles and tamping down holes into which they had rolled from sheer exhaustion. Creeks which had not before been noticed were exposed, lined with corpses. These creeks ran for miles between flax and toi-toi which lay down crushed, in crooked sheaves. By contrast the cabbage trees stood starkly, their upper branches gnawed bare by sheep that had stood on ten feet of snow to reach them. The frosts persisted, plating the ground with ponds of rime. The living died in scores, feebly tapping the crust for the tussock they could not reach.

They found Droo, quite close. He was engraved in the snow. He was holding a crust of pie. Mackenzie had to chip it from his fingers. They buried him quickly before the flies came, with his bullock whips beside him.

Mackenzie was leaving for Seagull. Frances saw him off. He said the merinos he had left there would be safe. She said he was trying to comfort her. They spoke of Droo. 'It was he, wasn't it, who attacked you in Australia.'

'Ay. But I forgot him that when I saw the way he learned to drive they team.'

'Did he suffer?'

'Twas a natural expression on the face, lass.'

It was possible for them to be quite still together. He had taught her that.

'Thee knows of Brandy,' he said.

'Mr. Sparrow told me. I always knew. He could not survive the freeze. You know—I prayed for his return. Yet I always knew that when he seemed most alive to me, he was most dead.'

As she spoke, Mackenzie's dog reached out a paw and touched her.

'Thee has aged, lass,' he said. And then, because she was sad and he wanted to leave her as he had found her, that day on the plateau, with her throat drawn up and the underlip trembling, he said: 'Thee should get thaself an man.'

But she would not flare. She had a purpose. She gave him her mother's ring with the owl seal. 'For Mary,' she said. And ran quickly inside.

He went off whistling to cover his embarrassment.

Sparrow came to say goodbye. He had been to the pa. He did not say very much, except they were all alive. He permitted himself a joke about the prayer books. They were using them for kindling. He rode off on a horse barely strong enough to hold him.

A few days later a note arrived from Blueskins. Polson was trimming his beard at the breakfast table.

'It will be about the ball,' Frances said. 'I shan't mind.'

'But you must go.'

'Not without you, papa.'

'Anyway,' she said, remembering that the Hays had lost four thousand dead, 'it will be a cancellation.'

But no. He showed her. The ball would be held notwithstanding. The word was underlined.

'You know Francie. I may be well enough to go after all. The Dewhursts will be there, we may even persuade them to let Rose travel back with us.'

'Would you like that, papa?'

'Yes,' he said with the scissors held open. 'Yes, I believe I would.'

His beard had turned quite grey.

On the eve of the ball Polson wrote a note to Miss Peebles, to go with the socks. '... You said once when we were rather silly (we were talking about fibre) that the most attractive thing about me, apart from my love of knitting, was my inimitable flair for falling down whenever I attempted to accomplish anything. You added that if ever I succeeded in the colonies it would be quite unwittingly and the shock to my temperament would be so great that I would sail home in disgust. Well, my dear, in a way you were right. For I have not succeeded and I intend to stick it. The philosophy is not mine; it was invented, I believe, by the Serahin Arabs—they went to war on the principle of failure. It has come to this: two-thirds of my flocks gone and one man. He died "with his feet wet", which is the highest compliment in these parts. Two more are leaving,

Moffet and Drake-Draper. I liked them best, for they have tried to understand. Self-improvement is not, I have said before, required reading for the university of these latitudes. I shall miss Draper. He was a good baker. One other must go, and he is the best of us. His flock alone has survived entire; he brought it down today. Not proudly, but the men would not look. It is a miracle. But the men do not want miracles, any more than they want leaders. His superiority excites contest which touches false pride, and breeds inferiority and shame. And I am no alchemist. He is a Celt, yet I believe were he an Englishman it would be the same. Here at last you see the decadence of Empire. There is no room here for peers any more than for servants; every man must do so much and no more, no worse and no better than the next. His crime is to do everything superbly well . . .'

In the end Polson had decided to abandon his plan. It was irresponsible, his capital was gone, it was not, as Sparrow had said, a solution . . . etc. But none of these things had weighed with him. In the end his conscience had proved stronger than his principles. He would return Mackenzie to Hay and be reconciled to himself. It was the only way. He would dismiss Mackenzie after the ball. Polson looked forward to the ball now, if only to see the expression on Hay's face when he told him.

Yet it was not the whole reason, he knew. Between his daughter and the shepherd there had always been a familiarity. Now quite suddenly there was something else, Polson hesitated to give it a name. Whatever it was, it was leading to the one disaster he really wished to avert.

THE ball was held in the Hays' woolshed, a great barn where normally presided the most up-to-date wool press in the antipodes. The woolshed had been converted into something exquisite—exquisite was the word on all lips—from the beribboned stage hung with red damask to the japanned lanterns set discreetly along the alcoves and the imitation chandeliers made of candelabra and papier maché which hung in seven rows, slowly revolving over the sanded floor. The ball was rumoured to have cost a thousand pounds: what with the band, the staff, a supper served continuously in three adjoining rooms, and the rest of the establishment (three storeys, heart of totara) given over to companies of maids for the sleeping arrangements, since none of the guests would depart before daybreak. It was a beautiful night, transparent and cool. The ballroom was away from the homestead, along a gravel walk lined with flowering ribbonwood and karamu. But behind the trees Polson noted mounds freshly dug for animals, heard the diminished cries of the carrion birds hovering in dark squadrons about the shelterbrakes where everything hung three ways. A slightly fetid odour hung in the air—and with it, something of the courage of the pioneer of Blueskins who had dared to greet catastrophe with such extravagance. It was this, Polson realised—a morbid curiosity to savour a man's misfortunes—that had drawn half a province to the ball. The drive was ranked with carriages, carts, gigs, traps of every description. Long after midnight they kept coming. Polson discerned in the remarks of the gapers a flatulence and an air of disenchantment; they did not believe, they said, that there *could* have been a storm (for in the lowlands the kowhai was blooming). Polson was glad Donald Hay had seen fit to disappoint them and said so to Arthur Dewhurst. Indeed, went further and called Hay, Prince of Squatters. Dewhurst postured in surprise and then spent half the night wondering if Polson were a saint or if some special code of honour had arisen among mountain dwellers of which he, singularly, were ignorant. But this of course was before Whitehouse arrived. Polson spent the first hours weighing up young Hollis, whenever he could persuade those green socks to abandon his daughter; and wandered about the house admiring Lady Suffolk's porcelain. At her request he inspected the spinet which she wished to sell to a Prussian baron—the baron having travelled especially from Wellington. Once, finding a corridor furnished with ladies' elastic sided travelling boots and the floor below with a row of filthy wellingtons, he experienced a sudden desire to exchange the rows, but mastered the impulse and returned to the ballroom. There he made friends with an Irish policeman playing the violin and was given a lesson on the dulcimer. In the crowd he had no chance to see Donald Hay; indeed the Hay brothers seemed to be avoiding him. Not until after midnight did they come upon him, almost formally, with the news that two days before Matthew Whitehouse had resigned as Superintendent. Polson was annoyed, the more so since he was convinced that of all the people at the ball he alone had been kept ignorant of the fact.

Towards midnight Frances thought she was going to be sick. She was giddy from dancing and, declining to walk outside with Dick Hollis, left him brusquely in the middle of the floor and went to the house alone. At the time Polson learned of Whitehouse's resignation Frances was in an upstairs bedroom, resting. Her nausea had passed. She was lying on the brass-posted bed asking herself why Rose had not come, when a familiar long neck, iridescent, white, unadorned, glided into the room. Mrs.

Dewhurst, with a conspiratorial glance about her, checked her glide; and then continued it almost into Frances' arms, her own extended stiffly like cart handles in a mist.

'At last. I have found you alone. My deah—and you have been dancing *all night*?'

Startled by the melodramatic entry, Frances coloured to the plum of her moiré gown. She was thoroughly rumpled. Her shoulders were uncovered. For no reason, except that her under lip was shaking, she knew she would be angry with this woman. 'Ceaselessly,' Frances replied.

'It was a young man you came to escape, I'll warrant.' Mrs. Dewhurst had disposed herself on the end of the bed. She was sitting on Frances' fichu.

Frances drew up her legs under a pile of cloaks. 'Yes, it was. A surveyor.'

Mrs. Dewhurst dabbed her nose, and breathed through it.

'Rose's young man,' Frances said pointedly.

Mrs. Dewhurst had not come for this discussion. She had come to impart. 'Rose is unwell,' she said. Her hands clenched. Then her eyes opened.

'Aha, I said to myself. When I saw you paired. Aha!'

Frances sat up. 'Dick Hollis is a pest.'

'My deah.' The vehemence of Frances' tone did not escape Mrs. Dewhurst. 'Quite in character,' she thought, at the same time wondering how she might turn the girl to her purpose without appearing to pry.

'Tell me,' she said, clasping Frances' hands, 'what *is* a foot?'

'Nothing. I slapped his face, that is all.'

'Capital. Simply capital.'

'You do not understand, Mrs. Dewhurst. I slapped him that he might return to where he is wanted—to Rose.'

Mrs. Dewhurst did not despair, although she stopped smiling. She accepted the rebuke. Her turn would come. Aloud she said, 'I did not wish Rose to come, Frances. Besides, Quentin has a cold.' In a mixture of pride and punishment Frances said, 'I think Dick is rather sweet really.'

Just then a Maori lad came in to tend the fire. To her surprise Frances saw that it was Billy. He went out without noticing her.

Frances was silent and Mrs. Dewhurst saw her chance. 'Your father, I thought, was looking quite ill just now.'

'Oh he often mopes at balls, Mrs. Dewhurst.'

'Perhaps not exactly ill. Rather, I should say, *distrait*. It must be Mr. Hossack's new post. Or, it could be the native question. Those wars. Dreadful, dreadful. And that Canterbury should be called upon to send volunteers to quell those *fiends* in the north! It is understandable—your father not being at his best, I mean. I keep forgetting that you've had bad weather. And no news. You have been quite cut off, I hear. Frances.'

Frances was smoothing her gown beneath the cloaks and puzzling about Billy.

'Then again,' Mrs. Dewhurst was saying, 'it could be the shock of Mr. Whitehouse's resignation. After all, they were at school together, weren't they? Whatever it is, I said to Arthur, it must be dire. Nothing less would cause Amos Polson to break a plate.'

'Papa did that?'

'Just now. In the card room. Delft. No, I beg your pardon—it was Rosenthal. I saw it with my own eyes. There had been a meeting of some sort, and your father was left by himself. If you are looking for your shoes, my deah, they are under the bed.'

Mrs. Dewhurst said ahem or something like it. Frances sat very still and thought. Then:

'You said something about Mr. Hossack?'

'Well.' Mrs. Dewhurst uncoiled her neck and sat bolt stiff with her hands pointed in her lap. 'Mr. Hossack has been made Land Commissioner and Mr. Whitehouse has resigned. Furthermore—'

'Mr. Whitehouse! But when?'

'Two nights since. Furthermore—now you must not question, my deah. Only believe.' Mrs. Dewhurst moistened her lips. The poor girl knew *nothing*. 'Now. Mr. Whitehouse has resigned because of Mr. Hossack's new law, yes. I have it right. You see. The appointment was not popular, as Arthur had predicted. No sooner had Mr. Hossack been appointed than he promulgated—I believe that is the word—a completely new regulation for the land. I don't know what it is, my deah, but the sheepmen were furious. And without waiting—my deah, it hadn't even been gazetted!—the sheepmen rode up and forced the council to meet extraordinarily. A pitched battle! Mr. Hay demanded that Mr. Hossack table his regulation. Mr. Hossack refused to table his regulation. The sheepmen then turned on

Mr. Whitehouse. There was this article, it had been in all the papers. Frances. The agriculturalists championed the article and attempted to chair Mr. Whitehouse round the room. *Then*. Mr. Whitehouse denied having written it and said he was pledged not to reveal who had. Mr. Hay said he had proof that *your father* was the author! Shouts and cries all round—I think I've got it right. Mr. Banfield tabled a motion demanding that a deputation wait upon the Governor in Auckland and Mr. Erk, he is the leaders of the small-holders, he is a rather vulgar man, Mr. Erk picked up his chair and broke it. The motion was lost—not all the sheepmen could attend, you see. Because of the weather. Mr. Whitehouse declared the proceedings inexact and went home. And Mr. Hossack was dusted, literally dusted off the table into the waste paper basket, Frances.' Mrs. Dewhurst paused for breath, and to observe. Frances was trying to calculate the effect of the resignation on her father. Mrs. Dewhurst's lavender complexion was suddenly quite close, as were her teeth. 'So you see. Frances. We too have had our little storm.'

'Resigned?' Frances was fastening the bows on her shoes.

'Now there is something else.' The older woman patted her arm. 'Do discover. He is very grand tonight, in his blue cloak, and *so* clandestine—'

'Mr. Whitehouse is here! Why didn't you say?'

'He is canvassing all the sheepmen. It is an omen, I said to Arthur. I have a soupçon—oh, do straighten your gown, my deah. Before you rush off. That's better. It is not true, is it, what they are saying—?'

Frances turned.

'I mean—that your father is ruined?'

Mrs. Dewhurst breathed through her nose. But with satisfaction, absorbing the girl's icy stare. 'Of course not. *But*. You see, just now. Mr. Whitehouse and Mr. Burcher and Mr. Hay, all poring over a map. I caught the word "hinterland". I am sure that some plan is afoot.'

Frances saw through the interrogation now. She tossed her head. 'Plan? Oh that's papa's idea. He thought of that ages ago.'

Mrs. Dewhurst gave a shrill cry and clutched Frances' arm. 'I was right, it is he! Your father. The Grey Eminence. I knew it all the time. But Frances. How splendid for you.'

Frances had slipped from the room. Mrs. Dewhurst was left on the bed. She stood up, dabbing her eyes which were more watery than usual. She had achieved her object. She had produced an effect. Her pale opalescent form seemed to touch the ceiling, and was almost heraldic. After a while her jaw began to work up and down. It was surprisingly loose.

Frances ran down two flight of stairs. Her arms were bare. She had forgotten her fichu. Her father was not in the card room. There was only an old gentleman spilling snuff who detained her for nearly five minutes by describing his journey from Christchurch, reclining on a feather bed on top of a cart. He complained that the colony was too young for balls. He was quite drunk.

She ran to the ballroom and back to the house again, trying all the rooms. In the library a woman was being violently ill under a row of boars' heads. She wore a purple creation resembling hide with Jim Crow figures picked out in gold. Nearby and quite unperturbed sat the chief surveyor, Mr. Burcher, with maps before him and a thick blue pencil in his hand. He waved to Frances abstractedly, and suggested she try the north supper room. She went out with the distinct impression that he had been drawing maps on the top of his bald head. The supper room was full of people and melting wax. Frances began to sneeze. She was jostled. She caught a glimpse of Albion Hay and Murdo Banfield talking in an alcove. There was also a young man in uniform. Albion Hay was knocking the casement with his walking stick. She began to question people at random, distractedly; her movements became less and less certain. More people entered. Mr. Whitehouse strode in, wearing a cloak. He walked right past her. Then he stopped, turned, bowed to her and continued towards the alcove. As Frances was leaving she was accosted by Mr. Plankton. He was eating mousse. It appeared to be coming out of his ears. He drew some moa stones from his pocket and said he was particularly anxious for her father to see them. She escaped by burrowing under a table. In the corridor she met Mr. Burcher again. 'No luck?' he said. "I should try the ballroom again.' Then the chief surveyor held up his thick blue pencil, erect as a flag, a few inches from his map and said, as if continuing a conversation: 'It is impossible to come upon the mountains from Odessa, quite impossible. Or am I mad, Miss Polson?' He looked at her so benignly that she almost blurted out something. 'You must ask my father,' Frances said and hurried on. 'Tell him,' Burcher called after her, 'it is the library, not the card room. We shall be there directly.' He disappeared into the supper room.

Once outside Frances forced herself to walk. 'So that's it,' she muttered. The air was tranquil. The trees waved with a pearly softness that seemed to descend directly from the thin swishing stars. People sauntered under the trees laughing, phantom sounds, picking up their dresses for the dew. In that grey softness the animals hobbled along the drive were less than solid, evanescent. And the mountains, overlying the roof of the woolshed, quickly fading.

There were about seventy people still in the ballroom. 'He *must* be here,' she told herself, fobbing off two young men and moving crabwise towards the musicians. Pieces of gauze and streamers were hanging from the chandeliers in filmy clusters. The dancers appeared chimerically, like well-mannered swamp hens stepping over stones. Hollis caught her, his carroty hair less dishevelled than angry. She smiled with relief and took his arm.

'Dick—help me to find my father.' She gave him a tug that was more of a jolt.

'You,' he said, 'are a caution. I want an apology.' Then he saw that she was in earnest and said, 'There he is.'

'Where?'

'By the stage.'

Polson was sitting on the edge of the stage partly screened by the big drum. As they approached he jumped up. 'Good. Francie, you're just in time. Um—' He turned. 'Hollis, be so kind as to do me a service. They will be along presently. Tell Hay I shall meet them here—there, that table with the roses will do, in the far corner. And when they are ready wave something. In the meantime, I intend to dance with my daughter.'

They made a few steps, then she stopped and studied him. 'Papa, you are not ruined, are you?'

'No, my girl. At least—not yet.' He smiled and they began to dance again.

'I was so frantic and worried. And here you are, quite cheerful.' (No, not quite, she thought. His feet keep losing their way.)

'An hour ago I was black as Albion's stick. That man had the manners to threaten me. There was a meeting, and I am afraid I walked out. There will be another one in a minute. I did it deliberately; I needed to think and I needed to talk to you. But—you had better tell me what you know.'

She told him what Mrs. Dewhurst had said.

'The trouble is,' Polson said. 'Yes, that is accurate enough: the Dewhursts have been pestering me all night, that is why I was hiding. The trouble is I no longer know where Matthew stands. I had a private word with him, but we were interrupted. Even so he was rather curt. It's understandable. He is worried. I have never seen him more worried. I know *why* he resigned — mind you, a verbal resignation only. He means to hold it over the Governor's head: either Hossack is recalled, or he goes. One difficulty is that nobody, not even Matthew, knows the precise content of Hossack's memorandum which sails for Auckland by tomorrow's packet. One thing is certain: gridironing is finished. And so, I fear, is cheap land. We may have to sell, my dear. Still, we don't know. Their fear is — I was thinking about this just now. I rather fancy Hossack may be acting on instructions from London and be about to revoke all the existing pastoral licences. And then it is they who will suffer. Their titles are, to say the least, somewhat shady. Now — you see, my dear, they lay all the blame at your father's doorstep.'

'Your paper?'

Polson nodded. 'It might be amusing if only Matthew were not susceptible to their arguments. He says my paper was too strong, which is nonsense. I am quite sure that Hossack's mind has been made up long since. By the by, would it upset you if we had to sell?'

'You mean the house, everything?'

'Everything.'

'Yes it would, papa. Very much.'

'Good. That is one thing clear. I like you in this mood. Now they want to blackmail me. Enter Polson's Plan. They are clever. It is all quite carefully done. They seek an escape route, an insurance. The land behind the mountains. It will always be cheap land, must be; and no rigmarole over native titles since there are no inhabitants.

'But, papa, we don't know that it *exists*.'

'I am coming to that. The amusing thing is that they are now convinced that it does exist. And the more I profess my ignorance, the more they are convinced. Even Matthew suspects me of half-truths, even he. There is so much trumpery and rogue dealing in their world they cannot conceive that anyone should be truthful and disinterested. If I had but half the subtlety they attribute to me I should by now be a very rich man. It's rather flattering.'

'I think that is Mr. Banfield now. Coming in with Mr. Hay.'

'Which Hay?'

'Mr. Donald. They are talking to Dick.'

'Dick Hollis,' Frances said.

'Oh yes. Well there is time. I am enjoying myself. It is a long time since we danced. What is that perfume?'

'It is only gillyflower.'

'Ah. Remind me to tell you of the spinet; it has the same scent. I think it's jacaranda. If this business goes well, I mean to buy it for you.'

'Papa!'

'Don't scold, and above all don't seem nervous. I mean to keep them waiting. In a moment they are going to put to me a proposition. So I fancy. And they will want an answer.'

'They want the key to our mountains.'

'Something like that. Has Matthew come?'

'No.'

The music stopped.

Frances said: 'The point is, do they know your real motive?'

'No. I think Matthew has been decent there.'

'Papa. Look at me. *Must* the journey take place?'

'No my dear, it mustn't. Except that there will always be a journey; and I would rather it took place under my auspices than theirs. We are back to my original argument.'

They began to dance again.

'What will you tell them?'

'I don't know, Francie. It depends really on you.' He looked at her severely. 'Is there a pass?'

'Of course there is. You believe that.'

'Ah, I believe. And the natives say. But *is* there?'

Frances was silent.

'Believing is no longer enough, Francie.'

'It is enough for me.'

'Once, you said there was a pass.'

'To tease you.'

'And now? What has he said since?'

'But—' Frances stared at him open-mouthed. 'Haven't you asked him yourself?' She saw that he had not.

'No, my dear. And for the life of me I cannot think why. But if I tell them that, they will suspect even more; and by God, girl, we must make them believe something tonight. Mustn't we?'

Frances said lamely. 'He is committed to finding it.' She felt miserable.

'Yes, yes. That isn't the same thing. Oh very well, you have answered my question.'

'But papa, surely! That is the answer. If you don't believe, how can you ever know? How can you ever know anything? Isn't that what the journey is all about?'

Polson was silent. His lips were compressed and he was frowning. His frown extended down the bridge of his nose to a point upon her throat. It was a waltz but he was barely dancing. She knew that at this moment he was making up his mind. She kept thinking of Droo's remark when her father had once attempted to drive the bullocks. 'Thir you doesn't know where you is from Adam's ox.'

'You are shivering,' Polson said.

'I have this faith, papa, this habit of thinking. That it will succeed—' Over his shoulder she saw Dick waving. She went on: 'And even if it doesn't succeed—'

'What is that at your neck?' Polson said.

'It is—it is greenstone. Mackenzie found it.'

'It came from up there?'

'Yes. I told you that.'

'I had forgotten,' he said absently. 'They are ready?' he added.

Frances nodded.

She could tell them all at the table, could feel their impatience; Thomas, droopy-eyed and appraising, lighting a cigar; Albion Hay sitting back chin on stick, the corners of his mouth turned down in an impassive smile—unlike his brother whose irritation always ran to his fingers which played, in pyramids, about the table-top; Whitehouse, grey and patrician in his green-lined cloak, tapping his pipe; that supercilious young man in uniform, it must be Banfield's son; and Banfield himself, disputatious and hirsute as a Turkish bey, and twice as round. It is not a nice feeling, she thought.

They had reached the stage, revolving indolently, when the Irish policeman leaned over and played an obligato to them. Polson looked up and brightened. 'Good, they are all there then. And Burcher has his maps. You know, Francie, they were looking at those maps in the card room; Burcher has the rivers picked out in red, like the figures on Mrs. Buckle's gown. As I went in I heard them saying, "It doesn't exist, a pass simply doesn't exist." I took Burcher's pencil and I drew a great blue line through the middle of Seagull Rock. He went off and studied that. When he returned he was quite annoyed by what I had done.

'They *are* getting impatient. D'you remember what Mary, your mother, used to say? She used to quote an Irish proverb. "It is to please himself that the cat wags his tail." Well, we shall please ourselves and keep them waiting a little longer. Twice more round the floor.' With that Polson picked up his daughter in a valse musette, and kept her at it. They were still turning when the music stopped.

'What will you tell them?' she said, preparing to leave him.

'*We*,' Polson corrected. He took her arm. 'I think, Francie, that we shall tell them the truth.'

There were two bottles of Chablis on the table alongside an enormous vase of tulle roses. The waiter had spilled a bottle. As they approached, Lady Suffolk left the group and Hollis brought another chair. The men looked askance at Frances. But rose and bowed perfunctorily. She was introduced to Nathan Thomas whom she had never met. He had a petit suisse beard and extraordinary nostrils. Everything about him was cadaverous. Banfield presented his son in the uniform of a volunteer, he was going 'to fight the niggers'; and descended, shimmying on his chair so that he almost fell off. Frances sat down rapidly, feeling scared. Her father was next to her talking affably and taking snuff, as he always did when nervous. He was talking about the spinet. How absurd that men couldn't control their feelings better in all those tight-fitting clothes, she thought. She felt a rankness of power coalesce and focus on her father. They would not look at her, any of them. Except for Whitehouse who touched her hand and slipped his cloak round her shoulders as he leaned across to Polson. She heard him murmur '*Cede repugnanti* . . .' or something like it and her father say, 'Certainly not.' Whitehouse chuckled in a nettled way. She could smell the gardenia in his buttonhole. Burcher, Hollis and Whitehouse were at one end, with the maps; Thomas and Banfield opposite her. Murdo Banfield's bulk, constantly shifting, began at the clavicle and projected across the table. The Hays were at her left, Albion Hay at the head. Albion Hay sat well back, one leg twisted and one shoulder raised, his eyes thin and bloodless, smiling sardonically. He had for Frances the fascination of a croupier, and she could not take her eyes from him. He held his glass, pointedly, his tongue playing over the rim, waiting for Polson to finish.

'I was right, Donald,' Polson was saying. 'Tell Lady Suffolk it is a Haward. Pepys had a Haward. He paid £6 for it. But in your case I would advise Lady Suffolk to sell it for not less than seventy guineas.'

'All right,' Hay said. He glanced at his brother, as did the others. Nathan Thomas was blowing smoke lazily through his nostrils. His lids drooped, as did his beard, which lay on his face like stubble left too long in the sun. Yet he was not asleep. His bulbous eyes had the intensity of a voyeur's. Albion Hay lifted his glass and said without taking his chin from the stick: 'We thought we should like to drink to the journey, Polson.' He did not seem to open his mouth.

'Why, yes. There can be no harm in drinking.' Polson's eyes were curiously awake as they drank. He was watching Whitehouse.

'We've got an offer, Polson,' Banfield said. 'And you'd better hear it.'

'Good. For I have none.'

'We can put up four thousand pound. And that's straight,' Banfield said.

'Dear me, that is almost as much as I was offered on a previous occasion.' Polson glanced at the next table where Arthur Dewhurst was sitting with his wife and Lady Suffolk. 'Yes,' he added innocently. 'It was an Australian.'

'This is a fair offer, Amos,' Whitehouse said quietly. 'I advise you to accept. More than that I cannot say.'

Polson said, 'It is a perfectly fair offer. But it is really beside the point. In return you wish me to indicate a pass that I do not know to exist and to give you unrestricted passage across my land for an undertaking which I do not believe, for private reasons, to be morally sound—at least until there is some form of responsible government in Canterbury committed to the interests of the natives. More than that I cannot say.' Polson smiled at Whitehouse, but the latter did not return the greeting.

'I am sorry, gentlemen,' Polson said. 'But I decline to join you.'

'Mad, mad,' Albion Hay muttered. 'In that case—'

Nathan Thomas laid a scroll on the table. He unrolled it and said distantly, 'Here are the signatures of twenty-six smallholders who are dissatisfied with conditions in Christchurch. When Hossack's new regulation becomes law they will walk onto your land. Understood? We shan't stop them.'

'And this is the counter-offer?' Polson spoke to the older Hay. 'I shan't mind that, Albion. I have no doubt that the signatories are real, as I have no doubt that you—some of you gentlemen—have incited them not to contain their patience. No, I shan't mind. Indeed it will be rather pleasant to have new neighbours.'

Polson could not tell from Albion Hay, whose eyes while not leaving his own rapidly scanned the table, if his bluff was succeeding. The silence lasted. Polson was perspiring. Idly he took a rose from the vase and stood it in his glass of wine.

The silence was intolerable.

At length Whitehouse said, 'Well, gentlemen. As I foretold, there is nothing to be done—at least until I return from Auckland.' The tone, which Polson judged to be of defeat, reproved them all, including Whitehouse himself. Whitehouse was angry at the attempted blackmail, angry at Polson for his obstinacy, angry at himself for having bothered to mediate. The man was tired and perhaps, his hands were fluttering, perhaps he was regretting his resignation. Polson was sorry for him.

Banfield was wheezing. 'God blast it,' he said. 'I haven't come fourteen thousand miles to be humbugged by the likes of you, Polson. You haven't sweated boots drainin swamps and improvin boundaries like we have.'

'That is so,' Polson replied. 'But then, I've always regarded myself as a tenant, not a landlord.'

Banfield lost his temper and swore, as Polson had hoped he would. Then he said, 'Say your mind, Polson. There's summat at back of it.'

'There is, gentlemen.' Polson spoke pleasantly. 'And it concerns the one man on whom the success of your scheme rests.'

'You mean Mackenzie, I suppose.'

'Yes, Matthew.'

'Let's drink to the beggar then,' Banfield said. 'For I'm damned if I can see way in this light.'

'Yes, let's,' Frances said.

They drank, with a kind of fumbling acquiescence.

'Where is he?' Thomas said.

Polson waited until the latter had put the scroll away. 'I want to be quite explicit,' he said. 'I stand aside from your venture. But I am prepared to give you Mackenzie to do with him what you will.'

'No,' Frances said, suddenly shrill.

'I am quite prepared,' Polson said.

Albion Hay said, 'Now why should you do that, Polson?'

'Yes why?' Thomas said.

'I am not his keeper, gentlemen. I am sure Donald has told you that.'

'I've said nothing.'

'Then it is time I did. The Scot is in my employ by a subterfuge. He belongs, if he belongs anywhere, to Blueskins—to this station.'

'You did not tell me that, Amos.'

'No, Matthew. I was sure that you knew.'

'What are your terms?' Albion Hay spoke acidly.

'Terms? Don't be silly. I haven't made an offer, I have stated a fact. I stole the man. Now I'm giving him back.' Polson turned to Thomas who was peering at Burcher's map. 'You asked where he is. He is on a mountain. As soon as he comes down I shall post him, here.'

Whitehouse stood up. 'Well, gentlemen. I think that solves your problem. I shall be getting back. The mail-boat leaves tomorrow and I mean to be on it.'

'Just a minute.' Donald Hay leaned forward, tapping his fingers down. 'There's no access from Blueskins. Hollis—you've explored the back country. Is there access from here? Or from Banfield's? Or from the east?'

'No, sir. I don't think so.'

'Don't you see? The only way to the pass is across Odessa, and he's barred that.'

Albion lifted his shoulder and appeared to wince. 'It's dead coinage, Polson, and I won't have it.'

Polson sighed. 'I thought you might grumble at that. Yes: my property is barred. Still, I'm sure if a way exists through yours Mackenzie will find it. If not—' He spread his palms and let them fall with a gesture of finality. 'If not, then you will have to wait.'

Frances looked from one to the other. Things had been going so well, and now they were all wrong again. Some of the dancers on the floor were looking, moving quite close. The band was playing dawn music. The lights were going down, deepening the camouflage that played over their table. Whitehouse was uncertain. Her father had shaded his eyes, playing with the tulle rose. How contradictory he was. How web-like! He had always loved counterpoint and now—she bit her lip; now she was beginning to suspect his duplicity herself. *Would* he give up Mackenzie? With a start Frances realised that the others were looking directly at her.

'I am afraid,' Polson said, resting his cheek on one hand and inclining his head, 'this means shifting more responsibility onto you, Matthew. It comes to this: If Matthew's bid succeeds and Hossack is recalled, the moment of urgency is past. If not, then I am sure you will all see to it that I am the first to suffer. If the others might see your map, Mr. Burcher? Thank you. Initially I shall forfeit the eastern basin, that marshland and these hills. And all my northwest boundary as far as—here, that rock: these river deltas, all this basined land to the gullies and onto the plain that confronts the rock. This rock, Seagull. Seagull is the gateway to the alps. North of it, those fan-shaped plateaus, I would retain. But everything south and west of it, those ranges, that great ribble of plain, all those concourses and streams which Burcher has picked out in an unidentified floral pattern, I would cede. There, gentlemen, is country enough for sixty expeditions to manœuvre; and there is your access.'

Polson was bored. He drained his glass. He was bored with the whole business. If at this moment Mackenzie had appeared he would have taken him on the stage and given him away publicly. There were about twenty couples left on the floor. As he looked he saw a figure wrapped in gauze descend from a chandelier and cross the floor towards him. His boots made no sound and he passed so close that Polson drew back in his chair.

But it was not that, not the shepherd's proximity nor even the enigmatic grin he wore that made Polson start: he believed he saw his wife's owl seal ring on Mackenzie's hand. Absurd! Whitehouse was bending over Frances, murmuring in her ear, taking back his cloak. He kissed her hand—it was one of the endearing things about him—and Polson heard him whisper, 'The next time you attend a meeting, my dear, bring a rug.' Frances was waiting for her father's signal to leave. But he was drinking—that was his third glass in succession. He looked as if he had seen a ghost. The men were looking at the map, over Albion Hay's shoulder. Burcher was drawing on his head again. Polson half rose to farewell Whitehouse. He did not hear what Whitehouse said to him. He managed to say, 'Good luck, Matthew,' and sat down again. He knew he should leave, but he had this feeling that he should remain, at least until the buzzing in his head went away.

'Mind you,' Polson said, causing them to raise their heads, 'I have this doubt. I cannot promise that Mackenzie will co-operate.'

Albion Hay's voice rose shrilly. 'For money, Polson, a peasant will co-operate with anything.'

'No,' Frances said, quite loudly.

She had risen. They were all looking at her. Out of the corner of her eye she saw Whitehouse, halfway to the door, stop, mumble to someone and then retrace his step. Lady Suffolk was with him.

'No,' Frances repeated. 'He will not co-operate—with any of you.' She said it flatly like a man, watching their suspicions rise to the surface again as in a looking glass. It was as if he had spoken through her. She knew a scintillating moment of power. They stared at her, half-fearing, half-believing.

Just then Lady Suffolk appeared. 'Amos—I have been waiting for you to finish. Amos, there is someone at the door. He is asking for you.'

Frances felt her whole body stiffen, and heard her father say Yes in a most unnatural way.

Lady Suffolk said, 'I would ask him in, but he is rather—you understand.'

'Of course,' Polson said, and walked unsteadily to the door.

The dancers were forming quadrilles to an air from an early French opera. The melody kept fading and returning on the strings of a bass lute. Frances was conscious that a number of people had gathered in the aisle. Also that a piece of streamer was fluttering over the door jamb where her father had gone out. It appeared to be trying to catch up with its reflection. But the shadow had a way of evading the streamer, of keeping just in front. Or was it the shadow that could not keep up?

'I do hope, my girl, it's nothing serious.' Whitehouse had returned and was standing beside her. For some reason they were all standing, except Albion Hay who had crumpled the map and was sitting sideways rubbing the ferrule of his stick across his nose. It was a heavy stick, tipped with silver. The heel, pointing upwards, kept hitting a chandelier, making the candles flare. Frances watched his fingers turn slowly white, blanching from the tips downward.

Polson returned and sat down with his hands on the table.

'It was Mackenzie, wasn't it?'

'No, my dear, it wasn't.' Nobody spoke. Polson stared before him. The words, when he spoke again, seemed to come from his lips some seconds after they had been formed. 'That was my manager. I am afraid, gentlemen, that my daughter is quite right. Mackenzie will not co-operate, not even with me. He has gone.'

Frances was slow to understand, as was everyone else.

'I don't understand, Amos.'

'Gone, Matthew. Quite gone. Gilliam has been to Seagull. There is no one there.'

For an instant Frances' heart leaped. Mackenzie had not come. But he had done something far, far better. Not even the look on Albion Hay's face could stifle the note of triumph in her voice.

'Good,' Frances said.

Albion Hay's face was so contorted as to appear misshapen. 'You mean—don't you?—that the journey has already begun.'

'I am afraid, Albion, that it looks very much like it.'

'*Looks* like it!' The other was suddenly standing, his saurian features full of a bitter loathing. 'Don't you see, don't you see what he's done? How he's tricked us?' With a sleight of hand remarkable in one so small he spun round and brought the stick down hard across Polson's knuckles. 'Rogue, rogue!' he cried, losing all control. He flung the handle at the bystanders.

The stick had broken. Polson regarded the blood on his hands.

Hunched forward, he appeared to be considering whether or not he should rise.

'Oh no, gentlemen,' he said, turning to them. 'I assure you, the trick is on me. You see, Mackenzie has taken all my sheep with him.'

And he remained like that looking up at them with his head on one side, like a bird; and gradually the pain that he felt was replaced by an expression reminiscent of the idol surmounting his stilthouse. Polson's face wore a droll smile.

BOOK TWO

THE JOURNEY

It was not true (the Hatter said later) that Mackenzie had taken all Polson's sheep: he had departed with only the five hundred merinos. Even this however was not the whole truth, although the Hatter could scarcely have known this. Mackenzie also took a bullock. He found the red bullock Venus bruiting along the river flats and he took Venus to carry his load. It was a mistake. The storm had left the beast skin and wind, and at the first stream it lay on its side and that was the end of Mackenzie's flour. The ox was his first mistake. His second mistake was to believe that he could remove a party of sheep into another country and bring them back unharmed. His third mistake was to imagine that he could bring them back at all.

It was a frosty October morning when he left Seagull. The land below was a gaunt porridge; and as he climbed into a sun sharpened by pinnacles of early gold, he did not doubt that gold was what they would find, or something like it, where they were going. He was pleased with the sheep, except for the slowest which was a bottle-shaped ewe with a band at the belly where the fleece had not grown. She kept sidling in the wrong direction and he thought, She is mourning her lamb that is down half-weaned by Gilliam. He did not think they were being followed, although he could not be certain what the sheep thought. The animals climbed in a race, breaking through the ice for toeholds, snorting and pawing. They had survived the storm in caves; now they hurried up the ravines on new levers snatching mouthfuls of green from the trunks as they went. They did not give him a care until the fifth day. On that day they entered the high canyon. Once, he had had no mind to put sheep up this gorge. He had thought it plain and he had thought it impossible; then he had remembered his forefather putting five hundred clansmen into battle and had matched the merinos with the men, and decided. Now, at the entrance to the gorge, his fears returned. A white torrent guttered from the base, silvered with ice and dirty at the edges. 'Now begins thy usefulness,' Mackenzie said to the dog, wetting his lips. He peered upwards. In six months all had changed. The gorge was a street of weddings, alabastered and silent as an apse. No crackle sounded. Then the ox lowed and snow was in his face; he drove Venus protesting, with his crook, up the descending flurries. He had with him the dog, the bullock and a sooty ewe —he had left the rest to graze on the helmets of islands at the entrance to the gorge. The bullock made tunnels as it climbed and the trees shook. Frozen birds toppled from the branches and the dog paused to tear one from the snow. But no precipice fell. The bullock scrambled on, groaning. It was shy at the knees. The knees shook with the cold. 'Tha weak-kneed, stupid-nosed, crying, turnip-ended mite!' Mackenzie cried. Venus had fallen twenty feet and started an avalanche. 'Mite!' he cried again, and Venus leaned up against a tree as if she had been put on the dole. 'Only the tree saved thee,' he thought, and stared at the river below his feet. The river had begun to sing. High up, branches stirred and the air seemed to quicken with hidden vibrations. Was Spring coming already? Wouldn't it wait for a man to mount? Furious, he hit the bullock on the nose. Venus gave him a look so reminiscent of Droo's that he took pity on the beast and sent it home. Later it occurred to him that he might have sent with it a note to the girl or at least unstrapped his blankets, but at the time he was glad to be rid of it. The brute was scared.

He looked up. The dog and ewe were already specks. Every few yards they tumbled, gripped scrub, shook themselves and went higher. Of the two the dog was the nimbler, but the ewe was unconcerned. 'That one will deliver us,' he thought. It was a satanic beast: one-eyed, quite black and a long dirty tail. He had chosen it to lead the flock because of its faulty sight; caution was wisdom. And because it reminded him of the seer he had known. He called it Christy after the seer.

He reached them at the waterfall. The water hung just as it fell, frozen, standing out from the cliff like a frayed bellrope. A ledge of ice barely three feet wide passed beneath; twenty yards on, he remembered, was a belt of bog pine where they might camp. He crawled through, staring into depths of shining glass —he could see down fathoms. The tree roots massed under the ice and the suckers reached onto the cavern floor. He stood up. He stood up too soon. His swag caught and he fell against the frozen arch. Going down, he saw the whole sheet move out from the wall and crash to the river below. He was lying on his back with his head and arms in space and the dog holding him by the haunch of his trousers. After that he cut steps with the tomahawk, and sent the dog and Christy back for the flock.

He waited, huddled under the precipice. The air was growing warm. The waterfall began to drip and the wetness soaked through him. High up a crepitation sounded; tapers glinted; coronals shook and descended in flurries; boughs bent in the crepuscular light; boughs creaked; and the feeling deep within him grew of a dam about to burst. He waited.

The first mob came quickly; the last with an intolerable slowness in semi-dark, wreathed in falling snow. They came in files of fifty, Christy at the head; and he counted them over the ledge 'ho, ho, ho,' spoken very softly between his teeth, and couched them steep under the pines. He shared his sodden biscuits with the dog after her tenth trip, and spent the night against a tree, hearing the crashes of the river. He thought the mountainside was lifting. But in the morning it was still there, the sheep lumped together like boulders in that peculiar giddy way that only melting snow can suggest. The hillside was straked with red and black dirt; snowberries and yellow anise had appeared, everything else had slid into the river. The river ran a bright pipeclay. Down there—they had waded in whole; now (he heard the roar) the river damned the gorge completely. 'We mun clear out,' he said, rousing the flock. And they climbed all day with a sense of peril.

For two days scrub held them and he came to hate the black olearia that grew in fences twenty-five feet high. Nothing stayed with the foot, neither root nor slate nor the sticky argillite clay, everything fell and was torrent and the hollow roar never left them. Nothing saps an animal more than the terror of noise, yet the animals' terror was less than his own: snorting, they sprang upwards out of the path of falling boulders with the adroitness of goats. Some of the boulders were as big as churches. He saw that the river had piled them, heaped confusedly together, almost to the treeline. At length when they seemed to be gaining on the ribbon of light overhead, the walls arched in blotting out everything and they were forced down a steep rampart that shone wetly in the gloom. It was straight shingle to the river's brink. The sheep slid down with an insolent pride that made his lips shake. But they would not enter the water. There were thirty yards of ink to cross, flat calm, in the lee of the rampart; the rest was watershoot, a lather of arching turbulence. Nor would the dog be persuaded to swim underneath it. She shrank into the rock. 'God save us,' he cried, snatching her up. He would never forget the look she gave him as he launched her flying into the air. Then she was persuaded. A rat and a ground owl watched her arrival from the far bank. He flung Christy and the rest followed. He went last on buoys of flax. He found the animals tearing up plant life that bloomed marvellously in dense shade; he lit a fire and dried out for the first time in a week.

They were three more days getting out, because of the miracle of Spring. It was the worst miracle he ever saw. The country was too new; they cross-trekked; they walked mostly with their heads in their feet; and he said to the dog on the day of rest, 'Thee has never seen God make hills with an worse whetted saw nor this.' 'What d'you expect?' the dog inquired. 'D'you expect crags to lie down flat?' 'No,' he said. 'But I would give mine front teeth to graze in an field of turnip.'

He saw the needle opening in the sky at the same moment that the eagles found them: they careened low over the backs of the flock and he put up his stick as the talons swept to a wing's width of his face. The eagles floated away on an up draught. Now the needle was very close. It was two pillars buttressed by slabs of rock. 'Green lass, green,' he said, for the opening was the colour of a Persian heaven. He climbed with a tearing heart and one boot failing, and the word Victory was on his mouth. But he did not utter it. He stood beside one of the pillars dejected.

'We might just as able have gone to market, lass,' he said. Beyond was nothing but blankness and fog. There was no vegetation of any kind.

The sheep had gone past him, growing faint in the mist. As he followed, he remembered thinking it was night and dropping his oilskin. Then two voices swam about him. One upset his swag, spilling his things and drew him back. It was coppery, clove-scented, a voice that he knew. It said, 'Avoid'. The other was a wheedling note and plucked him on, saying 'Believe, believe'. That voice he also knew, although it was the voice of a sibyl. But the worst of it was that his mind paid heed to neither, it sank to his feet and they carried him on regardless. Mesa-like structures loomed and his feet did not have the sense to skirt the bases but took him up, onto the stones, and one boot gone. He stumbled across and there facing him was another structure. Or was it one of the pillars? He stared at it. He was back where he had started and there was the dog holding out a bruised paw with a thorn in it, utterly bewildered. 'You are very careless,' the dog said, 'to lose your things.' He removed the thorn. 'Unclean,' the dog said. 'Unclean.' He felt his face, it was covered with sores. Then the pillar spoke, 'Avoid, avoid' and the scent of cloves was in his mouth. She was beside him. He locked the girl in his arms, crying bitterly. 'Woman,' he said, 'Mine woman' and they murmured together incoherently. But he did not fling himself back into the opening that presented itself. What transfigured everything was the image of a hag's face in the shape of a tree, and the rich wheedling tones beckoning him on—'Believe, believe'.

He woke. The dog was licking his face and the sun was beating down. The flock was bleating. He was lying on a mound of sprung thistle, bootless, and a colony of rats was devouring the biscuits. His belongings were scattered over an area. He found his boots, then the candles and oilskin, his knife, the holdall ... he went from one to the other, trying to recollect. He set his legs apart and gazed up at the slab of ash-white limestone set upon the pillars of yesterday. Drawn up at one end, wings outspread, was a solitary eagle with a bad-tempered nose. 'Have we come through unscathed?' he thought. His eye followed a string of ants on the ground. He spun about. Here were jumbled stones. They led in a line, like ancient breastworks, to a low saddle; and there in the gap were the mountains. 'Mary!' he cried, as if to battle, and rubbed his eyes. 'Mary begotten!' (To distinguish the other.) He broke into a run. As he ran he slapped the sheep to warm them and gave them the words of Isaiah, '*This is the way, walk ye in it.*' Black Christy and the leaders were already there, also the dog, as he came up the incline. The dog was looking out with her back to him, her tail waving like a bottle brush. She was turning her head gravely from side to side, as if the immensity of what lay beneath was too great to contemplate. And so it was. 'Mai-reee!' He cried once more. His voice dropped into total silence.

He hesitated to go down. Between discovery and possession there is always a moment. It seemed a crime to interrupt a primeval stillness. Something plucked his sleeve and he heard the fluted voice, half heard the coppery tones, but he could not catch the words. Then a hawk plummeted down with a petulant scream and rose again from the ground with weighted talons. And in that struggling speck, an atom, he saw the whole. His blood surged. He passed a hand across his beard, 'Come lass,' he said. ''Tis an mortal place.'

So they went down, a man, a dog and five hundred sheep, although it did not occur to him to count them until some days later. He was surprised to find they were all there.

It was the colour of honey.

It was not a plain, nor a basin, it was more nearly a continent. It stretched away on the left hand further than the alps. And the alps were the whole horizon from north to south.

Eleven and twelve thousand feet high, they broke the clouds like the uplifted camps of armies before a battle; and the sunlight, striking off the tents, revealed grasses in zones of more than honey: amber and blue and silver, and the trailing bronze of sea vetch that hangs on the ebb of a great spring tide. The dog led them down frisking easy, into the north west corner, and everything was as natural as ever it was. The ground was corrugated, never quite level, with a shifting hardness that puzzled him. The sharpness of the light made him catch his breath. It sharpened the tussocks the length of fifty mile, though he guessed it was nearer five hundred—it was bigger than

Australialand. Certainly it was nearly as big as Scotland. Had the Polson *seen* all this? Bleary-eyed little Polson? If so, the Polson was a very great man.

Yes, but what had caused it?

At the north-west corner he was stopped by terraces at the base of the mountains—the river had sprung up again. The mountains were black and strange; furrowed where streams gushed out but otherwise strange and black. He could not reach them. So he set up a cairn in the north-west corner and inscribed the letter P on it. And in the bark of a solitary rimu he cut *POLSON'S LAND* in letters four feet high.

In the morning he told the dog, 'I mun take the news down. An thee stay guard the flock, thee wait.' The dog had brought him a game hen. She shook the feathers from her mouth and was gone. When he had eaten the dog was a mile off, driving the flock hard into the south. Didn't she understand 'wait'? The wee whore! He halooed. He was two hours getting to her, marching under a rampart. By then his temper had abated and instead of punishing her he read her a lecture. 'The curious thing lass is—nay beasts. Nay mammals, look. There is an bat an its nest of fleas: an the native rat; an the black rat that I ate last night baked in the jacket.' And that, he told the dog was all. It was a land of birds. The dog sniffed. She would get on. She knew the birds. They were unnatural: hopping instead of flying or gliding through the brush or appearing from rotten logs with phosphorescent beaks or hanging droop-eyed in the branches, they scared the wits out of her when they did that. It wasn't natural. It wasn't hunting. So little notice did they give her she might have been a lemur.

But that, he said, was part of the mystery. Look. And he took her up onto the terraced rampart to see the river. It was the same river had walked with them from the Pacific, he said. It had begun as a fan of shingle. As the plains mounted, it had dug. In the foothills it had cut steps and raised terraces, those barred ramparts above Odessa. Emerging from a ravine, it shed grazing. Whenever it tired of cutting it shed a basin or a delta. The hills were delineated by its skins. As it laboured to reach the alps it deepened, until suddenly it merged pitch with the bluffs of that gorge. It had cut that pass. Breaching the top of the range, it had gathered itself for a final assault, had failed and died. 'So I thought, lass. But wait.' As he led the dog up, he imagined the land buckling—fissures appearing, to be clothed in forest; crevasses, to be hollowed by the wind and become tarns; the air, steeped in a hail of falling rock. The animals had perished every one, but not the birds. The birds were the messengers of the spirit, look. Then the seeds had nurtured on the decaying animals and the grubs had come, all the lizards and insects, in order to feed the birds when they returned famished and out of exile, after first dusting themselves.

'So thee sees, lass, how the birds has multiplied? The animals has died so the birds shall live.'

They had reached the top. They stood on high shoulders.

'An all this, lass (he pointed) yon river has done, look.' For, emerging from the pass, the river clearly did not die—it began again, serpentining, repeating terraces, each uniformly stepped and higher than the last. They rose in tablets of blue shot with bands of yellow ochre and quartz, the quartz white as milk: perfectly parallel, perfectly symmetrical. From these shoulders the tablelands overflowed like granaries. He looked down, following the river's course to the point where it lay far beneath them, an imperturbable green. He counted them. There were twenty-six terraces on each bank, layered like salted pancakes, rising to 2000 ft above the bed. 'That high we are, lass.'

A few miles south and the river twisted, expiring into the snows whose polar caps annihilated everything.

'So in them (he remembered the words of Polson)—in them is everything beginning?' Up there was the river born? Then the mountains by destructing were lifegiving.

Then the mountains, he told the dog, are a parable.

Then (he was quite logical) the cause of it all was a parable, was God. 'Is that what tis, lass?'

The dog sneezed (she was quite wayward). She would not look at him. She pouted her cheeks in the gargling way that she had and flounced off the terrace in the sunlight. 'Just like a woman,' he thought. He laughed, simply to be high in the antiseptic air. He named the river the Hewer as he had named its realm Polson's Land. Then he went down to cross it from north to south without giving the bleary-eyed founder another thought.

The Hatter claimed (later) that Mackenzie was twelve weeks in that land. The Hatter said he found twelve notches cut in the man's chanter, and from that he assumed. But the Hatter's

THE JOURNEY

account is not reliable and it is to be doubted that he ever discovered the chanter. In any case Mackenzie did not cut a mark only on the Sabbath, he made notches on other days too.

There were two ways to cross the plain. One was to continue as they were along the western edge, a way of obstacle. For every few miles the snows sprawled, extending an arm, a rib, a humped fellfield. The other route lay down the eastern edge under the bluffs of a frontal range, and was scarcely more attractive: it was miles off and meant recrossing the plain. In the end the dog decided. She set the sheep on a path of her own, diagonally towards the middle.

At first hawks troubled him. They wheeled over the backs of the leaders, both the falcon and the bigger loping harrier. The harriers filled the eddies, watching from on high, until the falcons drove them off and returned alone. He blew horrible notes on the chanter to let them know he was about; and the falcons mistook the chanter for a weapon and soared out of range. It was an eagle that made him cross. It dropped so rapidly he had not the time to open his lips, and it drove a talon in the side of a ewe that he called Delilah. Once he had seen an eagle bind a roe deer in Scotland, and the deer had won. Now he watched, fascinated. The flock was ahead of him, moving out of a wooded gully when the eagle struck. The ewe turned screaming and plunged back into the trees, beating itself and the eagle against them as it ran. 'Ha!' Mackenzie cried, and ran into the wood, following the sound of crashing. The ewe ran a mile. He found her in a pant with a ghastly smile on her face, standing. Her side was raw. The pelt was bared from neck to rump and fixed to the end of the pelt was a talon and one half of the eagle. Nearby, attached to the bole of a tree, was the other half where the vulture had clung in an effort to stay the ewe. The ewe had not been stayed and the eagle had been torn asunder. So it had been with the roe.

'Thee has an pretty gallop,' Mackenzie said to the ewe. He laid back the pelt and stitched it and treated the beast with unguents of flax and crushed herbs, and waited for her to die. The ewe recovered and they travelled on.

It was curious how he came to trust the dog. At first he had worried for her remembering the parable of the animals and the birds, and gave her little attentions, more than was wonted.

Sensing this, she in turn became more affectionate and he would discover her hairy pads or an ear flap laid on his chest in sleep. Or again in dreams, when she appeared close, unreasonably staring, with eyes like shocked plums. Now, though the ground was broken, and cut up by blind creeks, he trusted her implicitly. Her route never deviated. When the first of the oystercatchers came, flying in V-shaped formations towards the Pacific, they confirmed the dog's route. They drew a straight line to the centre. As he walked Mackenzie poked the ground; he turned up axeheads and flint knives and pieces of greenstone — godheads like the one at his neck. 'Thee has been here at another time,' he told the dog. They seemed to be following an ancient path.

So he let her be, and she would be lost in the grasses for hours on end. For the first time he was free to look about him: to watch the locusts rising long-legged in billows, until the whole honey-coloured fastness was covered with a veil; to see a branch snap clean under the settled weight of their swarm; to observe two gossamer white moths embracing on a flax leaf; to notice a tuatara lizard or a carabid. The way was alive with weka, the obese ground hen whose fat preserved the flax sandals he made every second day, and his feet. Beady eyes followed him with a walrus squint: on looking into dustbowls he discovered owls with green whiskers. They screamed '*Ta-aa!*' as he passed. The very slowness of the march was invigorating. Migrants confirmed their route daily, passing inland, and long afterwards the peaks would echo to a microtonic piping: the gargle of the curlew, the creak of the stilt, the plangent chorus of the tiny wry-billed plover. But nothing impressed him as did the high whistle of the godwits piercing the haze of those still October evenings.

Every so often a basaltic boulder reared like a megalith, and he would fix that and count his paces to it; again he would fix the horizon, another megalith or a dead tree clustered with purple black berries, and march towards it. Every day he did this. But in that altitude and in that light, the distance they had to travel seemed in no way to diminish. They marched by the light. The noon light was white, dead white; it made him purblind. As the peaks crowded in and the still whiter peaks behind, he would feel his eyes recede sharply and rub his twinging brows, and stop. Everything stopped. The sheep clotted together moodily.

The dog lay still. Even the lizards, baking among the smoother pebbles, looked at him with little gasping sounds. He would wear the opossum rug and all his clothes to keep the heat out and look for a stream. The creeks that gathered silt tasted of zinc. He would find a clear pan and lie head down till the fishes stared. The light of morning was scarcely less intense. It burned back off the snows, drawing the horizon to him, so that he had only to lift a hand, it seemed, in order to touch it. The light at daybreak was best—they would march ten miles in two hours. In its amber rays the silt on the riverbeds, dried to a fine powder and hollowed into dunes, revealed an underlying richness of shot velvet. These dunes shouldered the dry watercourses for miles and as the sheep passed in the early morning ghostly against the tundra, the silts ran in showers beneath their hocks: silver on copper, bronze on rose, dove grey on rowan red. The afternoons were often grey and sultry and they would march to nightfall. In the evenings a haze would descend through which only the mountains were visible, rising like islands in a fog. Seldom were the clouds absent. They came and went with the suddenness of the locusts. They nourished the whole landscape. It was the clouds, he realised—the scud and race of them—that made the country unlike any he had ever seen.

He never marched the Sabbath. He would find a stream and read aloud from the Book of Psalms; for the land in its variety seemed to him not unlike a psalm of David. He would kneel on the bank and intone the psalms out loud, first speaking and next wailing, in the eldritch way. Then he would say a prayer and jump into the torrent, stark naked.

He became aware that the ground was tilting; as they marched towards the centre it seemed to dip mysteriously out of sight. At the same time the dog muddled him. Her pile had been terribly torn in the gorges and at first he thought she was troubled by sores. He would discover her on a knoll, standing in a frieze, tail dragging, searching the flock from afar. Then she would rout them in circles, distracted. 'I am dissatisfied with their movement,' she explained once, when he had criticised. She continued her incursions, as if engaged in irregular warfare. He watched her. She was at odds with herself. For two days they made scarcely any progress. Once, crossing a riverbed in blinding sand, she flung herself onto the backs of half a dozen sheep and all but drowned them. 'Thee will cast thyself into swamp and become a taniwha like Tamatea's dog,' he roared at her. In camp she sulked, sitting apart from him. One night in camp she raked the flock entire. The animals had arrived winded and ill-tempered, drifting out of a cold wind like lumps of timber congealing with the tide. They had sunk their immense triple chins under cottonwood. Now they rebelled. Out of fatigue they plunged, snorted, reared through the thickets; he saw them streaming under scudding clouds into the open, the dog in pursuit. He stared into the moonlight, weeping softly, for he had seen horses go mad after eating loco weed in the Australian desert, leaping over tufts and dying in agony, shunned by the rest of the herd. He believed the dog was approaching that condition. But in the morning she ate sowans with him and showed him the flock. It was grazing in five lots. After sowans it moved off the same, in five lots, and all the day maintained that order: the front lot with Black Christy, the second lot with the ewe with a wart on its nose, the next with the ewe Delilah that had the pelt all stitched and a broken horn besides, the fourth with the big ringstraked ewe that was speckled and spotted like Jacob's cattle and the final lot with the longtailed ewe that missed her lamb and was the forlornest lot of all. Now he could at a glance tell the distribution of his forces — for they couched by night the same as they marched by day, in lots — and he told the dog praises for drilling them in such a royal fashion.

Like himself, she was much given to orderliness.

Yet now he grew careless. They had been marching for two weeks when he missed his spare shirt. He had dropped it. Likewise his socks and a penknife. He threw away his fork. His rat trap he burned for kindling. He did not know why he did these things, often he did not bother to cover his feet. A pair of sandals made from flax lasted two days. When they fell off he would walk on, not noticing, until a smell took him. He would see his feet and be appalled. After he met the berry, he grew more careless than ever.

There was a purple black berry that he strangled in a bag to make wine. It grew on a bush like a salt bush. But it occurred also in parasitic clusters hanging from the boughs of petrified trees. He began drinking the berry juice when he had nothing left for staple but fern root. (He had brought supplies for two weeks. The last, his sowans and sugar, had gone to the rats. Then he had skinned the rats and boiled them in the wine as a form of protest.) The berry wine tasted bitter. There was an aftertaste of bitter almond, but it seemed to sustain him.

'For courage,' he would say to the dog, raising his pannikin and grinning with an abnormally dark tongue.

Also it seemed to make the journey shorter.

As they descended between the ranges he began to dispute the march, turning the flock east out of clefts or detouring above bush that appeared suddenly in their path, invisible from afar. Yet however much he changed course, the ground dipped mysteriously to the centre. 'Tis the berry, lass,' he would say; until it was a joke between them. The dog would have none of his drink, until they came to the desert. Here the berry grew plentifully and he was glad of that. He found he could no longer do without it.

At first he barely noticed the change. He had a little water in a bag made from a sheep's bladder, and a spare pair of sandals. Gradually the grasses faded until only a pallid vetch showed and as their hunger mounted the sheep, conservative of stomach, refused the change of diet. Then the extremes intensified—a glacial cold by night, a pitiless heat by day—and he thought of turning back. Not for the sheep, whose insulation would have contained infernos, but for the dog. Yet she it was who led them on, almost gaily, husking over the hot stones with an ease bordering on insolence. Again he thought: She has come here in another life. Given a choice of direction, he would stop. At a crevasse or channel that faulted three ways he would stop, bewildered. She never hesitated. It was as if some desert mechanism came into play by which she bypassed the heavy thought processes necessary to man; and though her bruised pads and stuttering glances cried out constantly for water, she never chose badly. The berry helped her—he made a jelly with it and bathed her pads. As for the sheep: they clambered on one another's backs to reach the fruit whenever it grew down, self-engrafted, from the trees. It was greed, not thirst, he thought, watching them bite through to the black kernel. Their lips turned negroid and at night the camp stank of fetid almonds.

It was not true desert but a torrent causeway of ancient riverbed and moraine, and waterless: a dry shingled torrid place. It was shaped like a gigantic fan, ever widening, and capped with steppes of glacial silt, steely in the early frosts but already smoking by mid-morning as if the sun had touched an invisible paper lining. The sides seemed to thrust back the flanks of the very mountains. After two days his eyes stung as if scorpions inhabited them. He cut his blanket for a cape, with slits for the eyes and another for the nose, and wore it like a keffiyeh, *sur tout*. Peering out he saw the peaks, that imperfect frontier, shimmer, wobble and finally disappear. In the shingle's glare the horizon turned quite white. He thought they made four miles in the morning and another two at evening. The moon had waned. Night marching became impossible. For a time he ate rats and occasional grubs. Then they too disappeared. His sandals perished. As the heat intensified, the sheep rolled over exhausted or sank into old flood licks. The floods had thrown trees into the bare arms of other trees, grotesquely embracing, host in turn to colonies of ants whose castled pyramids swayed petrified in the air. All sense of familiarity vanished. He had never knowingly sought civilisation or history. What was civilisation if not a footprint on the land? History? It was within him. But nor had he sought this—this descent into Nowhere. At every turn the way fell, yet always the horizon curled up at the edges, like a saucer. The dog's confidence maddened him. 'An shall we get *out*?' he shouted, taking her by the neck. He had stopped—a perfectly level place. She shook him off. In despair he sat down and began squeezing the berry. Fifty berries made a mouthful. Two hours' squeezing slaked the dog. Another two hours of it and hope revived in his own feet, hope lay nowhere else. His feet were blistered, but they ached only dully and each day less and less, like an old dream that recurred each day about this time. It was a childhood dream and it left him slack: no one had told him that hope might lie in the layers of an inherited memory. He saw a place, a thorn tree on an island in a loch. People had burned seaweed there and purple asphodel and nearby in a fold of hills was a copse. But the tree was paramount. The tree was encircled by a wall of stones and the trunk and boughs were studded with nails on which hung tatters of ribbon and clothing. Alongside was a well where his father had been cured of a raving. Lunatics were taken there without consent. Nearing the island they were flung out into the loch, then pulled back into the boat. Landed, they were led up with a rope tied to their middle and made to drink of the well. Then an offering was made to the tree. He had gone there as a boy secretly, taking a dog that was mad. It was night. He climbed the wall and the spirit spoke to him.

'Ah, boy, what is your wish?'

'The cure of madness,' he said.

The spirit sighed. 'Make your hands into shovels and return to the earth as a worm; all is forgotten.'

Then the well vibrated with a hollow sound. He ran to the stone orifice and saw a white face peering up at him from crystal depths. It was strangely inviting. But he put the dog in the well instead, and the next day it died.

There was a change in him after that. He did not grow bags under his sex, as other boys did; though he was strong as they were. The Douglas, his master, said there was a word for it and that it was a punishment for drowning the dog; but Mackenzie regarded it as a curse of nature for his forgetfulness. He had left the tree without offering so much as an acorn.

And why, he wondered later, if the tree made boys sexless, did they call it the place of light?

The dog was licking the juice from his chapped feet. Mackenzie woke — or rather blinked at the eye of a tuatara lizard. The lizard was baking at his feet. It was lime green. Its centenarian skin had folds of rhinoceros yet it was no bigger than his finger, and it curled into the ground out of his reach. So worms turned, he thought. He dug down with his fingers. It was still warm even under the earth. Did God dwell there? Or some other spirit? He remembered what the Maoris said — the earth, they said, was greater than the sky, the body was greater than the spirit. Otherwise Maui the demigod would have lived as a bird. Instead he chose to die as a newt, he was crushed even as he crawled up between the thighs of the Earth Goddess.

'Ay, an twas a grand death,' he mused, meaning mysterious.

He stood up, feeling in some way magical, like the well behind his thoughts. Everything shimmered. Pieces of sky fell blustering over a dry sea and far off (he began walking) in a fold of three hills was an oasis topped by a great tree. He saw it clearly: a place of water and grey-green bush, and the tree brightly waving. Then it vanished.

The dog slopped down, craving company. He fondled her neck. The white blaze, the languid eyes reminded him of the face in the well; made her somehow exciting to him.

He gave a bitter laugh. 'No sex, lass. No sex, an I would lie with thee, an it be unnatural.'

She was restless, in some way desperate: though not in heat. A sly desperation, wanting to get on. 'I canna, lass.' I am sick, he thought. 'An so are they,' he said, watching the sheep nudge the wretched gravel, weakly staring at their own bile. Their hocks ran a livid green. He had noticed the scouring before. They would die without water.

Savagely he cut a boil from his foot, and spat. His mouth tasted of bog iron. 'I am sick, lass,' he cried, knowing it for a lie, and burst into tears.

Whenever he was overcome he did childish things. There was a cleft nearby. He climbed up and sat in the opening with a bent back and his legs curled up, like a worm. There was nothing magical about his thoughts here: only a girl brightly gartered, bending at a trough sluicing the water from a bucket down her flowing black hair. Yet even as he tasted the cold water and the mingled scent of gillyflower, the mirage came back and a voice called, entreating, from the desert. It brought him rocking to his knees with an almost palpable strength, as if the sex force were returning. The dog had seen too—he caught the sly grimace, the knowing stare, and he fought the dog as he fought the vision, putting it from him. 'I will go back, I *will* go back,' he muttered. He wanted none of this second sight, this immortality that sat like an inherited sore within him. He wanted his senses back.

Also he wanted a bowl of the girl's motherly soup.

The dream passed, leaving him limp, and the dog licking his sweating soles. 'Terrible lass, to coop in daylight,' he said; and was quite unable to get up. So he sat in the cleft all day looking on an empty sea, without ever understanding that the price of freedom is loneliness.

A storm came. He saw the dog look up, the black cloud descending and the dog race tail streaming to bind the sheep. One minute she was running and a string of petrels flying over her, the next everything was gone and the air black with flying insects. He could not see his hand in front of his face. The inside of the cave was a baker's oven. He put his head between his knees, heard the sound of trees shiver and split, felt the holocaust as the living streams wave on wave collided with his face and hands; knew the sickly revulsion of dead and dying in his mouth, his ears, and staggered out into silence. The wind had died, although he would have said there had been no wind. A brown dust was settling. Lightning displaced the ochreous void. Shapes formed. And there out of sliding darkness the glaciers were revealed, stretching themselves lazily on a sheet of pure lilac. Below him, curiously formal, was the litter of dried plums where the sheep had stood; and a little way off the flock waiting, like a multitude praying.

In the morning they continued.

He watched the scouring of the sheep increase with a sense of dread. Their craving for water grew intense, as they marched their throats parted in a dry rattle; nor did the sound cease in the night. Surprisingly they maintained their discipline of five groups; but at night they congealed (absurd, he thought, with all this space around them) and he cooped in the midst of their stinking bed, out of sympathy.

The berry only increased their agony, he discovered. He beat them off whenever they tried to reach it. The vetch persisted and he wet his tongue on the dew of the leaves. But the sheep would not touch it. They were selfish brutes. They were selfish about dust bowls. Yet in other ways they did bravely. Often, discerning a patch of vegetation, hebe or onion weed, the strong would butt the weak towards it; and whenever a ewe slumped, another would station herself alongside and wait patiently for the first to rise.

Water there was. They would come upon fissures clothed in scrub, the sides sheering to a cold stream; and no way down. Or they would look up into rain forest, (the marvel of green after the glare of shingle), forests beyond chasms, remotely gullied under the alps; and no way across. It rained in the mountains and once a cloud burst behind them. He drove the sheep back amid jets of steam to find the moisture already dissipated.

So they continued, a dim little army, along the labyrinthine path that led only the dog knew where.

One day he stopped and stared. There beside him was a footprint; his own. They were crossing a sand flat. His mind, always pictorial, drew a small but useless comfort. Still the way was stony, pitted with flints and the interminable eroded channels and here and there a knoll of grey bunch grass; and only an occasional ti palm to break the endless glare. Still the horizon fused white and seamless with the mountains and there was no reality but the long hours of marching: the pebbles under his feet, the rasping bleat on the stones, the morning halt and the slow crushing of the purple fruit; the profound sleep, wine induced; then the road again, the stench of steaming pellets, the dog's tail waving.

He cared for her daily, and neglected himself. He did it for the self-sufficiency in him that was male and his true state of health; and because afterwards that state would be judged by the heart of his companion. Whenever he dropped retching to his knees, she rounded with agonistic glances and herded him on, like a sheep. He dropped things now with that carelessness of an emptied mind that seemed almost a condition of survival.

He found a horse potato that he had overlooked. The ends had perforated the bottom of the bag and each day they grew a little towards the ground. He looked regularly to see if they would curl upwards towards the sky. 'Twill rain then,' he thought.

He became fascinated by the ants and crane flies that nestled in his toes. As he walked his knees knocked together negligently, but the ants clung, coating the scabrous feet with a warm and microscopic insulation. They fed the illusion that he was in some measure protected, though the comparison with Solomon never occurred to him. After a time they discovered the awful forest of his legs and climbed up underneath his trousers. The next morning he woke to find them gone and a wood pigeon sitting on his knee, giving thanks for a surprising meal. It flew off tumbling into the south.

'Saved, lass, saved,' he said, taking it for a sign. But no omens were repeated that day, only the gravel beds projecting frontally, like strips of withered orange peel. That evening the dog brought him a bird, a poor stilt with a broken beak, long dead. But looking on the flock, he could not eat it. He cooked it and gave it to the dog. She opened her mouth and remained like that, clutching the pinion between swollen gums and staring at the fire with a maniac concentration. He left her and walked into the night alone. The animals stirred hardly, their lapped chins drooping to the stones. They had not the strength even to face out of the wind. 'An if I hadna been baptised I would be no better than thee,' he said, walking on into the night: angry at their bloodied lips, at their mute submission, angry that he could not explain what he felt—that some vile retribution was at hand. Retribution for what? As he walked he laced and unlaced his fingers making cat's cradle, as if to unravel the mystery. It was difficult to make, walking and no twine; but easier kneeling in some dim growth. 'O great God,' he prayed. 'Give me force to know mine enemy.'

The cat's cradle would not come out. He had played it since he was a child, and it would not come out.

It came in the morning. He was kneeling in rank weeds. Companies of white birds were saying 'greep greep' to his face and studying their reflections in a pond of water. He got up with a hobble and a 'ho ho ho,' the silliest sound he ever did. But his fingers for a reason he could not fathom were knotted together, and he fell face down in the swamp. 'Blue Jesus,' he said, and plunged again. The water was all blue. He gobbled it. After that he smiled. He had not smiled for so long it hurt. He continued to smile into blue Jesus and waited for the water to inform him if he had changed. When the water settled it informed him he had not changed, and all his teeth were present. Then he ran, hurling rocks to tell the others. Indeed they came, when told.

The next morning he gaffed an eel and it was forty feet long. He baked it in sections and laid it in his bag where the flies found it by noon. His bag was a stink pot and all the ends of the potatoes had turned up.

Subtly, imperceptibly, the feeling of the landscape was changing. Pale flutings came out of the ground and ghost moths reappeared at his fire. The vetch thickened. Mosaics of snow-grass appeared touched with alluvial sedges and whipcord and the fugitive bloom of the windgrass flower. Dry stones persisted. But beyond the steaming pellets, fetid in his nostrils, he sensed the odour of quicker things. The air grew sharp: he could taste it, blow saliva. His feet, ugly pennies floating aimlessly beneath him, became weighted, planted on the flints, knowing pain again. And with the birds, familiarity returned.

Birds like porcupines darted from crevices and waddled obsequiously at his side. Rails sounded. And out of the flax, its voice mewling through a dense and hairified nose came the obscure honk of the kaka.

Yet the dry stones persisted.

He had made camp. (It was the day the rats returned.) He had crushed the tips of a shrub called coronita—it was the bush his Lord was always pictured against. He had set the leaves to boil. He was slumped by the brush fire inhaling the aroma and was watching the shadows which grew quickly, as they always did at this hour, when a beak like a condor's beak came up his leg and lodged a claw in the owl seal ring on his little finger. The girl's ring sparkled and the kea screamed for possession. Wearily he knocked the bird down. Without complaining, it snatched up his tinder box and studied it with a claw in front of its face. Mackenzie sat up. The bird left the box and entered the firelight. Now it seized his pannikin, chuckling its wings on which the greened feathers splashed with vermilion hung like warped slates. He watched it. He watched the eager inquisitive eye. Suddenly it sniggered, bringing all its relatives. The keas came in a flock and studied everything in sight. His limbs stirred, as if invested by contagion with a new thirst for knowledge. He was suddenly awake, overturning the fire and marching with the moon. The keas guided him. He made two rests before dawn and in the morning they were still beside him. Thereafter he marched surrounded by a perpetual green cloud, splashed with the blood of the underwing.

The way was deepening.

In the afternoon a light drizzle fell. Then the rain stopped. He stood on top of a knoll. 'There is an tree,' he said to the dog. His voice was knotted. Down there was a riverbed: above it, in a fold of three hills, was a clearing. The tree rose from the clearing like some gallant vessel of the sun. A harlequin tree decked in reds and colours of sea mousse. And a spreading tree, beckoning with outflung arms.

'Tis the place of light,' he muttered.

Mackenzie put out a hand as if to ward off a vision. But it was not a vision.

He left the knoll and entered the riverbed and drove until he was exhausted. In the morning the tree was still there. Low sandstone tells had appeared in the bed, isolated tablets that led off the shingle onto the clearing as guideposts. Now rising, now falling, they appeared as grotesque statues topped with a goat's beard of leafless shrubs. At each statue he stopped to peer round it, the way a horse peers. The tree was always there. Nor did he fail to notice how its presence rejuvenated the land. The rubbled spurs had softened to domes. In them pebbles clustered like shooting stars: garnets, jaspers, mother-of-opal, and the clouded gems of chalcedony and clove-veined marble. As he walked his head butted up and down against his chest. Brazenly he plucked toi-toi and waved the torch heads in the air to announce his coming. Now the flock was behind him. He had outpaced it. 'Ha!' he cried, as grebes and crested pigeons came down to guide him. 'Tis real.' The birds were the true messengers of light. 'Tis real,' he said again, and stopped.

The tree was just above him: aerial, witch-like, thorny.

He observed how everything slumbered. As he climbed the mound he seemed to pass into a different, a more tranquil zone. To the last he doubted — everything he had ever known or forgotten or feared of childhood was here, even to the coloured beads hanging from the lower branches.

The sheep came up in five lanes, bleating like mortals. It was difficult to know what he was saying, the haggard figure that preceded them and stood babbling before the tree. The babble was lost in the bleatings and the blunt scrapings of the knife as he took the first animal by the throat — and eventually (for the knife was very blunt) severed it, and smeared the lower branches, all that he could reach, with a royal red dye.

Apparently the dog knew. She trotted up with a certain majesty of unconcern, a hindleg lifted, and sniffed the dead ewe and then put the flock to browse. Finally she sat down by one of the cairns ranged about the tree with her front knees crossed. Only when the sky had darkened and the birds awoke, shaking down their tassels from the branches, did she join the man. He lay sprawled at the base in an attitude of fulfilment, head down, arms flung over a root, like a lover.

For a time he was very happy there. He had food, he had shelter, he had clothing. The tree and its environs gave him all these things. By day he was naked and at night he wore a shift from sheddings of bark. Her umbrella shade broke the heat and he slept curled in the alleys between her feet. Her feet were gnarled, sprawling for a hundred yards in every direction; the alleys between, cloudy with moss. A whitish moss covered the clearing. He left the tree only to fish. There was a woodland lake below the clearing studded with conical islands. It was milken of the same milk whiteness as the clearing. But on some days it was black with the fish migrating there. Bush ran steeply into it. From the edge where he fished spear in hand he looked up to a small decked wood, so secretly contained in the hills as to seem originally planted. Above, the sheep grazed to the summits. He was content simply to watch them, slumbering on the cushion moss, accepting the tree's fecundity, incurious as a convalescent. The tree glittered with lianes of hidden suggestion; yet he never inquired. He had only to reach up a hand to feed from the berries that hung down in purple chaplets; the odour was sweet to his nostrils; yet he resisted the temptation. He would extract a lice from his beard and cry, 'Holla!' Yet he never tortured the vermin for scavenging his cheeks, he saved them for the stick birds that descended at evening. In that sanctuary he would commit no outrage. He touched nothing, disturbed nothing and he never ate a hedgehog. And so for a time he was content.

It never occurred to him that he had found that primal source of which the native Wiremu had once spoken. The past was obliterated, the future held no cares for him. There was no future. How could there be? In the world of childhood the present is eternal; there is no difference between the natural and the supernatural; nothing therefore is strange or fearful. He was never afraid.

Only the dog was suspicious. She grew jealous. Her rowan eyes continually roved the upper branches whence came the sound of sighing. He explained, 'Tis the birds, lass.' For he knew that they came to the tree each spring to sigh for the soul of their great ancestor called Moah or the frigate bird. This was Moah's sanctuary. 'True lass, look.' Together they stepped out the cairns that encircled the mound. On each was imprinted the wingless form of a giant bird, besides smaller drawings of human rites and human hands. The drawings had been scratched into the stone and then blown with ochre. They were of a great serenity. The cairns were ranged like shields; they protected the tree even as the tree protected the land below. It was the birds had raised the cairns, he explained; as it was the birds who had warned him not to touch the berry. The tree stood very stiffly, they said, on certain points of honour.

Every second day he entered the lake and washed away the lice that still clung to him. Some days, lying under the tree, it was so still he could hear the silken cords of the diadem spider crack. On the Sabbath he stood the Book in the tree and read from it. He knew the shorter Catechism by heart and could intone the 50th Psalm with a certain lilt and decency. He liked especially the first part, 'For every beast of the forest is mine . . .' and when he hallooed it, wailing across the lake, the sheep liked it too, he could tell the expression on their faces. One day at the bottom of his bag he found a tiny hoard of fern root that he had hidden away even from the dog; he showed her, saying, 'I canna remember, lass'—and he could not. Although as a child he had hidden away crusts of bread, every night, against starvation. Several things like this he could not recall and he asked the tree for his memory back. The tree shook her foliage drowsily. 'Not yet,' she said. He came gradually to resent the spirit that dwelt there.

At first he had thought it necessary to guard the tree; and had prowled about her brandishing the crook in both hands to smite the forces that might come against her. All children know this game. It is called King. But after a time, when she saw that he touched nothing, disturbed nothing and never ate a hedgehog, the tree came to trust him and told him not to bother. So long as he kept her secret, she said, she was inviolable. And indeed he saw that she had a kind of wholeness, uniting earth and sky; for everywhere he looked the nectar of her blossom, budding in spikes of scarlet trefoil, was reflected in the landscape.

'Is thee old?' he said, for sometimes she spoke to him in the voice of a hag. 'I am ageless, laddie,' the spirit replied. And she added in the voice of a young girl, 'And so are you.' 'Me?' For some reason his thoughts turned to his sister, Mary, who was dead. He saw her in the manes of toi-toi waving below the clearing. Mary had always worn her hair long and undone in the spring, shaking out the tresses that the tassels of the maize might grow in a like profusion. 'Me?' he said. 'How?' The tree laughed and told him to stop his prowling and be content.

Yet even as he ceased his daily patrol, he grew restless and longed to penetrate her secret; as do all children whose games are taken from them and who begin to pry instead into the source of their immortality.

He began by tapping the trunk. He discovered it was hollow. The trunk was wrapped in an aerial casing of cables that grew down from the sky; but the spirit that dwelt there was always screened by the host of birds entwining her limbs. Perhaps the mystery lay with the birds. He began to watch them when they descended after dark. At evening the tree would sigh, touched by the lightest of breezes, and lift her arms to undress as if the burden of her benevolence—so many birds, so many lovers— was intolerable to her. First the herons would descend, blustering into the rainpools, and an alarum grebe that lived entirely alone, gliding up and down in the eddies of the branches like a cliffwalker; at the same time from the trunk there issued a pulsating stream of insect life—carabid, weta, rove beetle and glistening glass moth. Then came the kaka. 'When can I know the secret?' he said to the kaka. 'When you rot,' the kaka replied, and began grinding up roots as though in pain. Next he asked a ventriloquial crow. 'Not yet,' said the crow, calling down the saddle-back and the wedge-tailed huia. 'Not yet tee-hee,' echoed the other foragers, warblers and riflemen, pipits, black and pied fantails, creepers, robins, fern hooters, hopping back and forth dring-drang dring-drang on the larvae infested roots. The cockatoos didn't help him, neither the redhead nor the billycock yellow; they arrived drunk and fired flower buds at him. A kakapo waddled out, swore in the ricegrass and told him to go to sleep and indeed by now the birds were coming and going in such confusion, he was both giddy and drowsy, and quite unable to blow the chanter in tune for the keas who enveloped him in a ring of steel blades. The keas told him nothing; when he played they simply put their topknots askew and pshawed round his fire. As the night progressed he barely heard the chime of the bellbirds, rising in canon. Yawning he fell asleep ignored by everyone, except perhaps by the cormorant, stiffening to attention in the rushes. And so it continued, night after night. Sometimes, starting at the hair-raising clatter of laughing petrels, he would stare wild-eyed about him, remembering his purpose; but always he fell asleep again. In the morning the clearing would be void, the tree sagging into the earth in a kind of ecstasy while from within came a sound of tittering as the creatures squirmed and nestled back into the hollows of her body. Once he woke in the dawn to find a kakapo, out late, grinding up fern root with a steady attention to business. 'Now I shall see,' he thought. But the kakapo was too quick. It raised its wattle, swore and flung itself inside the trunk. The tree heaved, causing the waters of the lake to splash; and Mackenzie, rising with a frustrated joy in his heart, raced about the trunk. In vain. He found no recess, no secret cave. He wondered. Long he wondered. 'Escape!' the dog said. 'Nay, lass.' He thought: 'I will grow up. I will stay here till I am grown up. Then she canna refuse me.' But the longer he remained, the younger he became; his cheeks filled out, the pockmarks on his neck disappeared. And the healthier he grew, the more his restlessness increased. He grew furtive. He slept by day and prowled by night. He disguised himself in leaf-mould and stole about the trunk to find a nook, a cranny by which he might penetrate. He was always discovered. The tree never slept. In a fit of anger he blew on the chanter and beat on the bole and cried out in a boy's voice, 'I am *ready*!' But the spirit only laughed at him.

One night he woke in fever. He was lying in a furrow and felt the ground go spongy. He crept forward. The tree was golden in the moonlight and shivering. With each quake a shock passed through him from his hair to his sex. He stood absolutely rigid, an adolescent fever pouring between his legs, exultant. The fever lasted. He gloated. For as the ground sagged and the tree tossed in sleep, he felt her pores opening to receive him. 'Victory lass,' he chuckled, bending to part her glowing flanks. As he did so he received a sharp blow. There was a claw in his face and wings were flailing his head like the whirlwind. He sang with the pain and went limp. When he looked again the birds had gone. Herons were dozing on the lower branches and high up sounded the mocking of the petrels, inexhaustibly kleeping. Waterfowl were settling on the lake and the shadows of the cairns shortening. The tree was still, gently dozing, and all the glade was filled with the immaculate purling of her slumbers.

'Escape,' pleaded the dog.

Mackenzie flung himself down in a fury.

He went up onto the hills and there were three lakes running down, and the plain unfinished. The dog had assembled the flock, was moving off; but he told her to wait while he fetched his belongings. He returned to the tree and remained there, he did not again join the dog. 'We mun wait, lass, till the tree blooms full,' he said. For though the berries grew ripe and succulent, its flowers were yet unborn. Each morning a brush-tongued pigeon flew low to taste the nectar, inquiring of the buds, 'Ready? Are you ready?' And Mackenzie replied maliciously, 'Not yet.'

The tree bloomed full and the air grew heavy with the efflorescence of her odours, apricot and peach and the crushed kernel of the bitter wineberry. The pigeons plundered the scarlet envelopes whole without bothering to insert their brush tongues, and the other birds ate the berries openly (since they were ageless) and spat the pips into Mackenzie's beard and became inebriated. The tree bloomed and he did not leave, neither he nor the dog. By now the flavour of bitter almonds had driven him to madness and he too had begun to eat the berry. 'Prisoners,' Mackenzie tittered, watching the birds sag with the weed of contentment on their lips and hang upside down in the branches; plainly they were prisoners of the tree. 'Prisoners, lass,' he piped. The dog slunk into the shadow of the cairns and would have nothing to do with him; plainly he was talking of himself.

'I canna leave now, lass,' he said distractedly. For answer the dog ran loping round the tree in ever watchful circles until he became dizzy watching her and fell over, like the birds. As for the dog: she who had grown sleek and lankly feathered became again haggard as from the desert, a fretful shadow; and her eyes, hooded, mistrustful, disdainfully peering, were forever slanted upwards. He tried to comfort her and failed, as the Christian will. (It is only the Moslem who grants the dog spiritual insight and the power of discerning Azrael, the Angel of Death.) In the end the dog was forced to steal the secret for him.

A storm came in the night. Waking, Mackenzie saw the ice-dust spout upwards from the mountains, heard the tree fumble and shiver and great pieces break off and fly to long distances. In that deluge that followed all her bark seemed to have a tongue, was rasping and tearing. Then it was that the dog sprang up and darted inside. She returned bringing him a stone. She disappeared and brought him another. And another. The tree laboured. And the dog stole. And when the storm had abated Mackenzie was sitting back against a cairn with his two hands cupped and the bright stones brimming into his lap.

'Look,' he said. And 'see how they shine?', although the dog was no longer there. 'Take one, take two, take three bright stones . . .' He began to sing a children's song. He sniffed.

There was a smell of burning.

He glanced slyly at the tree. Now, he thought, she cannot hide the secret any longer.

The tree had suffered certainly. Her casing was torn to a smirch of fibres and her arms hung awry, weeping almost to the ground. But of the wound, the secret place where the dog had entered, there was no sign. Instead the roots had bubbled up, huge cracks had appeared in the ground; and all the cairns save one, the one under which he sat, leaned inwards. A froth coated the ground and the ground itself was barbed with prongs. Most strange of all, from the vents nearest the trunk a dry foam was issuing in puffs. He thought it was steam. Then as he watched he saw the smoke run: first to a root, then into the trunk and finally upwards where it reappeared as a bluish tongue of fire. The tree burned and Mackenzie waited for her living cries. None came. 'Brave, thee is brave,' he said to the tree, standing and stretching himself, for it was yet early. Idly he threw a stone into the clearing. As it fell it was swallowed up and a white spar appeared, swirling upwards through the crust. It spun slowly, hung a moment and then toppled. The tree groaned. 'Aha!' Mackenzie shouted with glee. He threw a second stone. Another mast appeared, hung and fell. 'Stop,' the tree cried. Mackenzie laughed and went on throwing stones into her lap.

He had backed down without realising. He was standing in water. Turning, he saw that the lake had risen. The water was lapping gently. There was yet room for him to escape round the lake margin and make onto the hills where the dog had herded the flock and was waiting.

Mackenzie chuckled and waved to the dog. He had one stone left. He examined it carefully, noting the small polished figure with the pot belly it was shaped to resemble. The figure had a sere coldness and shone green — baleful in that light. He clasped it tight in the palm of his hand. Now stones were rising from the ground of their own accord, in reels, inflicting a torture greater than any he had conceived. They rose incandescently, leaving a feathery wake like dolphins leaping from a sea of ice; and as each cluster fell masts stood up through the gaping roots, now singly, now jointed like dancing skeletons, and the tree groaned horribly. The air was tainted as from a charnel house and the birds mewed plaintively. Kneeling behind the cairn, Mackenzie grinned. Now he knew. The masts were not masts at all but bones, grave bones. Moah's grave, Moah's treasure — all was here. Yes, but the smell, the sickly dry odour — whose flesh was that? Were humans interred here? Wiremu's people? Yes, yes, people had lived here, yes. But why did the tree suffer — to signify regeneration or to mark the dying of the race? The fire was a portent, certainly; but of what?

Mackenzie was done with questions. Strangely elated, he was dancing about the cairn, eating berries and rubbing the green stone figure against his cheek. As he danced he sang a song of St. Bride's Day, which is a song all children sing to their favourite tree, for he knew trees: he had seen men marry trees and beg their pardons for felling them, he had seen girls adore them and women kiss them and sacrifice marten to them and beat them with rods of hickory and then pray to them in order to be delivered of the dangers of childbirth.

Every village, every race had its tree where the souls of dead forefathers resided and guided the future of the living. Oh yes, he knew trees. But he had never known a tree that consumed itself voluntarily for the sake of men, dark little Maori men at that. Such altruism was beyond his comprehension. So he rejoiced in the tree's agony. In one way he pitied the tree since he was responsible for her pain. Yet he could not stop chuckling and dancing about on the points of his toes, the way gods do, since it is only gods who hold in their hands the power of life and death.

He glanced at the stone figure in his hand. He had intended saving it for Wiremu, as proof. But —

'Shall we throw it, lass? Shall we end her misery?'

The dog was tugging him back. The tree leaned over. Her feet dug and the craters yawned as she fought to regain her mastery of earth and sky. Mackenzie held his breath. Slowly the tree righted herself.

'Twould be kinder,' he said.

He wanted to fling the stone, he wanted to fling it badly. Then the tree would lie down and surrender herself to him. Then he would be immortal. But he did not fling it.

A little thing stopped him. He had left his pipe at the base. For that and that alone he would prolong her torment. 'The chanter, lass.'

But the dog would not go.

'Then I mun go mine self,' he said.

The distance to the tree was eighty paces. 'Cold lass,' he said starting forward. It was cold, walking on bones. He had taken a dozen steps when the dog was upon him, tearing his ankles. He turned to cuff her and she shrank. She shrank to her stomach, shaggy and bristling, with her muzzle pointed and revolving in a slow arc as if she were following the spoor of some gigantic wraith in the sky. He looked. Nothing at all, the sky was a blue dome. Then he heard. Far off, muffled, the sound of drumbeats, like wings beating on velvet.

Only the echo remained.

When the sound had passed over he was lying flat beside the

dog, talking to her in the Gaelic. He was talking gibberish. He was also trembling. He rose sheepishly, cursing his impotence and his mortality. Then he escaped.

He reached the safety of the hills and he stopped running and looked down. He was surprised to hear the spirit's voice still speaking, albeit wheezily, from a pillar of smoke. Of the tree itself there was no sign.

He entered now the other world. He saw the grasses return, wheaten, and crossed them: he descended by three great lakes, one sapphire, one emerald, one ashen, and barely paused to fish although they were teeming; he passed through groves of kowhai extending from riverflat to mountain, he saw the glory of the landscape in spring. And when he came into the south and saw the native huts, he knew at last that he had reached the limit of that journey which, according to Polson, no man had ever seen.

From afar he saw the carved storehouses standing up on legs like the ruins of ancient cities; and the huts huddled beneath on a bed of caked mud. He put up a signal. 'Strange,' he thought, 'that no one comes to meet me.' For the Maoris lining the riverbank opposite regarded him moodily. No, someone was coming. A raft was crossing.

'My dear, you look famished,' said the putty-coloured man as he clambered out. He tipped the water from his galoshes and raised his beaver hat in salutation. 'Are you well? Your lips are blue. Have you been eating almonds?

'I heard your bleating,' he went on, looking from Mackenzie to the torn and trailing fleeces and back to Mackenzie again. 'Jump on. My dear, you *are* ill, I didn't think I'd have to carry you.' Somewhere from among the huts a bell rang and the watching natives vanished from the bank. 'You mustn't mind them; they want to decontaminate you, don't you know.'

Mackenzie lay on the raft, his mind reeling. Suddenly he sat up. 'Wiremu,' he said hoarsely. 'Take me to Wiremu.'

'Of course,' said the other, smiling. The smile did not reach his protuberant eyes. 'Of course. But first, come along to my house and tell me about the tree. Elsa and I have been expecting you.'

Polson did not want to arrest Mackenzie. He would have nothing to do with it, he told the inspector and forbade him to issue a warrant. The inspector, who could not understand why in mid-summer Polson wore three waistcoats, went away and made inquiries. These inquiries were quite thorough. He learned, for example, that after waiting a month for Mackenzie's return Polson had obtained a mortgage on his original flock and bought a fresh mob to replace that stolen; that his wool clip after that December's drought had barely covered living expenses and wages; that when the first smallholders had invaded Odessa and set up their V huts his effective pasturage was reduced by a third; that Taylor and Kerr had been drunk for a fortnight and had then walked off; that when rain did come it came too late for Polson had already sold his dying flock at a loss and engaged fresh hands at salaries he could no longer afford. From all this the inspector concluded that Amos Polson was a ruined man and would in the end be obliged to sign the warrant, if only for reasons of self-respect. Arthur Dewhurst was less certain.

'Is the matter pressing, inspector?' Dewhurst said.

'The fellow's sighted, sir. Three hundred miles to the south, in Otago. It is incumbent on me—'

'Quite. Inspector, there have been other sheep thefts. D'you attribute these to the same man?'

'No.'

'It would be well to,' Arthur Dewhurst observed. 'It would strengthen your hand.'

'You can do nothing with Polson then?'

'Can you bend a nail, inspector? Polson is not, I am afraid, a public spirited man.'

'But he lives in *Canterbury*, sir.'

'*Up*land Canterbury,' Dewhurst corrected. 'He is of a singular breed.'

'I don't understand, Mr. Dewhurst.'

'It pains him to air his grievances.'

'He must be made to air them,' the inspector said.

Arthur Dewhurst, on reflection, thought so too.

So on consultation did Stoddart, the editor. He agreed to publish an article ('*In the matter of the theft of five hundred merino ewes, and the near-discovery of an inaccessible alpine province by the pastoralist and benefactor, Amos Polson . . .*') The euphemism, near-discovery, was Dewhurst's idea — though not the ambiguity. The police inspector hoped that the article would create demands for a summary arrest; Arthur Dewhurst hoped that it would result in subscriptions to the Transalpine Railway of which he was a prime mover. They decided to delay publication of the article until Polson came to Christchurch.

The Polsons arrived at the Dewhursts late in February.

'I intend to help you,' Arthur Dewhurst said, over breakfast. Polson shook his head.

'What will you *do*, Amos?'

'I shall see my creditors.'

'And after that?'

Polson shrugged. He picked up a piece of toast and bit it. 'What d'you suggest, Arthur?'

'Lie low. Trust in me. Whatever happens, don't sell.'

Mrs. Dewhurst glanced at her watch. It was the morning of the cricket match. They were all going.

Frances spoke. 'Who on earth said anything of selling?'

'Nobody, child,' Mrs. Dewhurst said. 'But your father is in straits — and Arthur presumes to offer advice.'

'The best advice in Christchurch,' Polson said. He added casually, 'I have read the article, Arthur.' Arthur Dewhurst said nothing. He wiped his chin, removed the Bible from the table and settled over his prunes. He had not seen the article yet; he had given the morning's paper straight to Polson. The latter's mildness was encouraging.

'It will make no difference,' Polson said.

'Stoddart's work, Amos. It's good, isn't it?'

'No, on the contrary. It is bad.'

'Oh?'

'Have you seen what is placed next to it?'

'No.'

Polson handed him the newspaper.

Dewhurst's face fell. 'This is shocking.'

'Arthur. Explain.'

'Your husband, Emma,' Polson said, 'wishes to have me canonised. I cannot conceive why. He has proclaimed my unfortunate circumstances — most tactfully, mind you — and then he has codified the elements of my plan to uplift the natives. The exposition is admirable, Arthur. Unfortunately, Stoddart has printed alongside in bold type a series of atrocities committed by the Maoris in the north, including the murder of a missionary.'

'Ghastly, my dear. Simply ghastly. Stoddart is a fool.'

'He would have been, Arthur, had he suppressed the war report. Luckily he asked my advice. I told him not to.'

'You *knew* about the article?'

'Of course. Since the plan was dead, I saw no reason why it should not appear. I was rather naughty: I corrected your punctuation.'

Dewhurst put down the paper. 'You know what you've done? You have put a noose round your own neck.'

'Possibly. But the noose was always there, Arthur. It will be interesting to see, now that I have put the rope in their hands, if they know what to do with it.'

'You had better not come to the cricket ground today.'

'Why not? I'm looking forward to the match. They won't lynch me' — he glanced wickedly at Mrs. Dewhurst — 'not if I stay with you.'

Mrs. Dewhurst gulped her egg. Her husband ate his prunes one by one and arranged the stones on his plate.

'Besides, the game's the thing.' Polson's eyes glinted equivocally. He took his daughter's hand. 'You mustn't worry, Francie. No man is bankrupt until he is declared to be so.'

'But what *will* you do, papa?'

Mrs. Dewhurst smiled at the admission and ate a rusk.

'I expect my creditors will allow me a week or so to make up my mind.'

Presently Mrs. Dewhurst said by way of contrast: 'Lionel has done well.'

'Damned well,' Arthur Dewhurst said.

Lionel won't help, Frances thought. His time is taken up with Rose.

Mrs. Dewhurst considered her two guests. They neither of them looked well, she thought; they seemed drugged; anxious to discuss their predicament yet unwilling to confide, restive.

'Tell me, Amos,' she said suddenly. 'Why won't you have the brute arrested?'

'Because we think he may return. Men of his kind don't buckle.'

Frances said, 'He has skin like a dunderfunk.'

'Ship's biscuit,' Polson interposed politely.

Mrs. Dewhurst simpered. Then she glanced at her watch again and took Frances off to dress. Arthur Dewhurst said to Polson, 'Tell me frankly: do you think he will return?'

'No,' Polson said.

'Did you see the inspector yesterday?'

'No.'

'Then see him today.'

'Arthur, please do not involve yourself.'

'Don't be a fool. I'm involved already.' Dewhurst smiled uneasily.

Arthur Dewhurst gave Polson a honey roll and drank three mouthfuls of camomile tea. He was wearing a towel at his neck and after each mouthful he mopped his face with it. Then he ate some nuts and several sticks of celery, deep in thought. Finally he fixed Polson with an apocalyptic stare. 'Don't sell,' he said flatly. He was prevented from saying more by the arrival of Rose who reminded him that the tilbury was not available and all the horses were being blistered. They walked to the cricket ground.

It was the Town versus the Natives—or, as some said, Hebrews versus Tara's Eleven. Tara's, because a warrior of that name had returned from the skirmishing in the north covered in suspicion and wounds, and was reported to be playing; Hebrews because at the dedication of the cathedral—mullioned chancels and stained panels from nave to porch—the bishop had pronounced on divided loyalties citing Hebrews, 'One race, one people', and then in a nervous aside had announced himself for umpire. The game was a symbolic occasion intended to cement harmony between two warring races (there being patently no war in Christchurch) and Polson had no doubts that it would. Whitehouse was somewhere in the war zone as emissary or government agent; he had never reappeared in Christchurch; rumour had it that he had taken up in Wellington with a lady; Polson had dismissed the rumour and awaited news of his old benefactor in vain.

The war in the north island was far from his thoughts. He reached the ground in much the same state as he had reached Christchurch: with no fixed plan, a slight stoop, white gloves and a dilapidated beret which said defiantly: 'Whatever society requires of me, I shall perform the opposite.' Which was why Arthur Dewhurst was uneasy. To him Polson had the air of a man about to commit suicide. In fact Polson was vaguely elated. The mood had come upon him about five weeks since. A report had reached him of a yellow-bearded dervish wandering wild among southern natives; and Polson, seeing much in little—or rather in the colour of a beard—had begun with peculiar energy to drain a swamp, engaging labour and advice and working spade in hand himself alongside the gangers. He had before him the prospect of a vast dyke like Antonius' Wall, with a chain of wells stretching over his blistered land, and he worked with a moleish energy since the report meant at the very least that his sheep had been sighted. When the inspector arrived, confirming the report, work on the swamp was redoubled, as was the expense. Until the day Lionel arrived from the Australian goldfields haloed with success, leading a long-trousered Afghan hound which he claimed to have won in a raffle. The gangers laughed at the hound and they laughed at Lionel's claw-hammer coat; and Lionel, an incongruous blend of neighing public schoolboy and Australian game-cock, laughed at his uncle's penury and declined cold toast for lunch. Over dinner he announced with acid logic that he was not fitted to dig in wet holes ten hours a day; nor was he inclined to invest his capital in a like manner, since no minerals were at hand.

Next day he returned to Christchurch, taking with him the sleek bearded hound whom, Frances said, he much resembled.

Work on the swamp was abandoned. Polson did not despair. He was like a man pinned to a snowball racing for a cliff, knowing the penultimate exhilaration before one parts company with the world and one's fellow men — for that, he imagined, was what bankruptcy would be like. He took out his paints again. He read Chamfort. He put all Arthur Dewhurst's letters offering help and his creditors' letters and his agent's letters refusing further credit into Frances' old iron pot and threw the pot out of the window. He rethatched the house — 'for the winter', he told Frances; but really it was for a new owner. He finished the summer with the usurping farmers' V huts dotted about him like teepees, debts amounting to £1300 and a mattock in his hand, flaying a contagion of thistle which had travelled from his home county, Norfolk, in a mattress belonging to one of the new tenants. Then he had come to Christchurch. He had in fact already seen his creditors; had made his preparations quietly; all that remained now was to sell the homestead. The end in sight and acknowledged, Polson felt nothing but a slight intoxication. On the way to the cricket ground he picked kakabeak for the ladies and smiled at the arrangements: a raddle of bunting decorated the tussock bowl; a pavilion had been built; the Maoris had set up stalls. The festive air pleased him and he tried not to think of the newspaper article. People would cut him, that's all. Well and good. He wanted to be alone, to walk with Frances in the sunshine, to enjoy the game. It would be their last outing before sailing. In the event he did none of these things. As he entered the ground people came up to him holding the *Christchurch Gazette* and shook him by the hand. His creditors smiled obsequiously. Far from being shunned, he was taken into the bishop's stand and acclaimed a hero. Hence his disgust.

'Foah,' signalled the bishop, who was a real bishop in whiskers and moist chins, and a circular straw hat on his head. As the ball flew by, Rose and Lionel drew back. But Frances remained quite still. Then she staggered and fell over.

'Are you alright, Fran?' Lionel's equestrian figure bent over her. He wore high boots and a gaping silk blouse and his voice showed concern, for he was not ungallant.

Frances righted herself. 'Perfectly,' she said. It was ridiculous.

A moment before she had been staring at the tops of the cabbage trees, then—without warning they had appeared to burst into flame in the shape of a dog and breathe upon her. But whose dog? she wondered. Mackenzie had been far from her thoughts. 'Perfectly thanks. Just a silly premonition, Lionel. Something fiery hit me and I fell over.' She rubbed her cheeks in a dazed way. They had turned carmine. 'Heat stroke, I suppose.'

Rose nudged Lionel. 'But the sun is behind a cloud.'

'Gord,' Lionel said affectedly in the Australian way. But he could not take his eyes from Frances. Bareheaded, she stood looking into the distance in a trembling way that was suddenly attractive.

'Hit you, Fran?'

'Scorched me. I had the impression it was a dog.' She laughed.

After a silence he said, 'But not this dog, Fran?' And he persuaded the Afghan hound to lie on its back with its trousered loins in the air. The hound's name was Dibs and its breeding, he said, dated from 2000 B.C.

They had walked round the area and were standing apart from the other spectators, looking down the crease. Raucous shouts came from Maoris sitting nearby under trees. They were cooking. Frances turned and saw that the batsmen were there. The Maoris were batting.

'The natives are losing,' she said; and again Lionel and Rose stared at her, for they had none of them paid attention to the game since lunch.

'How do you know?'

'I don't, Rose. And yet I do, you see. Something happened to me when I fell over, that's all.' To Rose the voice sounded muffled, as if a strip of muslin lay between them. Rose linked arms. 'You mustn't be frightened, dear.'

'Frightened? I'm always like this when I am reminded of him.'

Lionel had heard of the shepherd. Who had not? His nostrils twitched and he rubbed his barbel beard quite deliberately along Rose's bare forearm, nuzzling her bangle as he did so. Frances' prim glance amused him.

'Was he a good man?' he inquired.

'I thought Christchurch had told you that. No, Lionel. He was wicked, quite quite wicked.'

'Oh everyone knows that, Fran. I mean—was he correct?' He smiled a small indelicate smile.

Frances coloured and glanced away; and Rose, nudging Lionel fondly, said: 'Fran, it's time you thought of other things. You say yourself he's gone for good.'

'So are we, Rose.'

'Don't be so stern. What do you mean?'

'I don't know yet. We're travelling, that's all.'

Lionel frowned, flapping his blouse and exposing mosquito bites on an incipiently downy chest. His long face slanted away to the bishop's stand where Polson was talking to a grazier; nothing amiss there. Something, Lionel told himself, is going on. Either that or the girl is peculiar; her eyes had the sharp lustre of iodine.

'Are you going far?' he said.

'Quite far, I think.' Frances toyed with the hound. With one white shoe and one mauve stocking sunk in its chaps, she seemed to be wearing an enormous slipper. 'That is, papa is travelling, not I. I am terrified he will do something rash. And I can do nothing to help him, nobody can. Except wait. Is it always like this, Lionel?' He shrugged. 'For a woman, I mean? I hate it. Waiting—it's all we're fitted for.' She stopped teasing the hound. 'Yet I can wait, you see.'

'What are you waiting for?' he said.

'Signs. We all wait for signs, don't we?'

Lionel raised an eyebrow and gave one of his neighing laughs. 'O well done!' he chortled, for the bishop's son had bowled a chief and the chief, being very fat, appeared to have wound himself round the stumps. He had to be prised off.

'I told you the natives were losing,' she said.

Lionel was smiling down at her, taking her by the shoulders between thin wrists and looping the tip of his tongue invitingly. 'I may have cut-glass manners and pointed shoes but I am not a prude,' was what she understood from his glance.

'What do you want?' he murmured.

'Once,' she said, pursuing her signs, 'I saw him sitting under a tree in sandals. Now the tree isn't there any more.'

'What do you really want, Fran?'

'I want—' she began, and her voice trailed off. He had begun, before Rose, to caress her. For a moment she was soothed, simply to feel a man's arms.

'You're thinking about the convict again,' he murmured.

'Of course. Does nobody understand what he is doing?'

His underlip went slack. 'I thought you were worried about your father.'

'I am. You don't understand either of you what Odessa means to him. He mustn't sell it, mustn't!' She broke away and stood shaking. Rose gulped, smarted and then, ever practical, took the little bottle of turpentine Frances carried and began dabbing the spots on Lionel's chest. Small things tantalise cousins. Lionel now found himself studying Frances' nose which he had thought priggish. It was not, it was retroussé and it puckered. He continued to ogle her. 'Come to town then, if Odessa defeats you.'

Another native had gone to bat. People were tittering; his pad was on the wrong leg. Frances had regained her composure. 'It's very hard for papa. Because God, you see—he seems to want to have as little to do with us as possible. I know Odessa's only—'

'It's only a shack.'

'I know, Lionel.'

'Then walk out. Come to town. It would be nice to see more of you.'

Rose had taken Lionel's arm possessively. She remembered a saying of her father's—'When in doubt, win the trick'—and decided it was time to make an announcement.

'France. I shan't be coming when you go back to Odessa.'

'Odessa!' Frances laughed shrilly. 'Will it be there, Rose?' She stopped. 'But why? It's all arranged.'

'I know, but we—' She rubbed her bangle along Lionel's sleeve expectantly.

Normally Lionel would not have minded announcing the engagement. He had enjoyed the escapade with Rose that prescribed it and he was not dishonourable. But taken unawares, he was embarrassed. He stared uncomfortably at his cousin.

Frances' eyes, clairvoyant as a cat's, betrayed the truth-seeker. Suddenly she understood and embraced Rose. 'I'm so happy, so happy for you Rose.' They wept a moment, happily; and Lionel, buttoning his blouse and feeling trapped, waited for his congratulations which duly came. 'Mind you make her a good husband,' Frances said, at her most matronly. Lionel's look was frosty.

'Good,' Frances thought. And suddenly saw that her father was talking to a policeman.

Another Maori was out, caught; and the hound, rolling about

arched topknot and forequarters together with a distinct clapping sound.

'I sometimes think,' Frances said, 'that I want one thing for my father and another for myself.'

'You're confused.' Lionel seemed to sneer. 'Sell. As you say, it's only a shack. Tell your father, sell.'

'No, Lionel. I want for him independence and—and the dignity of being allowed to find his own way out, like Mackenzie. That's what I meant when I said papa's travelling. All day people have been fawning over him with their little schemes, their railway, their niceness. "Sell," they say. You're the same. "Come to Christchurch. Be like us." They will corrupt him in some way. People shouldn't be allowed to touch a man like that! But they will, they are. And he will give in for my sake.' She was talking wildly, striking her fist in her small palm. 'A woman doesn't want that, Lionel. A woman is—is different. She is not allowed to enter your world because it's considered not appropriate. She can only love. You ask what I want? Ask Rose. *That* is what I want. I want to taste, to know.' She looked quickly from one to the other. 'I simply want to know *what it is like*.'

It was a poor thing to say. But having said it she was defenceless. Rose was flattered. She shifted the bangle up her bare arm until the flesh bulged. Lionel said nothing. Taking Rose by the arm and the hound by its silver chain, he led them both away.

Frances minded. She minded the snub. She minded the white dress and the white shoes with heels that clicked and the rust and black braided jacket that made her conspicuous as a monarch butterfly. She stood defenceless and unhappy, holding the bottle of turpentine, and looked for another sign. The sun shone clear above massing clouds. Heat weather; storms in the alps; and beyond the ground, pale fires on the hills. The game dragged on, scored with the shrill of cicadas and she wondered if insects lived that high, in the alps; and how long it would be before they found him. 'Please, no flies,' she whispered. 'No flies please.'

She minded that there were no more signs. But most of all she minded being alone.

A tug roused her. A child with a cockle in its mouth had snatched the bottle and run off to the Maoris seated behind her. 'Don't, don't drink that.' She caught the child. 'Why not?' A brown hand grasped her wrist. 'It is spirits?' 'No, turpentine.' 'A great pity.' He did not rise. The grasp tightened. Smoke rose from the turf, mingled with the heady smell of taramea and, she thought, of beer. There were about fifty Maoris. The bottle of turpentine was passed round; everyone sniffed; they stared at her for a moment then resumed watching the game. Cockles were cooking.

'Sit down please, Miss Polson.'

She obeyed, conscious of her neatness, her whiteness, yet strangely at ease in the rival camp. A bedraggled crone moved over. 'My mother,' he said. The old woman, on her knees, bowed and gave Frances a handful of cockles; then continued stirring the fire with a cricket bat.

He wore a cloak, was handsome, proud, with a curved nose and full lips parted in a half-smile of scorn. Only the chin was tattooed. She remembered the malevolent smile, as she remembered the impeccable voice and the ring of black curls that gave him a bearing. He kept one shoulder twisted away from her.

'We met at the ball, Miss Polson.'

'Yes. Your name is Tara. You are the one who said he would shoot my father.'

'Perfectly. But now I shoot missionaries instead.'

'And when will you stop shooting missionaries?'

'When they stop selling our land. They tell us to look up to heaven—'

' "And they take the ground from under our feet." I know the proverb. It is what they say in the north. It is the reason for the war, isn't it? But the missionaries are not to blame.'

'They were the first. In the beginning was the Word, Miss Polson. They have broken it.'

'One missionary,' he said, 'I do not shoot.'

'Oh. Which one is that?'

'The one who gives me this.' He picked up a musket lying beside him and shook it.

Quietly and insistently he began drumming the tussock with the heel of the stock, in time with the others who were tapping down sticks and stumps and bats and chanting softly, for one of their number on the crease was skilful and kept hitting the ball into the sun, breaking up the field.

'Aie!' cried the old woman softly. More stumps were down. The fallen batsman came in and another batsman ran out. The chanting continued.

'You are losing?' Frances said.

'Of course.' Again the smile of scorn, as he beat the ground with the musket. But savagely now.

'*Heh, heh, mana toi* . . .' the others sang. '*Heh, heh, mana toi* . . .' sang the mother, hitching her calico skirts and wiping Frances' blazer where cockles had spilled. 'Heh, heh, sing girl—sing. Heh, heh . . .' The old woman, on her knees, wobbled her buttocks; and Frances laughed. Then she began to sing with the others. At the sound of her coppery treble the old woman cackled, squirting cockle juice through her teeth, and Frances overbalanced. Her legs shot up. The giggling she caused! They sat her up and brushed her down and she was gathered into them: squeezed, carefree, a little self-conscious but singing again, humming rather—not for the game, the game was nowhere; but for the song. Nobody cared about the game. Except Tara, she noticed. 'Him next,' the old woman said to her. 'Him last.' She jolted her son. 'Sing!' she commanded. But he would not sing. He continued to beat the ground with the musket, his eyes flashing over the group like adders' tongues. 'Cowards,' he hissed. 'Big warrior,' somebody jibed. 'Big son, big stupid son. Fight the Engerlish.' From under her skirts the old woman broke wind. They were laughing at him.

Then he pulled on a cricket cap and stood up. Another wicket had fallen. In the peaked cap he looked ridiculous. Someone gave him a bat. It was a native bat with a carved handle. 'Miss Polson,' he said, bending over her—and the clipped tone was perfect. 'My English is better than my manners; and your manners, being English, will permit you to accept this as a token of our defeat.' He gave her the bat. Throwing off his cloak he strode towards the pitch, carrying the musket in his right hand. Roars of laughter followed him.

As the cloak fell away Frances saw why he had been sitting queerly. He had only one arm. The left stopped above the elbow. The stump was raw.

'O Tara!' the jibing voice cried; and whispered in Frances' ear, 'I am his friend.'

'Is he mad?'

'He is mad to think we go back to the war with him. We are harvesting the kumara and the maize. Now we are doing it. And Tara is saying, "Come to the war." So we laugh. We would rather play cricket. But not with a musket. O Tara! The ball is too great for your barrel! See? They refuse him.'

'He is a chief's son?'

'O yes, o yes. In the north he is famous. Nobody else gives his arm away like Tara does. You understand? The English are firing their cannons, poom-poom! poom-poom! Then finish. You understand? No more munitions. No more balls. "You miss!" Tara says. "Try again." He takes back the balls to the English. O fine, very fine warrior. Tara is walking away and the English soldiers blow his arm off. Now, see? He is angry and fights them because they refuse him to play.'

But no: Frances saw that the bishop had intervened. 'One race, one people'—he pointed jocularly to the banner waving above the stand. All was well. The fielders had moved in close, poised, like white herons ranking on a pool; and the batsman, bare, his grass skirt invisible, crouched down to receive the ball.

The pitch was towards Frances, end on. Tara held the musket by the barrel. She saw that the stock barely covered the stumps and that he could not, with one arm, hold it steady.

The first ball was wide. As it passed Tara yawned and swung the musket lazily about his head, like a caber. He glared at the fielders and faced the bowler again with his tongue extended, taunting him. The next ball was also wide. Tara put his backside out and laughed. He leaped into the air, landed lightly and spat, obscenely. A growl came from the spectators and the fieldsmen moved closer, their hands abnormally slack and large. The third ball bowled him. Tara did not move. At the last moment he lifted the stock clear of the ground and allowed the ball to take the middle stump.

Jeers sounded, and clapping. Some of the male spectators had picked up clods. The bowler, continuing his run, tore off his cap and made to fling it in the batsman's face. He stopped when he saw the musket pointing. Tara had raised the stock to his shoulder. As he sighted along the barrel, resting it on the stump of his left arm, Frances saw his face. It was quite possessed and quivering in every muscle. The laughter had ceased. Tara swung the barrel in a deliberate arc and the field emptied to the margins. The bishop had retired first; he stood in a space below the pavilion, head bowed under the absurd straw hat.

She could hear the banner flapping above the crowd. 'Only fire,' she prayed. 'Fire.' Anything, anything to shatter the complacency of this town, this mob. This polite mob. They were not even running.

Then the old woman staggered onto her feet and the gun fired.

Everyone was looking at the smoking barrel. It was pointed above the pavilion. The banner was shot away, except for a strip of white hanging down containing the one word 'Hebrews'. Tara lowered the barrel perceptibly and held it, still smoking, pointed at the bishop's chest. Then he turned and walked off the ground.

The game ended then.

Walking home, they none of them spoke of the incident. Instead Mrs. Dewhurst met a farmer. Arthur Dewhurst revealed himself. Lionel learned about toot and caressed Rose in the thickets; and Polson, dragging his steps, reflected that in the end society claims its own, even the misfits. Frances got lost.

They were spread across the plains in a line, like beaters. The sun had left a subdued warmth in the earth. It had stripped the tussocks a peculiar ruddy colour; the light was peculiar. Clouds hung in dull sheets, awaiting the afterglow. Native huts were hard by in coverts of fern and toi-toi, and no sign but the shouts of the ferryman to tell them that the river was at hand.

'I take it,' Mrs. Dewhurst said, 'that Polson is serious, Arthur.'

'My dear. The Polsons are *sailing*.'

'Then—finish with him.'

'Emma, he is distressed. He's got that hunted look.'

Mrs. Dewhurst glanced sidelong at Polson who was advancing erratically in the background in the manner of a bumble bee. Arthur. Remember Rose's wedding, we shall need every penny. Don't sidle away. Arthur. Every penny. On no account offer him money.

Arthur Dewhurst gave his wife a pained look and waited for Polson to catch up.

Mrs. Dewhurst furled her parasol and struck out for the river. She was sorry now that she had suggested such a roundabout way home—everybody spread out, apart; nobody was helping her to gather wildflowers at all. Every few yards Mrs. Dewhurst bent down to gather flowers. She wore blue and a quantity of tulle and whenever she bent the parasol stood up behind, like a rudder. She overtook Frances in a patch of moonwort. 'You're too sad, child.'

'Yes. He has just told me. My father is weak, Mrs. Dewhurst.'

A ghost of a smile lit the older woman's face. She reached out a hand, as people do who are touched by a new confidence. 'But human, Frances. Only last night Arthur was saying—you had been talking to him in the kitchen and he said, I think I have it right, that he was afraid your father might turn out to be a saint. Never mind, he isn't the first to give in.'

Frances shook slightly. 'Odessa isn't sold *yet*.' Mrs. Dewhurst withdrew her hand and her face assumed its usual columnal form.

Rose and Lionel came up, oblivious of all but the soft light and themselves. Rose was humming. 'What is that song, Rose?'

'Ditty, mama. Lionel's ditty.'

'Ode to a one-armed—Sing it, ducks,' Lionel jested.

'O the Maori was a devil
He ate both flesh and bone-o!
He stole the heart of a white man
And cooked it on his stone-o!'

                              Rose sang.

'Chorus, Lionel,' she lisped.

'And the white man tamed him, O!
And the white man tamed him—'

'Lionel. Stop. You are not to encourage her.'

'Mama, it's true. The Maoris killed a missionary and took out his heart and ate it. His name was Falkner. It's in the newspaper.'

'That was in the north, child.'

Lionel said coyly: 'What *is* it about the north, Mrs. Dewhurst?'

'Lionel. You must never forget that although you live in the sticks, as we say, you live in Canterbury; and heah we have every class from peer to peasant, and we are educating the natives to be—something different.'

Frances said, 'Mrs. Dewhurst means, Lionel, what your song says. They will fit in.'

'Exactly, Frances. They will fit in somewhere. They will have to.'

'*Won't* they, George?' Mrs. Dewhurst said.

George Sunnaway, a wandering farmer leading a rope with nothing on the end of it, looked round sulkily.

'Have you lost another cow, George?'

'Betsy, Ma'm. Und missed t' game.'

'We won,' Mrs. Dewhurst said.

'If you sees er, Ma'm, she is strorberry.'

'There's something in the swamp,' Rose said.

'Brand her, George. Brand her!' Mrs. Dewhurst called to the departing farmer. 'Now there Lionel is the perfect case of an Englishman who won't leave his notions behind him; won't fit, you see. Will not. He brought out a very special cow valued at forty pounds at home. "Lock it up," Arthur said. But no. On the first night he let it out to eat where it pleased, and it died next day.'

'Tooted,' Rose explained. Lionel was mystified. 'There'—she indicated a bush with shining leaves and purple black berries— 'that's toot. It kills stock.'

Mrs. Dewhurst nodded sagely. 'Will not adapt, you see—' But Lionel and Rose had gone on.

'Like your father, Frances,' she added. But Frances too had slipped ahead. Mrs. Dewhurst put up her parasol, faintly bothered. '*Sailing?*' she thought, and wondered who was paying for the passages.

'Something has frightened you,' Arthur Dewhurst said. Polson kept stopping to guide the bigger man round the birds that were nesting in their path. 'I want to know why you are running away.'

'And I, Arthur, want to know why you are determined I shall not.'

Polson's smile met the buttoned twill and ran upwards, all the way to his host's three chins. It always seemed to him he was a guest in Dewhurst's garden, even though they were together on the open plain. The smile no longer deceived Dewhurst. Soon, he told himself, watching the blinking eyes, soon he will break. 'What did you tell the police inspector?'

'I told him to go to the devil.'

'That is not what he said to me.'

'Very well. I told him to do what he liked with Mackenzie, that I was done with the whole thing.'

'Did you sign the warrant?'

'I signed.'

Dewhurst nodded, pleased. Polson was changing. 'I have never understood what you admired about the fellow, Amos.'

'Have you never thought what might exist in the mind of a man whose people were driven out by sheep?'

'I don't follow,' Dewhurst said.

'Sheep, Arthur, sheep. Landlords. Improvement. *Us.* That is

THE JOURNEY

what the Clearances are about. That is what the wars in the north are about. I admire him because, unlike me, he will not compromise. He also has a vision. *I* don't know what it is any more than you do, except that he's making a journey, and he should be allowed to finish it in peace.'

'And now you no longer wish to see the end of it?'

'No,' Polson said, 'I don't.'

'Have you the money for the fares?'

Polson hesitated. 'Yes.'

'Once, Amos, I said to myself: "Here is a man who is not an island but is making himself into one." You seemed to be winning the struggle. Now — as I say, something has frightened you.'

'Foolish of me — ' Polson had walked into a bush like an artichoke. He turned waving a bloodied wrist. 'And yet — do we change? Do we?'

'Once you begin something, Amos, you see it through. It is the only philosophy I know. You are changing, you know. But you cannot order a man's arrest and then run, oh no.' He performed a breathing exercise and exhaled, shrewdly. 'Mind you, if you stayed you might be lionised. You might even be asked to stand for Parliament.'

'I have, already.'

'Then why so bitter?'

'I should have thought that a man who fires a dart publicly at the very core of society's hypocrisy is immediately an outcast. But oh no. Let the dart become public and he is at once everybody's darling. That's what appals me, Arthur — this popularity, this insidious benevolence.'

'I don't understand.'

It was on Polson's mind to quote Chamfort: 'A man must eat a toad every morning if he does not wish to discover anything more revolting by evening.' Instead he said, 'You and your confounded article! Fifty people came up to me today offering help — not because my sheep were stolen, not that; but because they were stolen by a man who went *behind my back*. All gentlefolk understand that crime. There was even a dowager, the late rector's wife — the one who sits in the garden and makes your wife kettleholders — who asked me to arrange a public flogging so the children might come.'

Arthur Dewhurst did not know what to do with his jacket. He shifted it from arm to arm. Finally he draped it over his head.

'Go on,' Dewhurst said. He could afford to wait, now that the convert was half-way home. 'You said once, Amos, that you wanted recognition.'

'For my idea, not for myself.'

'What exactly was your idea?'

'Haven't you read your own article? My God, you have charm, Arthur.' His voice was weary. 'I should like to have persuaded you all to put the natives first and yourselves second, even for a moment. To make you aware that there was in yourselves this *possibility* of change.'

'People are aware, Amos.'

'Shall I tell you what they're saying? They say, "Here's a man who has tried to save us from ourselves. Huzzah! What a man." That's what they say in public. In private they say, "Huzzah! He has failed, thank God. Now we are safe." '

'You exaggerate.'

'Arthur, in the north the vicars' wives are demanding ten natives for every white man killed. War, Arthur — war full scale. In Canterbury the pilgrims fret because the Governor can't excuse himself to christen their railway. Exaggerate?'

Arthur Dewhurst was looking ahead. He was chairman of the Railways Concession. He said, 'I am afraid we shall never agree on the native question.'

'There is no native question. There is a policy of extermination: smite and spare not, and reward the survivors with cricket caps. The only question now is whether there will be any survivors.' Dewhurst exhaled blandly, secure in the recollection that all the great civilisations had resulted from the expansion of Empire, thus soothing in piece the wounds inflicted in war.

'Try and understand, Arthur. My plan, like the native question, has ceased to exist. I am no longer concerned with the natives. I am concerned with mending my own failures.' The voice died off. The eyes, peering insistently at the ground, looked up. 'Rather, I was —'

'Until other people began mending them for you.' Dewhurst chuckled. 'It has been my experience, Amos, that people who rail against mankind quite as much as you do, do not end by committing suicide.'

'Sailing is suicide,' he added softly. 'Moreover, if you do sail, you will lose Frances.'

Polson nodded, suddenly contrite. 'I think, Arthur, if you

don't mind, we should move on. That lark is waiting to build its nest.'

As they continued Dewhurst felt a slight pressure. Polson had taken his arm. They were passing rickety fences of sticks tied up with flax. Brown faces peered from the open yards, and young women carrying gourds turned to stare, leaving their pointed breasts in profile. The earth was chirruping. Pulsing with a marigold of yellow and mahogany blazers—the earth was alive with birds.

'No trees, so they nest in the ground,' Dewhurst murmured. 'Once I was lost here, this very spot. All bush—very silent and strange. Not nice, Amos. So I cut it down. My bush, of course. But the birds, you see, adapt very quickly. It is always the birds, isn't it, who adapt first?'

'Amos,' he went on, still talking in the same muted voice and waving to his wife on the bank below where the punt was crossing, 'let me tell you what you will do. You will return to Odessa. You will burn and fence and farm it properly. You ask how? Last night Frances came to me in distress. I gave her money— for, let us say, "contingencies". That is the first thing. Second: as an anti-feudalist and a supporter of close settlement you are not, I take it, opposed to progress as such? Good. Then, that is second: you will support the proliferation of the railway. Third: you will do this understanding that you are not a failure. Failure is the opposite of momentum. Momentum is progress, change (I'm not talking of spiritual change). Nothing stands still. Whether you like it or not, you are the very embodiment of change. Since that convict disappeared and your Promised Land with him, land values have trebled, shares have risen, endowments to public works have multiplied, to say nothing of those to the Church. There's hardly a gentleman in New Zealand who isn't aching to own an inch of soil in Canterbury. Your doing, Amos, yours. People are *genuinely* grateful to you. You still doubt me? You still doubt that change is real? You're changing now as I speak—have been changing, in fact, since you left the ground; I mean, since that madman humiliated his people before the whole town. You saw then the stupidity of private rebellion. In a land of niceness (I accept the accusation) and fair play, rebellion is stupid. Another thing. Lionel. Now Lionel: he said an interesting thing. He says you haven't failed. He has a phrase, he calls you "the conscience of the age".'

'Me?'

'You were too quick, too sharp with him at Odessa; you forgot to discuss your plan with him. I didn't. Lionel is interested in politics. He needs a platform.'

'He would do it for self aggrandisement.'

'Does it matter? Nothing, Amos, nothing is achieved by self abasement. You are interested in goodness. So in my little way am I. I do good works. I try to, my conscience tells me to. But I know very well that the root of my conscience is not disinterest. The *fons et origo* of all my goodness is the ego. You spoke to me once about the Lord Jesus Christ—'

'Are you giving me a lecture about God?'

'No. I am talking to you about the ego. You are the only man I know who has none.'

'It is easier,' he added, watching Polson take out a brush and comb his beret, 'to be a hero than a hermit. You've gone bald, Amos?'

'Perfectly bald.'

'You will learn to expose the fact to the public since it was done in their service.' Polson had not been spoken to like this since his father died. He rather liked it. 'And what,' he said, 'has all this to do with the railway?'

'One moment.' Polson's eyes, suddenly waken and bright again, startled him. Dewhurst spoke quickly. 'At the ground I watched you. Of all the graziers who congratulated you, you shook hands twice with only one. Nathan Thomas.'

'Well?'

'Let's be quite clear. I said just now that you're changing. So you are. But you are not like us and never will be. You are a man who has built a home in the heart of perdition and more than anything else you wish to retain that home—that, in your heart of hearts, is what you want.'

'I—I simply want my sheep back, Arthur.'

'Your sheep, your self-esteem, your daughter, your home. *You-wish-to-retain-Odessa.*' Dewhurst might have been giving a spelling lesson. Polson noticed his hands: their normal pinkness was discoloured, as if the owner were in pain.

'Very well. I admit that.' Polson had taken out a lady's purse. Dewhurst's eyes narrowed.

'Where did you get that?'

'Frances gave it to me. It contains the money you gave her

last night. Arthur—why do you insist on forcing decisions from those whose way of living makes them your natural enemy?'

'What are you trying to say?'

'That I am not a saint. Also, that I want an explanation—you see, in reality you care nothing for me or Frances. If we sailed tomorrow your life wouldn't alter a jot. Your concern is that I retain Odessa and that I retain it with your money. Why?'

'The railway,' Dewhurst said defensively. 'It is, if you like, my vision. Amos, the line has reached Christchurch—ten miles. Ten miles is nothing! It must go on, Amos. And on. It must cross the island. To do this it must cross your land; it must cross the mountains. Odessa is the gateway. You have said you welcome the railway. I need your support. Your popularity—it matters to me. But now: there is opposition. There is Nathan Thomas. Thomas and his satraps will block the scheme—not because it is unworthy but because it's *mine*. I detest the man. Amos—I've sunk everything I have in the railway, all my capital. I cannot afford interference at this stage. It would ruin me.'

'Amos, you are quite right. I lent Frances the money as a ruse, as a means of persuading you—'

Without a word Polson handed Dewhurst the purse. After a pause he said, 'Thank you for being honest with me.'

Arthur Dewhurst's jacket had remained posed on the dome of his head. Inside it his features appeared clotted, as if he had been discovered on a windy corner. 'I am thoroughly humiliated,' he said. Out of the corner of his eye Polson saw Mrs. Dewhurst gesticulating from the bank. Suddenly he burst out laughing. 'Arthur—it's no crime to admit that your life is governed by profit and loss. Just as mine is ruled by indecision and—' Polson rose abruptly on the points of his hilows and descended again—'and subterfuge.'

'Yours?'

'My dear man: I asked Frances to get that money because I had too much pride to ask you for it myself. I told her I needed it to secure Odessa. I lied. It was for the fares. You might never have seen it again.'

Polson's gaze focussed on a point of waistcoat which seemed at that instant ready to burst; he imagined the tidal juices that it clothed turning sour.

All the buttons ran to meet him. With a gulp, Arthur Dewhurst embraced him.

'Then you'll not sail? You'll keep Odessa?'

'If you like.' Polson stepped back. 'No—no, Arthur. You see. As well as irresolute I am also stupid. I cannot keep Odessa because I have just sold it.'

'Where? When?'

'At the cricket ground.'

'Thomas?'

Polson nodded.

Arthur Dewhurst burst into tears. 'Blast,' he cried.

They were halfway across on the punt when Arthur Dewhurst remembered to say, 'It's all signed then, Amos?'

'Hardly.' Polson, watching for the landing stage, could not understand why Frances had gone ahead. She had crossed without them. He turned. 'No, no, nothing's signed. We do that tomorrow.'

For the second time that day Arthur Dewhurst hugged him. Slowly it dawned on Polson what the other was suggesting. 'It seems very strange, Arthur. But then, as you say, if nothing is set down on paper—'

'How much, Amos? How much?'

'You see.' Polson was a little diffident. 'He just gave me a bill of exchange. I think the figure is seven hundred pounds. But really, I think I ought to give Thomas a little more to buy it back again. Would two hundred pounds be an embarrassment?'

Arthur Dewhurst did not embrace Polson a third time. He simply handed back the purse.

Frances ran on. The plain was bare on this side of the stream, white as gypsum paste where old swamps had dried. There for a mile and more the stream meandered over flat plain into Christchurch, like a canal. But here—now the plain became scrubby and barricaded with flax, sheltering the drear little whares. She parted the rasping blades. Islands of watery raupo lay before her. Flax and more flax, not dense but canopied; and silent. She hesitated.

'Not that way, *chil-d-ddd*!' She heard the remembered cry of Mrs. Dewhurst, saw the widow's peak nose stark with disapproval as she had taken the punt without waiting; and then, landing, darted away from the track leading to Christchurch. Now, alone at last, Frances laughed softly to herself and stepped

THE JOURNEY

into the swamp. She slid to her ankles. Slime everywhere. She kicked off her shoes and carried them. Once she stopped sunk in mire, hot to death, holding the flax, trying to think things out. Sailing? She could not, would not believe it. Her father had been joking—he wouldn't use papa Dewhurst's money for *that*. She passed on, lifting her feet, her thoughts racing. She paused. Interrupting her thoughts was a space, wrapped in bush. She scrambled up a rooted bank and entered the clearing. It was gilded in the strangest light. The afterglow had begun. The glow found the tops of the bush, filtering down in curtains stained violet. All filtered, all vibrant—yet totally still, totally silent. Again a remembered voice: 'You got to be alone, lass, in the twilight.' Mackenzie was right. These last moments presaging the southern night were the most beautiful on earth. She started. 'Who is it?' Flinging round at a crackle. Nobody. There was a path through the trees, overgrown; a patch of leeks, wilted, also overgrown; a smell of over-ripe citrus. She sauntered down the path eating berries and grapes. Vines everywhere. She ate indiscriminately. The berries tasted of almond, half almond, half pumpkin. But bitter, the pips were bitter; and queer. She was starving. 'Who is it?' She peered ahead, frightened. It was behind the persimmon. Then she laughed, clapping her shoes together. 'Go home! Mr. Sunnaway is looking for you at the bog.' The cow looked up, a necklace of berries running from its nose. 'You look just like Droo. Go home. Shoo!' The cow gave Frances an opulent stare, groaned and lay down. Further on was a porch, some immeasurable building. Trees hung over it like a wreath. As she went forward a shadow passed along the verandah and bent over the step, tall, dishevelled and vaguely familiar. She was about to call out when her blazer caught. Freeing it, she had to lean against a trunk, momentarily giddy, pressing her sides. Looking down she saw her dress, her stockings, the mildewed earth, everything turn yellow with the emulgence of abandoned fruit. When she looked again the man had gone. Now there was a boy sitting on the step. Aged eleven or twelve. Something about the attitude, the knees drawn up to the stomach, the hands drooping like faded lilies, made her catch her breath. He wore duck trousers. Only the hands and the trousers were visible—and the face, staring at her. It was the face of an idiot. 'Hullo,' she said, going forward, 'Would you like some?' The child smiled feebly and took the berries, even that was an effort. His face was flushed. Once before she had seen a boy like this, in England. Her father had been working in the parish of St. Bartholomew in Birmingham when he was considering taking orders. One night they had gone to a slum. A family was camping illegally. The police were there. And then a boy had entered carrying coal, grimed and bestial and with a high flush, and turned his eyes on her. The boy had screamed when the police put them on the street.

Why didn't this one scream?

A woman came onto the porch, wearing slippers.

'It's alrightey. He got the sump.'

The woman was real. She had long trailing hair and thick lips; she smiled with the sumptuous thickness of her middle years; she was Maori. Suddenly she slapped the child. 'Not eat berry. No berry, no!'

'Want to come in?' the woman said.

'Thank you,' Frances said. But she could not get up the steps.

'You alrightey?'

'Those berries — are very strange.'

'Who is it?' a man's voice said, and a dog howled as if tormented.

'Some missey. She got the wet feet.'

He came out brusquely, holding a gun.

'Ogodlordalmightey! Quickey, Bernard.' And the missionary, stepping down, caught Frances as she fell.

'It's the pips. The berry's harmless.' The man at the window was writing.

'Yes.' She was terribly thirsty. The mattress she lay on was twisted, the air was stale. The room was full of half-made beds and there was a fire. The smoke made her retch, and vines looping across the two panes of window added to the closeness. Frances felt the closeness of the bush as an oppression and sat up uneasily.

'Feeling better?' Sparrow was leaning on a high desk at the window, writing in a book. He scarcely turned.

Frances nodded, tasting peppermint they had given her earlier. The bitterness at the back of her throat had gone. The woman was in the room crooning, supposedly to a child, but she could not see either. There was a bed next to hers littered with papers, and another bed; between them a door slightly ajar, against which the boy was sitting. He was drawing. He smiled vacantly at Frances; then, leaning back, he pushed the door open further. Irregular sounds came from behind it; and something else, a smell. Sparrow pulled the door to and returned to his desk. At his back was a bed and another door, made of slats; beds and doors and harness rings and old clothes, it was like a barracks. Sparrow put down his pen. He went to the fire and spoke with the woman in Maori. Now he was beside her. 'Drink some more. You'll feel better.' Frances thanked him. The mug was scalding. The liquid was herbal, astringent, but the mint in it was good. 'What does it cure?'

A rich gargling came from the fire. The woman was laughing. 'Everything,' she said, and went on crooning. Sparrow smiled, showing his yellowed teeth. Then he said, 'You shouldn't have come.'

'I said I should, Mr. Sparrow, to see Mervyn.'

'You came alone?'

'Yes. There is no one with me. The others — I was worried and ran on. I left them. Mackenzie is lost, you see. Oh, everything's gone wrong. I don't want to talk about it.' She stopped, noting his puzzled air, and extended a hand. 'But it's alright. I'll go presently. Nobody knows.' At that he relaxed and drew up a stool.

'Yes, that is Mervyn,' he said, glancing over his shoulder. 'He is dying. He draws a lot. And that is my wife. And that is our child.'

'You alrightey now?' The woman joggled a baby boy and gave it to him to hold. Sparrow took the child and began to fondle it, suddenly engrossed. The woman unslung her shift, sat down, and threw back her hair to reveal the thickest nipples Frances had ever seen. Sparrow gave up the child and watched contentedly while it was suckled.

'You have changed,' Frances said.

'I have shaved my beard.' His voice had lost its edge, like his wristbands which were folded back and tied with wire. He was less stooped, less cadaverous than she remembered; his black choker hung to his knees and she could not tell if he wore a collar.

'I didn't mean that. I meant — may I say that you seem more contented and because of that more honest?' She frowned. It was the wrong word. But he laughed aloud. She said quickly, 'Are you still a missionary?'

'My dear, I am in hiding!' He chuckled evasively. 'But yes, yes—yes. Only—' He turned to her. 'When I left Odessa something occurred to me. I wonder how it will strike you. You remember the Lord said, "Suffer those who are lost to come unto me"? Now, supposing he meant "Suffer the lost ones to cry out and I shall go unto them"—what then?'

'There is a different emphasis.'

'Precisely. I would be glad if you would explain it to your father. Assuming of course that he inquires.'

'About you? Of course he will.'

Sparrow was bending over the child.

'Is it a boy?'

'Yes.'

'He has your eyes,' she said. 'You're very fond of him, aren't you?'

The missionary was silent. Presently he said in an altogether different tone, so softly that she barely heard the words, 'I am going away.' And then, abruptly: 'Does your father care for children?'

'Yes. Why yes, I think so.' She could not follow him now, neither the changed tone, the abrupt questioning nor the half-stifled 'Thank you' that he gave, looking straight past her.

'Strange you should say that. Papa loves children, especially boys. He always wanted one of his own.'

'Thank you,' he said again.

In the silence that followed Frances turned and saw that the boy Mervyn had stopped drawing. She put down the mug.

'What is it?' Sparrow said.

'I thought I heard voices.'

'It's only the printing press. It goes all the time.' He paused and she saw that the old habit of fingering his black glove had not left him. 'I shall probably take it with me when I go. Yes, probably I shall. And from time to time I shall send your father messages.'

'Messages,' she repeated. 'Yes. Of course.'

'From time to time,' he added.

It was very strange. Then there was that noise coming through the wall behind Mervyn, sharp and irregular. Now there were sounds from beyond the verandah also. The missionary had heard. The woman rose with the baby and went out.

Frances stood up. 'I think perhaps my father may come after all. He will be looking for me. If I may—?'

'Of course, my dear, of course. Take the candle and wait for him on the verandah. I would rather not meet him, not today. Goodbye.' He smiled shyly and was gone.

Frances was about to step outside when something made her turn. In the far corner a latch clicked. The boy Mervyn was standing, fluttering a piece of paper. He was beckoning. She recrossed the room. 'For me?' He nodded, his glaucous eyes shining. She set down the candle and bent over the paper. It was covered in thick pencil strokes resembling long sticks. Or rods. She could make out nothing else. 'Thank you,' she said, puzzled. He stood aside, pressing open the door as he did so, and beckoned again. The door led onto another verandah, narrow and arched with bush, open in places to the sky. Light showed from a door at the far end. 'Oh, you mean the printing press? Of course.' It was not until she had passed along and was standing by the lighted door, listening, that she began to question the sounds within. 'How curious,' she thought, and was turning back when the door opened, a stifling heat enveloped her and she saw in a flash what the drawing had intended she should see.

'Good evening, Miss Polson.' He stood filmed in cordite dust. He pulled the door quickly behind him.

'I—I am sorry. I wanted—'

'Yes, Miss Polson? What did you want?'

He was still wearing the cricket cap. He had been drinking. His face and chest were daubed with ochre and as she backed away he came towards her, holding the stump of his arm stiffly. He was quite naked.

'Peeping, Miss Polson?'

'No.'

'Little pee-ping spar-row. What did you want, Miss Polson?'

'I want—' She held to the rail. He was almost touching her. They moved cat-like together, his lips thrust to her ear. She heard their icy rasping, the crackle of dry paint as her fingers slid backwards along the railing, then nothing: only a wild drumming that rose from under and burst in foment on her brain.

'You want perhaps . . .' He was eeling about, flaunting his belly and loins. 'Perhaps?' He gave a lascivious grin and, suddenly sweeping the white cap from his head, hung it down low. It hung jibbering—obscenely white and jibbering before her. He laughed softly.

Even then she did not scream. She had read somewhere that human ingenuity in the face of prolonged terror is great. She was carrying, now, now she remembered (why not?) a pair of shoes. These she threw. They clattered of course. (Why of course?) Anyway he lurched, something white fell. (Did it?) And a hand, small as a leaf, was dragging her back, back through total darkness, was fleeing with her through the house. Yes, yes, but who howled?

'Was it *you*, papa?'

'It must have been. That's better.' Polson was sitting beside her on the step in the umbry light, brushing dirt from her face and blazer. ' "Tooted", the woman said — you must have eaten more than the berries. How very odd, I thought it applied only to cattle. Feeling better now? Of course it was me, Francie. You ran right past me. Then you flumped on the ground, just there.'

'Have you got the bat?'

'Bat?' Polson peered at her.

'There was a bat. I must have left it.'

Then: 'Papa?'

'Yes?'

'Why did you howl?'

'Howl? My dear girl, I've been sitting here like a mouse for twenty minutes waiting to tell you my news. A Maori told me where you were, then I met a dead cow. Strange. The Maori told me Sparrow lived here. He hasn't come, you know.' Polson rose and took his daughter's arm, liking the fierce way that she clung, staring up with a sense of aboriginal wonder at the trees and the moon breaking through.

'The woman left me a candle."

'Candle?'

'Yes.' He chuckled. 'But I had to douse it. I was being eaten alive. D'you know, Francie? The mosquitoes here are much worse than they are at Odessa. Come along.'

They were going home. It was two days later.

'What did you say?' Polson shouted to Frances. 'Heavens, hold on.' The trap swayed on hinges of rust and Polson, gripping the reins, rose up like a puppet; a moment later he descended on the piece of stretched sacking and the two girls, who were also sitting on it, were projected into the air. Frances settled with hilarity. Rose gulped. Rose was coming with them after all. Polson had insisted. He kept apologising to Rose for the fog and saying, 'Hold on.' The unsprung tilbury that he had acquired jolted through the ravine. The horses, two new greys, were barely teamed. Now they were climbing again. 'What was that, Francie?'

'I said you haven't told me everything. When papa Dewhurst said you were "sound" together, does that mean partners?'

Polson nodded, perforce: the way was so bad his chin and neck bumped together continually. 'Sound, Amos—soun-ddd!' Arthur Dewhurst's parting cry lingered in the fog like a bad joke. Yet what a comforting ring the word had! And by God, he would be sound this time, for Frances' sake. He winked at her muffled features. The shock of that night, the vagrant coltishness, the delusion of an arsenal in the bush, had receded. She wore a bemused half-smiling expression, and though he had not told her the extent of his compromise, he had the feeling that she approved.

'Yes. I am the junior partner,' he said.

'Then he—he will control everything?'

'Oh no. Far from it, m'dear. I have insisted on much. I have reserved the right, for example, to be proprietary about the emotions.'

'Stop teasing me, papa.'

'Didn't I say? Young Hollis is coming.'

'As manager? *Dick Hollis?*' He nodded. Her face lit up.

Yes, decidedly she approved.

'Also,' he said—but just then Rose was sick again. Rose, who had not travelled in the grey stone country before, pleaded with them to turn back. In her suffering she imagined herself tooted and prayed to die by the wayside in a strawberry mess, like the cow.

'Change of diet,' Polson said, pulling up for the twentieth time.

Frances held the girl whimpering over an abyss. 'It's the air, Rosie—simply the transition. It will be easy when we get there.'

No, thought Polson, catching his daughter's eye: not easy. Neither easy nor difficult—but *easier*, for us both. And because he was going home he winked at the girl who thought she was a cow, and drove on into the mountains.

Mr. Huntley-Shawcross had been described as a Hatter, a name sometimes granted the gold seeker or the remittance man. But he was more than that. Hatters do not normally speak Peruvian dialect and wear green spectacles, although it is possible they may be given like Mr. Shawcross to breeding mice. Mr. Huntley-Shawcross was a cultured man. He was a member of the Philosophical Society of Bath. He was on the maternal side a half-brother to Neüstatter, the famous geologist, whose lectures on the Australian goldfields of the 1850s occupied so much space in the London newspapers; he was also related to an unmarried Unitarian named Palfrey, said the father of Californian botany, who introduced the *sequoia gigantea* into Britain and commonly wrote four thousand letters a year. Although he never met them, Mr. Huntley-Shawcross owed something to both men. Indeed they account for the fusion of the two basic elements in his character: the arboreal and the mineral. Peru was a digression in his travels, but an important one nonetheless, for it was there among the Shipibos of the Ucayali region that he encountered a mythological tree of the universe. He had of course read of it — the cosmogony of the ancient Chaldeans and Egyptians was not unknown to him —

but in Peru, where he was for a time under the influence of the ayahuasca drug, the concept took a rather unusual form; and he became imbued with the idea of a mother lode, hidden at the base of a cosmic tree of light. In his subsequent search for gold, in California, in the Andes, in the volcanic isles of the New Hebrides and the camps of the Bendigo diggers, Mr. Huntley-Shawcross was forever craning into the soul of the primitive to catch the sign of truth. In Australia for example, among the pictographs of the aborigines, he encountered a phallic tree which affected him with an intense almost physical pain. The top-most branches were in flame and the lower half embedded in a pool of yellow dust. Unfortunately the source of the tree itself was not revealed. In New Zealand however he found a tribe of nomadic Maoris whose concept of a cosmogonic tree almost exactly coincided with his own.

These natives were unutterably simple. They had a curious history. In the 1830s, harried by war-like tribes from the north, they had retreated south. They were a remnant. They identified themselves with a tribe of hunters, tall and auburn-haired, who in remote times had inhabited a lost land between the alps, eating the flesh of the moa and the fish of the lakes. Oral tradition did not explain the mysterious death of their ancestors; it merely granted title to their land and told them they would be delivered there by a stranger who was a reincarnation of the fertility god they worshipped. This was a quaint figure with a pot belly not much bigger than a teapot. Retreating south, they had attempted to plant the figure on the top of a mountain, but a storm came and they were forced to abandon him halfway up. For a time they inhabited the coast. Civilisation turned them inland. Once they were converted. A Baptist mission led by one Maximilian Flight found them. Mr. Flight was a wizened gentleman with retractable spectacles and a turned-up collar of the kind sometimes seen loitering at second-hand pastry stalls. He gave them English lessons, Bibles and soap. The soap was an afterthought. Mr. Flight gave them 48 lb of brown Windsor soap and the natives ate the lot and were sick. They abandoned Mr. Flight. When they had retreated as far as Otago and could go no further they found he had given them measles as well. Prospectors entering these remote gorges found the tribe camped in a gloomy valley, between a rampart and a river, on a bed of caked mud. They found them shy, illkempt, phthisic, half

Christian and malleable only when plied with rum. A Roman Catholic priest, who came later, found them degenerate but not difficult to reconvert—save one, an aged specimen with a mobile face like a monkey's, called Wiremu. Mr. Huntley-Shawcross who came about the same time found them charming, especially the chief who had taken the name of St. Kemp. Mr. St. Kemp was a drunkard. He had the mind of a child. He liked his latest visitor and set him up in a cave. He liked to visit him there and see the mice; he liked the violin on which the man from Bath sometimes played to him; but most of all he liked Mr. Huntley-Shawcross for his rum. It was there one day that Mr. Huntley-Shawcross showed the chief a pictograph he had discovered on a wall of the cave. He did not tell the chief he had done it himself. Mr. St. Kemp looked. He saw an ochreous figure painted on the wall with long hair, snake-encircled, coiling between earth and sky. The Medusa image puzzled him at first until he stood off and recognised the parasitic serpents as branches. The effect now was tree-like and distinctly female. Perhaps the chief thought he saw the Earth Mother, perhaps he did not. But his bleary and disconsolate eye opened very wide and he confided much in the man from Bath. He told him for instance of the golden blank, the fecund land his tribe had sought for generations; and of the coming of a stranger who would reveal the womb of the Earth Mother herself, having first turned her over and lain with her in order to regenerate the race.

Some prospectors might have laughed. Mr. Huntley-Shawcross did not laugh. He knew he was on the edge of gold-bearing country. He respected symbolism. In the metaphysical leaning of the savage mind he discerned the fusion of two other elements, one botanical, one mineral, which had for so long eluded him. He made some notes, reflections. He observed among other things that as regards the origin of mankind the Maori had evolved a scheme which was supremely imaginative. No other system had evoked the source of cosmic mystery quite so suggestively. Sometimes the key, the begetting agent, was a tree and sometimes a pillar and sometimes the body of the Earth Mother herself. In Maori myth symbols were frequently exchanged. The form of the dream, however, was always the same. There was a place at the end of the last great journey on earth leading down to the source of ultimate light and universal wealth; and the way was barred only by the Po or Unknown.

So wrote the little man from Bath in his journal. The notes were found later, under a decomposed mouse. It is not surprising that a man so mytho-poetically inclined should believe in this place and desire it for his own. What is surprising is that a lapsed tribe in the depths of Otago should inform him, so soon after his arrival, that the moment of delivery was at hand. Such coincidences, in the experience of the much travelled Mr. Huntley-Shawcross, were exceedingly rare.

Mackenzie woke slowly. Out of his dreams a putty-coloured face descended. It wore a hat and was not quite in focus.

'They want to take you from me,' it said; and Mackenzie smiled at the putty-coloured man in the beaver hat. He wore india-rubber galoshes with rough soles over kneeboots, and tiny creatures nestled in his beard. In point of fact, Mackenzie told himself, I am among the Little People.

'But we shan't let them, shall we?'

'Nay.' Mackenzie belched and tasted a familiar bitter-sweet kernel. 'Look,' he said noting the cave drawing. 'Look man. There is an stem. There is an tree stem growing on yon wall.'

The other leaned forward and crooned: 'You remember?'

But Mackenzie's interest had strayed. 'What is that?' he said, indicating a glinty ledge.

The little man rose crossly. 'Those are my portable soups. We shall need them. Listen carefully. I also have a supply of tinned beans, pickles and sago. And some novels. I have the complete works of Thackeray and the *Pleiad*. I can't leave my Thackeray, and I must have my clothes line and my violin. And my gold dish. You have your dilly bag. I shall take the utensils and the beasties and you will carry Elsa's cage and the books and the bird bath. Everything else you will put in the dilly bag, we shall manage nicely. Shan't we?'

Mackenzie smiled. He was floating. Something hopped from his beard onto his chest and began pecking. He stroked it.

'You remember Elsa? Elsa has missed you.'

Mackenzie nodded, not because he remembered but because the budgerigar was so evidently happy among the lice that grazed there.

'Profligate little fellows, aren't they?' The little man took a toothpick and probed about under the sick man's brows, spearing the vermin and then suffocating them in the strands of his own trailing beard. Besides mice, the beard contained a quantity of toothpicks. Mackenzie had never seen so many toothpicks before.

'I hope you don't mind my green spectacles,' the man went on. 'The light is very strong and I must keep watching.' He went to the opening, parted a sack curtain and peered out. Wreathed in the fumes of a small pungent fire, he hovered there as on the lip of a kettle; then he removed his spectacles and sat cross-legged as before with his beard folded on his lap, and regarded Mackenzie with a cockley and meticulous eye.

'We leave tomorrow,' he said.

Mackenzie liked the man's voice. It had a honeyed flavour, familiar as the taste in the back of his throat. He felt his lips. They had vanished to the gums. He put up a finger and two teeth fell out. He eased himself against the wall. Curious how he did it without moving. His joints cohered musically as if oiled and the music was repeated in his ears. Birds sang. Birds flew. The cave was layered with skins of light like the inside of an onion, rotunded with ledges and birds and the homely labels of portable soups. The nectar in his mouth transported him. He himself was floating to the cupola, guest of the Little People — high, high above the Imp who presided with a cockley and meticulous eye, and was so kindly.

'I was thinking,' Mackenzie said.

'About the tree?'

'Food, man. Is there food?'

The little man's eyes narrowed. 'We shall come to that in a moment.'

'What on earth is up with the mosquitoes?' he added, picking up a churchwarden and hurling it. The bowl of the pipe clattered against the rock wall, disturbing a bat. Several parakeets cooed. 'The mosquitoes are very bad. I have been very good to you, Mackenzie, letting you sleep; you didn't notice them. *I* cannot sleep. I have to get up and dress and go to bed again.'

'Why is the ankles swelled?'

'Scurvy. I have dressed them with a lady's kid glove.'

'Nay. Tis the chains.'

'Of course, the chains. I am sorry about the chains.'

They were not fastened to anything but they were very heavy and Mackenzie could not move his legs, although he tried.

'The ankles, look.'

'The lice, my dear. They multiply, don't you know? Don't *scratch*.' He leaned forward and slapped Mackenzie, his voice rising to a whine.

Then: 'It is great pity you brought none of the gold with you.'

'I am nay thief.'

'But you are, my dear. A very fine thief indeed. You told me about it. I have written it down, every word. Listen. "Fire springs from her loins and her valleys are paved with gold." Poetry, Mackenzie; your dreams are poetry. It is all in the journal.'

'Tell me — is there water.'

'Why?' Mackenzie said idly.

'For washing the stuff.'

Mackenzie was silent. His eyes had fallen into their sockets. Roving about they assumed the luminosity of periwinkles set in courses of ashlar; passed blankly over the wall painting and came to rest on the pit fire at the entrance. An iron pot sat on bars; below, food was roasting. Saliva ran from Mackenzie's mouth.

'Those sheep of yours in Scotland,' the little man said. 'That was a beautiful theft. And the dog, she is a theft too —'

'The lass — where is she?'

'Best of all,' the other continued, 'are the sheep you brought. O a lovely theft! D'you know, my dear, it takes three of those savages to slaughter one of your animals?'

'They are cooking the flock then?'

'My dear, you must be famished. Have some mutton.'

Mackenzie reached out eagerly, but the portion was set beyond his grasp. 'Give it me.'

'On second thoughts, you are better without.'

'Put it in the mouth, man.'

'Don't whimper. I shall give you mutton when you tell me the way.'

'Ay,' Mackenzie said, without interest.

'You see, if you do not tell me, I shall be obliged to give you to Mr. Kemp. He is the chief. Mr. *St*. Kemp, if you please. He dresses entirely in English costume and is very fond of whites.'

''Tis him cooking the flock then?'

'But of course. To tell you the truth I am rather frightened of him. Now he — shall I tell you a secret?'

'Ay. Oh ay, an it passes the time.'

'He is preparing a feast in your honour. The tribes are assembling.'

'Ay, an tis a grand honour.'

'My dear, you don't understand. You are to be the middle course.'

Mackenzie dislodged another tooth. A wan smile crossed his face. Beyond the entrance he could see a sill of red cliffs. He could see a pa, the tops of huts. And above the pa a small cultivated field. 'I was thinking,' he said.

'Thinking?'

'I was thinking. I havna seen a patch of turnips since Scotland.'

The little man scowled and drew the sack close. Then the scowl vanished. Mackenzie had become excited, chuckling and scrabbling at his chains with small ineffectual movements. His eyes were fixed on the tree.

'Ah, ah! He remembers! Elsa, our friend remembers.' The little man sprang forward, the budgerigar pressed to his cheek. He bent low to hear what Mackenzie was saying. As he did so the budgerigar flew out from his fingers and disappeared under the hat. The mice ran from his beard and hid in a frying pan. The little man stood, listening. 'Bother,' he said. Very quickly he took an olive-coloured bottle and poured half the contents down Mackenzie's throat. Then he lit a candle. When a moment later the curtain was parted to reveal an elderly Maori in European dress bearing a pail of milk, the little man was seated at the patient's head reading in honeyed tones from Thackeray's *Book of Snobs*.

The visitor's moley eyes searched the candleglow for the form of Mackenzie. Then their owner, having satisfied himself, made the sign of the cross and set down the pail.

'You are early, Kemp.' The little man did not look round.

'Yes, sir.' The chief continued to regard the sick man disconsolately.

'Well?'

'The litter is ready. In two days the star Vega is in the moon.'

'Indeed?' The little man's voice was pinched, no longer sweet. 'You see him, Kemp. Putrid. Look, come closer.' Mr. St. Kemp did not move. Debauched pagan that he was, he preferred to treat of his messiahs whenever possible through an intermediary. 'The fool isn't fit to travel to the end of your nose.'

The nose was a sore point with Kemp. Like his faith and his culture, it had been broken: the debauch that had damaged it was recent and the chief rubbed his gut remindingly. His tongue was dry.

'He is not a god, you know.' The little man filled a pan with rum. Mr. St. Kemp shuffled up, took the pan and retreated with it to the doorway where he drank greedily.

'In fact,' the other continued, 'he will probably die.' As he spoke Mackenzie retched violently. Mr. St. Kemp paled. He had been a fine old man, less corpulent than fronded, and hoary. He was mostly hair and twist now, squashed into a triangular bend that was accentuated by a pair of ballooning duck trousers that stopped tight on the calves. About the nose were arraigned hoods of fat, rolled in moustaches, suggestive of distemper or a badly combed walrus; and the eyes that started in their pouches were quite bloodshot.

'That is why, Kemp, I have decided. I shall be your guide. You are very lucky.'

'Lucky?'

'He has told me everything. You understand what that means? . . . My dear, I know the way. I *know*.'

Mr. St. Kemp shifted on his canvas shoes through which the toes protruded. They were big toes. They, no less than his person, were undecided.

'Don't slouch.' The voice, frugal as hide, pulled the old man up sharply. 'And the next time you visit me see that you dress properly in a shirt and braces. This is a private residence.'

'When—?' the chief began.

'When I am ready, Kemp.'

'The people will want to see him before leaving.'

'Now that is interesting, that. Unfortunately I must refuse. There will be no crying in this house.'

The big toes became planted. 'It is necessary, sir, to wait on the truth before it departs.'

'Kemp, you are a fool. You think he will die of grace, you are wrong: he will die of sin. It is a punishment for touching the berry of your sacred tree. Perhaps you have heard of the Chilean tree, *coriaria ruscifolia*? The seed of the berry induces a high state of fever, suppuration of the tonsils, then delirium, disintegration. See how the fingernails have begun to drop out? The effect is similar to that of the Peruvian tree drug, ayahuasca. The

Mexican drug tlolocopeti is also related. Sometimes it merely affects the medulla oblongata causing paralysis of the brain, but often'—the eyes hardened—'often, Kemp, the disease spreads. It would be dangerous, I fear, to bring your people here.'

'Dangerous?'

The little man stood up. 'I must give the beasties their supper. Did you remember to strain the milk?'

The chief nodded dumbly.

'Kemp. I have had an amusing thought. You had better sacrifice the dog. The animal is likewise contaminated.'

'But the measles is over, sir. The priest has come and we have got rid of the dirt.'

'Over? Measles! O Kemp, this is worse than measles. O my dear Kemp. You must never underestimate the diseases of the white man.'

'Wiremu will be unhappy, sir. He is very attached to the animal.'

'As you wish.' The man from Bath took the pail and poured milk into a dish.

'I talk to the elders, sir.'

'Talk by all means.' He clapped his hands. From the ledges and the hidden places a scurrying of specks, white and brown and magpied, converged on the dish and the plashing of their small tongues was as the carillon of foam caps beating on a distant shore. The chief watched with a shy fascination. When the mice had nearly done the man from Bath lifted his hat and the budgerigar flew down to tap the grains he had sprinkled in the dish. Taking up the book he sat down by Mackenzie's side and continued reading where he had left off, his frugal voice rising and falling above the tin chorus like a gull's. Presently he turned to the figure in the doorway.

'You may go now, Kemp.'

It was dusk when Mackenzie woke, into candlelight. The slurred light, the close wombed walls, the smell of meat newly roasted warmed him; and he lay, hands pressed to the pit of his stomach, in order to empty it for the food he would shortly receive. There was a plate of mutton set before him. At length, rising on an elbow, he lunged towards it, but as he did so the flame vanished and with it, the plate. Now the flame lit the wall opposite, the glinty soups on the ledge and the great dawn tree whose tendrils sank to the white of the little man's hair. The latter sat in an embrasure with an antimacassar at his head, stitching a length of calico into a bag.

'What is that?' Mackenzie said.

'This is your winding sheet. Please call me Barney.'

'Barney,' Mackenzie said.

'And the smaller bag is for the dog. It is a custom to bury both together.'

'Ay, master and hound; tis custom. Are they coming then?' The little man smiled.

'Food, man,' Mackenzie said.

'Then again,' said the little man, moving the plate just out of reach, 'I might persuade them to spare the dog—to guide me, you understand. Since you will not accompany me—'

'I canna travel, Barney, without food.'

'You will come then? O splendid! We shall travel together.'

Mackenzie put a hand to his brow as if to control a great thought. 'Why?' he said.

'My dear, you have the appetite of a mouse. I never knew a man who cost me so little to keep. Also—you know the way.'

'I know the way to *her*.' Mackenzie held up the ring he wore and gazed at it. Somewhere in that pale blue fire burned a memory, could he but grasp it.

'Mutton?' The man called Barney edged the plate forward. Mackenzie grasped, and his nails broke on rock. He wiped his brow, damp with vermin, and slithered over the rock pallet, on his side, reaching. He did this many times. Bewildered, he sat back. 'Barney, the plate is travelling.'

'I shall give it to you when you tell me about her. *Her*, you said. See? I have it written down. *Her*. Now. It cannot be the girl.'

'Nay.'

'And it cannot be the dog.'

'Nay.'

'Nor your sister, she is dead.'

'Ay, Mary is died.'

'Then'—the little man lifted the candle and his fable, pitch and gold, seemed to radiate above them—'Then she is here?'

Mackenzie gazed at the spangled tree. ''Tis a worry not to know, Barney. Ay, if thee say: that mun be her.'

' "Coppery", you said. "She turns and opens on soft nights." You are a great lover, Mackenzie, you see what the ordinary mortal does not see. It is a pity that the art of observation is disappearing. It is due to the spread of education. And then? On the ground, under the earth, among the roots, what then?'

'Glow-worms.'

'No, Mackenzie; those are the meteors, very poetic. "Trailing glow-worms in the night sky", you said—poetic, very; I have it all down. But what do you see when she turns over, when she *opens*?'

Mackenzie gave a sigh. He saw then. Looking into the flame of the candle, he saw a rain of pollen descend over his land. In the end of his journey he saw the beginning.

'Oh ay, beautiful,' he said. 'When she turns.'

The gnome was staring at him in puzzlement and wonder. Mackenzie was turning the ring in the candlelight—it had a life of its own, this jewel: a memory of coppery laughter: of hair spilling over him at the fire, hair that was not jet but tangled copper with tones of laughter, tangling his thoughts like dust...

'What is beautiful, Mackenzie?'

'Copper and pollen and dust,' he burbled. And the little man sat up.

'Dust?'

'Ay, dust, man. Yellow dust.'

Barney was delighted. His cockley eyes glinted. He began to caress the lines of the tree with his fingertips except for the little finger of the left hand where the nail grew abnormally long and with which presently he began to conduct, hopping about. In a trice the mice ran from his beard and entered the dance, also the budgerigar. As he hopped, he crooned:

> Gold is for your mistress
> Gold is for your tree
> Gold is growing in the earth
> Gold for you and me

'NAY!' Mackenzie roared suddenly.

There was a whinny of rubber as the galoshes came to rest.

'But, my dear. You and I—we share.'

'An share is right. The sheep is the Polson's, but the land is the tribes'.'

'But the tree, Mackenzie, the tree!'

'Tree? Don't be cripple, man; tis the golden floodplain I am telling of. Tis Polson's land an the girl's, and after that tis the tribes'. There is nay tree.'

'No tree?' With a squeal of rage the little man leaped on Mackenzie's chest and began to cuff him with the fist of his beard. Mackenzie slid down. It was a tiny weight that he felt, a tickling, tiny blows. He slid down. He could not stop himself. O the kaleidescopic images he saw in that descent! He slid sixteen inches and was arrested once more by the ledge of particoloured soups. He was aware of no weight leaving his stomach, of no menace in the atmosphere nor flame at the entrance nor of the little man's sudden attention to the pot that smouldered there. More properly it was a cauldron, set over a pit with a handle on either side. It was old with caulk and fumes of tar. But more probably pitch since from pitch comes a form of lampblack; and it was this which had formed the basis of the little man's rock painting. The tree itself, nestled with birds, was faithful enough to the rambling of Mackenzie's dreams; but the tap roots, wedged in yellow ochre, were ridiculous. Gold, as we now know, though it may lie at the root of wisdom seldom lies at the root of trees: and perhaps the man from Bath realised this at last. Taking up the pot in both hands he glowered at the drawing and moved as if he would fling the contents and destroy it utterly. But then, stepping over Mackenzie's body with the pot held high, he saw the latter's eye, fixed on the tree with a rapt expression; and the innocence of that deception infuriated him. A toy smile lit his lips.

'Soup?' he called softly, and Mackenzie looked up.

'Set it down, man. Set it down, tis brimming.'

'El-sa?' The man's smile faded as the budgerigar, its grazing pattern disturbed appeared, with awful clarity on the victim's brow. Sharply now, 'Elsa!' Obediently the bird flew up and disappeared inside the cauldron. 'Elsa?' he whispered. 'O *E-L-S-AAAA*!' The scream roused Mackenzie, as the vessel fell. It fell sideways beside his head and did not break, being of iron, although the molten liquid spilled. The liquid splashed the wall, entered the nitches, clogged the cracks, fissures, mosses, all the sinter, and rose hissing towards the cupola whence it fell soundlessly in gouts onto the sick man's head. One gout, the size of a potato, dropped at the little man's feet where it rested like some larval excrescence on a floor of new varnish. Sobbing, he turned the hump with the stem of his churchwarden. But Elsa was no longer recognisable.

The cave had grown mealy and dark, as from a simoom. The

candle, kneeling in a pool of transient gold, had expired almost immediately. Mackenzie lay with his hands to his eyes, writhing.

'Come closer,' the little man said. He was quavering like a goat. Mackenzie advanced with a soft fury, hobbling. Chained, the ring bolt dragged free; and moaning, with a purple blotched face. Still he advanced obediently into the light, for light he could see.

'Closer?' The little man wheedled. He held a glowing brand and pointed it, at twenty inches. He had never blinded a man before and such spectral courage advancing as a moth to the flame made him wonder if he knew to go through with it. Still he quaked. 'You understand, my dear? It is because of Elsa. Say you do—o say you understand!' He gibbered and held the brand to plunge it one way; then his head twisted round in another way, astonished. A sound like the popping of glass reverberated in the vault. It was only the fly of spittle. But Mr. St. Kemp, who had come unseen, had spat magnificently. For an instant his blubbery lips were identified at the entrance in the shape of a halo. The chief and his followers had arrived bearing torches and a litter in order to sit, mourning, unto death. As was custom. Mr. St. Kemp was wearing a korowai cloak over braces and had entered first, with one finger pressed to the right nostril. But instead of snuffing up the odour of sanctity emanating from the dying god, as intended, he had spat. Seeing the antics of that bereaved goat, and his god (gruesome spectacle) shifting in agony. And now, finger still poised, he sniffed the air and considered silently the possibility of action. Did he detect some ineffable imprint of evil? At all events he spat again and considered a moment longer. Debased paganism and laodicean Christianity will try the keenest wits, but dull old Kemp was rather fond of the title he had lately caught from the Catholic missionary—Jerubabbsel, the priest had baptised him: Old Bible. Therefore he sought in a kindly way for some Biblical formula to arrest the sinfulness that he detected before him. Sin, the priest said, was punishable only after death. But that did not ease the conflict in Mr. St. Kemp's soul. Gods punished gods, reward was here and now; conduct, not consequences, was what mattered. As he thought this Mr. St. Kemp felt better. So he acted by the conduct of his race and gave an order. His followers, one of whom was carrying a mussel-shell, stepped forward and carried out the command with an almost apostolic faith. When they had castrated Mr. Huntley-Shawcross they rolled a stone across the entrance to the cave and left him there.

Father Bataille was puzzled. He knelt in the round bark church that the natives had built for him and he prayed. 'Holy Jesus grant me a sight of this abomination that walks among us that they call *atua*, spirit of the ancestors, that I may battle with him and bring him to Thee cleansed and purified . . .' Father Bataille was a man possessed of few, if chosen words, no chin and an enormous backside. He was a big man with a large panelled face and as he prayed he sweated; the church was built on layers of old mud eruptions and an invisible powder, blowing off the floor and through the grass-lined walls, invaded his garments and presently he began to scratch and stopped praying altogether. He thought about the natives. The Maoris called him 'Your Very Great Gentleman White Man' and he rather liked that. Fate had brought them to him in sickness and death, and he rather liked that also. In his opinion disease was to faith as yeast to the dough: and he had cured all that, more or less. The one thing he had not cured was ancestor worship. Some vague anthropomorphic spirit stalked the pa—and the priest was troubled. He thought about Wiremu whom he did not like. Wiremu called him 'Your Immense'. Wiremu was a mystery. Wiremu was the only one—the thought stung the priest as he pictured the slight twisted form with the stooped lids—Wiremu was the only one who had not been baptised. Why? Father Bataille was suspicious. Then there was the dog Wiremu guarded. There were other mysteries too: the sheep, for instance. The priest picked a speck from his eye and smiled, remembering how many of the beasts the natives had sold in order to furnish his church—a sign of true faith. His eye moved over the altar which had about it an air of gilt and dim gingerbread which reminded him of his village church near Lyon. He nodded with satisfaction. How compliant the New Zealanders were! Tribes, to Father Bataille, were crafts moored to satanic banks; and Mr. St. Kemp's tribe, more punt than craft, had been barely floating when he arrived. Tapus, mourning rites, totem worship, tattooing, ceremonial wailing—he had cut them all. (Save one.) And the result was this church fashioned in rural simplicity even to the window sashes: not a shred of degradation, not a sign of native carving in it. The priest nodded again; at the same time he offered a prayer of silent thanks to the Baptists.

'If only,' he thought, 'Wiremu had contracted measles with the rest.' His suspicions about Wiremu revived. The more he thought about him, the more he longed to kick him into grace and the more that cantankerous monkey face annoyed him.

His eye passed to a tableau behind the altar. It was a picture he always carried with him. It showed a chronological tree in the form of a cross. Christ was on one side amid heathens, blessing the tree which was the true Faith; and the Protestants were shown as the lopped branches to be cast into the fire. At the bottom was the crest of his mission, *Eslaf*, L'Eternelle Société de Lyon pour l'Annonciation de la Foi. Suddenly a thought came to him. The priest rose, dusted a bulrush from his skirt, crossed himself and went out. He passed along the reed huts until he came to one larger than most, ducked low and went inside. The occupant was lying on a mat.

'Wiremu,' said the priest, 'I have been thinking of something Jerubabbsel said to me yesterday. That tree of yours does not exist.'

Wiremu's face did not contort as it usually did into a rascally grin. For one thing he had a pipe in it; for another he was playing draughts, a game popularised by the late Maximilian Flight, and without an opponent he found that a considerable strain. Also his head hurt. He took the pipe from his mouth, licked the juice from the chiselled underlip and spat. Then he returned the pipe to the gap in his front teeth.

'Is the tree there, Wiremu?'

Wiremu pressed his nose flat with his forefinger, and pondered. Why was the priest so stupid? They had had this dialogue before.

'We are bound to it, your Immense.'

'How, mon vieux?'

Wiremu explained with difficulty. Strictly speaking, he said, they were not bound by the root but by the navel strings of their ancestors which had been hung upon the boughs at birth. In sympathetic association the tree had grown fruitful and so had the tribe. 'So the people will return to the land that grows it and multiply, your Immense.'

'Ah yes. But Wiremu, if you grow sick, will the tree help you then?'

Wiremu turned, his eyes suddenly baleful; and the priest, bending down, observed the whites as if he would lick them. He stepped back—carefully, for the dog was under his feet. 'The trouble with trees, Wiremu, is that they grow old and die. The tree is dead, mon vieux. Explain to me, if it is not dead, why the tribe has fallen into barrenness?'

Wiremu could not say.

When the priest went out, squinting into the sunlight, he was much pleased. He waved to the boy Moses, Wiremu's son, standing in his monitor's smock beside a disused whare. Odd, the priest thought, how the lad is always there. But back in his church the thought left him and he knelt to give thanks for the efficacy of his mission; past, present, and future. His mind ranged over the whole state of the Church in New Zealand; and pausing to acknowledge his debt to the Protestants, Father Bataille remembered once again Mr. Flight, the Baptist, who had delivered Mr. St. Kemp's tribe up out of measles. He recalled the night of his own arrival. There had been two deaths that day and a profound awe had attended him as he knelt, missal in one hand and a powder dark as oxide in the other. The powder he had sifted into an iron vessel and from this he had brewed a mysterious concoction, gently stirring. It was half liquid, half jelly. Such was its fragrance, the natives had begged to be allowed to drink. Father Bataille had refused. For two nights he refused. On the third night when the corpses were stinking and the natives prostrate with grief and fasting, he pronounced the spirit risen from the vessel and permitted the chief to taste from a silver teaspoon. Hot chocolate blancmange, the priest knew, was a restorative and no chief had ever failed to ask for more. So it was with Mr. St. Kemp. From there to the draining of the vessel was but a queue of teaspoons, and conversion to Rome but a natural consequence. Protestant Bibles were burned, prieux Dieu distributed and the iron vessel consecrated as the headstone of the new church. Father Bataille had buried vessels from the headwaters of the Waikato to the Puketoi Ranges, his crest was known from the golden sands of Takaka to the domed hills of Otago; he had exorcised Lutheran consumption, Anglican influenza, Wesleyan dysentery, Congregational pox and, as recorded, Baptist measles; and whenever his detractors had complained of a lack of scruple he had always replied, raising his bronze voice and pointing to the infants wasting in the damp raupo huts, that Rome had merely come to the Antipodes like the plague.

Now in his church he prayed powerfully, doubting not that his battle with the last stronghold of Satan was at hand. Wiremu would come to him; one glance at his eyeballs had told the priest that Wiremu had jaundice.

In the meantime Mackenzie lay hidden in a disused whare, curing.

Perhaps Wiremu was meant to be the flensing tool of the tribe, since he was the simplest and mangiest besides one of the oldest. He had in any case no choice since all the news of the *atua* came to him from his boy Moses, and Wiremu was impelled to pass it on. He told the tribe of an increasing stench of sanctity, of a lifegiving tree where birds dropped like fruit, of an outrageous march before them: signs synonymous with the rude oracle so long awaited. The people received the news secretly and secretly they made preparation, some weaving, some plaiting, others sending for the pearly shell of the paua to inlay the shanks and hooks of weapons. For it was known that their ancestors had been fowlers and fishermen. In the daytime the people dressed in European costume and sang the Sanctus, and in the nighttime they made preparation.

But now Wiremu's mind was thought to be tottering; the tribal tree was none other than the burning bush—*of the Bible*, he claimed. He was confused, and the priest was daily with him. Tree, bush, who was right? Wiremu? Or the Dreamer? Some said, perhaps the land after all is only a dream; and others, all the gods are as one but the fear of the Lord is wisdom. And they began to debate among themselves. Still, not all doubted. For a time they continued to make preparation for the journey ahead.

Mackenzie did not want to leave the whare. They had set him apart; they had imposed restraints in the manner of one who is both holy and dangerous, since in the native mind the qualities go together. He lay on a mat in an airless hut twenty feet long; there was a tiny opening at ground level through which the boy Moses crawled to tend him. His eyes were bandaged. Each day the boy invited him to remove the bandage ('If you are a god,' the boy said); and each day Mackenzie's courage failed him. He preferred the dimness of the bandage and the safety of the whare. Yet, although the whare insulated him from the problems of the world—of men—it only seemed to plunge him deeper into them. If he went out, would he see? Would the people follow? Would he remember the way? What he had gone through to get here no ox would endure. The return seemed more difficult, immense. He felt wretched.

There was a mystery about himself. 'Who am I?' he said one day. And the boy, who was dressing the bark poultice on his temple, said:

'They have a name for you.' He sniggered.

'Ay. An what is that?'

'The Dreamer.'

Mackenzie nodded to himself. He dreamed a lot (and out loud), but afterwards he could never remember what he had said. The boy would not tell him. He wore a crucifix over his white monitor's smock and he was on that account a little proud. He said that he was happy in the Lord—and hearing him sing the canticles in Latin in a voice keen as a girl's voice, Mackenzie believed him; but when the boy said that the people were happy and feared the priest more than they feared him, Mackenzie—that, he did not believe. It was only the boy told him so. Nobody else came to see him.

'Healing?' the boy said.

Mackenzie was silent, thinking about the boy's father, Wiremu. There was a mystery about Wiremu too. Wiremu, like the Polson, was dependent on him. Then why did the man avoid him? Why didn't he bring the dog? In his wretchedness, Mackenzie was confused.

'Here.' He took from his bag the jade figure. 'Show thy father.'

''Tis from the tree,' Mackenzie said, and would say no more. The boy took the amulet outside into the light and recognised the figure with the pot belly that was the emblem of the tribe. He decided to keep it for himself.

When the boy had gone Mackenzie knelt at the opening. Chanting came from the church. By his nose a lizard clicked. He felt the dry earth and the blue sky and he listened for the note of his flock. A single bleat sounded. 'One,' he muttered. And again, 'One,' fiercely, as the note sank into the Latin chant. Now he grimaced, slyly—the chant was hollow, their hearts were not in it. Slowly he rose and shuffled the length of the hut and again back, half a length, returning exhausted to his pallet. But he was pleased. 'Yesterday,' he told himself, 'I stumbled. And the day before I fell. Today it is only the eyes that pain. Tomorrow—'

'Tomorrow,' the boy Moses said when he returned, 'Tomorrow Wiremu will baptise.'

Mackenzie asked the boy to repeat what he had said. He thought the boy was lying.

The boy said, 'He will baptise. He will baptise, Elijah.'

'Did thee give him the greenstone?'

The boy said his father had no use for the charm and went away to play knucklebones. Presently he crept back. Mackenzie was turned aside, looking shrunken.

The boy spoke gingerly. 'Are you a god?'

'Nay.'

'Because if you are, my father says—let me take off the bandage.'

'*Nay!*' The boy disappeared. But not before he saw that the other was sweating, in his vehemence, and very much afraid.

When the boy brought his supper Mackenzie was lying cramped in the same position.

'Boy,' he said. 'Where was I before I was here?'

'In a cave.'

'Cave?' He barely remembered. Then, fidgeting with the string at his neck: 'Tis dropped at the cave then.'

'What?'

'The ring. Tis gone, laddie.'

The boy giggled. 'There is a ring on your finger.'

Mackenzie felt. The ring was there. As he touched it he knew a spasm of pain at the lids. He sat up heavily. 'Boy. Tomorrow I want fern root and eel meat. Bring it and put it in the bag.' Suddenly the boy was on his knees, blubbering and chafing his hands, imploring him not to leave. Mackenzie steadied the boy, rubbing him at the armpits, feeling the fine elastic skin under the loose garment and stroking his hair which was short and springy like a girl's. 'Nay, laddie. I mun return.'

'Where?'

'To her.'

'There is no tree!' blurted the boy.

'*Her*. Her that give me the ring.' Remembering the girl, he put the boy from him. She had sleepy eyes. They were hazel. And long curled lashes, fine as catkin. There was a dimple on her chin.

'No tree?' He chuckled. It came back to him now, he had left it burning. 'Boy, tomorrow thee sees it, an everybody.'

The girl would see it too, perhaps.

Something else about her, he remembered. Once they had wrestled, out of doors. He had lain upon her feeling nothing, no plumpness, no buds. But then. Later in a storm they had lain again. He had woken to find her leaning over, smelling of wood smoke; hair in his face and a softness on his chest, a round soft plumpness. Suddenly the flavour of pendent berries was in his mouth and he wondered if hers were the same, ripe on one side, green on the other.

She would be waiting.

As the taste of the berries returned, he no longer isolated her from the tree. The tree — the girl — the journey: all was joined in the source of the land and in the fertility of his mind, all was one. And his mind, like his legs, was growing strong.

But his eyes?

'Healing?' the boy said.

The pain had gone, leaving a slight headache. Mackenzie touched the scars beneath the bandage where the pitch had scoured. They were festering. They felt like rotting peaches.

'Tis an prison, laddie.'

'He will never heal,' the boy thought.

'*Never* heal?' Wiremu, the boy's father, said.

He was sitting beside his hut, head down, smoking. He looked at the boy with one eye, while the other flickered wanly at an errant evening sun. His eyes were yellow and lidless. Two teeth protruded on either side of the pipe, like bones, and he began to laugh. In laughter as in sickness Wiremu was more ugly than usual.

'He, he,' he said, laughing. 'No journey, boy. No journey now.'

'Therefore you can baptise,' the boy said eagerly. 'Baptise, baptise quickly.'

Wiremu drew up his spindly legs which were mottled as if cast in different metals, and stopped laughing.

During the night Wiremu was taken with abdominal pains

and nausea, and sent for the priest. Father Bataille dosed his anaemic frame with calomel and Epsom salts; afterwards he gave him hot chocolate and said that if he lived it would be the Lord's doing. In the morning Wiremu was much restored.

Mackenzie smelled the smoke from the oven stones almost as soon as he awoke.

'Today is the feast of Elijah,' the boy said. 'The women are preparing the pits.'

Mackenzie said nothing. Then: 'What do they eat, pork?'

'Sheep.'

'Sheep?' He grasped the boy. '*He* told me the flock was died.'

'Sold, not died. Some are left.'

'How many?'

'Don't know.'

'Look, boy.'

'Can't tell, too many people. Fifty, sixty.'

'Is Christy there?' Mackenzie was strangely agitated, his fingers clicking together in the clay dirt as he bent beside the boy at the opening. 'Christy, the trusty one.'

'How do I know it is trusty or it isn't?'

'Black, boy. The black beast.'

'Can't see, too many people.'

'Look beyond, look.'

'Beyond is the red gorge.'

Mackenzie gave a long sigh. 'Ay, an the bendy river,' he said.

'You came that way?'

He remembered now. Forgetting Christy, he was full of remembering and spoke aloud, telling the boy the way he had come. The boy listened.

'An lastly tis fell moor, look; tis all graves. Thy ancestor was given to fighting, boy. Has thee not seen the graves?'

'No.'

'Not the pit caves under the bluffs?'

'No.'

'Not the prints of Moah thy ancestor slew?'

'No.'

'Thee has *never* seen the moor?'

'Thee neither?'

The boy was weeping.

'Thee has sold thy birthright for an cross, boy.'

THE JOURNEY 343

The boy stood up from the opening and beat his fists on the man's back. 'Jesus is not *there*,' he cried. 'The tree is not there!'

'But it burns, laddie. The tree burns and is not consumed.'

The boy pushed the man sideways. Mackenzie lay on the earth and stretched himself like a cat. 'Go an look,' he said. 'Go an look on the mountains.'

'Not true!' the boy sobbed. But he went all the same, he crawled out of the hole and sat with his buttocks covering the entrance and 'Nothing,' he said. 'Nothing,' he called through the hole, keeping his eyes shut.

'Throw away thy cross an look again.'

The boy hesitated to remove the cross. It was a big gunmetal cross reaching to his lap, and painted scarlet. Not far away were the women. Half-turning, he said a prayer; then he slid the string from his neck and hid the cross in the folds of his garment. Tremulously he looked out. He looked out over the backs of the women and the smoke of the women's fires, he looked right into the mountains of the western sky. Then he smiled. The mountains were there the same as ever, and nothing else.

A bell rang. From the hut the boy saw the people leave their fires and their pipes and their branch shelters at the river and go into church, among them Wiremu in a white shirt and sandals; saw his father go in Wiremu and come out Elijah; heard the great shout 'Elijah!' as his father knelt to receive the blessing and he knew the joy that was the joy of his people united in the Lord. For there was none that had not been baptised save Wiremu. Outside the church they sang a final hymn and the boy, rising, fixing on his cross, sang with them, beating his palms jubilantly on the wall of the hut that the man inside, Mackenzie, should know the people were truly united and the mountains the same as ever, and nothing else.

Afterwards Mackenzie asked for the dog. The boy brought a message from his father instead. 'He says take the dog, if you go away in the night and give him peace.'

Mackenzie would have gone out then, blind as he was, to end the whole business; but he had to lie down. Queer things were happening in his head: a queer dinning of the eyes and ears, as if they swung on bell ropes. He could not understand it and, absorbed, holding his head in the heel of his hands, he nursed the pain until he dozed. He did not hear the sheep brought down.

There were six sheep before the block, where the women

waited at the ovens; and the first, shaved at the neck ready for Wiremu to slay in the name of Elijah, since it was his feast. Watching, the boy thought his father slayed it very badly; it took four blows. One of the women taunted him for his weakness and Elijah took off his shirt. 'He will never give up the axe now,' thought the boy, as they gave the old man a second sheep to warm his pride. The taunts rose in yelps, this sheep took seven blows; and after that Elijah brought them to their knees with laughter. Truly, the boy mused, my father is pleased to kill badly, for no man is that weak after baptism. And he was thankful they taunted him only, keeping their distance, for his father wielding the axe was not himself. His face was hollow as a broken saucer and he was drunk in a blood bath when he had done. 'Six,' he cried, breathing coarsely, and staggered over. No one pushed him. Two men dragged him from the wrack, a riot of colour and puny shame, and gave him no more heed. The two went on quartering with their knives, the women laying the portions in the hot stones and pausing to lap the new blood from a dish as they worked. 'By Jesus,' Elijah could be heard saying, 'by Jesus,' mocking their indifference and boasting that the next he would sever with one blow. The boy knew he would have a seventh merino yet. 'Seven,' Elijah cried. 'Six for the Holy Ghost and seven for the chief.' 'Only to humour him,' Mr. St. Kemp said; and he permitted a seventh ewe to be laid out. It was then, as his father was raising the axe, that the boy ran forward and threw himself across the block. For the seventh was a black sheep. 'Enough,' said the chief, freeing the boy and the beast, both. 'Enough,' commanded the priest, as the black ewe bounded away. The priest arrived from a broken rest, roaring at Elijah. Elijah had taken a rope and was beating the boy. With his son's smock held over his head he was lashing him on the back with the same jerky action he had used upon the sheep. Father Bataille stopped that with a clout and a bronze harangue.

'Not my fault, not my fault,' babbled Elijah; on his knees, suddenly contrite. 'Blame the Dreamer.'

'Drea-mer?' intoned the priest, intensely curious. For the silence that word produced on the people was remarkable. '*Show me the Dreamer*,' Father Bataille said. He was too quick, he saw that; the people turned away, muttering, farouche. And at the same time too slow: as they drifted away, leaving the meat half covered, one of them, the chief, put his foot in Elijah's mouth and twisted it, so that Elijah for a long time was unable to show anybody anything.

Elijah was made to kneel until he confessed. He was made to kneel before the church with his forehead touching the ground and broken mussel-shells under the kneecaps. The people accepted the idea of repentance; it was Christian and they understood that. They were shocked by the mussel-shells. But the priest had a need to shock them; and besides, he had tried the method in New Guinea using shark's teeth and found it to be effective.

It grew dark and when the boy took Mackenzie his supper, flitting quietly through shadow, Elijah was still kneeling before the church. 'No feast tonight,' the people said. 'Elijah will never tell.' The boy Moses however contradicted them. He brought word that the Dreamer was absorbed and without appetite but had said that Elijah would tell by morning.

At that season there were yet no snows. But the west wind blowing through the gorges was bladed with rime and even a priest, trussed in rugs with an oil brasier at his feet, might have complained. In the morning when the people looked, the space before the church was empty.

'And I have wished (Elijah said) to worship the *atua* in order to return to the land of my fathers and hunt the fish in the lakes of my fathers and shut out the foreign devils from our midst.'

'Explain the foreign devils to Our Lord,' the priest said.

'The white man. What sin is that, please?'

'Apostasy,' muttered the priest. 'You have confessed the sin of apostasial barbarianism.'

Elijah admitted it. At two o'clock in the morning the pain in his kneecaps was unbearable. The priest absolved him of apostasial barbarianism and suggested a cup of hot chocolate.

Elijah asked for a second cup to placate the *atua*.

'Saint Diable, he is *real*?' the priest said. Elijah explained that he was in a hut thirty yards distant.

Three o'clock found priest and confessor crouched together at the brasier, praying for the abomination in their midst.

'He is sick, Your Immense.'

'Elijah,' said the priest, bidding him rise, 'he shall be cured. He shall be cured in the Faith.'

Elijah was, like most of his tribe, genuinely attracted to the Latin chants which so much resembled his own; he was also by nature an indolent man, a nomad by pressure not preference. At this moment sitting rug-enfolded on the priest's camp bed, drinking hot chocolate, he was growing comfortable; and the thought of admitting the Dreamer, the *atua* of his torment, into the comforts of the Faith was irresistible. 'He, he,' he said. Later when his cup had been filled for the third time and he had been given an osnaburgh shirt Elijah was persuaded, in order that the sheep might be restored to the rightful owner, to fetch the police.

'Boy,' Mackenzie called softly. 'Take it off.'

'The priest is coming,' said the boy. Fumbling with dirty fingers.

'Off!'

And the cloth fell.

'Dear Mary,' Mackenzie said. For he did see. Aeons of light struck at his temple with the force of a flat-bladed sword. A myriad of deckled shapes, massive silhouettes, fan bright; posts and planks and a knitted face toppling; oh a boy's face, close cropped, adze keen; cusped lips gaggling, opening wide. 'Dear Mary,' he repeated, in daylight and in tears.

After a silence: 'Thee has an flatter nose than thy father, boy.'

'Were you frightened?'

'Ay, laddie. Frightened to death. Now put it back, the light tis cruel.'

Light? It was barely dawn. Mackenzie settled the bandage and the boy ran into the small starless morning to tell his father. His father was nowhere to be found.

Half-way across the marae, Father Bataille waited for the chief to dress and accompany him; for he might have need of protection. Mr. St. Kemp led the priest to the hut and pushed him through the opening, like a wedge. Father Bataille was unprepared for so feeble a spirit.

'You look ill, child,' he managed, touching the scrofulous face with the hem of his garment. Choking also on the waste bucket.

'Ill?' Mackenzie sat up in a great glory of dirt.

'I am here to cure you, child.'

'Nay. Curing I *am*.' Two tiny orbs, grottoed in cavernous blisters, took in an enormous cube of priest and a chief, panting upright by the opening, a mask of blubber and strain. For some reason Mr. St. Kemp was wearing a panama hat and his white duck suit.

'Today,' Mackenzie said. 'The land, tis there.'

'Today,' ogled the chief. 'Today' repeated the voices outside. And again, *today*—passing subdued, elongated in the pewter light.

'Whose land?' The priest stepped back, a cambric handkerchief before his face. The man was a keeper of flies.

'Ours, father—' the chief began. But the priest silenced him with a look.

'The land on which they have honest title, man. Tis theirs—' Mackenzie covered his eyes from the light. The priest stood easier. Those penetrating orbs had a candour which disturbed him.

'Saint diable.' He took Mr. St. Kemp aside. 'Who lives there? Protestants?'

'Nay,' Mackenzie interrupted. 'God.'

'God,' Mr. St. Kemp repeated tonelessly.

Such conniving certitude enraged Father Bataille. He pushed the chief outside and grasped the tempter.

'Man, thee is scented like an woman's belly. Go away.'

'Of course, child. But first answer me a question. Are the sheep yours?'

Reaching up, Mackenzie found a lobe of fat and pulled it. 'Nay man. But the pasture—tis theirs.'

'Merci,' hissed the priest, and escaped.

He emerged smiling, dusted his surplice, white and gold, and sailed heedless through the throng like a lily of the valley. Inside his dwelling he mopped himself and prayed for the return of Elijah and the police.

Mackenzie now, blithely, feebly sweating, was suddenly cold. 'Boy,' he called. There was no answer. And a little later, hearing a commotion: 'Boy,' he called again, needing a shirt. He was naked but for the jacket. In the dilly bag he felt his Bible. He wanted that—there was a sign, a word on the flyleaf. The writing was faded, disjointed. On the flyleaf his mother had written,'*Behold thy God hath set the land before thee: go up and possess it,*' and as he spoke the remembered text he thought how simple it was, would be, if only they would come. Come? They would carry him up. He had a great need to be carried.

'Boy?'

There was no answer.

'You say, constable, that he is known to you?' Father Bataille had refreshed his face in milk and was pomading his wig.

'Watching for weeks, father,' said the constable, who had pimples and a corporal's dignity. He had ridden hard from a gold strike nearby, he said; an escort was coming from Dunedin. 'Although, if you don't mind, father, I'll take the man now—'

'Settle down, lad,' the priest said, watching him prime a muzzle-loading pistol with swollen joints. The boy was nervous. The priest set a bottle of cognac on the bedside table and told the constable to wait until he was needed.

The constable said, 'Why is the dog muzzled?'

'Because it bit me. But the man is not dangerous.'

The constable relaxed and settled down to drink the brandy.

It was yet cold, and the people were glad to gather by the fire Elijah had kindled at the priest's bidding for the delayed feast. They wore their bright cotton gowns and striped osnaburgh shirts, and grumbled a little that the meat of yesterday was barely warm. Elijah sat on the edge of the blaze, brooding and rail-like; not eating. The people ignored him, gnawing and spitting and talking among themselves. 'He is arisen, the boy has seen,' some said. 'Ah,' said others, 'he is cured.' 'Then why does he not come?' ventured the women. The priest when he arrived was jolly. He encouraged their appetites and their gossip. He noted that while some were expectant, others were apathetic and most were undecided. All, he perceived, were awaiting a sign. So he listened and said nothing and answered their questions with a smile. 'I shall sit with them,' he told himself. 'Good is in the sitting, evil in the action.' It was a favourite text. Soon, he reasoned, they will be sated and fall asleep at the fire and the constable can remove the fellow quietly. Yet he half-hoped, such was his longing to cast out Satan *positively*, that it would not happen as gently as that. Elijah was his messenger.

On the edge of the fire Elijah stood and pointed at the hut.

'Look! He comes!'

The people turned. And indeed something stirred in that opening, a flurry. No, they were deceived. A trick of the light.

'Look!' Elijah called again, shaking his finger at the western sky. Again the people turned. They saw nothing. The sky was a vault of pewter without meaning.

'He, he,' hooted Elijah. 'He, he!' He rolled about, fingers in his gapped mouth, hooting with laughter.

Then Elijah did a surprising thing. He tweaked the priest's ear.

Father Bataille had large ears. In repose they lay flat along the panelled jowls like a spaniel's; now however (as the people laughed) they twitched and splayed outwards and as (very quickly, before even he was aware of it himself) the priest stepped backwards into the fire, they gave to his voice a peculiar amplification. Softly and insinuatingly he addressed them, his fog-like garments, only the sleeves protruding, transfigured in smoke. For he was not a coward. He spoke in the fire, veiling their heresy in tongues of scorn; then, singed but unharmed, he spoke in the open, explicit: 'Only great men, my children, become religious by contemplating the vast mystery of Nature — great men and fools.

'This barbarian: is he a fool?'

'No father,' Mr. St. Kemp replied.

'Is he then a great man?'

'He is a god,' the people said. 'And he has seen the Burning Bush.'

Father Bataille was prepared for this. He held up two pictures. One was a tableau of the mythological generations of the Maori in the form of a tree, and was aflame. He beckoned to the chief.

'Lay it on the fire. The bush burns and is not consumed, the *atua* says.' The priest smiled benignly.

Mr. St. Kemp straightened his panama hat and took the picture. He wore his English suit of white jean, white cotton stockings, shirt and shoes complete, and he faced his people with the picture in his hands and nobody spoke.

'Why do you hesitate?' said the priest.

'He, he,' said Elijah. 'Do it. Then the *atua* will arise and pull the other ear.'

Mr. St. Kemp laid the picture on the fire and it burned to ashes.

Then the priest invited him to burn the second picture which the people also recognised, being the picture from the church and showing the Lord surrounded by heathens in holies.

'Burn it and fear not,' the priest said.

Now the chief's hands trembled, facing the tribe. But he obeyed the priest.

When the flames had licked around it the priest removed the canvas, which was of painted amianthus cloth, and displayed it undamaged. The priest listened to the murmurs, he saw that the people were moved. He held them a moment in prayer. Then he sang: '*The mighty God, even the Lord—*'

'Hath spoken,' said Elijah with undue reverence. And all in a moment they were chanting in tumult. '*The mighty God, even the Lord—*' But the priest interrupted them, the fervour was ominous. He spoke a more sober text. '*The former things are passed away . . .*'

'Away, away!' sang the women. The cry rose. They would not be stopped. The cry rose and Elijah goaded it. 'Away, away, burn and fear not! He, he, burn, burn!'

'Away the land!'

'Away the dream!'

'Burn, burn!' shouted an old man whose hair was falling out.

'Stop,' cried the priest.

'Burn the Dreamer, he, he,' shrieked Elijah. He was cavorting and lifting the priest's smock, so little did he understand. His fang teeth were bared in lascivious delight. 'Heretic,' mumbled the priest. And amid the derision, the yelped frenzy, could be seen the priest flailing his great arms, cuffing Elijah the way one cuffs a dog; Elijah grovelling, Elijah falling, running and falling, crumpled, by the river; yolks of eyes starting, narrowed, maniacal; women leaping, seizing lighted faggots and leaping towards the opening. Horrific, their belling cry: '*Burn the Dream—!*' Belling—and broken. Mackenzie had appeared. He appeared from the hut at the same instant as, at the opposite corner, the constable appeared from his; and they stared at each other without ever realising what it was all about. Father Bataille realised. Believing at that moment in the undesirability of guiding the people other than in the direction in which they were so obviously leaning, he took inspiration from the half-finished phrase and thundered: 'Not the Dreamer but your dreams. Burn your dreams!'

It was such a novel concept that the people hesitated. Turning from Mackenzie, the faggot bearers glanced at their chief who nodded, abstractedly, and crossed himself. For in them Mr. St. Kemp knew himself, wanting to protect Mackenzie yet fearing to, owning in their half-crazed automaton state that part of himself that also craved release. Release—but how? By obedience, yes yes. Obedience was greater than rebellion. Yes, yes. Burn the dreams! Yes, yes, he nodded excitedly, and Mackenzie was forgotten. One of the women clasped her husband's digging stick and threw it on the fire. More digging sticks followed, a chevroned amulet. One snatched off a comb and another a flax loincloth and the boy Moses, once sad and now delirious, waved his jade emblem and added it to the blaze. 'Yes, yes, burn the past!' They ran to their huts, ransacking them, bringing forth the possessions they had stored against the journey into the past: capes, kits, weeders, reels of ivory, tubular beads, rubbing sticks and weaving sticks, totems, toys, gourds, snares, lures, traps, some brought toothbrushes in error and others topknot feathers, tikis, talc hatchets, carved boxes, cloak pins, flake knives and flensing tools, cutting tools and caulking tools, phials of ochre, shark oil, hooks with wooden shanks and hooks inlaid with mother of pearl, and fine dogskin mats—they cast them all into the burning, chanting and stamping in the release of exaltation. And the sparks whirling, Mackenzie forgotten; and 'God is Love' sang the priest to the chief's 'Hallelujah'. As Mr. St. Kemp lumbered up, bearing a huia cloak. For a moment the chief stood, stroking its down, the pouches beneath his lids enormous. Then he flung the cloak, which was plumed with the feathers of the huia and the white heron and was an ancient cloak and a lordly cloak, flung it up and out and onto the pyre like a dying swan, and all sang lowly through his 'Hallelujah', his or the priest's, the voices joined and lowing. And they remained like that singing 'God is Love', their voices muted and their hearts breaking, watching the flames sink to the level of their voices, into ashes, until the dream was ended.

Absurd, thought Mackenzie, as he went towards the fire, the way they shrink from me. He called out, leaning on the stick. 'I am no miracle bringer.' Perhaps they are drunk, he thought. They stood back. They had left a path—it stretched clear across the pa to the river and the lightening gorge. But he could not take it. He stared at the hooded eyes, the queer yolked lids, and he sat down oppressed by light and smoke and a grand prickling of the scalp. 'Perhaps they are dead.' For no reason he thought of a bit lamb he had owned once, the mother had abandoned it.

It had blundered onto his own hand, and the comfort of that strayed faith had impeded it for the rest of its life. It died prematurely, flabby at the edges. The people were like that. As yet he had no premonition of death himself, of finality. The priest was motioning to someone. The strange thing was that as the constable stepped up and fumbled with the handcuffs, Mr. St. Kemp intervened. Mr. St. Kemp on the whole had not much conscience, but what he had was guilty. He might not hold his tribe to the promised land. He would yet hold the priest to his promise. So he said to the priest, 'Baptise him.'

'We wish,' he told Mackenzie.

'An what I wish, man, is Bring the dog!'

Mr. St. Kemp did one more thing. He sent for the dog.

'Father—' the constable said. But the priest smiled. His hat was broken and his wig hung aslant, but he was smiling and regarding his fingernails.

'Baptise? Of course. You must kneel, child.'

Mackenzie was conscious now, hearing the voice of unction, that he could put his trust in no man; that the people, waking to his feebleness, were crowding him and also hating him—hating themselves, they had to hate something. And that they were tall, very tall. 'Fear Him!' they cried, pressing him down. Yet they had barely touched him, and they scattered. The dog was among them. A hare's leap, and they did scatter—at her or at him. Mackenzie guffawed softly, hugging her up, the lovely beast, and rubbing his cheek the length of her wizened pelt. He held her a long moment, shy and intimate, removing the muzzle, cradling the wise head, the rose ears, weeping at what they had done to her—she had been a dog once. They had made a space around him and the dog—she troubled them like a good witness, he could tell that. Now she licked his face, face and brow and stubble of blisters crowning his head where they had shaved and not healed him; and he continued to guffaw softly, knowing suddenly no fear. For one thing, sitting there now under his blanket, he was taller than they. He told the priest, 'Give her thy blessing, man.'

'Witch,' muttered the priest, strangely immobile.

Her tongue then was a kind of shock; and the shocks he was feeling were without mention.

He said it sprucely, wickedly. He told the priest to baptise her, the dog, instead.

'Constable,' said the priest.

'An she is one of God's creatures,' Mackenzie said. 'Give her an piece of the holy bread, she will eat it—an does she not eat Christ?'

'Certainly,' Mr. St. Kemp thought.

Father Bataille was having a trying day. 'Your god perhaps the bitch eats, but not *my* Jesus!' Then: 'This is the man, constable. Arrest him.'

As he spoke the priest felt his knees give. His rozet blew up. The constable breathed scarlet, not moving. A gust, some furnace breath touched him. They all felt it. It was after all a cool morning. Sungold certainly, but cool. And abominably still.

'What is happening?' said the constable.

Mackenzie could not explain it. The dog was glaring, glaring at *him*. And he—all he had done, thinking her about to spring, was put a hand up to his face. The blanket had slipped from his shoulders, his eyes were scalding. The people were staring at the man on the ground whose features were irradiated in firelight. All the livid dark skin was peeling. The scars and pestilential blotches were peeling and dissolving in foam—the man was foaming. Moisture and pus were running off the crown of his head and the cheekbones and seeping into the beard. The beard itself was damp and the ends suffused with a bright liquid which fell in drops onto the man's chest. As they watched, the drops became a stream washing over the hands folded at the navel. And the man was whole and smiling at them.

Mackenzie had a slight headache. He stood up.

'Anew,' they said. 'He is anew,' and were arguing among themselves.

The dog sped away. There was a path again; now he could take it. Mackenzie walked. ''Tis God's handiwork,' he thought, snatching his crook from the boy Moses and walking. He could see clear to the running gorge and the mountains, the mountains were unmistakable. Mackenzie did not walk well—so many plucked and fustered at his side; yet he walked. 'Then you do not fear Him?' Mr. St. Kemp mouthed, into his ear. He shook the chief off; striding. 'Thee worries, man,' he thought. 'Thee worries, thee thinks, thee waits, thee acts not, thee looks out of thy bleary eye with thy head on one side and thy hat on one side that is not even thine own hat, thee is nothing original, thee is an obscenity, thee is an upside down obscenity person that fawns and farts in borrowed pants, thee is that, thee—thee has burned thine inheritance and now, *now* thee talks to me of Faith, thee is not worthy to suck at the raw end of mine dog!'

'Fear Him?' he said aloud. 'An who's Him?'

'God,' puffed the chief.

'Tell us,' said the boy. The boy was clinging to one leg.

God? But how could he tell them about that when God was in him and all round him? He was smelling again the creamy panicled smell of the cabbage trees hoarded by the river. 'To understand God,' he wanted to say, 'you must know the kingdom of the glow-worm that lasts an hour and of the tuatara lizard that lasts a century, you must know these things in all their parts until it is as if you were standing not over not under not alongside but inside these things, looking at them through and through, *then*—' he gave a hot laugh—'Then, that is God. You know him then as you know the picture of your own face. For you are *in* God.'

He said that, I am in God. Not pridefully or even spiritually but reflectively, a reflection of the force that was pouring through his body. At this moment, he thought, I am God.

Later he remembered having passed a bundle, a crumpled landmark on the ground and saying 'Who's that?' and pressing on. Now he was alone. A bubble of angry sound burst behind him but he did not look back. Ahead of him the dog had drawn the sheep under the red cliff, and was waiting. 'Ha,' he muttered, noting a black speck among the rest. He was alone, running free.

He had forgotten Elijah.

They had not forgotten. As they passed the crumpled form they had fallen back, first one and then another. In their hatred they remembered; and, remembering, they turned aside in sullen rage and fell upon him with stones. The last to turn back, hearing his father's cries, was the boy.

Elijah tried to tell them about the tree. He sat up gobbling words in a bloodied mouth, and 'Look' he tried to say, that they too might see the column of smoke rising over the peaks in the sungold air. But this time they would not look.

Then they were there, bending over him: the policeman, the priest, the chief, running up, and the boy, running back. They were all there then, wailing, on the death of Elijah. Mackenzie did not look back.

IN his haste he broke his fast on lichen and sucked moisture from the tubular root of a plant like scorzonera. Then the blunt red walls of the gorge enclosed him and he moved warily. A sharp breeze came up the gorge and his eyes throbbed intermittently. Yet his mind was clear, fashioned to a plume of smoke rising in the west; and his sight was refreshed by the occasional sight of that plume. He thought he drove towards it well enough. The question arose on the fourth day: did he? Two nights previously he had woken with the flock around him and heard a laugh. Shapes were flitting down the smooth cliff walls. They vanished in the direction of the pa. In the morning, twelve sheep were missing. The same had happened on the next night. More ewes vanished. So the fact remained. He had left the pa driving a flock of forty-five ewes. Now on the fourth day he had barely twenty. Mackenzie hurried out of the gorge, as from the scene of a crime.

A small range led out. It rose from a bend in the stream in a razor's back, forming a watershed between the interior and the high tablelands. A day's march and the range turned on itself at right angles, sweeping due west. At the same time a line of gravel cliffs met it from the north-east. Between the range and the cliffs, bleached to the blue of the pale meadow clary, was secreted a moor. It gave directly onto his land.

So he remembered. He remembered the moor and the glacial stream that eroded it. He did not see the moor until he was directly on top of it. It slanted upwards, elbow shaped, the stream suddenly white on the windgrass and the glaucous green of a salt bog. He forgot the bog. Red rimmed, he slithered down a long gully and bathed his face in the stream. The cold water revived him. He discarded his rags and began delousing himself. The sheep came off the tops ravening. They plunged into the warmer air like goats, made for the stream in a pod, full twenty, stopped abruptly, turned, sighted some rosetted herbs, and ran straight into the bog. Six sank at once. A dozen more stopped on the edge. They stood with their heads turned away, not bleating. Two more were stuck fast when Mackenzie came up, waving his crook. 'I am quite naked,' he thought to himself, running and prodding. 'I am lighter than the sheep.' The mud swallowed his crook as if it had been a strand of wire and he was suddenly standing on his armpit. He withdrew his arm. It was like extricating himself from a vice. He squatted on mossmound and shouted to the two beasts struggling only five feet from him. He felt strangely irresponsible. It was not his fault. The dog sat beside him, tranced. She placed a paw on his knee with her eyes turned obliquely towards the centre line of her head, as if apologising. For no reason he swung round and caught her a stinging blow. He did not know why. It was not her fault. He was angry. He took the dog by the hindquarters and flung her forward. The forepaws dropped on the nearest pelt and the ewe reared up before the dog could grip. He flung the dog away. The ewe stood teetering on her nose, her lips grazing the slime. She began to snort, as if snorting alone would save her. Mackenzie had once seen a ship sink. He thought she would drown like that, and she did. Her nose settled, first the beard, then the lips and lastly the horns. Her stern came up. She slid down with small sucking sounds, her hindlegs trundling the air to the end, like paddles.

The other ewe stood half submerged, balanced. It was the one Delilah, the one that had killed the hawk. Each time she struggled black mud oozed up and she was sucked lower into the quagmire. She seemed to understand this. She stopped threshing and laid her face flat on the slime with an indolent eye towards him. Finally she rolled over and lay in it, as if enjoying herself.

'Tha stupid beast! Tha stupid beast—' He started up, tears running from his cheeks, and walked slowly forward. A sound of wingtips checked him, a purling, infinitely remote. Something brushed his face. He put out a hand to ward it off, at the same time he walked forward into the mire. 'Very effiekayshus that thtuff,' Droo the bullocky had said once. He remembered what Droo had said. 'If you go down in that thtuff the only thing to do is práy.' He remembered. He advanced with a sort of fixed horror on the sinking sheep. He knew he was being drawn in. Then the dog knocked him sideways.

He crawled away numb with fright and lay for a long time on his back staring at a sky that was curiously mauve. And void.

'Tha' stupid beast.' He sat up. He was really very tired.

The sheep lay on her side and looked at him, sinking slowly.

'Tha' stupid beast.'

He walked away and left it.

Later when his drawers were dry he put them on. He looked at his coat which had been bright with patches and was now grey as the scorzonera plant. It was pitifully inadequate. He thought if he cut off the sleeves he might cover his legs with them.

Why was he worried about the coat?

Presently the sheep came up and then the dog and formed a crescent, as if to protect him — as if he was somehow deficient in the art of survival. 'Tis not,' he told the dog, recalling the clout he had given her, 'that thee is losing thy master. Tis they—' he addressed the sheep—'that is losing their shepherd.'

He was twisting the coat in his hands. The cloth tore.

He began to whimper.

Then he pulled himself together and crossed the creek, intending to camp higher up. He put up a swamp bird and, pausing, watched the dog run it down. 'Dodo, dodo,' he cried, although the dog could not hear and the bird was not in any case a dodo. He had forgotten the name of it. The bird ran, flapping its wings. It was incapable of sustained flight. The dog would outrun it. She always did. Then why did the widow's peak bill continue to bob up and down?

The dog could no longer outrun it. Eventually she brought him a moorhen. It tasted sour.

Instinct told him to move higher, onto the gravel cliffs. But what instinct? The evening was warm. Here was a hollow. He laid his fire in that.

That night the creek rose. Once he woke to find the crescent of sheep stirring and the black beast Christy ogling him with her single bright eye. Later he woke again half stifled. The air was full of harrier hawks. He watched them settle on the swamp, each a dozen feet from its neighbour, and dropped off again thinking how light the sky was. Later still he heard the hawks banging along the cliffs and prepared to move. But when he woke a third time he was still lying, the dog burrowed into his armpit, and rats were pouring over his chest in the direction of the cliffs. The rats had eaten his only candle. He sat up intending to follow them, remembering that in the cliffs, halfway up, were graves, refuges, overhanging alcoves filled with corpses, the lips worn smooth as river shingle — and, dozing, he was very comfortable, very, and forever. So he thought, stumbling after the rats and eating them up, a tail at a time, in return for devouring his last candle. And then — miracle — he was sitting at a table with a napkin and fork and other things he was not accustomed to, having a discussion with the girl. 'Which is best, lass, when starving,' he said. 'Drowned rats or boiled grubs?' 'Best for who?' 'Best for thee.' 'Don't "thee" me,' said the girl, as he ate her petticoat. 'Don't "thee" me. Anyway the sheep are drowned, not the rats.' Then they fell into the fire laughing and found the grubs roasted, not boiled. At that the fire gave tongue, coiling the girl's hair into tree branches, and Mackenzie really woke and cursed himself for feeling nothing from nothing. Water was all round him. He was alone, the sheep already swimming and the dog frantic. He knew about freshets. A creek might rise forty feet in half an hour. Then again — he shivered — it might not. The creek was turbid. But up there — as he looked he saw the snow wave advancing, bank and bank, and heard the sound of crashing. 'Then again, tmight,' he mumbled; and ran. First he waded, then he ran, then the river plucked him up like doll's ticking and hurled him under the cliffs.

He climbed twenty feet into a cave, and there were birds clinging to the crevices. 'If the river rises, twill be an case with us, lass,' he said. It was some time before he realised that the dog was not there.

The river rose and he climbed higher, into another refuge.

This too contained birds. They were all large birds. Companies of blades, poised murmurously, shoulder to shoulder on the floor. As he crawled in they moved over, as if they had been expecting him.

After a time the murmuring ceased. It grew marvellously still. Presently a white flippered penguin floated in.

It began to rain.

He thought the water was receding.

On his knees, he dozed. Stirring, he saw that he had cut his hand. But it did not bleed. Only a little dark blood oozed out. He was too weak to move, and too cold. He was crouched between two rocks, cleft like a badly made coffin, gripping something moist and puckered. He stroked it gratefully: 'Ah tis thee, lass.' Nothing else could be so soft. But it was not the dog. It was only his dilly bag.

He had saved *that*?

Time and again he had asked himself what he would do if the dog were taken from him. He had replied by saying that he would find the nearest dule tree and hang himself on it. Now he did not believe, he simply did not believe. She would be hunting. Hunting? He looked down, peering over the lip, and a sense of helplessness came upon him. The waters were still rising.

All that night he remained in a crouch. He told himself, 'If I lay down I will sleep, and if I sleep I will not find the dog.' And again, when morning came, 'Tomorrow.'

'Tomorrow, when it stops raining, I will find the dog,' he said. 'But today I will coop in the cave.'

The birds left. But the rats stayed. They had fine pink eyes and made a sound like men shuffling cards. Soon, he thought, they will inhabit me.

The water when he looked out was swirling a few inches from his nose. It was muddy. He tried to imagine the reason for its being there. He failed. He failed to concentrate, as he had failed to concentrate on the problem of the dog and of the sheep; instead he thought of the girl and the jets of fire springing from her hair like branches.

A tree was swimming towards him. It passed the cave perfectly upright, trailing candelabras of berries on the water. That was something to think about.

The sky was slack. The rain continued.

He found some fern root and crawled inside. He pounded the root slowly into dough, as if he were building cathedrals; and masticated each mound of dough thirty times before swallowing. He thought about hunger. There was a pigeon with a broken wing. All day it had brooded in a corner, afraid. Now it was restless, seeking escape. He stared at the pigeon for a long time before he realised that in order to eat it he must first catch it. His hand travelled forward, the fingers spread, and they remained like that—he was staring at the torn flesh, at the waxy pallor of the hand that would not bleed. Yet his palms were sweaty. Could a man be cold and hot and hungry at the same time? 'I am hungry,' he said aloud to the pigeon. 'But I am not that hungry.' As he spoke the pigeon darted forward and pecked his thumb.

That was hunger.

There was something in the bag that he might eat. As he fumbled with the draw string he found that he had not the means to untie it. His brain sent a message and somewhere along the line it faltered. His fingers would not respond. There was no sensation, only cold.

That night the birds returned. It continued to rain. There was no firewood. The birds would not lie down. He developed a sort of plurality of the senses, hearing everything he said twice over. He spoke incessantly, the girl beside him now, always there, and he spoke always to the girl; although once he said, 'I am sick of *thee*,' meaning the cave. He thought if he did not die that night, he would never die.

In the morning all the birds were perched in tiers on the lip of the cave. At a sound they flew off, and the dog walked in holding a piece of timber in her mouth. Mackenzie sat up with a start, bumping his forehead on rock and bleeding with it, yes, yes, he was bleeding alright; and yes, yes, it was wonderful, blinking away the blood to look at her, yes, yes, yes. Yes, he was very much alive.

He built thirteen fires that day. No sooner did the dog arm him with twigs than he burnt them; and no sooner with sotted quail than he singed and ate them. He ate himself to sleep. He woke in darkness, snored again, rolled in the fire, roared, sneezed, laid his hands on the embers, felt nothing, poured fat on the sores between his toes, stripped, coated his body with grease, saw his face, the face of a hangman reflected in the wet walls, put out his tongue, belched, scrambled outside, saw clouds wind-whipped, saw gravel, the rain on the gravel glinting in sunlight, was blinded, sang nevertheless, for the river was going down, felt a constriction in the chest, slipped, held on, knew shooting pains from ankle to groin, beheld a perpendicular sheep eating ribbonwood bark, alive and eating, saw a second sheep, then a third, counted three more white on the dark cover and a black one, bouncing stiff-legged down the cliff towards him, cried, overbalanced, and was violently ill.

He left a vomitoria of mud and moraine, and five sheep drowned, and walked out of the moor in three days. The down journey had taken him three hours. The soles of his feet were blue sponge and though he bound them with grass and flax they were suppurating and raw within the hour. He had to stop every mile or so to rest. Each halt confirmed the articles of faith that remained to him. They were three. First was his body, that was a constant—the knowledge that he must exert it and gain the next point of rest, in order to proceed again. Second was his mind, that was fickle—the knowledge that he must discipline it: once it had gone off without him and he had caught himself walking downhill in the wrong direction. Direction. That was the third, direction of march.

The tree waved to him now, hanging up: a smoking mare's tail behind the ridge leading off the moor. Behind and to the left. So he said.

The dog said no. The dog stole right.

With the dog he had always had a special relationship. Their trust in each other was implicit, especially in crises. But now in the open they kept each other at a distance. One would pause and give the other a look, yet the question inherent in that look was never answered. Each continued as before, as if afraid of inquiring closely into the other's motive.

He had confided the flock to her utterly, as he had the question of food, the pit for the night and the lesser problems. There were seven sheep left. Christy the leader shied at obstacles: the least fissure in her path and she stamped, backing down with upcurled lip, then she sat licking her hoof; the ringstraked beast had developed ulcers; a third sneezed all day; a fourth, with long thin horns, was consumptive and had to be lifted onto its feet after each halt; the rest were lame.

But the dog moved them.

Persistently she stole right into the east. When he was not looking. When he was resting. When he was behind. She slid thus, minutely. It was unfair. Once he said, 'Thee has no *right*!' He spoke furiously, laying to the west. Everything—his faith, his stick, his bleeding feet, all westward. He insisted. She was shocked, the beautiful cur. She left the seven and came to him, inclining her head full mouthed. 'Bodily,' he thought, 'thee has lost grace. Tha coat is an old muddy stuck on an old broom. All tha' beauty has run to tha' head.' The piled leonine head, grave and pre-eminent, seemed to soften. She gave him a paw. She licked his feet. She gave him the full red owl of her eye and the rose of her ear with perfect acuteness. Then she slid the flock minutely into the east.

He corrected the drift. But the ascent was slow and there was an afternoon of fog. When they had traversed the rubble and got onto, as he thought, the ridge he found they were hanging to the sides of a new-made canyon. They emerged through a blanket of snow totara above a valley he had never seen before. The mist cleared. They were miles off course. And his tree was nowhere.

The dog was already shifting, scattering the seven through the pines to the valley. The valley led nowhere, he could see that. It was some minutes before he realised the extent of her betrayal. He picked up a stone and hurled it. 'Mad,' he screamed. 'Come back. Thee is mad.' Sadly he watched her go. She slid down herding and bullying, shadows of eight on the clay-slate rock, seven plus one; far below she crossed a torrent, some fissure on the darkening floor, and stood a moment looking up; then she plunged into the tundra. The bleating grew dim. They were gone.

Mackenzie turned into the west, resolved to sight his land by nightfall. His resolve lasted only to the bottom of the canyon. He stared at the interminable clay-slate rocks that rose up on the other side. He could see the ridge. He had only to climb in order to gain it.

Morning found him still there at the bottom of the canyon, sitting with his head in his hands. A noise woke him, swung him round. He thought the dog had returned, but it was only stones falling off the calcareous cliff. 'Bitch.' He laughed bitterly to himself. 'The wee, horrible bitch.'

He began to climb. The west side of the canyon was banked with dull Lydian stone. Half-way up it began to snow and a sort of ague gripped him. 'Tis slow you are, laddie,' he said, wincing as he clambered out onto the ridge. A blast of wind threw him against a boulder. He had to brace himself. Only then was he aware of a surrounding whiteness. 'Tis snowing,' he said aloud. 'Whatever season is it?' Strange, he thought when a moment later the sun shone, throwing light as through a rotten vest, how near they seem. He could see the alps. The cold air rushed upwards, fanning the spaces between the peaks with the radial intensity of peacocks' tails. 'Mun get on,' he said. 'Mun get on.' But the hand that steadied him against the boulder had frozen. Part of the flesh clung to the rock as he straightened. His head swirled and the throbbing, when it came, made him run. He ran ten yards and collapsed. Before him towered the ridge, a succession of morainic blocks, humped and deformed like rampant cattle. But then—he got onto his knees—he saw the signal. Through the flurries of snow and the mountains that came and went with the inconstancy of a rainbow he saw it clearly, a blueish plume. As he watched a strand detached itself, was animated, assumed a shape—a neck, a brow, foils of jetting hair—and floated over the intervening space towards him.

'Avoid—' The coppery voice sank into the valley of the east. Eastward?

Eastward lay Odessa.

Mackenzie passed a hand over his brow. He felt clammy but no longer faint; his headache had lifted. Grumbling to himself, he picked up his stick and stumbled back after the dog.

He found the dog playing step-down by a flooded stream with her mouth full of fry. She had gone barely a mile up the valley. The sheep were tearing up mouthfuls of fresh dock herb, as if from some lingering recollection of the Sierras concerned to devour the valley entire. He thought they looked bloated. 'Cast, thee will be, my dears,' he thought. And then his relief at finding them changed to bewilderment. They were five only. Two were missing. He glared at the dog for her neglect. She seemed unconcerned by the loss, replete as she was with fry and the sunshine melting the snow on the pale tussock floor. She blinked at him like a woman who has taken off her spectacles, and waited; while he gorged on fish and calmed himself into some sort of condition for marching. Marching! It was easy. The dog led him round a truncated cone steaming with ants and huhu bugs. The ground was uncommonly luxuriant. There was no resistance. There were recesses, cross currents, overlapping fronds through which they slipped insubstantially. But they could not cross the flooded stream. They returned unceasingly, for the stream doubled back, to the point where they had begun. The steaming cone was always there.

It grew hot. His jacket parted at the chest. He discarded it foolishly.

Two more sheep strayed, two lame ones.

He sat down to open a blister and found he had mislaid his knife.

He knew where the knife was. He had stopped, unslung his bag and used it to carve the name of the girl on a log. Now, when he looked, he could not find the log.

'An the dilly bag, where is it?' He rounded on the dog. The bag and the Bible in it and the knife, were they lost?

He blamed the dog now for everything.

The dog kept out of range. Whenever he looked at her like that she kept out of range of the crook.

'Thee is lost,' he burbled. 'Thee has lost tha' sheep, thee has lost tha' bag and now thee has lost thaself.'

The dog went away and returned with his jacket. He planted his crook and draped the jacket over it and sat under the jacket in desperation. After a time the play of light on the grasses began to fascinate him. In the long grasses he saw a girl's hair flouncing and once again the voice rose above the cicadas and tempted him. Sourly he twisted the girl's ring on his little finger. He tore at it. But the joint was swollen, he could not rid himself of the ring.

He started up, cursing the dog. 'Thee is bewitched, the wee whore has bewitched thee! The valley leads nowhere.'

So he turned from the valley a second time. This time the dog came with him—she, and the three sheep that were left.

Only Christy got up the side of the canyon. The other two, the ringstraked beast and the ewe with thin horns, fell off.

'One, lass,' he said, stumbling along the ridge. Christy came on meekly. With her one eye she advanced cautiously, hanging out her sides and stepping stiff-necked round the cattled blocks as if she bore calf. He stopped to wait for her. She stood in the wind, arching her horns. She concealed nothing but the fact that she stood in the wind, barely standing. Every few yards she put her tongue into a crevice and licked the bare trap-rock. He pitied her.

'One,' he complained, and went on.

'See lass—my star?' he said on the following day as they descended onto the open floodplain. 'See?' He pointed to the smoke. It was only a puff, he was sorry to say. The dog made a sound, a queer little sharp intake of breath, mucus ran from her nose and she tried to drag him back. He pushed her off easily, her jaws had the soft putrescence of a puppy's. He told her they had to return to the tree in order to collect his chanter, although until then he had not thought about the chanter at all. The dog made no further attempt to reason with him. 'Only believe, lass,' he said. 'Only believe.' Her pads were festering. He became aware of it in one of the rivers when the flax bundles he wore buoyed him clean out of the water and the dog straddled his chest to float him down. Then it passed from his mind.

The cold in the rivers revived him.

The smoke was growing.

On the second day he noticed that the dog's sight was waning. Christy had strayed. They were approaching the second lake when he saw the sooty ewe making into a clump of dead forest and he had to *tell* the dog. Even then she did not sight the beast at once. She recaptured Christy after a long time.

The next day Christy walked out of their lives. It had been a long day. He had risen damp and sweating from the frost that coated his bark suit and pounded some fern root and got on until it was too hot to march. They had rested by a ford. The rivers were going down. He smiled a little at the snow flowers that were coming to view, lighting up the shingle beds and the fellfields between the lakes. In the afternoon they continued. The black ewe was on his left, dragging a fleece that weighted her to the ground. She walked straight, grinding her teeth, regardless of obstacles. At dusk when they stopped she trundled on with a grim stepping motion, looking neither left nor right, leaving a crooked swathe in the grasses behind her. Mackenzie spoke to the dog. He could no longer tell if her gaze rested on the sheep or the flies or the westering sun, nor could he summon the energy to rouse her. So he sat rubbing the roof of his mouth with a stone; and the dog sat; and the ewe Christy walked on out of sight.

The next day which was the fourth day he fell, without bothering to put up his arms to break the fall. The dog was ahead of him and did not notice. He staggered up quickly and continued. A little later he did it again. His knees gave and he pitched forward without a thought until the gravel, forced into his nostrils, made him gasp. 'What on earth is the matter with me, lass?' His legs had yellowed, the skin was curiously shadowed. His ankles were puffy. When he touched them the print of his fingers remained.

Now he used the stick, and leaned on it.

Yee-yaw, yee-yaw. He narrowed his gaze to the thin shadow just ahead of him, the dark hull and the white paw facings yawing from side to side ... The lakes ended and the plain began again, strongly, sieved with the dry watercourses he remembered.

'See, lass,' he said at the end of the fifth day. 'How near it is?' The dog was sick, needing water. He commanded her to *be well*. In the morning the smoke was nearer. 'An hundred yards, lass —an hundred yards!' He said, to encourage her.

There was a little water in the riverbed. He carried her towards it. She grew hysterical, scenting the trickle; and lay in it, panting. He wet his face. 'See, lass, there is yon tree. An they stone blocks that is our guide, look.' The ancient tablets ranged before him, stations of the tree. But the dog would not look. He was impelled to explain. 'See, I would go back. I would take thee to the girl by the east road. But I understand the girl—she is *not* waiting. An yon valley road is easy. Now the tree, lass, is difficult. The tree, I do not understand—an therefore in her I *believe*, look.' It made no sense what he said, the dog rolled in the shingle. 'Fleas,' he thought. 'An she be proper sick.'

'An get up,' he cried. 'Free we are!' He looked out over the plain, shading his eyes. The snows came and the snows melted, the lizards emerged to drink the dew and all the foolish piping things enjoyed this sun, this emptiness, these peaks, unbroken as a line of prophets. Somewhere a hawk dived. Nature lay in a perfect balance. He thought it about the best thing nature had done to any land.

'An get on,' he said, as she slunk to her feet. But the dog fell behind.

'An hundred yards, lass!'

He could feel the heat. The earth was redolent of the decaying matter of bitter almonds, the mound soft and warm. The heat warmed him deliciously. He looked back. The dog was a smudge. He stopped and she stopped. He moved and she moved. 'Ha!' He laughed. She was in fear. He was not imperilled.

He fell several times, going up. 'What saves a man, lass, is to take another step. An each step — is — different — '

He stood upon the clearing. Did nothing threaten him? All was changed. The chanter was not there. The cairns had gone. No birds greeted him. The tree was silent — submerged in a milkfloss of fine sand, turned upside down like some old hag with her feet in the air. Only the tap roots showed, waving tentacles; craggy on the bare plain.

Smoke issued from them in queasy coils. Creeping forward, he caught a glimpse of two red eyes in the riverbed far below; then the fumes enveloped him in a lurid haze. 'Come an be charred, lass,' he joked, picking up a stone and touching it to his rib. It left a brown depression but no pain. The feeling of warmth persisted. The tree was dying, certainly; extinguishing itself in signals of fire that would open this land to all men — he corrected himself: all the whites, since the browns were unworthy.

He managed the last few yards in a lope, shambling up on hands and feet. 'Now how am I to embrace thee?' he said waggishly. All his life the spirit had kept him at arm's length; now, he decided, having come this far, he would salute it properly. He peered about. He was unobserved. The spirit slept, mute as the dog. So he took a root and tweaked it. 'An if thee murders me' — he meant to say — 'thee murders tha' land, an we shall be croolly murdered.' But at his touch the very life came. As when, at the lowest ebb of a great tide, all the world is drained from its orbit and there comes a wave, a sudden urgent little wash and the world is reconnected by the thread of an invisible power — so now the ground began to heave and pullulate and the tree, coiling its spidery arms about his waist, drew him gently down. As he sank a susurrus of piping reached him, perhaps of birds vagrantly harmonising under the earth; a breeze touched him; he heard the muffled wingbeats; and he recognised at last the glooming frigate bird that swept down from the alps, annihilating everything.

The dog saw his struggles. She might have been indifferent to the music of his laugh. He did laugh once. She saw the hands clasped as though he were stripping a knuckle, saw the blue flash as he flung the ring in a wide seminal arc. As the mineral dropped in front of her she heard the high tinkling laugh. Then the tree vanished. The mound was bare. The grasses pulsated with fire and all around a great cone of light stalked the sky. She went forward and sniffed the ring, and perhaps she understood. For in the end she was neither mute nor indifferent. In the end she threw back her head and howled, like a dog.

Orakau entrenchments
29th March, 1864

My dear Polson,
I send this with Whitehouse. He is a good man, less misguided than most. But he does not like me. By arming the natives I have hastened his failure as an envoy.

I have, as you once prescribed, 'crossed over.' Tomorrow or the next day there will be an engagement. We are few, but the Maori world topples and he will have his Thermopylae. The issue is clear and I am afraid. God grant I do not desert like the solitary Greek.

The money is for the boy's education. If he asks, tell him it is from the sale of guns. I know you do understand even if he, growing up white, does not forgive.

What do you call him?

Yours, towards God,

Bernard Sparrow (né Enwright)

Sparrow did not die in the battle of Orakau (as Polson heard from Whitehouse later), although the battle occurred at the time and in the way the missionary predicted. He was killed on the preceding day when a young Maori chief whom he had taken for a godson shot at a stray dog. The missionary was crouched in a trench with his hands in his ears and thought it was over, and looked up just in time to receive the bullet through his temple.

Polson called the boy Bernard.

About the year 1875 a man of short stature wearing a white turban and three waistcoats might have been seen walking the streets of Christchurch. On one side of him strolled an old dog with white paw facings and sluggish eyes; on the other was a half-caste native boy—a foundling, some said—carrying a tripod and a leather bag. To those who had known the man fifteen or twenty years before, he seemed not to have aged at all; although the lines, drawn tight like quill strokes about the streamy sucked-in eyes, might have indicated that he had cried much. The man walked with a jaunty step, talking occasionally in Maori to his young assistant, and rising and falling on the points of his hilows. He gave the impression of being able to see through solid objects: which was nonsense of course since he, like the dog, was nearly blind. Still, he was a noted photographer.

Dignitaries came to his villa to be photographed in the garden or they came to see the dog. The dog was famous. Latterly it had become illustrious. In 1869 the Duke of Edinburgh visiting the city had upset his own procession outside the villa and entered the garden in order to be photographed shaking the dog's paw. After that the stream of visitors was unending. Churchmen also came to the villa to inspect the School for Foundlings which the man had begun. They were not admitted. The School, which occupied a secluded corner of the gardens, was thought to be free and to contain mostly Maori orphans enticed away from northern tribes who had lost their lands in the Wars. The details, the methods of recruitment and so on, were known shortly afterwards when the man died and the school was closed. They do not concern us here. But at the time the school was functioning there were many rumours. Only one vicar gained admittance to the classroom, and that by stealth. He was horrified to discover he was talking in a foreign language; the pupils spoke only Maori. 'Retrograde,' was the word he used when he staggered back to the mayoralty and made his report. 'Still,' said Mr. Dewhurst, the mayor, in his caressing tones, 'he is old now and almost lovable, and his ideas can't hurt us any more.'

Polson's photographic walks (his villa was in the east) invariably took him past the mayoralty, along Disraeli Street to Victoria Market, across Albert Square and thence, via the Society for the Liberation of British Deer and Songbirds (where the Hunt Club celebrated its ball) to Derby Lane and the river. Whenever he paused to peer through the lens that the boy would set on the tripod, knots of people would gather. Strangers, noticing the turban and thinking him wounded, would ask if he had been to the Wars. Polson would reply, 'No, I was never there.' Others, having him pointed out for the first time, would approach and take his hand. 'Polson—of Polson's Land?' Polson would admit it. 'Then do tell me, since nobody else seems to know—what is the meaning of that procession of strange stones leading onto the mound?' To these Polson would raise an eyebrow; then, whistling up the dog and continuing upon his walk, he would reply inconclusively, 'I cannot say—I have never been there.'

Sometimes his voice had a hint of fatigue; and sometimes of drollery. All the same it was true; they had named the land for him and he had never been there. The reason, as Polson once told his adopted son, was simple enough: he didn't like trains. He could hardly have expected Bernard to understand the other reasons.

True to Polson's prediction, Canterbury had not succumbed to the follies of the northern districts. While the northern settlements had built a war, Christchurch had built a railway. Nobody had foreseen that a handful of ill-equipped savages would keep five regiments of British redcoats at bay for half a generation before laying down their lands. It was a sufficient pause. In fifteen years Christchurch had extended its railway from the plains to the brink of the promised hinterland. A dog had guided them in the end, and the land was found to contain such unbounded pasturage that the first graziers were misled in their measurements by up to 45,000 acres at a time. In five years all of it had been taken up—chiefly by fires. The new men burned everything in sight. The birds were consumed first since they were wingless, and the lakes were mysteriously polluted, and millions of fish and waterfowl died. Erosion set in and one or two small mountains fell down and most of the medieval shelters containing rock paintings were destroyed. Undismayed, the new men continued the war on nature to the death. Then came the day when the birth of the first brood of English blackbirds was recorded in the *Christchurch Gazette*, and the cheques taken from the first army of sheep rescued their masters from thoughts of an obscure martyrdom. Then the new men spoke in a voice of fatigued clarity and declared the original landscape to be at last unrecognisable.

The tablets, those weird obelisks with prehistoric countenances, survived however. They were called Polson's Stones. But the land itself was not named until the railway dawned.

The opening of the railway (the Dewhurst Concession) promised to be a lively affair. In fact the engine never got there. It ran out of water on Erk's Hump behind Odessa Station and all the Notability, fourteen carriages — plus one (for the band and the native dancing girls) — had to be returned to Christchurch facing in the wrong direction. Polson meantime had gone to Europe.

He was in Lucerne when Frances' letter came with the news of the birth of his first grandchild, a girl. In the same letter she wrote of the train's reversal, and Polson smiled his grim little smile all the way over the San Gothard to Ticino where he studied the blending of ebony with ivory in those marvellous wayside shrines. In Milan he ran into Donald Hay, now Sir Donald. The two men saw each other at the same instant across the parquet of the Gallerie and each for a second hesitated. Polson felt a twinge of — not exactly bitterness; his brows knitted. Then the moment passed. He smiled. Hay threw out his hand. 'I said if I came to Italy I should find you, Polson, and by God so I have. I'm off to Germany tomorrow.' Hay had developed a new strain of sheep and was invited to display it before the King of Württemberg; then on to England where Victoria had claimed it for the Royal stud. They exchanged news. Time (and the knighthood) had lessened the friction between them. As they stood under the Gallerie, sun-dappled and talking, Polson remembered he had once dubbed Hay, Prince of Squatters; and a saying came to his mind: 'He knew the temper of the age, he knew his district — now he is a wealthy man.' He nodded to himself without rancour; he found he could still admire the shrewd professional in the man who had once sent smallholders against him, the man's energy ... Hay was charming. 'I envy you Polson. By God I do. I may have got this—this Sir thing for helping the industry, but nobody's put *my* name on a map. Surely you've heard?'

He had heard, yes; in Frances' letter. Polson blinked, and declined Hay's invitation to lunch at Orsini's. Then he went off to buy a new improved rat-trap. In Milan he also bought a camera; and in Rome he enrolled in the photography course with Brandolino. Later in Marseilles, where he took ship, he photographed Garibaldi; and was invited onto the official balcony for the great Incendiary Evening held to mark the General's raising of a new army. Polson watched the scene quietly and on being asked his opinion of the Illuminations told the General that, compared with the ignition of the Mackenzie tussocks, he found them rather dim. But of course Garibaldi did not know what he was talking about.

Polson returned in time for the birth of his second grandchild, also a girl. Polson's Land was already in the schoolbooks. In Christchurch he set up his photographic studio and regarded from afar the unfinished struggles of the British army in the north and of Dewhurst's rail gangs in the west. It seemed to Polson to have developed into a race. In the end Dewhurst's gangs finished first. A softer pass to the mountains was discovered and the railway engine, Pride of Canterbury, prepared to make its official plunge through the gap amid general rejoicing. Polson was summoned to ride in the foremost carriage with the official party. A public holiday was declared. Water tanks were installed at thirty points along the route. This time there was to be no mishap. There was none. Polson however contrived to miss the train.

'You've ruined their pleasure,' Burcher said.

'Nonsense.' Polson smiled and drew his cape over his knees. It was the afternoon of the day in question. The two men were sitting at the club by the fire. It was a cold spring day and the top room shook a little with the wind coming up the stairs. Both men wore horse blankets. The chief surveyor had a pile of leases beside him. Polson was writing, in his turban.

'I expect they will get along very well without me,' he said.

'You should be there,' Burcher insisted.

Presently he looked up. 'Sausage?'

Polson waved the offer aside. A moment later he changed his mind and asked Burcher to toast another. He accepted the object and examined it gingerly for the distinguishing marks of Burcher's silver compasses. He ate ruminatively.

'You should have told me, Burcher.'

'I couldn't. It was a secret.'

'I had no idea they were unveiling a statue to me. You should have told me.'

'Would you have gone?' a burred voice said, and Whitehouse slid quietly into a chair beside them. The tone was gruff.

'No,' Polson said, glancing round. It was on his tongue to say, 'Why aren't you there?' Then he remembered. It hurt him now to see his old friend. The urbanity had gone. Years of office in the north, served too well, too honestly, had embittered him.

'Sausage?'

Whitehouse thanked the surveyor and turned to Polson. 'Yet you care.'

'I care, yes. I care that they spoil, that they deface, that they reduce the promise of something different to a single unedifying greenness. Why do you sigh, Matthew?'

'Perhaps because I no longer care. Perhaps because the tragedy of this country no longer affects me.'

'Tragedy? What tragedy?' Burcher passed the sausage.

'That she was settled by the English.' For at heart, Whitehouse knew, the deficiency was not a want of decency but a failure of the imagination. The Polsons, all the mockers and dreamers, would go. The sameness would persist. New Zealand would become a land of followers—fanciers not seekers of truth; and in the end Polson's Land would merge with the rest and become what it deserved: a little English country garden, with a woollen border.

'I only dropped by for a moment,' he added. Yet he remained slumped in his chair, ignoring Burcher's mumbled reply and Polson's stare, his grey brows drooping over half-closed lids. No, he didn't care. He was exhausted. The Government had sent him north to mediate. Sparrow's tribes had spat at him. They had spat at him. They would fight. They would drive the white man into the sea. *Ake, ake, ake*. On and on and on. Poor fools. The Government had gun-boats now and field artillery. Whitehouse had resigned, had stood again as an Independent,

THE JOURNEY

had been beaten by a saddler. Then the carnage had begun. He had had enough. He was going home.

'Strong country,' mumbled Burcher. He had the leases spread round him and kept going to the window, shaking out his maps.

'What are you doing?' Whitehouse said to Polson.

'I am writing my will.' Polson was doing precisely that. 'When is it you sail?' he inquired.

'Tomorrow. I only dropped in to say goodbye.'

Polson said nothing. Whitehouse fidgeted with his pipe, then got to his feet. They both found it difficult.

Polson said, 'You know Matthew, I don't care that much. I don't really care a bit.'

'Don't you?' Whitehouse extended his hand. 'Well — goodbye.'

'Don't go.' Suddenly Polson swung on Burcher. 'For God's sake, stop rattling those papers. Take them away, burn them.' The old surveyor looked up open-mouthed.

'Leave him alone, Amos. He's doing his job.' Whitehouse permitted himself an acid smile. 'Why should he burn them?'

'D'you remember seven years ago, we sat in this room, Matthew — what you said? You said, "The land isn't there".'

'I thought you would have been the last person to bring that up.'

'And I said' — Polson rushed on — 'I disputed, I produced evidence. "There," I said, "the responsibility's no longer mine, the proof lies elsewhere — with the gods." Well, d'you remember what the firstcomers described, what the dog showed them? A whole tract ravaged below a mound, split by a chasm — split and bared for miles, as if scoured by a great frost. What was there before, Matthew? You don't know. Burcher doesn't know. Nobody knows, except one man. And about him the gods are silent.'

'Well?'

'All I'm saying is that you were right, as far as I'm concerned the land does not exist. For me, it doesn't. D'you follow?'

'No, I don't follow, Amos.'

'Fellow's cracked.' Burcher was on his feet waving a spike of leases on the end of his compasses. 'It's *there* all right. Lookit this, Polson — 126 names all claiming 42 titles. See? And another thing, that Hollis — he was a damn good surveyor till he married your daughter. Tell him that from me. He's got Hossack's boundary climbing a perpendicular mountain. Jesus save us, he's out by seven miles.'

Polson chuckled. His son-in-law was fond of the same expression.

'And Mackenzie?' He felt Whitehouse's hand grip his arm. 'What is your opinion, Matthew? I've always wondered.'

'The fellow was sighted, escaped, took ship. There are witnesses. Your sheep were sold. You yourself identified the brand.'

Burcher spoke. 'The bugger ran all right.'

Polson said nothing.

'You don't honestly hold after all this time that he intended to behave honourably?'

'Not intended, Matthew — *did*.'

'Then how do you explain his failure to return?'

'It's interesting, isn't it? I mean, how everybody has come independently to the same conclusion.' He went on quietly. 'I think he did not return, Matthew, because he was diverted along the way.'

Whitehouse and Burcher exchanged looks. And Polson drew a weary smile from his old friend when he added: 'I've always believed Matthew, that the gods reveal only to those they love.'

'Train's coming,' Burcher said.

Polson went quickly to the window. 'All of it?' He could not count the wagons. He could only see the smoke, a faint blueish plume. It was somehow familiar. They would be here shortly. Frances, Dick, the children . . . bursting in. 'Papa! Guess—' Watching his face. 'You're busted — busted in bronze, like Garibaldi.'

'Really? How many waistcoats?'

'Frree-ee!' Podge, the eldest would scream, laughing till the wainscot shook. Then they would go back to the villa for tea — crumpets, oat cakes and cream — and spend the night together. Polson blinked. It was a better future than he deserved.

'Don't come tomorrow,' Whitehouse was saying beside him. 'There's no need. Write.'

He felt, without looking, that Whitehouse needed to slip away. Yet he did look. There were frets of tears in the older man's eyes. He stayed a moment longer at the window, filling his pipe.

'I shall miss this view,' Whitehouse said.

At the door they shook hands. 'Oh, and Amos.' The vestige of a twinkle was there. 'If ever you do reach a conclusion about mortality, you will keep it to yourself. Won't you?' He was gone.

Polson returned to the room. It seemed stale and empty. He gave a shrug and scuffed the floorboard with the side of his shoe. Then, seeing smoke emerging from one of the chairs at the fire, he ran across. But it was only a moth sliding up and down above Burcher's bald pate. Burcher, sunk in the chair with his boots on the fender, ignored him. Polson picked up a magazine, discarded it. The steward entered.

'Boddy,' he announced.

'Mr. Whitehouse has just left,' Polson said.

'Not for 'im. *Yew*.'

Something about the steward's expression made Polson question him.

'No tit,' the steward said.

'I beg your pardon?'

'Got no tit, sir.'

'Male?'

'Neuter, sir.'

Polson hesitated. 'Show him up.'

His first impression on seeing the bent sprig of saffron advance in a grovelling position was one of revulsion; and on hearing the squeaky voice introduce itself, one of pity; but he did not dismiss the intruder at once, and ordered drinks.

'Two, my dear,' the man said, and squatted like a weasel. He would not sit. His facial muscles, loosely distended under the tiny lurid eyes, twitched constantly, and he wore his hat. One hand was clasped in his jacket pocket. Polson thought he held a pistol and placed himself with his back to the grate.

The man swallowed the first cognac and set the second on the floor beside him. 'For my friend,' he explained.

Polson waited.

The beady eyes flashed into the corners of the room. Suddenly he giggled, and brought them to rest again on Polson. 'I have come,' he said, and Polson had to crane to catch the eunuch sounds, 'to know an answer. You are Polson? Please don't interrupt. I knew him, you understand? I knew *him*. He spoke of you. He spoke in parables, he spoke of a tree in the kingdom.'

'Which kingdom?'

'Don't interrupt. Croesus' Kingdom, of course. Then he said, the Scots devil—he said, "It does not exist." Now—' The little man had grasped the poker. With a bound he sprang upward, catching Polson by the collar and hanging there, one foot on the fender. 'Now tell me the *Truth*!'

'Of course,' Polson said, and braced himself. He was reassured by the frailty of the grasp. 'Of course. It is a pity you didn't come a moment ago when Whitehouse was here, we were talking of that very thing. The truth, I believe, does not exist separately, just as the land does not exist separately. For you and me it exists only, so to speak, in the dream.'

'Don't—Please don't lie to me.'

'The land is not there,' Polson said steadily. He felt the grip tighten, and then relax.

'O good—o *thank* you.' He was backing away, raising the beaver hat. 'O good, good, good. I am so glad. You see, had it been otherwise I should have been compelled to—' The voice became incoherent. As he reached the door the man took a shrunken object from his pocket and rubbed it pathetically against his cheek. Polson caught the words, 'Elsa and I . . . really rather tired of looking . . . Must excuse us—'

When he had gone Polson picked up the remaining cognac from the floor and sipped it thoughtfully. He glanced at the fire.

'Well?' he said loudly.

There was no reply. Polson came closer. On a whim he drained the glass and placed it, lip down, on top of Burcher's bald head. He stood looking at it, absorbed. The chief surveyor slumbered on.

There were three children now, at Odessa.

Podge was drawing with a crayon; Mary, the younger sister, was making cat's cradle; little Toss slept, head at his mother's side, half-buried in leaves. They were picnicking. Below the edge of bush where they were sitting dozed the station cob; also the buggy with Drake-Draper in it, reading a book. Draper had come back—he was the only one. Frances and Dick had kept him on as a sort of nurse. They gave him wages in beer and books and he read, even when baking. The children adored him.

Podge said, 'Can I have it now?'

'If you ask nicely.'

'*Please.*'

Frances passed the ring to the child and watched her dip the owl seal in berry juice and then stamp the bottom of the drawing which was spread on her knees. Podge was seven, and had pigtails. She licked the rest of the juice from the seal and regarded the acquamarine stone a moment. Then she slipped it behind her back.

'Was my name always Podge?'

'No, we just call you that.'

'Why?'

'I suppose, because you're like your father.'

'He waddles, doesn't he?' Mary said, and stuck out her tongue at Podge. Mary was six.

Frances held out her hand. Podge gave up the ring unwillingly. She watched her mother slide it back onto her right hand.

'Can't I keep it?'

'No.'

'It's magic, isn't it?'

'Yes, Mary.'

'You promised to tell us about it.'

'Later. Now hurry up, one more play and it will be time to go.' Frances gave them the last of the Fry's soluble chocolate and shooed them into the trees.

Left alone with Toss, Frances wondered why they had come. It was years since she had been. The little scathe of beech overlooking the valley was as dreary, as sodden, as stunted as ever. She was not one for reviving memories. Marriage had erased poetry. Yet she was very happy. Her hair, piled in soft caps on top of her head, had achieved the lustre that comes with children and the comforts of an abundant household. Dick was good to her — and practical. She had few problems. She had grown ample with Dick, a little well-to-do, even (Mrs. Dewhurst's word) a little vulgar. They lived now where the pa had stood, above the end of the valley. After old Hue died the natives had drifted to the towns. Dick had razed the huts and totems and started afresh, except for Sparrow's stone church which was now the woolshed. One or two natives had come back. They had gazed in wonder at the timbered homestead, three storeys, and a chute on the elmy side to put the laundry down. Then they had gone away. She had forgotten their names, except for Billy. Billy had appeared one night in the rain, a ghastly shape, clinging to the tree outside her window; he was weeping. He had begged to be taken back into service. Dick had put him to fleece picking. Shortly afterwards Frances had found him digging up the garden which was the old burial ground. He said he was looking for his ancestors. He made a speech, quite a long one. They did not exactly dismiss Billy, they sent him back to town, to a school. He came back, however. He helped in the laundry for a time. But he proved shiftless, not that he stole much; just little things. Finally he had followed the new men into Polson's Land, as a porter.

'Shiftless,' she thought; and sighed. Instinctively her gaze lifted over the valley to the poplars. A cavalcade of poplars led up to the house from the bridge, where Hollis Road crossed the old ford. She could just see the top of the house. After twelve years the elms were halfway to the third storey, growing well. From her room the trees hid the valley, mercifully. She had not realised before how ugly the valley was from this side—the double line of poplars, their wintry forms staked on the hill line, gave it the air of a squalid shipyard. The ugliness was almost breathtaking: a scatter of fenced farms, of dirty sheds, of matted ditches and manic gorse, of higgledy-piggledy wagons and engines and railway lumber. There was a mill now, built to serve Hay's Forest for the little clapboard townlet on the margin of the swamp. Also a dyke forty feet wide running the length of the swamp, Erk's Dyke. Not nice. Neighbours were nice but nice neighbours were few; and even the vicar woke her at four when he rose, together with the smallholders, and commenced shooting rabbits. The hills were black with rabbits, besides grasshoppers and the little excrescences of erosion (she smiled, remembering the fires she and Rose had lit—they said the erosion was due to the fires, but really it was the deer); the deer hunters came on Saturdays, in packs . . . But really it didn't upset her. Once, when they had demolished the old homestead and her father had gone to Europe, she had found herself waking in the early mornings wishing that the sky would fall in fog to cover man's depredations. But not now, she told herself; none of this had the power to upset her, not now.

The sharp cry of a weka (how alien!) startled her. The wind soughing in the branches gave her an eerie uncomfortable feeling. She shifted. Little Toss woke, his face creased and baleful in dreams, grimaced, then rolled over abruptly and slept again. Somewhere in the gathering dusk the whistle of an engine sounded. Frances relaxed. Next week she would take the children to see granpappa, a lovely ride. The mushrooms would be up, the guard would stop the train and they would all get down to pick them.

'The only thing is, Toss,' she found herself saying aloud, 'I do wish they hadn't put the railway depot *there*.' Her father had cried when the homestead came down. ('A nice bright depot, what colour will you have it?' the engineer had said. 'Red and yellow, like a boiled sweet,' Polson had muttered. They had been as good as his word.) The depot was just below her. Strange, she thought, how the dairy had survived. Crumbling now, the walls defaced; but it held. Remarkable, considering that her father had set the snowgrass on the roof so that all the water ran inwards. The last time she had looked, there was the tin bath. A tramp was sleeping in it.

The children were coming back. She closed her eyes.

'Pixies, pixies!' The children leaped whooping, coroneted in bay leaves, their faces daubed wineberry purple. The elder snatched the ring from her finger and ran.

'Bring it here, Podge.'

'Pixies steal!'

'Bring it *here*!'

The child ran screaming. The next moment she tripped and the ring flew like a wasp branching from her hand.

'Where is it?'

'There.'

'Where Podge?'

'It fell.'

'Where?'

Podge whimpered. Her cheek was cut. The mother shook the child until the blood froze. 'Where?' Podge only screamed. Mary giggled. Frances slapped Mary tartly and told her to fetch little Toss. Toss was bawling.

They searched about the damp stems for half an hour. Finally Toss found it, embedded under some twigs.

'Mary, give Podge some of your chocolate.'

'Why?'

'Because I frightened her.'

'I'm alright, mamma, just cold. Truly.' Podge had crept into her skirts, they all had. She sat under the beech, still holding them, still shaking.

'Why are you crying, mamma?'

'I'm not. Not now. Don't sniff, Podge.'

There was a silence. The tip of the sun held orange, momentarily expanding; then sank slowly under the peaks. The shadows spread unevenly. Podge's chin shot up.

'You promised to tell us.'

Frances made a little movement of annoyance. 'All right. Promise not to interrupt?'

'Promise.' Three pairs of eyes loomed, like pit boys entering the light.

'Well then—it came from a fire. It came out of the earth, just like Solomon's ring.'

'Whose fire?'

'Rose's fire.'

'Not yours?'

'Mine too, we were both there. Rose was staying with me. We made a man tell us where the longest tussocks were and rode out. We made little fires first. The great thing was to see who could make the biggest blaze.'

'Who was leader?'

'Rose was. Hers always burned best. We took turns. There were some pretty little groves of ti-palms on a terrace. She burned them all. Once the stem caught the first spark, the poor palm would bend and hiss and sway and then, gip, away it would go in a shiver like a linnet; and suddenly there was a black pillar, and another, and another. And the flames ran on up the hill. I was jealous. All my burns stopped in a bare patch.'

'Didn't the birds mind?'

'I'm coming to that. Rose burned the terrace and then we made tea. We had our little kettle. Then I saw the basin. Grass to here—no, *here*. It was over the horses' heads. Fern, and Irishman. And Spaniard. And pigs! Wild cats too. Gilliam said they were dangerous. They were *not*. Absolutely screaming human screams—'

'What were?'

'The pigs of course. Running this way and that, they ran like ninepins. The trouble was, you see, we didn't know when to leave off. It was really quite late. We just left the tea. I lit first, although Rose says she did. At first we just dropped matches. Then we had torches, long brands—longer than that. It was extraordinary really what we did. The wind was lovely. My girth slipped. "Hurry," Rose said. Your Aunty Rose was always impatient. She was blacker than a sweep, but she was fearfully white. Her horse got burnt. The whole basin, you see, Podge. Every clump, every patch of fern, every kowhai—roaring. The basin was done, we knew that. We could see the moon. The sky was crimson. We rode for miles. We had some chocolate. We ate that. I don't know why we didn't stop. We lit the flats as we rode down, all the ridges, all the kanuka, all the flax, the ti-palms exploded like gold—magnificent really.'

'What happened?'

Frances was silent. The terrible thing was that even now, looking into those small bright eyes—even now the sight thrilled her.

'You see. First the butterflies came out, red and yellow and heliotrope. Then came the caterpillars, the lizards, the beetles, the cicadas, all the hoppy-hoppies. Then the rats and field mice. Then the wobblies, the weka and the kaka and the kakapo, all the dodo things that couldn't fly. I had no idea there were so many sounds in the earth, so many cries. We had to brush them off. The moorhens leaped on the horses, flaming—'

'Why didn't you eat them?'

'We did. We ate the pigeons. We were starving by morning. She stopped abruptly.

'Mary, you're chattering with cold.' She stood up, gathering her shawl. Suddenly she was swaying.

'Mamma, what is it?'

'Nothing. I thought I saw something in the trees.' She pulled her hair round her throat and tucked it into her bodice, like a scarf. She had let it down without noticing. 'Perhaps—perhaps I will sit down again, just for a moment.'

'But what *happened*?' Podge was beside herself, twisting the linsey hem into balls of terror.

'Nothing happened, darling. Rose was sick, that's all. It was the roast lizards. I told her not to eat them. She wouldn't stop.'

'But—the *RING*!'

'Oh this. Didn't I say? You see, the dog came back then—'

'And the dog brought it!' Frances smiled in a bemused way. Podge was very quick. Curious. Now that she tried to shake out the flames and think who had found the ring and where—it wouldn't come. In her thoughts the fire was still there, Rose being sick; and the dog, limping towards them out of nowhere over the charred stumps . . . In a way Podge was right. Frances stared at the six pervasive eyes and found herself saying: 'Yes Podge. The dog brought it.'

Podge fell silent, uncommonly so.

Toss said, in his hoarse little way: '*Gran*-pappa's dog.'

'That's right. Afterwards we gave the dog to granpappa. She was sick and granpappa was lonely. She'd been on a journey.'

'Who was the man?' said Toss, who had really not understood at all.

'No more questions, come along.'

'There was a man,' Toss said.

'Silly. You didn't listen.' Podge pulled him up. 'The *dog* brought the ring. She brought it out of the fire. *That's* why it's magic. The dog brought the ring in her mouth and gave it to mamma and mamma put it on and the fire stopped, and then the dog was sick.'

'Then there wasn't a man?'

Frances stood up. She was quite still. 'No dear. The man never came.'

She stood a moment longer.

'You're coughing, Mary. Take my wrap.'

'Mamma! It wasn't me.'

'Keep still. All of you.' Something was creeping towards them through the trees, and coughing. A thin rasping human cough. The sun had quite gone but the shapes cast by the tall moorish stems were distorted, lumpish . . . Again the rasping cough. 'Quite still now.' She had her hand over Toss's mouth and gripped Mary by the other arm. For a moment she believed that it was Billy, come to exact some insane vengeance. She stiffened.

Then with a cry the beast blundered right into them. Never, oh never, would she forget the moan that broke from that heroic and raddled throat.

'Ba, ba, ba.' Podge was equal to it. 'Dirty, dirty, dirty—mamma, look. A dirty black sheep!'

The children sang the rhyme all the way home, and vied with one another picking the wreckage and mud from its coat. Frances took the reins. Drake-Draper held the ewe.

'Jesus save us,' Dick said when they arrived. He called the hands. He took the ewe into the hall and stood it under the lights so they could see.

It had fifty pounds of wool.

Frances went to bed very early that night, pleading a headache. Later she had the fleece made into a rug and sent it to her father. She never again took the children for a picnic in the bush.